Praise for the Dark King series by
DONNA GRANT

"Loaded with subtle emotions, sizzling chemistry, and some provocative thoughts on the real choices [Grant's] characters are forced to make as they choose their loves for eternity."   —*RT Book Reviews* (4 stars)

"Vivid images, intense details, and enchanting characters grab the reader's attention and [don't] let go."
                                                        —*Night Owl Reviews* (Top Pick)

Praise for the Dark Warrior series

"The world of the Immortal Warriors is a thoroughly engaging one, blending powerful ancient gods, fiery desire, and touchingly human love, which readers will surely want to revisit."   —*RT Book Reviews*

"[Grant] blends ancient gods, love, desire, and evil-doers into a world you will want to revisit over and over again."   —*Night Owl Reviews*

"Sizzling love scenes and engaging characters."
                                                                —*Publishers Weekly*

"Ms. Grant mixes adventure, magic and sweet love to create the perfect romance[s]."   —*Single Title Reviews*

Praise for the Dark Sword series

"Grant creates a vivid picture of Britain centuries after the Celts and Druids tried to expel the Romans, deftly merging magic and history. The result is a wonderfully dark, delightfully well-written [series]. Readers will eagerly await the next Dark Sword book."

—*RT Book Reviews*

"Another fantastic series that melds the paranormal with the historical life of the Scottish Highlander in this arousing and exciting adventure."   —*Bitten By Books*

"These are some of the hottest brothers around in paranormal fiction."   —*Nocturne Romance Reads*

"Will keep readers spellbound."

—*Romance Reviews Today*

Also by DONNA GRANT

THE SONS OF TEXAS SERIES
The Hero
The Protector

THE DARK KING SERIES
Dark Heat
Darkest Flame
Fire Rising
Burning Desire
Hot Blooded
Night's Blaze
Soul Scorched
Passion Ignites
Smoldering Hunger
Smoke and Fire

THE DARK WARRIOR SERIES
Midnight's Master
Midnight's Lover
Midnight's Seduction
Midnight's Warrior
Midnight's Kiss
Midnight's Captive
Midnight's Temptation
Midnight's Promise

THE DARK SWORD SERIES
Dangerous Highlander
Forbidden Highlander
Wicked Highlander
Untamed Highlander
Shadow Highlander
Darkest Highlander

From St. Martin's Paperbacks

FIRESTORM

DONNA GRANT

St. Martin's Paperbacks

This is a work of fiction. All of the characters, organizations, and events portrayed in this novel are either products of the author's imagination or are used fictitiously.

FIRESTORM

Copyright © 2017 by Donna Grant.
Excerpt from *Blaze* copyright © 2017 by Donna Grant.

For information address St. Martin's Press, 175 Fifth Avenue, New York, NY 10010.

ISBN: 978-1-250-10953-8

Printed in the United States of America

Our books may be purchased in bulk for promotional, educational, or business use. Please contact your local bookseller or the Macmillan Corporate and Premium Sales Department at 1-800-221-7945, extension 5442, or by e-mail at MacmillanSpecialMarkets@macmillan.com.

St. Martin's Paperbacks edition / March 2017

St. Martin's Paperbacks are published by St. Martin's Press, 175 Fifth Avenue, New York, NY 10010.

10 9 8 7 6 5 4 3 2 1

To Viviana Izzo—
Thank you for helping me stay sane
and for being so amazing!

ACKNOWLEDGMENTS

A special shout-out to everyone at SMP for getting this book ready, including the amazing art department for such a gorgeous cover. Much thanks and admiration goes to my fabulous editor, Monique Patterson, who I can't ever praise highly enough.

To my incredible agent, Natanya Wheeler—here's to dragons!

Hats off to my street team, Donna's Dolls, along with the fabulous readers on DG Book Talk. Words can't say how much I adore y'all.

A special thanks to Gillian and Connor and my family for the never-ending support.

PROLOGUE

Long, long ago . . .

The stench of death and blood filled the air no matter how high Dmitri flew. Everywhere he looked, he saw another dead dragon with mortals cheering. It was gut wrenching. Everything the Dragon Kings had worked so hard for was being obliterated.

And by the very beings they had vowed to protect.

Time was running out. His heart banged with trepidation. Already, he'd lost several of his Whites in the never-ending battles. The loss pierced his soul, leaving a scar that would never heal. Their deaths would be a weight he carried for eternity.

The dragon bridge blazed brightly in the distance. The sky darkened from the swarm of dragons rushing toward the bridge. Each of the Kings was responsible for getting their clan to the bridge—including the sick and the old. No dragon was to be left behind.

Dmitri looked over his shoulder to see his clan behind him. When he saw his aunt falter and slow, he dipped one wing and turned to go to her.

"*Keep going!*" he shouted through the mental link shared by all dragons.

He came up under his aunt until she was resting on his back.

"*You shouldn't*," she said in his mind.

He ignored her and kept flying. They had no other choice but to get the dragons to the bridge so they could find another realm—somewhere. No longer could the dragons and mortals co-exist.

Yet, Dmitri wasn't sure he could let his family go. It was going to take more strength than he had. More than he was willing to give.

His gaze looked to the earth below. The humans were to blame. They were the ones who kept claiming more and more land, the ones who insisted everything was theirs simply because they wanted it.

Because of it, he was not only losing his clan and home but also his family.

The closer he got to the dragon bridge, the more he wanted to fight the mortals and claim the realm for the dragons as it had always been. Then he spotted a flash of gold next to him and looked over to find Constantine.

The King of Dragon Kings gave him a nod. In Con's royal purple dragon eyes, Dmitri recognized the same emotions within himself. Con's Golds had been the first to cross the bridge. If he could let his dragons go, then so would Dmitri.

He flew faster until he was leading the Whites once more. Sadness clogged his throat when his aunt rested her head against his.

His sister came up on the other side of him, his wing touching hers. The last few miles, he soaked up every moment he could with his family, because each beat of his wings took them closer to the dragon bridge.

All too soon, they arrived. He hovered near the bridge. His aunt rolled off him before spreading her wings and flying to face him.

"*I'll see you soon, nephew. I love you,*" she said.

He gave her a nod. "*I love you, too. Take care of our dragons until we can call you home again.*"

With fierce determination in her eyes, his aunt faced the dragon bridge and led the Whites over. Dmitri remained at the entrance, touching his wing to each of his dragons before they flew over the bridge.

His sister waited until the last. "*Don't worry about us.*"

"*You're in charge of them now.*"

She nodded. "*Aunt and I will do our duty and lead our clan until you can take your rightful place. Just be quick about it,*" she said before buming into him.

"*I love you, too, sis,*" he said.

A tear fell from her eye. With one last look, she flew over the dragon bridge.

Dmitri's heart shattered. Pain filled his chest, suffocating him until he couldn't draw breath. He watched until his sister faded from sight. Then, reluctantly, he tucked his wings and dove to the ground where Con and the other Dragon Kings stood in human form, watching the dragons leave their home.

Just before he hit the ground, Dmitri shifted. He rolled to his feet and raised his gaze upward. He'd taken the sight of dragons in the sky for granted. Within the hour, the last of the dragons would be gone.

None of the Kings spoke. The anguish was too great, too raw. Everything they were was being viciously and savagely stripped away.

The horror didn't end with the last of the dragons crossing the bridge. Now, the Kings had to destroy every dead dragon. They were erasing themselves from the realm—and the minds of men.

DREAGAN

Dmitri breathed in deeply as he entered the warehouse. The smooth, dry peat smell accented with oak filled his senses. Whisky.

It wasn't just Dreagan's major source of income. It was the essence of the land and the people. Every time he walked the warehouses where the oak cask barrels were stored, he felt pride in what they did.

He let his fingers trail over the barrels that had been maturing for seventy-five years as he moved down the rows. His mouth watered at the thought of sampling the Scotch. Stopping at the end of a row, he put his hand on the oaken barrel and squatted down beside it.

"Anxious, I see."

He looked up to see Constantine walking toward him. "Aye," Dmitri answered and straightened.

While the world might know Dreagan Industries as the global leader in Scotch sales, there was much more to those who lived on the sixty thousand acres than anyone realized.

For starters, they weren't human. They were dragons able to shift into the form of mortals and live among them.

But as with any story, it wasn't so cut and dry as that. Dmitri blew out a breath when Con reached him. The men at Dreagan were Dragon Kings—leaders of each of their dragon races.

As their leader, Con ensured that their true identities remained secret from the world. However, that was becoming more and more problematic.

One of their enemies—the Dark Fae—had secretly videoed the Kings in battle with the Dark. The subsequent release of said video showing the Kings shifting multiple times had caused a worldwide sensation—and brought the attention of every military and government agency around the globe.

"What's wrong?" Dmitri asked, noting the worry in the depths of Con's black eyes.

Con twisted the gold dragon head cufflink at his left wrist. "There's a matter I need you to attend to."

"Name it."

"I'm sending you to Fair Isle."

For a moment, Dmitri didn't breathe. "Now isna the time for more of us to leave. Asher is still in Paris at the World Whisky Consortium. No' to mention Anson, Kinsey, Henry, and Esther are about to head to investigate Kyvor."

It seemed that the Kings had adversaries coming at them from all sides. The Dark Fae and humans, but the most troubling was a banished Dragon King, Ulrik.

He was the instigator of most of the things happing at Dreagan. Unfortunately, so far, Ulrik remained one step ahead of them.

"I agreed with Ryder that in order to find out who from Kyvor sent Kinsey and Esther, the girls had to go there and infiltrate the offices," Con explained.

Dmitri still couldn't believe that Ryder wasn't going to be with his mate, Kinsey. Then again, as a computer mastermind, Ryder could keep an eye on Kinsey from behind his rows of monitors.

"They're all mortals," Dmitri reminded Con.

Con raised a blond brow. "Both Henry and Esther have sworn to aid us, and Kinsey is Ryder's mate."

"But the ceremony hasna been done, which means she's no' immortal yet."

"No one is more aware of that than Ryder. Frankly, right now, we can use them. Until Vaughn takes care of the legal papers to get MI5 and the news crews off Dreagan, our wings are clipped."

"I ken that. But we also know that whoever used magic on Kinsey and Esther to turn them against us can do it again."

"Ryder will protect Kinsey, and Henry will look after his sister. Asher is doing fine in Paris, so there is no reason for you no' to go to Fair Isle."

Dmitri's heart missed a beat. It had been so very long since he was last there. Would it be the same? Would he even recognize it? "What's happening on the tiny isle?"

He hoped it was Dark Fae. He was ready to kill more of those bastards. The Kings were still cleaning up the mess those evil shites had made on Halloween across the UK.

"I got a call from MacLeod Castle today."

That caused Dmitri to worry because, for the most part, those at the castle had remained out of the war. If they had reached out, then something must really be wrong. Thankfully, the Warriors and Druids were allied with the Kings. Each group had helped the other out several times.

"Have the Dark finally found the Warriors?" he asked.

Con gave a shake of his surfer-boy blond hair and adjusted the sleeves of his dress shirt before slipping his hands into the pockets of his pants. "In some ways, that would be better."

Better? This wasn't going to be good. An ominous feeling ran down Dmitri's spine like the fingers of Fate. There was no getting out of it—not that he would even try. "Spit it out."

"The call came from Ronnie."

The foreboding increased, twisting until it grew into a tight knot in the pit of his stomach. "Dr. Reid? Is she in trouble? Is she on a dig at Fair Isle?"

"She's well. Everyone at MacLeod Castle is fine. But there is a dig on the isle. Ronnie received a text from a fellow archeologist and friend about a recent find."

Dmitri folded his arms across his chest. It was Veronica Reid's "find" that had brought the immortal Warriors into her life, allowing her and Arran to fall in love.

As a Druid, Ronnie was able to locate hidden treasures beneath the ground, which had brought her to the attention of the Warriors to begin with.

"What find?" Dmitri demanded.

Con's gaze was steady, his face set in hard lines. Then he delivered the killing blow. "A dragon skeleton."

CHAPTER ONE

Fair Isle

Faith Reynolds never felt more at home than she did in the middle of a dig. Sounds of rocks being moved and dirt shoveled into pails filled the air, giving her a purpose—and a goal.

All around her, people talked and laughed, but she didn't hear their conversations. She was so deep inside the cave that the darkness and dampness that clung to everything didn't even register. Her focus was on something much more important. Something much more valuable.

Bones. But they weren't just any bones.

She moved the electric lamp and used the large cleaning brush to gently smooth away the sand and dirt to expose more of the jawbone. Over eighty percent of the head and neck had been excavated.

It wasn't until she'd discovered the bones of what was obviously a wing that she confirmed what she'd found—a dragon!

A week later, and she still couldn't believe it.

Nor did anyone else.

Since her funding came from The British Museum, they

continued to send other archeologists, biologists, and zoologists to declare her a fraud.

Except not a single one of those idiots had been able to do that. It made her smile. They wouldn't confirm it was a dragon, but they couldn't name it as another animal either.

For the moment, that was enough. She was sure someone would attempt to say it was a new dinosaur. By that time, she wanted the entire skeleton excavated and brought to her lab so she could study it more.

Until then, she wasn't going far from her find. She felt a connection to it that she couldn't explain or understand. As if she were supposed to be the one to finally give it peace.

Almost as if the skeleton had been waiting for her to discover it. She shook her head, inwardly laughing at herself. A firm believer in making her own destiny, her thoughts were vastly different than her normal scientific reasoning.

She enjoyed hearing all the local tales and legends, but they were nothing more than stories. Nothing about them was real.

This dragon, however, was something else completely. It proved that the animals had once existed. It would also confirm that all the myths about dragons having magic were entirely false.

Her excitement to share what she'd found made her want to hurry and uncover the remains, but that would be folly. Something could go wrong, or she might damage the bones. No, she needed to proceed cautiously.

It was too bad her mother couldn't be there to share in the delight. Molly had loved dragons so much that they were everywhere in the house—knickknacks, paintings, pillows, posters, wind chimes, and even a potholder. Faith never had to wonder what to get her mom. If it had a dragon on it, Molly Reynolds wanted it.

Faith looked up, her hand stilling as her eyes became

unfocused. All of her mother's dragons were now carefully wrapped and boxed away in a storage unit back in Houston.

She blew out a breath and blinked several times. Though it had only been six months since she'd walked into her mother's house for a day of shopping only to find that she'd died peacefully in her sleep, the hurt was still there.

The first thing Faith had done when she'd found the skeleton was grab her cell phone and dial her mom's number. Molly hadn't just been Faith's mother, she'd also been her best friend.

Faith had never cared that she didn't have a father, that he hadn't wanted her enough to stay. Molly had loved her enough that it didn't matter.

She swallowed, her eyes filling with tears. "Oh, Mom. If only you could be here," she whispered into the darkness.

Faith hastily swiped her cheeks with the back of her left hand. She sniffed and returned to her work. Little by little, she uncovered the rest of the jawbone.

She ran her hand lovingly over the head that was easily five feet long. The snout wasn't rounded, but narrow. And the teeth were incredibly long and sharp, particularly the canines.

As intriguing as the four horns—extending from the back of the head like fingers—were, it was the two sets of ridges along its nose that she found most interesting.

She placed her hand between the two rows and spread her fingers but couldn't quite reach either side. If the head were that large, just how big was the rest of the dragon?

"Dr. Reynolds," Tamir said as he squatted down beside her.

She jumped, startled by her assistant. Faith turned her head and smiled. He'd just returned from a visit with his family in Israel.

With his thick black hair pulled back in a man-bun and

his muscular body, every woman on the dig lusted after Tamir. Everyone woman that is, except her.

To her, Tamir would always be the gangly, awkward young man who was eager to learn from anyone.

"What is it?" she asked, rolling onto her side to better see him.

Tamir's dark eyes quickly looked away. "Another news crew arrived."

"Send them away," she said with a shrug.

"I tried."

She sat up. "Then just ignore them. They'll go away like the others."

"I don't think so."

"What aren't you telling me?" she urged as she got to her feet.

Tamir ran a hand down his face. "I found two men trying to get into the cave. Fair is small, Faith. Only seventy people live here, and the authorities aren't prepared for any of this."

That's when it hit her. "You think those men were going to hurt me?"

"It's certainly a possibility. There was something . . . odd . . . about them." He gave a shake of his head. "I can't explain what, but I sensed evil."

"Did you call the police?"

At this, Tamir looked away. "No."

"Why not?"

"I wanted to." He cleared his throat. "Then I couldn't."

"Couldn't?" Now she was concerned. This was very unlike him. Had someone threatened him? "Did they try to hurt you?"

Now Tamir wouldn't meet her gaze. "Just the opposite."

"They came on to you?" she asked with a grin. It wasn't the first time a man had taken an interest in him, nor did she suspect it would be the last.

Tamir nodded.

She laughed and slapped him on the shoulder. "What's the big deal?"

"I . . . I wanted them."

Them. Not him. *Them.* Since Tamir's interests ran exclusively to women, this came as a shock. And explained why he was so upset.

"Where did they go?" she pressed.

He shrugged and fisted one of his hands. "They walked away. Once they were gone, I felt like myself again."

She tucked a strand of blond hair behind her ear. "We can't help desire. Or fight it."

"You don't understand," he insisted, his gaze swinging to her. "I *wanted* them. I would've done anything to have them, but even during all of that, I felt their evil. I think the locals are right. I think there is magic on this island."

If there was one thing she couldn't stand, it was people saying something was magic simply because they were either too lazy or too ignorant to find a scientific explanation.

"It wasn't magic," she stated. "How long ago did this happen?"

"Thirty minutes or so."

She frowned, a thread of anger running through her. "And you're just now telling me?"

"I took a little break."

Which was Tamir's code for going off and shagging some girl. Since he was still visibly upset over the desires of his body, she didn't say anything else about the matter.

"Also, Dr. Reid called."

Faith hated that she'd missed Ronnie's call. They had become fast friends when they were paired up on a dig together—the first for both.

"Did she say what she wanted?" Faith asked.

"She's sending someone to help us."

At this, Faith raised her brows. "We have plenty of volunteers. Besides, you know I'm particular about who I let near my finds."

"Well, I might've told Ronnie some of the issues we've been having."

"With the reporters?" she asked, confused. "It's not really an issue."

"Actually, it is. You're always in here digging. You don't understand what's going on out there."

"Perhaps you'd better start telling me what's really going on."

He glanced at the dragon head. "There are some fanatics out there. Some who will do anything to see this skeleton. And . . . well, frankly, there are others who want to see it destroyed."

"All this over a fossil?" she asked in surprise.

"You're claiming it's a dragon."

She shot him a look. "I didn't claim anything. I've not told anyone about this dig except for Ronnie. It was one or more of the volunteers who let that tidbit leak."

"Then stop all of it by saying it's a dinosaur."

"I won't lie." She pointed to the head. "Does that look like any dinosaur you've seen?"

"New ones are still being discovered."

"So you don't think this is a dragon?"

He blew out a frustrated breath as his expression grew pinched and filled with tension "Faith, you know I'll follow you to the ends of the earth, and if you say it's a dragon, then I believe it is."

His words were meant as consolation, but he had no idea just how deeply they cut. The one person she expected to have her back was Tamir.

"We're lucky the cave is difficult to get to," he continued, unaware of her hurt.

"That will keep them out, and allow me to finish my

work." She turned on to her stomach and returned to brushing away the dirt to reveal the neck bones.

Tamir remained a moment longer, then he got to his feet and walked away. When she was alone once more, she rested her forehead on her hands.

The people she could deal with. There were crazies everywhere. It didn't matter if she was digging up a dragon, a dinosaur, or another King Tut. Some believed things were better left buried.

As for Tamir not believing that what she'd found was a dragon . . . That stung, but she was made of tougher stock. She knew what she had, and that's all that mattered.

The cave was difficult to get to. A person couldn't just walk into it. It took climbing skills in order to reach it. At first, she'd been upset by how hard it was to get to the entrance, but now, she was quite happy about it.

The crazies would be kept at bay until it was time to take the bones from the cave. But that was a worry for another day. There was no sense in wasting energy on that when she had other work to do.

Faith lifted her head and looked up at the bones once more. Why couldn't others notice what she saw? Was she seeing something that wasn't there because of all the dragon stuff her mother had had?

No. She'd compared the teeth with every known animal—living and extinct—and had come up empty. Nothing matched. Then there were the horns, again no match. And the wings.

There were no known birds—ancient or otherwise—that corresponded with the size. And she hadn't even uncovered the rest of the skeleton yet.

She touched the pocket of her windbreaker. One of the teeth was tucked away to run a carbon dating test. The longer she was near the bones, the surer she was that the dragon might be the oldest fossil ever found.

It was a theory, one that she was keeping to herself for the time being.

"You'll reveal all your secrets soon enough," she whispered to the bones.

CHAPTER TWO

Dmitri sat with his eyes closed, pretending to sleep as the plane bumped along. The turbulence was brutal and caused many of the other seven passengers to gasp and shriek during the flight.

The plane ride was only about thirty minutes, but to the young Scot sitting next to him mumbling prayers, it was a one-way trip that ended in death.

It was on the tip of Dmitri's tongue to tell the man that he should've taken the ferry if he was so sure he would die in the plane, but he decided at the last minute to hold his tongue.

By the time the small aircraft landed, Dmitri seemed to be the only one who didn't let out a relieved sigh. Then again, it was difficult to frighten an immortal.

He stepped off the plane with his leather bag in hand and glanced at the sky to give himself a moment to adjust to being on Fair Isle. The clouds were moving fast, the perfect cover for a dragon.

It would've been so much easier had he been able to fly here himself, but none of the Kings had flown during the day in . . . eons.

Ever since the video leak, Con had refused to even allow them their nightly flights on Dreagan. With the whole world's eyes seemingly trained on their land, it was a smart move.

But the Kings were less than thrilled about it.

Dmitri opened the mental link shared by all dragons, but right before he told Con that he'd arrived, he remembered that he had to look and act human.

So, instead, he took out his mobile phone and shot Con a text. It was all he could do not to roll his eyes. Con's reply was:

That wasn't so hard, now was it?

Bite me, he returned.

Putting the phone away, Dmitri finally looked around. In that second, he felt the strong connection to the land that touched his very soul. There was a reason it had been several thousand years since he'd last set foot on Fair.

Despite the passing of time, the land still smelled the same. Sea, salt, and wind. He closed his eyes, and was immediately transported back in time to when the isle had been his home. His dominion.

Of all the Shetland Islands, his family had chosen Fair to rule their dragons.

The waters had been deep and plentiful, the cliffs high and steep. It had been a wonderful playground for a young dragon to learn and grow.

While he had many wonderful memories of his time on Fair, it was the horrific ones that ruined it all.

"I should've never come," grumbled the young Scot as he walked past.

Dmitri opened his eyes and looked at the human. How very right he was. None of them should've come. But they had. Their arrival had changed everything.

The planet had been the dragons', but now, the humans had claimed it. He felt like an outsider on the very world he'd been born on. Sadly, that wasn't going to change anytime soon.

He walked into the building that made up the airport on the isle and spotted a young woman. "Excuse me," he said as he walked up to the counter. "I'm looking to get to the dig site on the west coast."

"Aye. Another one," she said with a nod of her tight red curls that fell just past her shoulders.

He glanced at the other passengers who were making their way to vehicles after meeting up with friends or relatives. "Another one? Have there been many?"

"Oh, aye. I can have Fergus take you. Fergus!" she shouted.

A tall, barrel-chested man with wild, dirty blond hair ambled in. He looked Dmitri up and down. "Another one?"

"Another one," Dmitri confirmed.

Fergus motioned with his meaty hand. "Follow me."

A part of Dmitri wanted to walk the isle. It was only three miles long, and a little over a mile wide. But he needed time to look around the dig site before he announced himself, so the walk would have to wait.

Thankfully, Fergus wasn't a talker. On the drive, Dmitri rolled down the window and took in the subtle changes that had occurred since he'd last seen his home.

There weren't many occupants on Fair Isle. When it had been his home, there had been no humans. It felt odd to see so many now. Houses stood against the constant wind, while boats drifted around the isle.

Everywhere he looked, there were mortals. A constant reminder of all he'd lost. He'd be lying if he said he didn't feel anger, but it was the misery of seeing his home turned into something else that fueled the fires of his rage.

In short order, Fergus pulled up to the site and simply looked at him. Dmitri hid a smile and gave the big man a nod of thanks before climbing out of the old Range Rover.

As he stood looking out over the barren scenery with white houses dotting the countryside, the sound of the SUV's engine faded as Fergus drove away.

Dmitri wished Con would've sent someone else. It was too hard returning—reliving the memories, knowing nothing was going to change.

Then again, that's exactly why Con had sent him. Few of the other Kings ever got to revisit their homes. How lucky they were. They didn't have to witness how the mortals had destroyed everything the dragons had once loved and cherished.

The force of the sudden fury that swelled within him took his breath away. If anyone had asked him even yesterday, he'd have said he didn't hate the humans.

Yet, the truth lay before him now. He blamed them for taking his home. Because of the mortals, the life of every dragon had been altered forever.

He didn't know where his family was. All he could hope for was that they were happy and healthy. Perhaps one day he might see them again. However, the reality was that that would probably never happen.

And how very sad that made him.

He drew in a breath, reining in his resentment, and turned around. The first thing he saw was the sea. It lay deep and blue and beautiful before him, expanding endlessly from horizon to horizon. How many times had he swum those waters, diving deep?

The wind buffeted him, urging him closer to the edge of the cliff. He heard the sound of the waves crashing against the rocks long before he saw them.

He couldn't help but smile when he spotted various birds riding the currents, diving into the sea for food, or nesting along the cliffs. Their calls mixing with the sounds of the sea calmed him, removing his anger—or, at least, lessening it. A glance down showed a pod of dolphins frolicking not far from shore.

Home.

Except it wasn't. Not anymore. Dreagan had been his home for countless centuries. Yet . . . Fair still pulled at him. It was his first home, the place where he'd been with his family.

The place where he'd been born, where he'd learned and loved. The place where he'd become King of the Whites.

The place where he'd lost it all.

"Can I help you?" asked a male voice.

Dmitri turned around, trying to place the odd accent. He stared into the dark eyes of a man in his late twenties. His skin was pale and his hair black.

"I'm sorry, sir," the man said. "But we need to ask everyone not working the dig to leave."

Dmitri gave a nod, recognizing the accent as Israeli. "I am working the site."

A black brow lifted. "I've never seen you before."

"Because I just arrived. The name is Dmitri."

A smile broke out on the man's face. "Ah. Yes! Dr. Reid said you'd arrive today. My name is Tamir."

Tamir held out his hand. When Dmitri took it, the young man eagerly shook his. He immediately noticed the calluses on Tamir's hand, proving that the mortal didn't mind getting dirty if needed.

"Come," Tamir said, motioning with his hand for Dmitri to follow. "Let me show you around."

Dmitri shifted his bag to his other hand and followed Tamir down a path that took them to a set of tents. The wind howled, pushing and pulling the fabric that was strung as tight as a drum.

Tamir looked over his shoulder and said, "We don't normally remain here overnight. The main tent is used to document the cave and collect any evidence Dr. Reynolds finds. But I always have tents set up in case of a storm or if we work late and decide to stay."

"You've a place in the village?"

Tamir nodded his black-haired head. "That we do. The food is hot and good, and it's nice to get a shower. That isn't always possible on these digs, you know."

Dmitri had no idea, but then again, he never minded sleeping beneath the stars—whether he was in human or dragon form.

Tamir reached a tent on the very end and tucked a strand of his hair that had come loose from his man-bun behind his ear. "I just had this put up for you. I already stopped two men trying to get to the cave this morning. You'll be a welcome addition to the group."

After ducking inside, Dmitri set his bag on the cot. Then he walked back outside and stood looking at all the people around the site.

Tied to a boulder were several ropes that disappeared over the side of the cliff. As he stared, a man climbed up the rope and set a bucket on the ground. A woman retrieved said bucket, and the man scrambled back down the rope.

"You aren't much of a talker, are you?" Tamir asked.

He glanced at the young man. "No' really."

"You'll get along great with Dr. Reynolds then."

"Tell me about Reynolds."

Tamir shrugged and waved a hand at the dig site. "This tells you everything there is to know about her."

Her. Dmitri should've known Ronnie's friend was most likely female. He'd hoped for a male. At least then he might be able to talk some sense into him. With a female . . . well, they tended to be more pigheaded.

"Why don't I bring you down to the cave?" Tamir offered.

It was on the tip of Dmitri's tongue to refuse. He didn't want to go into the caves he'd explored as a youngling. Nor did he want to see the skeleton. But he was there for exactly that. There was no walking away from this.

Every Dragon King was counting on him.

And Dmitri wouldn't let them down.

"Follow me," Tamir said enthusiastically.

He trailed after Tamir to the boulder where they got into harnesses. Dmitri could climb down it without any such aid, but he was trying to appear mortal.

When Tamir handed him the helmet, he immediately bristled. But he took it anyway. All he could be thankful for was that no other King was around to see as he snapped it beneath his chin.

He could only imagine what jokes Rhys and Kiril would make up. Thankfully, Dimitri was saved from being the butt of such jests.

With Tamir beside him, they made their way down the sheer cliff. Halfway to the cave, Dmitri stopped, his gaze locked on a set of claw marks.

They were faded, barely visible to the human eye. But a dragon would recognize them. His heart hurt as he touched the marks with his fingers.

"Did you find something?" Tamir asked.

He gave a shake of his head and proceeded down the cliff. All around him were signs that dragons used to inhabit the isle. For whatever reason, the mortals didn't—or couldn't—see them.

How then did Dr. Reynolds know where to look for the skeleton?

And how in the world had he missed destroying it?

It hadn't been enough to send the dragons away. After, every King had the duty of finding their dead and removing any trace of their existence.

Dmitri dropped onto a ledge and unhooked the harness from the rope. Then he removed his helmet. After, he simply stood, looking into the large opening of the cave.

The team had set up generators to power lights that flooded the darkness. He didn't need the light. But it wasn't because his dragon eyes allowed him to see in the dark, even in human form.

No, Dmitri could walk this cave blind. Because he knew every inch of it—and every other cave on the isle.

"Exciting, isn't it?" Tamir said with a wide smile showing even, white teeth.

All Dmitri could do was nod. Words would be too difficult with the swell of emotion flooding him—excitement to be home, hatred for having to leave to begin with, and guilt for all that he'd lost.

He looked down at his feet. Two steps would put him inside the cave.

Once inside, who would he find when he saw the bones of his kindred? In the chaos of battle and getting all the dragons across the dragon bridge, he'd barely had time to say farewell to his family.

Tamir was talking, but he didn't hear him. Somehow, his feet had moved of their own accord, and he entered the cave. With every step, he saw evidence of dragons.

Claw marks and tail marks.

He knew where the skeleton would be, though he allowed Tamir to lead him all the way to the very back of the cave. At least the humans believed it ended there. In fact, there was a hidden opening to the right a hundred yards closer to the entrance.

Dmitri stopped at the sight of the bones. He didn't care about the people around him. His attention was focused on the remains of the dragon that had been exposed.

Out of the corner of his eye, he saw movement and heard Tamir speak. It was by sheer will alone that he pulled his gaze from the dragon and looked down at the figure kneeling by the skeleton.

A woman turned, her sherry colored eyes locking with his. "Who are you?" she asked in a drawl he immediately recognized as Texan.

"The man who is going to keep you safe," he replied.

CHAPTER THREE

Faith let her gaze slowly run up the tall man. He wore jeans that hugged his trim hips and a thin, black, V-neck sweater that showed off every mouthwatering muscle that was honed to perfection.

His muscles weren't so huge that they looked ugly. But they were big enough to be noticed—and appreciated.

And she couldn't seem to stop appreciating them. Her gaze lingered on his thick chest, imagining her hands running over his pecs before sliding around his neck.

Her breath hitched as her blood heated. She unzipped her jacket to help cool herself. Then she looked up at his face. And what a face!

His wide, full lips softened the sharp lines of his jaw. Azure eyes framed with thick, black lashes watched her with a decided lack of interest. It was difficult to determine whether his hair was dark brown or black in the dim light of the cave.

But it was trimmed short with the top long enough to be parted to the side, the locks having a hint of wave to them.

She had a strange and overwhelming desire to run her hands through his hair and climb him.

Claim him.

Her knees threatened to buckle from the insane and decadent thoughts. The carnal longing swept through her shamelessly—and she embraced it.

Even as she feared it.

It took three attempts before she was able to have enough saliva to swallow.

"Who are you?" she demanded.

"The man who's going to keep you safe," came his harsh reply framed in a Scot's brogue.

Her gaze shifted to Tamir. "Excuse me?"

Tamir laughed nervously. "Yeah, this is what I tried to tell you earlier. When I spoke with Ronnie, she suggested someone to help keep the crazies out. So she sent Dmitri."

Faith looked at Muscles again and noticed his interest was squarely on the skeleton. Just as she was about to tell Tamir to send him away, she realized they could use someone to keep the loonies at bay.

Getting to her feet, she extended her hand to him. "Faith Reynolds."

"Dmitri," he replied and briefly shook her hand, letting go as if the contact between them irritated him.

She frowned and looked at Tamir before returning her gaze to Muscles. She fisted her hand to lessen the slight tingling across her skin from the contact with him. Again, she had the urge to touch him, stroke him. "No last name?"

"None needed," Muscles said. "Why this cave?"

"I'm sorry, what?"

"Why did you pick this cave out of all the hundreds on the isle?" he asked in a slightly lower pitch.

Faith's hackles immediately rose, shoving the majority of her lust aside. She didn't need to explain herself to anyone. So why she answered him, she'd never know. "I saw it from shore and wanted a look."

"There are five more caves you could've seen from shore. Yet you chose this one."

His blue eyes were penetrating, as if he were trying to see into her mind. She crossed her arms over her chest and lifted her chin. "I got lucky. If it hadn't been this one, I would've moved on to another."

"So you were looking for such a skeleton?"

Was that a hint of mockery in his tone? *Oh, I don't think so!* "I'm an archeologist. I look for anything."

"Do archeologists no' have a specialty?"

"Some, yes. For its size, this island has been more intensively studied by archeologists than almost any other area in Scotland."

"Is that so?"

She let her confidence show in her smile. "That's right. Did you know evidence has been found here to suggest Fair may have been settled by Neolithic people up to five thousand years ago?"

"And you came to find more verification?"

"It's what I do." No one was more surprised than she when she'd found the large horn and a portion of the skull sticking out of the ground.

"Just a wee bit of luck, aye?" he asked skeptically.

Tamir chose that moment to issue a nervous laugh. "Well, now that you two are getting along, perhaps we all should get back to work."

"Splendid idea," she said and turned her back to Dmitri of the no last name.

But she still felt his gaze on her. It was everything she could do not to look at him.

She took a deep breath and stared at the skull. The skeleton seemed to rest on one side, as if the animal had lain down and not gotten back up.

Returning back to her work, she was happy to hear the fading footsteps of Tamir and Muscles. A bodyguard. As if she needed such a thing.

Tamir worried like a mother hen, and Ronnie must have picked up on that to send someone. Despite not liking Muscles, Faith wasn't going to send him away. If his presence eased Tamir, then she could put up with the silent, accusing stare of the newest member of the team.

It wasn't long before she became engrossed in her work once more. With an earbud in her right ear, she listened to one of her many playlists, humming as she worked.

No one disturbed her. Every once in a while, she saw Tamir as he came in to check on her progress and help dig for a bit. If there was a problem at the site, everyone went to Tamir first.

He was an archeologist, as well, but he'd taken on the role of site supervisor from the moment he began working with her. Not that she didn't make sure he got his time in at each dig, too.

Many times, the two of them would spend hours, sometimes late into the night, working while everyone else rested and slept. It was how they got so much done.

She and Tamir worked well together. He understood her, and she gave him a lot of freedom. Now that he had his degree, he could go off on his own. A few offers had come in for him to lead a team, but so far, he'd declined them all.

It made her smile. Tamir had started out as just an intern for a semester, and now, years later, he was pretty much family. It was why it hurt so much that he didn't believe she'd found a dragon.

When she looked up at her progress, she sat back with a smile. All of the head and a portion of the neck had been exposed.

She stretched her neck and back. When she checked her watch and saw that it was seven in the evening, she knew why her stomach was growling.

By now, everyone would either be in camp or on their way back to town for dinner, drinks, and bed. She wasn't quite ready to call it a day, however.

Though she was going to have to work the kinks out of her back. She stood and took a deep breath as she closed her eyes before she lifted her hands over her head and put her feet together. As she released her breath, she folded over at the waist and put her hands on the ground, stretching her legs and back.

When she opened her eyes, she was shocked to find Muscles sitting on the ground behind her with his back to the cave wall. From her upside-down angle, she took in his casual pose.

Could he look any more comfortable in his surroundings? He had one foot planted, leg bent, and an arm resting on his knee as he watched her.

She straightened and turned to face him, taking out her earbud. "Do you need something?"

He gave a slight shake of his head.

Great. A non-talker. Usually, she liked that, but there was something about Muscles that just set her off. Perhaps it was the condemnation in his gaze, as if he were angry that she was in the cave.

She was absolutely, positively certain her unease had nothing to do with the fact that he had a mouth-watering body and face.

It wasn't like she was going home with what she found in the cave. It would go to the museum, though she would get credit for it. For her, it was the thrill of uncovering something from the past.

She decided to ignore him. This time, she put in both

earbuds and faced the skeleton. Her goal was to expose the entire neck in the next two days.

So far, the skeleton had been intact, which was surprising. Not that she was going to complain about it. A gift was a gift.

Dmitri still hadn't decided about Faith Reynolds. Her dedication to her job was unquestioned. He wasn't accepting her answer of just finding the cave, though.

To have chosen this cave above any others? This one, which happened to have a dragon skeleton inside?

While he'd walked the site after meeting Dr. Reynolds, he overheard conversations. Many of the volunteers didn't believe it was a dragon. They suspected it was a new species of dinosaur. The few locals he saw milling about were curious, wondering how the new find would help tourism.

He spotted a few "crazies" as Tamir called them, watching from a distance, but no one got close. Though he was curious about the two men Tamir had encountered earlier.

The way Tamir had acted as he spoke about the incident made Dmitri wonder if word hadn't somehow reached the Dark Fae.

Or Ulrik.

Once volunteers began leaving for the night, Dmitri found himself climbing back down to the cave. He'd expected to find Faith shutting things down for the day, but she continued to work.

He didn't want to be intrigued by her, but he was. If only his fascination had to do with how she'd found the dragon, he would discover what had led her to the skeleton, but that wasn't what kept his gaze locked on her.

It's not what kept his body strung tight as a bow.

She was average height, but there was nothing typical about her looks. Much to his dismay. His tastes ran toward the Fae since he preferred to stay away from humans. Yet, there was no negating the fact that lust burned through his body from the first moment her sherry eyes locked with his.

There was a . . . simplicity about Faith that he appreciated. No makeup was needed to enhance her natural beauty. At first glance, she seemed almost ditzy since her mind ran a million miles a second, but her intelligence and zest for life were apparent with one look.

Her sandy blond hair hung straight and glossy to her shoulders and was parted to one side with long bangs that she swiped out of her eyes repeatedly. The locks tantalized him by exposing the slender column of her neck and the delicate skin behind her ear.

Unblemished fair skin beckoned him to touch, to caress. To lick.

He clenched his teeth at the need that surged through him. When she turned, he watched the pulse at her throat and fought the longing to press his lips against it to feel the warmth of her body.

Her oval face held a look of innocence and excitement he hadn't seen in a long time. While her high cheekbones and sensual mouth added to her beauty, it was her eyes that caught him. They looked at the world as if it were a large sandbox waiting to expose its treasures.

His palm still prickled from their brief touch earlier. The shock that had gone through him had been electric. The charge surged through him faster than lightning and left him reeling—and aching for more.

Unable to look away, he watched as she stood and then bent over at the waist. The sight of her firm ass high in the air had the blood rushing to his cock. No mortal had ever had such an effect on him before. It unsettled him—and angered him.

He forced his eyes away and turned his mind to more

pressing matters. He'd been sent because of the skeleton, but there was something about Faith that didn't seem to add up.

The most important question: How had she known where to look to find the bones?

Faith became so engrossed in her work that she didn't hear others talking to her. Even when Tamir called her name, she was often too preoccupied with digging up the skeleton.

Dmitri had watched her for hours. In that time, he'd listened to her hum and watched her touch the bones with such reverence that it shook him.

Though he'd come to the cave to watch her, it gave him time with the skeleton, as well. By the size, he knew it was an adult. Which of his dragons had gotten left behind? They'd been his responsibility, and he'd failed.

The longer he stared, the more he felt the weight of regret. The world had been created for the dragons. It was their birthright, their home.

Yet they were no longer welcome.

And he feared nothing would ever change that.

The Dragon Kings who found mates with human females were lucky. Those mortals welcomed the dragons and the Kings. But most of the globe was made up of individuals who wanted nothing more than to destroy the Dragon Kings, imprison them, or run tests on them.

So he and the others remained hidden.

But the dragon inside him—the fierce, savage creature that he was—silently cried out for revenge. And his family.

Yet he kept it all locked away. He couldn't let it consume him, or he'd end up just like Ulrik: banished and cursed to roam the world in human form for eternity.

It was almost two hours later before Dr. Reynolds turned off the music on her phone and removed her earbuds. She collected her tools and cleaned them off before returning them to a leather pouch that she rolled up and neatly tied.

Then she adjusted her jacket, grabbed the tools, and began turning off the lights.

He got to his feet and did the same on the other side of the cave. One by one, the lights were shut off. As the darkness grew, he found he wanted to remain.

"What is it?"

He turned at the sound of Faith's voice. Her gaze searched the dark to try and see him. He glanced at the dragon. The need to stay with one of his clan—even in death—was strong.

"If you're afraid of the dark, I can turn on a light," Faith said.

Dmitri found a smile forming before he cut it off. "I'm no' afraid of the dark."

"Then what is it?" she asked again.

It wasn't like he could tell her the truth. Or could he? "I once lived on Fair. A verra long time ago."

"Oh," she said. "I didn't know that."

There was a lot she didn't know—and never would. Dmitri walked around her. The only thing that allowed him to leave was the knowledge that he'd be able to return the following day.

There were no words spoken between him and Faith as they put on the harnesses. But he felt her looking at him often, as if she were trying to figure him out. Perhaps letting that little truth out had only complicated matters instead of simplifying them.

He finally met her gaze as the light from her helmet shown in his face. Dmitri waited expectantly for the question he knew was coming.

"Do you have family here?"

He swallowed past the sorrow that lumped in his throat. "No' anymore."

"I don't have any family anywhere." As if surprised by her words, she hurriedly looked away and began the climb up.

Dmitri didn't want to feel anything for the mortal, but there was no denying the pain he heard in her words and saw in her eyes.

He followed her up the cliff where Tamir was waiting for them. He gave Dmitri a grateful smile and guided Dr. Reynolds to the tent where food awaited.

Dmitri stood, slowly removing the climbing gear long after Faith and Tamir had walked away. Memories were consuming him, overwhelming him.

He turned and faced the sea. He could hear the echoes of his family and other Whites upon the wind and within the rock. He closed his eyes as the wind moved seductively around him. How glorious it would feel to shift and fly above Fair once more.

To release his true self.

And plunge into his memories.

CHAPTER FOUR

Perth, Scotland

Ulrik stood in the middle of his living room, hands fisted at his sides and seething with rage. He wanted to destroy everything around him, to release the fury that was about to erupt from him.

And it was all due to Mikkel.

His uncle had meddled for the last time. Ulrik had had Asher right were he wanted him. Con sending Asher to Paris had been fortuitous.

Ulrik's plan would've worked if only the key to his entire plan—journalist Rachel Marak—hadn't fallen in love with Asher.

She'd promised Ulrik that she would tell the world about the Dragon Kings. He didn't take such pledges lightly. The oath bound her to him in a way she hadn't understood.

Then she betrayed him.

Too many treacheries left a mark. And for her betrayal, Rachel had given him no other recourse but death. Except Asher had gotten to her in time. Even so, Ulrik had planned to wound Asher and kill Rachel.

Then, out of the corner of his eye, he'd seen his uncle standing in the rubble of the warehouse.

Now, Mikkel knew his secret.

Now, Mikkel knew he could shift.

It was information Ulrik planned to use when the time was right. He was strong enough to take his uncle out, and had been for a while. But he'd been biding his time, waiting to discover as much of Mikkel's secrets as he could.

There was only one King of the Silvers. Mikkel may have coveted the role, thought he could take it from his brother, but the strongest dragon with the most magic became the next King. That wasn't Mikkel. It was Ulrik.

His uncle had hidden his anger well all those years. So well that Ulrik had never known how much hate festered in Mikkel's heart. After Ulrik's father died, Mikkel had attempted to leave the family and go off on his own.

Ulrik was the one who'd talked him into staying. Ulrik had been a different person back then. He'd seen the world as nothing but good and decent, a beautiful place in which to live out his dreams.

Now, he looked back on those memories and saw them in another light. Had Mikkel played him? Had Mikkel wanted him to ensure that he would remain a part of the family? Was that why his uncle had tried to leave?

Ulrik's anger grew because it was exactly the type of thing Mikkel would do now.

Eons ago, Con had warned Ulrik that his trusting nature would get him hurt. It seemed his old friend had been right—not that he would ever tell Con such a thing.

Ever since Mikkel had come into his life a few years before, Ulrik had played the part of subordinate well. There were several things he'd done to the Kings that Mikkel wasn't aware of.

So, who tipped off his uncle to his plans in Paris?

Since Ulrik didn't trust anyone, the blame remained with him. It had to have been something he'd said—or didn't say—to Mikkel.

But he hadn't spent the last thousands of years putting this plan into motion only to have his uncle destroy it all. There were still things happening that would put Ulrik ahead.

He looked around. If he remained at The Silver Dragon, Mikkel would destroy his shop and all the beautiful antiques he'd acquired through the years.

Ulrik stalked to his bedroom and yanked open the door to his closet. He had little time to get what he needed. Dressing quickly, he made his way down the stairs to the shop below.

He pulled open his bottom left desk drawer and took out the file he'd hidden. Inside was a list of names that he'd narrowed down to two. One of them was the spy Mikkel used on Dreagan.

Ulrik was going to discover which one it was. With merely a thought, the file disintegrated into nothing. Then he used his magic to spell the shop so that Mikkel couldn't wreck anything.

There was nothing in his desk or on the computer that held any secrets for his uncle to find. No, everything was in Ulrik's head.

He touched the silver band on his wrist and teleported away, his thoughts on one individual.

Ulrik found himself in the middle of a field with grass reaching past his knees. He looked around and saw the forest before him, a lake behind him, and mountains on either side.

But he didn't spot his quarry.

Not that he'd expected it to be easy. V never made anything easy.

He headed in the direction of the forest. For over an hour he walked until he saw a road. He followed it, staying in the woods, until he came upon the road sign.

"Sweden, V? What the hell are you doing?" he murmured to himself.

In no time, Ulrik came upon the town. He made his way down the center of the village until he found the pub. Inside, he spotted V. He sat in the back with a pretty woman on his lap, the female running her fingers through his long, dark hair.

V's gaze jerked to him.

For a lengthy minute, the two stared at each other. Then Ulrik turned on his heel and left. He made his way back through town and up a trail atop a hill.

He didn't have long to wait before V found him. They stood together, staring over the land as the sun sank into the horizon.

"How did you find me?" V asked.

Ulrik took a deep breath and slowly released it. "No' easily."

"You used magic."

He heard the suspicion in V's words. Ulrik faced him and nodded. "That's right. A lot has happened while you slept."

"Apparently," V said with distaste.

"I have all my magic returned."

"No' a gift from Con, I suspect."

Ulrik snorted. "No' hardly. I worked diligently until I found a Druid who helped me."

V nodded, folding his arms over his chest as he shifted to the side to face Ulrik. "I've heard Con in my head every day. He wants me to return to Dreagan because of a war you started."

"Why have you no' done as your King commands?" he asked with a grin.

V glanced away. "I've something I need to do first."

"So you plan to return to Dreagan?"

"Eventually."

Ulrik looked into V's blue eyes and smiled. "You sided with me once, brother."

"For a time."

"Because you knew the humans were a plague upon this realm and needed to be exterminated."

V's chest expanded as he inhaled. "Aye."

"Our dragons are gone because of them."

Calculating eyes watched him. "We made a vow to protect the mortals."

"That was before our dragons were slaughtered."

"Things can no' be undone," V said as he dropped his arms and turned to face forward.

Ulrik saw his chance and took it. "You're right. They can no'. But they can be changed. Con once demanded I fight him to be King of Kings. I declined because I did no' want the role."

"And now you do?" V asked, his head turning toward Ulrik slightly.

"Aye. I'm going to set things right. And once the humans are gone, I'm going to bring back the dragons."

V nodded slowly. "We could fly free again."

"Whenever you want. No more restrictions, no more pretending we're mortals."

"I was forced from my sleep to once more walk this world I want no part of in order to fight in a war. Again."

"It's a war I began," Ulrik admitted. "I did it to exact my revenge for having my magic bound and being banished from my home."

Turning his head gradually, V met Ulrik's gaze. "I was one of the ones who killed your woman."

"You also sided with me in the war against the humans."

"What do you want of me, then? You have your magic. You can release the Silvers."

Ulrik smiled. "Oh, that is coming, brother. But no' yet."

Blue eyes narrowed into slits. "You want me to return to Dreagan."

"Aye."

"I've something yet to do."

He looked around. "In Sweden?"

"I doona know where I'm going, but I'll know it when I see it."

"Tell me what you search for. I'll help."

V looked away. "Nay."

"Then find it, but soon."

"There's something you're no' telling me."

V had always had the ability to see into the unspoken. "No' all the dragons went across the dragon bridge."

"Your four Silvers."

"There was another."

V's head jerked to him. "Who?"

"My uncle. The second my magic was bound, he became King of the Silvers. Then the magic bound not just my magic but also Mikkel's so that neither of us could shift."

"It's been a race to see who could become King again."

Ulrik gave a nod. "Mikkel never stood a chance with me, but he knew he wasna strong enough to kill Con."

"That's why he kept you alive. How long have you known Mikkel was here?"

"No' long. He hid himself so I wouldna find him."

"I can no' imagine you were happy to learn that."

That was putting it mildly. All those years wandering alone when he had family there watching him . . . It infuriated him to know that Mikkel had seen him at his lowest. "I've been using him just as he's been using me."

"How so?"

"He looks like me, except for a bit of gray at his temples."

V shook his head as he understood the implications. "So the other Kings see or hear about Mikkel and think it's you."

"Some of it has been me. Some of it has been Mikkel. As I said, I've used him. I put plans into place thousands of years ago."

"Did he, as well?"

"Aye, but no' as good as mine."

"Kill him, then."

That had crossed Ulrik's mind on several occasions. "Mikkel can still be of use. I've got a plan for him that will keep Con's attention focused away from the very thing I'm going after."

"Which is?"

"The weapon."

A frown creased V's forehead. "What weapon?"

"Con has kept a weapon hidden in his cave that has the potential to destroy every Dragon King."

"Then why do you want it?"

Ulrik smiled. "The Dark wish to use it."

"You're playing with fire, brother."

"I know what I'm doing."

V ran a hand down his face. "So why send me back to Dreagan? To spy for you?"

"I can do that on my own. I've got something else for you."

"What is that?" V demanded to know.

Ulrik looked up at the darkening sky. "There are mates at Dreagan."

V's shocked expression was filled with abhorrence. "That can no' be possible. The spell—"

"That prevented any of us from having strong feelings

for the mortals was shattered the day I gained my magic once more."

"You know I can no' hurt the mates."

"I'm no' asking that of you, brother. I simply want you to gather them for me."

CHAPTER FIVE

Faith squeezed her eyes shut and counted to ten as she stood in the cave. Everyone around her was talking about Muscles. All because he had apparently stopped three people who tried to get to the cave the night before.

She'd done her part and thanked him. He'd mumbled something she hadn't understood and walked away. Had he not been there, she wasn't sure what would've become of the bones. She'd never expected someone to risk his or her life climbing down to the cave in the dark.

Several times that morning, she attempted to work, and each time, the conversation of those around her would break into her thoughts.

Everyone's mind—including hers—was on one person: Muscles.

This had never happened before. It didn't matter if she had her music on or not. It was like her brain was attuned to Dmitri's name, because when she heard it, she found herself looking for him.

Which made working difficult since his name was spoken every few seconds.

To help take her mind off him, she walked the cave a

few times. At the entrance, she looked over the water that slammed into the rocks below.

Her cheeks became numb from the cold wind blasting against her. She thought about calling Ronnie to thank her for sending Muscles, but with the wind, talking would be difficult. So Faith sent a text instead, promising to call her friend soon.

Faith returned the phone to the pocket of her windbreaker. When she turned around, she came face to face with Muscles. His azure eyes caught and held her gaze.

She looked up at him, mesmerized by the strength and intensity she saw on his face. He was ruggedly handsome, in a wild, reckless sort of way.

Something she found wholly appealing.

She was so shocked at her reaction, that she took a step back. In a flash, his hand reached out, grasping her arm and yanking her inside the cave.

Her heart hammered wildly, because in the second before he grabbed her, her foot had hit air.

With her hands latched on to his shoulders, she felt his warmth and strength. Seconds ticked by as they continued to stare at each other. His gaze was quicksand, and she was sinking.

He steadied her before dropping his arms. "You should pay more attention, Dr. Reynolds," he scolded and walked away.

Her mouth dropped open. Her embarrassment at nearly falling had turned to a profound hunger she welcomed. That was quickly replaced by annoyance at his words.

She lifted her chin and straightened her shoulders before she strode back to the skeleton, ignoring Dmitri when she passed him as he talked and smiled to a female volunteer.

"Insufferable," she muttered.

He barely deigned to talk to her, and he certainly never

smiled. Not that she cared what he thought of her or her work. Let him flirt with whoever he wanted.

Meanwhile, she was going back to her dragon.

As soon as she put her hand on the dragon skull, she was instantly calm. Faith sat with the brush in her hand, but she didn't begin moving the dirt away. Instead, she stared at the bones.

"Who are you?" she asked.

So many questions rattled through her head. What had happened to the animal? Why had they not found more skeletons? Had it died alone?

She hoped that once the entire skeleton was revealed, she would have some answers. For some reason, she became a little sad when she thought of the animal dying by itself.

"You're not alone now," she whispered.

Dmitri's enhanced hearing picked up Faith's words. He frowned, wondering who she spoke to. Surely it wasn't the skeleton.

He remained close to Dr. Reynolds for a number of reasons. The major one was to destroy the bones as soon as he could. He could've done that last night—or allowed the three who'd tried to get in to do it.

But he was curious as to why the dragon was there. And how it had remained behind.

His other purpose for staying close to Faith was because he had a suspicion that someone on the dig was letting people in. He ruled out Tamir quickly enough. Yet that left a couple of dozen others to investigate.

He roamed the area around the bones for a bit, studying Faith. She was a conundrum. The woman was obviously good at what she did. And while Ronnie's Druid magic led her to finds, he didn't think Faith had that ability.

However, she was absentminded and consumed with

her work. She often forgot to eat, and never kept up with the time. It was like she was in her own little world where it was just her and whatever she was excavating.

She never seemed to see Tamir move things out of the way so she didn't hit them, step on them, or impale herself. And now, Dmitri found himself moving things for her, as well.

Hell, he'd had to catch her before she plummeted to her death earlier. He hadn't said a word when she faced him, but her rounded eyes said he'd startled her. That wasn't reason enough to take a step back.

He gave a shake of his head. It was amazing that Faith Reynolds was still alive. If it weren't for Tamir—and countless others who looked out for her—she'd most likely have died long ago.

Usually, humans were more careful with their lives. They understood mortality and didn't wish to die. That concern didn't seem to reside within Faith.

He made sure there was nothing about that might get in her way before he climbed to the surface. He'd told Tamir he wanted to remain overnight to see if anyone showed up.

The truth was that he'd wanted to be alone his first night back on Fair. It was just by happenstance that he'd been there to catch the trio. Yet it proved that people would do just about anything to see what it was that Faith had discovered.

Since he hadn't gotten to talk to Tamir earlier, he took that opportunity now. The man stood off by himself, looking at an outcropping of the cliffs. Dmitri walked to him and found the archeologist with his arms crossed over his chest and his shoulders hunched.

"Everything all right?" Dmitri asked.

Tamir shook his head. "I can feel it again."

"Feel what?"

"The evil. They're back."

There was only one species on this realm that he knew exhibited such evil—Dark Fae. "Where do you feel it?"

"Everywhere."

Dmitri let his gaze roam the area. If the Dark were there, they were hiding. And though they could remain veiled for a few seconds, it wasn't long enough to keep hidden. "I'll find them."

Tamir suddenly turned his head to him. "Do you know how many digs I've been on with Faith?"

"Nay."

"Dozens. I can't remember another time where people have tried to see what it is we found like they have here. I don't understand."

"People fear what they doona understand."

Tamir nodded, glancing at the ocean. "That doesn't explain the ones who want to steal it for themselves."

"There are those who want to possess anything that could be magical or extraordinary."

"Yes, you're right. Faith is going to get hurt in this. I know it."

That, Dmitri wasn't going to allow to happen. "Nay, she's no'."

Tamir's black eyes met his. "I have your word?"

"You have my word."

That seemed to ease him, because Tamir's shoulders relaxed. "Perhaps I should hire more men to help you."

"I work better alone." He didn't need others to check on, nor did he want anyone watching him.

"Thank you, Dmitri." Tamir walked away.

Alone, Dmitri sat on a rock and watched the site. He took note of everyone and their movements, cataloguing them in his mind. By the end of the day, he had two people he believed were helping others get onsite.

One was a woman in her early twenties. She was tall

and leggy with brown hair cut very short. She flirted with everyone while doing all that she could to see what Tamir was documenting.

The other was a voluptuous woman in her mid-forties with long, black hair. She worked hard, mothering those around her. Yet her gaze was always on Tamir and Faith. She wanted to be in the cave, but Tamir had them on rotation, which kept her on land that day.

Dmitri didn't believe the two were working together. In fact, he thought they had opposing agendas.

As daylight faded, he walked the site, observing as people went off in pairs or small groups as they got into cars to return to town.

To his surprise, he found himself thinking about Faith and wondering if she'd managed to keep from impaling herself on anything while he'd been away.

Then he thought of her eyes. Such a unique, striking color. And so damn expressive. Everything she felt was reflected in her sherry colored orbs.

He stopped beside Tamir, who stood at a table with a large plastic bin about five inches deep. Inside the tub were items found within the cave.

His gaze locked on the small piece of dragon scale. It was no longer white. Time and the elements had faded it, but Dmitri would know a dragon scale anywhere.

"You staying the night again?" Tamir asked, not looking up from the clipboard.

"Aye. It's better this way. The sooner everyone realizes someone is here, the sooner they'll stop trying to sneak in."

"Or they'll kill you." Tamir looked up and frowned. "Are you sure you can do this on your own?"

Dmitri smiled. "Doona worry for me. By the way, do you have a list of names?"

"For the workers? Yes."

"Can I get a copy?"

Tamir shrugged. "I'll bring it in the morning."

"Put a mark beside anyone you doona quite trust."

There was a slight pause before Tamir said, "But I approved everyone."

"That doesna mean you didna change your mind about someone after they began working."

Tamir frowned and looked away. "You're right."

"Have you checked on Dr. Reynolds lately?"

"Not in a couple of hours."

Dmitri looked at the sea. "There is a storm coming."

"I don't see anything," Tamir said, searching the horizon.

"It'll be here in a day or two."

Tamir gave him a doubtful look. "Gotcha. I didn't realize you were a weatherman, as well."

"When you belong to a region, you feel the subtle changes in the air."

Dmitri walked to the edge of the cliff and climbed down, not bothering with the harness. When he reached the cave, a group of four workers was preparing to leave.

He gave them a nod, noting that Faith wasn't with them. Then he made his way to the back of the cavern. Just as he expected, she was right where she'd been the night before.

This time, she had both earbuds in, humming a slow tune as she worked. He found a comfortable spot and sat. There was something mesmerizing about watching her tedious work and listening to her hum.

Her hand moved slowly, surely over the area until, little by little, the bone was exposed. She never grew tired, or if she did, it didn't show. Every so often, she would sit back and look at the work accomplished, smile to herself, and touch the skeleton.

He found his gaze drawn to her shapely bum when she got to her knees and bent over to look at something. Desire stirred again, surprising him.

Then her humming stopped—and she began to sing.

He was transfixed by her melodic, ethereal voice. It was seductive, erotic, husky, and the most beautiful thing he'd ever heard. He didn't know how many songs she sang or how long he sat, listening.

Unable to help himself, he closed his eyes. He found himself relaxing, the worries about Dreagan, Ulrik, and the Dark easing away.

He couldn't explain it, but the entire scene felt . . . right. Her in the cave, singing. And him, listening.

Then she stopped.

His eyes snapped open to find her sherry gaze trained on him.

CHAPTER SIX

Faith hurriedly turned back to the bones. Finding Muscles in the cave once more was disconcerting, to say the least. She wasn't sure why he was with her so much, but there was no reason for her to complain.

Ever since Dmitri had arrived, Tamir hadn't been bombarded with the crazies. She was going to owe Ronnie big time.

She frowned, wondering how Ronnie knew Muscles. Faith had met Ronnie's husband, Arran, once. A strapping Highlander with golden eyes and a love for Ronnie that made women everywhere swoon and sigh.

Even her.

She moved aside more dirt with the brush as she thought about Ronnie and Arran. Marriage wasn't something Faith ever saw for herself. It had a lot to do with how she'd grown up. Her mother had been just fine without a man in her life, especially after her father ran off.

Perhaps that was why Faith never chased after guys. She'd tried relationships a time or two, but the men just got in the way of, well, everything.

She loved her independence and her job. Neither of which left time or room for love.

A quick glance over her shoulder showed that Muscles was gone. She blew out a breath of relief. He set her teeth on edge. Every time he was near, the air around her seemed to vibrate with intensity.

At least it did once she noticed him.

She crossed her legs and scooted closer to the bones. All day, and she'd only uncovered about four more inches. It was a tedious process because she wanted to make sure that she didn't accidentally destroy something.

It was why she didn't allow anyone to help unless she was present. Mixed in with the volunteers were students getting field experience, who were more than anxious to prove themselves.

The only way for them to learn was to actually do the digging, but there were some parts she didn't want them messing with. The neck was one.

Actually, if she had her way, she would have only Tamir with her. But she didn't get her way. There were rules she had to follow.

If only she had the money to fund her own digs as Ronnie did now. Faith might not be jealous of her friend's love life, but she was envious that Ronnie ran her own digs.

"One day," she whispered to herself.

Uncovering what had been hidden for generations was a passion. But it was finding funding and getting approval to dig from countries and influential people that managed to take a lot of the joy out of it.

Her job was a far cry from Indiana Jones.

That made her smile because that's what her mother had called her the moment Faith had decided she wanted to be an archeologist.

She turned up her music to help drown out her memories

while she worked. Soon, her mind was totally focused on the dragon skeleton and the secrets it had yet to share.

She imagined what its life had been like living on Fair. With more and more of the neck bones exposed, she could envision the island as a home to dragons, much as it was to the birds now.

She couldn't wait to see just how big the dragon was. If its head were any indication, it was going to be huge. Excitement and impatience surged through her. She wanted the entire skeleton revealed now.

Normally, she enjoyed the discovery phase. Each day exposing more and more of an artifact brought her such joy. Not this time, however.

Then again, everything about this dig was unusual.

Her hand stilled as she thought back to when she'd been standing on the beach. The numerous caves around Fair Isle were well known, with several extensively explored.

She still didn't know why this one had caught her attention. Or why she'd felt the overwhelming need to get inside of it immediately.

When she finally did step into the cave, she'd known. Even before she found the skeleton, she'd known that something was there, waiting to be found.

If she ever dared to tell Tamir any of this, he'd say it was some mystical being or force that had brought her to the dragon. When in reality, it was just luck.

Someone tapped on her shoulder. Faith jumped and jerked out her earbuds, turning as she did.

"Do you have any idea how late it is?" Tamir asked, a frown on his face.

She glanced around to see if Muscles was with him. When she saw no sign of him, she looked up at Tamir. "I'm gathering by your tone that it's really late."

"We're the last ones. Well, us and Dmitri."

Muscles. She wondered where he was now. "I'm not ready to leave."

Tamir sighed. "I knew you were going to say that."

"Bad day?" she asked when she saw the weariness about her assistant's eyes.

He gave a half-hearted shrug. "Just long."

"Go on ahead."

"I'm not leaving you behind," he said, plainly offended.

She smiled at him. "You've left me plenty of times."

"Not this time. Not this dig."

Why? What was it about this one that seemed to be affecting everyone? "This is just like any other dig."

"You know it isn't, so don't try and pretend otherwise." Tamir blew out a long breath. There were lines of strain around his mouth and eyes.

She got to her feet and put a hand on his arm for comfort. "Ever since those two men showed up, the ones you said felt evil, you've been on edge."

"Yeah, I have." He put his hands on his hips and shook his head, looking at the ground. "You're immersed in the dig, so you don't see everything."

"You usually tell me."

He threw out his arms. "You want me to tell you that some people are pissed? Fine. They're really angry that you're here and digging, Faith. So angry, I fear for your safety."

"I think you're being dramatic."

"You didn't encounter those men."

"And you're sure they were after me?" she pressed. "Or the dragon."

He stared at her a long minute. "I don't know. But what I do know is that they were the kind of men who wouldn't think twice about hurting you."

"All right." She swallowed, taking in Tamir's visible distress and the worry she heard in his voice.

Standing straighter, he asked, "Does that mean you're coming back with me?"

"I'll stay with her," came a voice behind Tamir.

A shiver went down her spine at the sound of Muscles' deep, sexy brogue. She looked around Tamir to Dmitri. He stood casually, giving no indication of how long he'd been there.

Her breath caught as she looked at him. He made her break into a sweat just looking at him. He was so damn gorgeous. And how she wished she hadn't noticed because it was hard to *stop* thinking about him now.

Tamir turned to Dmitri. "She'll work all night."

"No one will get past me," Dmitri promised.

And Faith believed him.

Apparently, so did Tamir, because he looked at Faith and asked, "Are you sure you want to keep working?"

"Yes." It came out as a croak, and she wasn't sure why. Surely it had nothing to do with being alone with Muscles.

Tamir's lips twisted. "Then I guess I'll see you both in the morning."

With Tamir's departure, she became all too aware that she was well and truly alone with Muscles. Their gazes met, locked. Half of his face was hidden in the shadows, and she had the urge to shine one of the lights right at him to chase away the darkness—and perhaps see what he was really thinking.

But it was never that easy. Nothing ever was, but it was particularly difficult when it came to Muscles. How she wished she knew why.

She cleared her throat and tore her gaze away from him. It felt as if she were sinking into his azure eyes when she looked at him. "I won't work too much longer."

"Work as long as you want. I plan on staying the night."

Unwittingly, her eyes returned to him. "All night."

A black brow lifted, a hint of humor softening his lips. "Aye. I will until the dig is finished."

"You're not worried about people attacking you?"

"They can certainly try."

His confidence made her want to smile. He completely believed what he'd just said. It made him infinitely dangerous, and reckless.

Somehow, the combination worked.

And well.

"I'll be making my rounds, checking on you from time to time," he said before he pivoted and walked away.

A smile now on her face, she turned and looked at the dragon. "That went much better than I expected. Who knew Muscles was so accommodating."

She put one of the earbuds back in place and nodded her head to the beat of the music. Without the distractions of people walking around her, asking her questions, or just talking, she was able to sink completely into her task once more.

Every grain of sand, every particle of dirt that she gently moved away from the skeleton was part of the story regarding the beast.

With each millimeter that was uncovered, more of the animal's saga was revealed. It was like slowly opening that last present at Christmas.

The joy she felt began to fade when she swept aside dirt with the brush and saw the missing piece from a neck bone. She hurriedly cleaned the area around it before sitting back to take it in.

She felt his presence a heartbeat before Muscles squatted beside her. Faith set down her brush as a heavy weight of sadness descended over her.

"It was a blade," Dmitri said as he ran his finger along the jagged edge of the broken bone.

"The attacker was beneath him."

"Aye, but I doona believe that is what killed him."

Her curiosity took over as she turned her head toward him. "How do you know so much?"

"I've seen these kinds of injuries before."

"It still doesn't explain how you know what you know."

"Experience."

Which could mean absolutely anything. She sighed, her eyes returning to the damaged bone. Her heart ached for the dragon. Who would want to kill such a magnificent creature? "You still don't believe this is a dragon, do you?"

"Have other dragon bones ever been found?"

"No. It took thousands of years for dinosaurs to be discovered. New ones are being excavated all the time." She mentally gave herself a high five.

"A storm is closing in," he abruptly said. "You shouldna allow anyone at the site tomorrow."

Her head swiveled to him. "We're safe inside the cave, right?"

"And outside? What about the people up top? Winds can get fierce here, lass."

"Nothing has been said about a storm," she argued. Nothing could disrupt her dig. She had a growing fear that once she left the cave, she would never be back.

Muscles got to his feet. "The wind is already picking up. Listen."

It was then she heard the howling. She put away her tools and stood. "It'll be fine. It has to."

"Have you ever been in a storm on Fair?"

She shook her head.

"You doona know what you're up against."

"Then tell me." She didn't know why she asked. Maybe it was just to hear his voice because she couldn't seem to get enough. It was his eyes, his face, his voice. That body. And the way he seemed to see right through her.

But she simply couldn't get enough.

He searched her face. "You willna believe me."

"Try me."

"Perhaps I should take you to the village."

"I'm staying," she stated firmly.

His lips flattened briefly. "I promised that no one would get to your skeleton. No one shall."

She looked at the dragon before turning her attention back to Dmitri. "I believe in science. I believe in facts and logic."

A small frown furrowed his brow. "And this has to do with the storm how?"

"Nothing." She swallowed, unsure why she was even discussing this with him. "Do you ever have unexplained feelings about something?"

"Sometimes."

"I don't. But I am now. I'm positive that if I leave this dragon, someone is going to destroy any evidence of it."

CHAPTER SEVEN

Dr. Reynolds was more intuitive than Dmitri had given her credit for. He didn't know how she knew he would demolish the skeleton, but she did.

"Nothing is going to harm you."

She cut him a hard look. "I was talking about the bones."

"Why is this so valuable?"

"It's a new find."

His gaze narrowed. "Is that all?"

"It's . . ." She paused, glancing at the dragon. "It's important to me."

It wasn't the first time he'd seen her eyes fix on the skeleton with such awareness and concern in their depths. He wasn't quite sure what was going on in that mind of hers, which was why he hadn't destroyed the bones.

Desire swirled within him once more. And not just for her body, but her mind, as well. He yearned to know what went on inside her head.

And he wouldn't mind seeing if her lips were as soft as they looked.

She lifted her chin. "Look, I don't need you to understand. You're being paid to protect this dig site. That includes whatever I find."

Without a doubt, he knew Faith wasn't a Druid. There was no magic within her slender frame. Was it just instinct that had alerted her to his intentions where the skeleton was concerned?

Mortals had that ability, but few listened to their subconscious. If her intuition was telling her that the bones were in danger, it was because she had a connection to them.

And that troubled him greatly.

What made her different? He'd felt it from their first meeting. It had taken him aback since mortals didn't normally affect him in such a way.

If it were some heightened awareness that had brought Dr. Reynolds not only to the cave but also to the bones, then that could spell trouble for her and the Dragon Kings.

Her pale brown gaze grew hard in the silence. "You don't even believe I've found a dragon. Why does it matter what the skeleton is?"

"It doesna make a difference what I think. It matters what the rest of them think. You're allowing word to spread that you've discovered dragon bones, and it has stirred people up."

She gave a roll of her eyes. "Oh, please. As if it takes anything but the change in wind direction to rouse the crazies. And for your information, I didn't let it leak about what I found. I didn't want anyone to know until I'd fully excavated the entire body and run all the tests."

He believed her. Dmitri wished it otherwise, but the truth didn't just hang on every syllable, it burned brightly in her gaze.

Standing before him was a mortal with a backbone of steel and determination stamped on every feature as she prepared to protect and defend one of his Whites.

It had a profound effect on him. One that left him temporarily speechless. Never had he imagined a human putting themselves between one of his Whites and an enemy. Except that he wasn't the enemy.

Though she couldn't know that.

His looked into her sherry eyes and wondered if she'd feel the same if the dragon were alive. There was a large part of him that suspected she would.

Unable to help himself, his gaze dropped to her lips. Passion for her trade and her beliefs smoldered within her, and he had a desire to discover if that same passion blazed between the sheets.

Even as his mind cautioned him on following the urgings of his body, his hands fisted to keep from reaching for her.

All because she gave a fuck about one of his dragons.

Dmitri wanted to dislike her and all she stood for. But he couldn't find a shred of loathing to grab on to, no matter how much he searched.

He shoved aside his desire when he saw her shiver. The temperatures were dropping rapidly in the damp cave. His head turned toward the entrance as his hearing picked up the distant thunder.

It would be hours before it could be heard by a human, but it alerted him to just how quickly the storm was moving in. If he didn't get Faith to the surface now, there might not be another chance.

A gust of wind howled through the cave as the waves slammed with brutal force against the cliffs, the sound reverberating through the stone.

She wrapped her arms around her middle. "I checked the weather. They didn't say anything about this type of storm."

"The sea doesna bend to the will of mortals," he said and walked toward the entrance.

She was two steps behind him. "Did you just say mortals?"

"Aye." No use denying it. Though he was going to have to watch what he said from now on. There was just something about her that made him forget his boundaries.

Faith halted ten feet from the moonlight-dappled opening of the cave as Muscles walked to the edge of the cliff. The force of the wind whipped around her even from her position.

Yet he stood like a pillar against it, barely moving while she had to take a few steps to the side. Her gaze was locked on him, on his stoic profile that contemplated Mother Nature as if he could tame it.

Oddly enough, she had a feeling if anyone could, it would be Muscles.

His head turned toward her, putting half his face in shadows again. His azure eyes seemed to glow in the glint of bluish light while his dark hair whipped about in the wind. Then he held out his hand.

She stared at his outstretched arm for several seconds before she took it. A current instantly ran up her arm. She jerked her gaze to his face, but he didn't seem to feel it. His long fingers gently wrapped around her hand, and he pulled her against him.

Faith gasped as the wind hit her. She turned her head away, burying it against the side of his arm. To stay upright, she had to cling to him.

She couldn't decide what she liked most—the feel of the heat emanating from him or the thick sinew beneath her palm.

Her eyes slid closed when his head bent, and his lips brushed her ear. He held her firmly, securely. The entire scenario made her body flush with unexpected—and unwanted—longing.

She burned from the inside out. Desire had never felt this . . . hot . . . before. Every nerve ending tingled as her breathing quickened.

"It's going to be dangerous," he said in his husky brogue.

Actually, she was quite fine where she was in the confines of his arms, his heat surrounding her even as the wind buffeted her with almost demonic force.

"I'll get you to the top."

Without a doubt, she knew he would. Muscles wasn't the type of man to give a promise and break it.

"But the rocks are sharp, and the wind vicious. I doona know that it'll be any better in the tent."

Faith had been inside a tent while the wind blew, and it hadn't been a pretty thing. She'd gotten no sleep that night listening to her tent strain against the ties.

She lifted her head and met his gaze. Desire rushed through her like a tidal wave. Their lips were so close they were all but kissing. And then that's all she could think about.

His lips moving over hers, teasing and nipping before plundering her mouth. Would he bend her back over his arm, hold her against him, or push her against the rock wall?

Her stomach fluttered at the thought. She willed herself to stop thinking such things, but the images were already there. Somehow, she had enough wherewithal to lift her gaze from his lips upward—colliding with azure eyes that watched her as a predator did its prey.

Was it the moonlight that allowed her to catch the threads of silver in his eyes? Or was it simply her imagination?

As if the storm would no longer wait for her reply, it sent a gust into her back that made her lose her balance. In an instant, he moved them out of the cave entrance and righted her.

Up against the stone wall.

Her knees went weak, her lips parting. She was panting and needy. He was still close, his strong hands holding
her steady. Desire heated her body as blood pounded in her
ears. Her hands held on to his shoulders with a death grip.

Slowly, she loosened and spread her fingers to feel more
of his muscles. She struggled to breathe against the tide of
passion that was rapidly dragging her under.

She wanted him. To know his taste, the feel of his hard
body naked against hers. To give in to the yearning and
the need that tightened inside her.

To surrender to the promise of pleasure.

"You're shivering."

No, she was fairly certain her body was on fire. The
words lodged in her throat, however.

"Come," he bade.

Somehow, she made her legs work as he guided her to
the back of the cave once more. Then he sat her down, rubbing his hands up and down her arms.

"Doona move. I'll return shortly."

"You can't go out there," she hurriedly said.

A crooked, sexy smile formed on his lips. "Of course,
I can. I willna be long."

He was gone before she could stop him. And with his
absence, the cold penetrated her clothes. Faith pulled her
legs up against her chest and sat huddled against the wall.

She knew the force of the wind. It was idiotic for Muscles to even attempt to climb the cliff in such a storm. Then
again, he had been unmovable against it.

Her gaze slid to the bones as her teeth began to chatter.
At least the rain hadn't begun yet. That would allow the
climb to be a tad easier.

Though the wind couldn't reach her so far back in the
cave, the sheer size of the tunnel meant that the cold fil-
tered in quickly, sinking into every space.

She pulled her jacket tighter around her, but nothing could stop the damp air from breaching her clothes. Inside her boots, she curled her toes that had begun to tingle from the temperatures.

Her lids slid closed. She wouldn't have been in this predicament had she left with Tamir. Instead, she'd continued working.

Muscles was right, she couldn't count on a weather app to know what would happen. But all of that was a moot point now. She was stuck in the cave.

Much as her dragon had been.

Odd how the storm made her realize how still the cave was. She wasn't afraid. Instead, she felt . . . at peace.

Her lids grew heavy, and it took too much energy to keep them open. She let them close as she continued to listen for Dmitri's return.

She must have dozed because she came to at the feel of strong hands on her arms. Faith forced open her eyes and saw Muscles in the darkness.

His hair was windblown, and his face was fixed in hard lines as he concentrated. She opened her mouth to ask what he was doing when he lifted her, but then she felt the softness of a sleeping bag.

She curled onto her side to find warmth even as he took off her shoes. That's when she noticed all the lights were out. A thick wool blanket was thrown over her before Muscles molded against her back.

As soon as his warmth cocooned her, she sighed in contentment. It was a dire situation, but somehow, he'd come through—just as she'd known he would.

He slid his arm beneath her neck before his other hand flattened on her stomach and pulled her more securely against him.

"You need warmth," he whispered.

Yep. Though she needed more than that. But warmth would do. For now. "Thank you."

"Rest," he ordered.

She wanted to argue, but as if on command, her eyes closed. Though she didn't go straight to sleep. Instead, she listened to the sound of Dmitri's even breathing while enjoying the feel of his body against hers.

They lay there for long moments while the wind and sea raged. Just as she was drifting off to sleep, she felt him move aside her hair.

The pads of his fingers caressed along her jaw so faintly she wondered if she'd dreamed it. Sleep began to pull her under, but she fought to remain awake.

She wanted to know if Muscles would do more. Because for a man who appeared to be made of granite, his touch was exceptionally soft and gentle.

More, she silently begged.

As if he'd heard, he moved aside her bangs that were tangled in her eyelashes. He then gently stroked down the curve of her ear.

"Sleep, lass," he whispered. "For tomorrow is yet another day."

CHAPTER EIGHT

Dreagan

 Rhi stood in the shadows, staring at the four large Silver dragons that had been sleeping away centuries inside a mountain.

The same mountain that was connected to Dreagan Manor. It was one the Dragon Kings used for special ceremonies, to gather before and after a battle, and, more recently, as a place to hide from the prying eyes of MI5.

Magic kept the secret entrance from the manor into the mountain from being found. The huge opening on the other side of the mountain would not be discovered either.

Because that's what dragon magic could do.

It was exceedingly powerful. So much in fact that they could've won against the Dark Fae just by using magic. That wasn't the dragon way, however.

Instead, they'd fought, utilizing their cleverness and inherent battle skills to outwit, overwhelm, and defeat the Dark during the Fae Wars.

Why then had they needed the Light?

The Kings had only required help then because they'd wanted to keep the mortals from seeing anything.

Now, thousands of years later, nothing had changed.

The Kings still needed aid to keep the humans from learning the truth.

Truth.

The word hung above her like the blade of a guillotine. She'd accepted the reality of herself after Balladyn had kidnapped and locked her in the dungeons of the Dark Palace. Even after he'd tortured her to turn her Dark, she hadn't lied to herself.

Both dark and light, good and evil, existed within every being across the galaxy. Sometimes one dominated over the other. Sometimes, the two sides continually fought to determine which would win.

Ever since she had released her magic to break out of the chains that had bound her and escape her prison, she'd felt the darkness growing inside her.

Balladyn, angry about her breakout, had pursued her relentlessly. Until she'd stopped running. Yet he hadn't wanted to harm her.

That's when he'd shown her his love. When he'd been left behind during battle and then taken by the Dark and turned, Balladyn had blamed her. His love had turned to hate. Yet, somehow, love had won out against the hate inside him.

So why then was she at Dreagan?

Truth. It all came back to truth.

No longer would she lie to herself about the Dragon Kings. If she could face the darkness growing inside her, then she could face her past.

Her gaze ran over the metallic scales of the dragons. The four were curled together so it was difficult to tell where one ended and another began.

A Fae wasn't supposed to love a dragon, but she'd done just that. She'd fallen head over heels in love with not just any dragon, but a Dragon King.

And he'd loved her in return.

All should've been right with the world. Except there was one who'd cautioned Rhi to think twice about such a "dalliance." With her family dead, she had devoted her life and everything she was to the queen and becoming the first female in the Queen's Guard.

Usaeil had warned that the Light, while allies of the Kings, wouldn't take kindly to one of their own becoming a mate.

It didn't matter how much Rhi loved the queen, she followed her heart. The kind of love Rhi had found was one for the ages. Their love had shone brighter than the sun, burned hotter than the biggest star.

Then it had all ended abruptly.

Rhi still didn't know what had caused her King to terminate their affair. The loss had nearly destroyed her. She'd wanted to die, but she pushed on with a hole in her chest where her heart used to be.

Usaeil had said it was for the best. Rhi then turned her attention to becoming the best Queen's Guard. She'd succeeded.

Life went on, it endured as it always had—and always would. The seasons changed, lives were lost and new ones born. She shouldered her unrequited love alone while whispers of the queen taking a new lover—a Dragon King lover—spread through the Light.

Then there was Balladyn. Rhi had taken him as her lover, hoping to turn him Light once more. Despite that, she was happier than she had been in a very long while.

She should've listened to her gut months ago, though. It was fear that the past was ruling her emotions that had kept her silent. Except now, she had proof.

Her gaze lowered to the magazine cover she held clutched in her hand. On it was a grainy picture taken through the window of a hotel room. Usaeil, parading around as her American movie star alter ego, was easily recognizable wearing a gold dress.

It was the man in the photo that drew Rhi's attention. Because even though he was half turned away from the camera, she knew who it was—Con.

Before Rhi confronted Usaeil, she was going to show Con the photograph. She wasn't sure if she was doing it to laugh in his face at being caught, or to see his reaction, though.

Perhaps a little of both.

She teleported into Con's office, not bothering to veil herself. He sat behind his desk, his head bent as he pored over some papers. A heartbeat after she appeared, his head snapped up.

He set down his favorite Mont Blanc pen and slowly sat back in the chair. Black eyes watched her carefully. "Rhi."

She noted that he'd removed the dragon head cufflinks from his French cuff shirt that was now rolled up to his elbows. The cufflinks sat within reaching distance.

His wavy, surfer-boy blond hair was disheveled, as if he'd run his hands through it several times. There were also lines of strain around his lips.

"You play a dangerous game," he said flatly. "Do you so easily forget that we've visitors on the estate?"

The humans. How could she forget? "I'm not that dim-witted. Unlike you. I made sure I wasn't seen."

"I gather since you're in my office that you want something."

"I thought you were smart."

His gaze narrowed, his brow puckering. "To what are you referring this time?"

It was no secret that she and Con hated each other. It went back to the days of her affair with her lover. And it wasn't likely to end.

She tossed the magazine on his desk. It landed with a thud before him. "Take a look."

He held her gaze for a long time before he looked down. Then he went utterly still. The waves of outrage were palpable as they poured off him with the intensity and violence of an erupting volcano.

His hands flattened on the desk as he slowly rose to his feet. Most called Con callous because he held every emotion in check. Rarely did he smile. His face could be mistaken for a statue because it seldom changed.

It was a singular event to see that mask slip and his emotions show as they did now. His black eyes burned with fury—and the promise of retribution.

"Who have you shown?" he demanded in a cold, deadly voice.

But she wasn't influenced by his show of indignation. "No one."

That seemed to appease him somewhat as his shoulders dropped. Yet the ire remained.

"By your reaction, it *is* you with her." Rhi gave a shake of her head. "You don't know what you've stepped into."

"I was handling it."

"Badly."

He slammed his hand on the desk. "I was handling it!"

Another burst of emotion. Rhi took a closer look at the King of Kings. Though he was trying to hold it all together, things were unraveling at both ends.

Con so effortlessly kept his emotions in check that it was easy to overlook him when there were others who didn't mind sharing their thoughts and feelings.

"Do you know why I left the Queen's Guard?"

"Because Usaeil tried to tell you what to do," Con said, closing his eyes as if seeking the serenity he'd previously had.

"That was part of it. The other half was that she's changed. She's different."

His gaze snapped open, pinning her with a look. "Why did you no' say anything?"

"It didn't involve you or the Kings. It was about the Fae." She gave him a stern look. "Aren't you always telling me to keep the two separate?"

"You Irish always hear things the way you want to hear them," he retorted as he straightened.

Rhi raised a brow. "And you Scots always do things the way you want, regardless of the consequences."

"What is that supposed to mean?"

"It means that she's wanted a King as a lover for a *very* long time."

"That's shite," he said with a wave of his hand, dismissing her words.

Rhi took a step closer to the desk. "Is it?"

Eyes black as pitch and as cold as ice met her gaze. "Are you saying she used me?"

"Yes. Just as I'm sure you used her. Unless it's true love?"

He didn't so much as bat an eye. Was it relief she felt, knowing that Con didn't love Usaeil? She was pretty fucking sure it was.

And it made her want to smile.

She held it in check.

Barely.

"What proof do you have?" Con asked.

"Conversations. She also asked me about my past affair with . . ." She trailed off, unable to finish. Damn, it shouldn't be so hard after all this time.

But the truth—that damn word again—was right before her.

Con nodded and blew out a breath. "The night this

picture was taken, she told me she wanted to announce to the Fae and the Kings that we were a couple."

"What did you say?" Rhi asked worriedly.

"I told her that wasna going to happen. Then she blamed my decision on you."

Rhi sank into one of the chairs in front of Con's desk with a snort. "Usaeil hasn't been to the castle in months. She's ruled our people for a long time, but she's never been so ambivalent about their welfare before."

"Do you think she had something to do with this photo going public?"

"Definitely." Rhi looked into Con's black eyes. "She might've also been responsible for posting the covers throughout the Light Castle."

Con raked a hand down his face and briefly closed his eyes.

"What does it matter?" Rhi asked. "It wouldn't be the first time a King and a Fae were together. There was my affair. Not to mention, Kiril is mated to Shara, which both you and Usaeil sanctioned, I might add."

"Usaeil wants to combine our races," he said in a soft voice as he looked at her. "She wants every King to find a mate with a Light to bind our races even further."

That's when it dawned on Rhi. "She thinks the Fae will be able to give the Kings children where the humans never could."

Con put his fists atop his desk and hung his head. "I need to find her."

"Why did you get involved with her? You knew things could turn out badly."

"My reasons doona matter."

"Well, you'd better come up with good ones because you can get away with not telling me, but the Kings won't take that dodgy shit you just shoveled my way."

He let out a long sigh. "I know."

"There is too much going on for this to be coincidence. The Dark releasing the video of the Kings shifting, Ulrik closing in on you, Usaeil acting weird, talk of the Reapers, and—"

She stopped right before she mentioned Balladyn wanting to overthrow Taraeth and become the new Dark King.

Con's knowing gaze said that he discerned she was hiding something., But he didn't push. Because if he did, he'd have to tell his secret, as well. Neither wanted to be put in that position.

"There's even more," Con said. "Ulrik attacked Asher in Paris. In dragon form."

Rhi's mouth fell open. All she could think was *holy shit*. That meant the battle with Ulrik was going to happen very soon.

"Usaeil won't stop until she has what she wants," she informed him. "And she wants you."

"She's going to be verra disappointed then."

CHAPTER NINE

Long after Faith stopped shivering and fell asleep, Dmitri remained awake. He told himself it was because he didn't want to wake her, but it was really because he liked having her in his arms.

That alone should've sent him as far from her as he could get, but it didn't. He briefly tried to determine why he remained. The answers were as complicated and ambiguous as his thoughts on Faith.

Around daybreak, the wind began to die down. The sea still churned, angrily throwing itself at the cliffs as if to pummel them to dust.

As he lay with Faith, he went over his two suspects in his mind. He needed to follow them, but he couldn't chance leaving the skeleton. Or Faith.

Someone wanted the bones. Ulrik or the Dark, it didn't matter, because neither was going to get their hands on them. Which meant whatever he was going to do about his suspects would have to be done at the site.

It would be easy enough to put up a barrier so that no Dark could get to the cave, but that would alert them that a King was there. That might incite a battle, and there was enough attention surrounding dragons as it was.

It was imperative that the Dark didn't realize he was there until he confronted them. Because the Dark would return. Though the Fae had yet to go after one of the humans, it was simply a matter of time.

A human soul was food for the Dark. Each time the mortal had sex with the Fae, their soul would be drained until nothing was left but the husk of a body.

That wasn't going to happen on his watch. Dmitri might've come to make sure the bones were in fact from a dragon—and then destroy them—but he found he was doing much more than that.

Perhaps if Faith knew exactly what she was unearthing, she might take another approach. Then again, the stalwart archeologist might just move ahead with more steam.

He gradually removed his arm from beneath her neck and scooted from under the blanket. Knowing that Faith was safe allowed him to leave the cave and look around the area.

The wind was a soft caress after the violence of the night. He climbed out onto the cliff and made his way to another cave. After a quick search to make sure there wasn't another skeleton, he climbed to the top and saw that the tents had all been destroyed.

His gaze looked far into the distance where the sky met the sea. They were being given a brief lull before the next storm made landfall.

He looked at the sun's ascent. Tamir and the others should be arriving soon. That gave him just enough time to walk the edge of the cliffs and the surrounding area to see if anyone had tried to come to the camp during the night.

Thirty minutes later, he had a pleased smile on his face.

No one had trespassed. Then again, the wind had probably kept those less adventurous at bay.

But it would've been the perfect time for the Dark. The fact that nothing had occurred worried him. It left him with an uneasy feeling that something was about to happen.

Much like Faith felt about someone destroying the bones. He might be the culprit there, but he wasn't sure who would come after Faith or the skeleton. Would it be mortals or Dark Fae?

It was another twenty minutes before he heard the sound of a vehicle approaching. He walked to meet it as Tamir and three others climbed out.

"What's wrong?" he asked when he saw the look of dread on their faces.

Tamir ran a hand through his hair and put on a baseball cap. He tugged it down low over his eyes. "There was an accident in the village last night."

"What kind of accident?" Dmitri asked as a young woman walked past him wiping tears from her face. His frown deepened as he once more looked at Tamir.

"One of the workers is dead."

The smile Dmitri had worn a short time ago was long gone. Dread filled him. "How?"

"We can't find any marks on him. He was just lying in his room, naked."

Dark Fae. Dmitri kept that tidbit to himself for the time being. He needed to hunt the bastards, but that meant leaving the site, something he wasn't comfortable doing.

"Where is Faith?" Tamir asked.

"In the cave. She worked too late to safely make it up the cliffs," he explained.

Tamir nodded. "The tents didn't quite make it."

"I secured the boxes of artifacts last night before the storm hit."

"Thank you."

Dmitri stopped Tamir as he began to walk past. "There is another storm coming, and this one will be worse. No one should be working."

"You don't need to worry. No one is coming to the site after Roger's death. Those with me came for what they left behind."

Dmitri hated that a mortal was dead, but it might work to his advantage. If the death was keeping the rest of the humans away, it could possibly send Faith along with them.

That would then allow him to destroy the bones and hunt the Dark before returning to Dreagan. His entire mission could be accomplished that day.

Why then did that make him a little sad?

"I'll see if Dr. Reynolds is awake," he told Tamir.

He didn't hurry on the climb down. And once in the cave, he wasn't sure if he wanted Faith to still be asleep or not. Halfway to the dragon, he saw that some of the lights were on.

So she was awake. He smoothed his fingers through his hair and lengthened his strides. Just as he expected, she was already back at work.

When she saw him, there was the hint of a smile on her lips. "Morning. I found the water and granola bar. Thank you."

"You're welcome. I have news."

She set the brush down and got to her feet, worry clouding her eyes. "And not good news by the sound of it. It's better to just get it out."

"Tamir arrived and said that a man named Roger died during the night."

She took it in, nodding absently. "Do we know how he died?"

Aye. "Nay."

"There've been only two other times I've had someone

die during a dig. There will be no working today. I should go to the village."

Just what he wanted to hear.

"Promise me you won't let anything happen to the dragon."

He stared into her eyes, trying to get the lie past his lips, but it wouldn't come. Finally, he gave a nod of his head in acknowledgement.

"I need the words," she insisted. "This is my livelihood. It's not about the fame or money. It's about learning the truth. There is truth here, and I won't have anyone stopping me from discovering what it is."

Her words had a peculiar effect on him. Somehow, he knew that if she were ever confronted by a dragon, she wouldn't run away screaming.

The next thing he knew, he said, "Nothing will happen to your dragon."

"Thank you." She then gave him a bright smile and walked away.

Dmitri looked at the skeleton. "What the bloody hell have I gotten myself into?"

He really wished he knew what it was about Faith that prevented him from doing what he needed to. Quickly turning out the lights, he followed her up.

Faith and Tamir were standing outside the main tent where the artifacts were kept. As Dimitri drew near, Faith spun around and pinned him with a look.

"You did this?" she demanded.

He looked at the mess of tents half folded in the wind, chairs and belongings scattered. "I took care of what I thought was the most important."

"You did amazing," she said in a soft voice.

The way her sherry eyes looked at him as if he were her savior made him take a step back. It was either that or grab her and kiss her.

"You took care of this in the wind when I didn't even think about it. I don't know how to thank you," she continued, tucking her sandy blond hair behind her ears.

He gave a shake of his head. "I was doing my job. Protecting the site."

"I'll send someone out in a few hours to give you some relief."

"I'll be fine," he told her. "I prefer it out here."

There was a hint of disappointment in her gaze. "Call if you change your mind."

Dmitri watched as they piled into the van with the bins of artifacts. Faith looked back at him as they drove away. He watched until the vehicle was no longer in sight.

Now was his chance. It would be hours before anyone returned. Plenty of time for him to return to the cave, shift, and destroy the bones with dragon fire. Nothing would be left but ash.

Then he thought of the neck bone with the evidence of a blade having punctured it. It bothered him that one of his dragons had not only been left behind but had also been wounded and died alone. Why hadn't the dragon called out to him for help?

It was a mystery he needed to solve before he could erase any evidence of the dragon. It gave Faith a brief reprieve that she didn't even realize.

He wasn't the type of man to give his word without following through. He didn't want to lie to her, but in the end, it was about protecting Dreagan and the other Dragon Kings.

The time alone would also allow him the opportunity to check all the other caves so there were no more surprises. He got two steps toward the cliffs when he heard Con's voice in his head.

Dmitri opened the mental link. *"Aye?"*

"I expected you home by now."

"*In truth, so did I. However, there are complications.*"

There was a beat of silence. Then Con asked, "*Such as?*"

"*There are Dark here. They killed a human last night.*"

"*You think they want the bones?*"

Dmitri snorted as he proceeded to the cliff before beginning his climb down. "*I know they do. The video caused a stir, but can you imagine if there are bones as evidence?*"

"*Our lives as we know it would be over. We'd either have to hide once more or leave.*"

"*I'm no' prepared to do either.*"

"*So the skeleton is a dragon?*"

"*Aye. He's one of mine. I saw a blade mark on one of the bones.*"

Con let out a long breath. "*But you doona know how he died?*"

"*No' yet.*"

"*I see.*" Con paused for a moment. "*And Dr. Reynolds? Will he be a problem?*"

"She *is something I can handle.*"

"*A woman. At least I doona have to worry about you since you doona find mortal women appealing.*"

Dmitri had to smile at the sarcasm dripping from Con's words. But that smile faded because the truth was that he now found himself attracted to a mortal. "*How is everything at Dreagan?*" When Con didn't immediately answer, he stopped his descent. "*Con?*"

"*There could be a . . . slight . . . problem.*"

For Con to even admit there could be an issue meant it was huge. "*Do I need to return now?*"

"*There's nothing you can do, even if you were here.*"

"*What the hell is going on?*"

Con started to speak, then paused. He did it once more before he said, "*I had a plan. It backfired.*"

"*That doesna normally happen. Who did this involve?*"

"I know the majority of you believe that I have taken a lover."

Dmitri dropped down into a cave and squatted at the entrance. *"I take this to mean that we were correct?"*

"Yes."

"Were we also correct in thinking it was Usaeil?"

"Aye," Con replied grudgingly.

He stood, taking in the news. *"What does this mean for us?"*

"My rule was that our affair was kept secret. She didna like that and secretly had us photographed. That picture is now on the cover of a magazine."

"Fuck." That's all Dimitri could think to say. Then he recalled why Con had begun the affair. *"What were you after with Usaeil?"*

"Information about the Light."

Dmitri wasn't fooled. There was another reason.

CHAPTER TEN

Faith fell back on the bed with the towel still wrapped around her from the shower. It felt so good to get the dirt off her and to be warm and clean again. Wet hair clung to her neck and face, but her thoughts were on death.

The ending of a life always had a profound effect on others. Some pretended it didn't bother them, but it was a lie. Someone passing out of this life into the next was a reminder of just how fragile the human body was.

And how quickly a life could be snuffed out.

Her thoughts drifted to the dragon bones. One of her mother's favorite sayings was that all life was precious. The dragon was just as valuable as a human life. At least, that was her thinking.

It was sad that others didn't share that philosophy. Though it was something Faith had learned to accept, since few rarely agreed with her thinking. They thought her too soft-hearted.

So what if she stopped her car to allow a butterfly to flit undisturbed across the road.

Why did it bother people that she caught and freed lizards, frogs, and geckos that regularly got into her house?

Who did it hurt when she pulled over and halted traffic to help a turtle make it over a busy street?

Her actions did nothing but help animals—and make her smile. Life was precious. Man may be at the top of the food chain, but that didn't mean they couldn't—and shouldn't—treat animals with kindness and respect.

She wished she knew if the dragon had been treated thus because she couldn't shake the feeling that something terrible had happened to it.

More answers were beneath the dirt, but she would have to wait another day to find them. For now, she was needed in the village.

Faith sat up and let out a sigh. The first thing she'd done upon arriving in the village was go and see the body of the dead worker. She hated that she hadn't remembered his name without being told. It wasn't that she didn't care. It was that there were so many workers and she concentrated on doing her job.

The truth was, her excuse was lame. She should know all of their names. These people wanted to be at the dig to uncover history just as she did. The least she could do was acknowledge them.

Not that she had that problem with Muscles.

Her thoughts halted at the image of him that popped into her mind. There was no reason for her to think of him. Why did he have to push his way into her head?

Now that he was there, there was no pushing him out. No matter how hard she tried.

She rose and dropped the towel before rummaging in her bag for clean clothes. Her determination was strong to forget about Muscles for the day.

Why then did she think about his palms running up her legs when she put on her panties? Why did she imagine his hands cupping her breasts when she clasped her bra into place?

Her mouth went dry as she recalled being within the confines of his strong arms. Her stomach clenched as she remembered how his azure eyes had watched her.

She bit her lip as her nipples puckered. Yearning—powerful and fervent—coiled lasciviously through her. It encouraged and compelled her to follow through with the longing within her.

Her palm flattened on her stomach and rose upward to her aching breasts as her eyes slid closed. She could practically feel Muscles' heat enveloping her as it had the night before.

How stupid of her not to take advantage of their time alone. She wanted him. And she should've grasped the chance that had been given her.

She was jerked out of her illusion by a knock at the door. Her eyes snapped open, and her hand dropped to her side.

"Faith?"

She was more than a little disappointed that it wasn't Dmitri's deep brogue she heard. "Yes?" she called out to Tamir.

"We're gathering below."

"I'll be right down."

She dropped her chin to her chest for a moment. In that second, she gave in to everything she felt for Muscles. Then she shoved it aside.

Dressing quickly in a pair of her favorite jeans that went everywhere with her, a white sweater, and brown boots, she was prepared to face death.

She quickly blow-dried her hair, added a bit of lipgloss, and a pair of gold stud earrings. Then she was out the door and down the stairs.

Tamir was waiting for her. He gave her a half-smile and held out her coat. As soon as she walked outside and felt the bracing wind, her mind once more went to Muscles and how he'd stood unmoved in it the night before.

"They're at the hall," Tamir said as they crossed the street.

Faith nodded. There were so few people on the isle that they had no restaurants or pubs. The only place to find anything to eat was the bird observatory. "I need to give the authorities the address to return the body to his family."

"I can take care of that."

"I should do it," she insisted.

As if knowing that would be her answer, Tamir pulled out a piece of paper and handed it to her. "It has all of the information needed."

"Thank you." She put it in her pocket and glanced at Tamir. He had worry lines bracketing his mouth and a frown that had yet to disperse. But it was the look of fear in his dark eyes that told her he was deeply troubled. "What is it?"

"Evil," he whispered. He came to a stop and faced her.

She halted and looked at him. She opened her mouth to ask him what he was talking about, but he spoke before she could.

"It's everywhere. Don't you feel it?" he asked urgently, his eyes darting around.

She put her hand on his arm, hoping it would calm him. "We've had something traumatic affect us. We're all feeling out of sorts."

"No." He gave a firm shake of his head. "We shouldn't be here or messing with those bones. The evil wants what you've found, and it won't stop until it has it."

"I'm not going to let anyone get to my dragon." She was a little taken aback to hear the anger in her words.

Tamir swallowed and looked away. "It's wrong. All of this is. We should leave and never return."

He walked past her into the observatory. She watched the door close behind him, shaken by the ferocity of his words. He believed what he'd spoken to the depths of his soul. She'd known Tamir a long time, and she'd never seen him like this.

Faith looked around the quiet village. The few people she spotted were all staring at her. Did they feel the same as Tamir?

Suddenly, she wished Dmitri was there. It wasn't just his calming presence, but Muscles had a way of looking at a situation. And right now, she could use some help.

It wasn't as if she could seek him out since he'd remained behind at the site. Perhaps that's where she should've stayed, as well.

Faith pivoted and walked to the house at the end of the road. With so few residents, there was only a volunteer emergency Coastguard team, volunteer firefighters, and a nurse.

She knocked on the door and smiled at the older woman who acted as nurse for Fair Isle. "Hi. I have the information to send . . . the body . . . home."

The woman's smile was sad. "Ach, dear. Police from Orkney will be here in the morn. You can speak to them about such matters."

"Oh, okay. Thank you."

She turned away as the door was closing. Apparently, the villagers didn't want her there any more than Tamir did. Faith drew out the piece of paper as she made her way back to the hall. She turned it around and around between her fingers.

How had—she opened the paper and looked at the name to remind herself again—Roger died? There hadn't been a mark on his body. He was young for a stroke, and since workers took physicals before being allowed on the dig site, there hadn't been a pre-existing condition. Though that didn't rule out a heart attack.

It wasn't unheard of for a younger man to suffer a heart

attack, but it was still odd. And for him to be found naked in his room . . .

Something didn't add up.

She looked back over her shoulder and saw a figure behind her. It was a man, and he appeared to be watching her. When she stopped and stared, he ducked behind a building.

Tamir felt sure that evil was there. Roger's unexplained death did tip the scales in that direction, but an autopsy could reveal a number of things. For all she knew, Roger had died of a drug overdose.

With a shrug, she turned and hurried out of the cold and into the hall. It seemed odd to see faces she barely registered at the dig site standing all around her.

As she walked among them, she heard them talking about Roger. Everyone seemed to have some anecdote to share about him. How he liked to quote movies and had an affinity for picking up all kinds of accents.

Apparently, he also loved to drink. But that could apply to many of the individuals in the building that night, so she didn't pay much attention to that.

She saw Tamir standing in the back corner alone, his gaze on the floor. His posture let everyone know that he didn't want to be bothered, and they gave him a wide berth.

Faith decided not to bother him either. She continued walking among the others, occasionally pausing to hear some story or another about Roger.

Most everyone liked him, though a few talked about how he would do anything to get out of working. That made her frown since he was a volunteer. It was a half hour later that she learned he had recently changed his major to archeology and was at the dig for extra credit.

Normally, Tamir let her know when someone was at a dig because of his or her major, and not because it was of interest. Did Tamir not know? Or had he just forgotten to mention it to her?

She put it aside and sipped her wine while she thought about her own mortality. With her mother's death a few months earlier, and now Roger's, it was nearly impossible not to think about it.

Which led her to think about finding more joy and happiness in her life outside of work.

Which, of course, led her to think about Muscles.

She blew out a breath. She really had to stop thinking about him. So she had a bit of a crush on him. Big deal. It wasn't the first time.

You sure about that?

Fine. So it had been a few years since she'd had a crush.

You want to tear his clothes off and lick him from head to toe. It's not a crush.

No, it wasn't a crush. It was inescapable, unstoppable, make-you-want-to-howl-at-the-moon desire.

And it made her heart skip a beat every time she thought about it.

She fanned herself in an attempt to cool down. It was pointless, but she couldn't stop herself. Just as she couldn't halt her thoughts from turning to all sorts of scenarios about her kissing Muscles.

Perhaps she needed to cool off. She made her way to the side door and walked outside. She lifted her face upward and took several deep breaths as the cold air washed over her skin.

She opened her eyes and saw the thick clouds rolling slowly in the sky. Muscles had said another storm was coming. The evidence sat above her, gradually building once more.

Last night had been horrid, and that hadn't even had precipitation. How much worse would it be when the rain did come?

She turned to head back inside when she saw two people walking away. One was a female she recognized from the dig. The woman had long, dark hair. Faith never saw the man's face.

Why then did she hear Tamir's words from earlier? *Evil.*

CHAPTER ELEVEN

Dmitri finished exploring the last cave. He should feel better that no other dragon bones were there, but he couldn't manage it.

With Con's news about Usaeil, and the picture of his King and the Fae queen together going viral all over the world, Dmitri knew he should be at Dreagan.

Then again, there was the matter of Dr. Reynolds and the dragon skeleton. Now that he was alone, he didn't worry about being seen and launched himself to the top of the cliffs with a jump.

It was the closest he could get to flying—for now. Even that little bit was a risk, and not one he could take often.

He walked the area where the tents stood with his mind in turmoil. The Dark were there. Dmitri could easily—and eagerly—take care of them.

Matter of fact, he was itching for just such a fight. The Dark had put the spotlight on Dreagan with the taping of their battle.

The Kings couldn't turn the tables on the Fae, because the Dark couldn't care less if the mortals knew about them. It was too bad the Kings didn't feel the same way.

His head whipped around when he heard the sound of a chopper. His heightened senses picked up the vibration much sooner than a human's would. And his enhanced eyesight was able to see the helicopter flying toward the airport.

It was most likely someone to claim the body, but with them would come a human who would soon learn that the dig worker died without explanation.

That would lead to an investigation into everyone at the site. He needed to get rid of the Dark well before then. One death was enough. Any more, and the spotlight would be shining on Fair Isle, as well.

Now that all the mortals were at the village, leaving the bones alone, the Dark would head his way. All Dimitri had to do was sit and wait for them.

He'd never been so relieved to have Faith and the others gone than he was at that moment. He would guard the remains of his dragon kin with his very life.

His head turned in the direction of the village. Faith was safe. She was surrounded by others who would watch out for her.

"She'll be safe," he said aloud.

But voicing his wishes wouldn't make them come true. Not with the Dark Fae walking around.

His oath to protect mankind drifted through his mind. He had the means to defend Faith and all the others on Fair, but to do so meant showing them who he was—the very thing Con had forbidden him to do.

How could the Kings continue to protect the humans and not do it in their true form? The Kings were constantly fighting with one hand tied behind their backs while the Dark—as well as Ulrik—had an entire arsenal at their disposal without caring who saw them or the outcome.

Dimitri turned on his heel and ran to the edge of the cliffs. He dove over the side, tucking his body to roll once before he landed on the ledge before Faith's cave.

He strode inside and checked on the bones before he moved into the shadows and waited for the Dark.

Because they would come. It was what they did.

"I'm sorry, but could you repeat that?" Faith asked the Deputy Inspector standing before her.

He looked at her with suspicious, dull gray eyes. "Fair Isle doesna get many murders with it having such a meager population."

"I understood that part." She was tired and frustrated, and D.I. Batson was not making things easy.

"When we learned about the lack of proof regarding how Mr. Thomas died, we brought in a doctor to perform an autopsy."

She nodded while the inspector spoke. "Yes, yes. I understood that part, as well."

"Then what part did you no' get, Dr. Reynolds? The section where I said there was no evidence of how Mr. Thomas died?"

"That's it. Right there. That part." She stared, waiting for him to elaborate.

He drew in a deep breath and released it. "I have nothing else to say."

"I'm afraid you've got that wrong, D.I. Batson. There is always some explanation of how a person passes away. Perhaps you need to find another physician. One that can actually figure out how Roger died."

The way his gaze narrowed had nothing to do with him taking offense to what she'd said, and everything to do with him hiding something.

"You know how he died." She took a step back, appalled. "Why won't you tell me? I may not have known his name, but he was part of my crew. I'm responsible for him. I have to tell his family."

"That has already been done, Dr. Reynolds."

She briefly closed her eyes as the truth settled around her. "He was killed, wasn't he?"

"He was."

"Why didn't you just say that?" she demanded, anger now taking hold.

Batson merely raised a brow. "I wanted to see your reaction. Everyone confirmed you weren't in the village last night, and when I went to ask the man guarding the site, I couldna find him."

Where was Muscles? But then she knew. In the cave. No way Batson would climb down to the cave. "Dmitri is standing guard over my find."

"That's what your assistant, Tamir, said, as well." Batson crossed his arms over his chest. "You didna kill Mr. Thomas."

"No, I didn't. But I would like to know how he died."

"His heart shriveled to the size of an egg."

Faith had known the reason would be horrific, but she hadn't expected it to be so . . . odd. "How does that happen?"

"It doesna. We're ruling Mr. Thomas's death a homicide."

She had been sitting in the nurse's front room for hours, waiting for the doctor to finish the autopsy. When she walked outside, the sun was sinking into the horizon behind thick, dark clouds.

There was a murderer out there. Was it one of her people, or a local? Did it even matter? A man was dead, a man that had been part of her team.

The first drop of rain landed on her cheek. The second, on the tip of her nose. She wiped off the two and looked upward. As soon as she did, the sky opened up.

She was soaked within minutes as she ran toward the

B&B. The dense rainfall made it difficult for her to see, especially with her head down. She slammed into the side of a motorcycle and grabbed her thigh, howling in pain.

"Damn it to hell," she growled and sidestepped around the bike.

She only got twenty yards or so before she ran into Tamir. Faith bounced back and looked at him. He stood in the rain, staring straight through her.

"Tamir?" she shouted over the rain.

He blinked and focused on her face. "Faith."

"What's wrong?"

"I don't know."

She shivered as the rain soaked through her jacket and sweater. Dmitri. He had the cave for shelter, but it wasn't right to leave him out there in this. "I need to go to the site."

"The storm is going to get worse."

"Exactly," she said. "Dmitri needs to be here with us."

Tamir stood there for a second more before he motioned for her to follow him. "We'll go together, then."

She didn't hesitate to rush to the van and hurriedly climb inside. As soon as the engine roared to life, she turned on the heat and rubbed her hands together.

Her mind drifted back to the night before and Dmitri standing against the wind as if daring it to try and break him. Muscles was the type of man who could never be broken.

He wasn't just strong in body. He was strong in mind and soul. She saw it in his eyes as he looked at the world around him as if it were his kingdom.

That made her smile. He would probably love that she thought of him as a king. What man wouldn't?

A king like him needed a queen who would stand just as strong. Someone who could bend but never break. The kind of woman she was not.

She wasn't ashamed of it. Life had dealt her a blow with her father, but the love of her mother had made up for it. Yet it was her father's actions that shaped the woman she was now.

Trusting someone enough to give them her heart was not an action she'd ever wanted to experience. She'd been infatuated before. She'd crushed on guys. But there had never been anyone who made her want to forget everything just to be with them.

It happened for some people. Those people who stood strong against the wind. People like Ronnie. And look what Ronnie had found? A love that even a cynic like Faith could see and practically touch it was so strong.

Faith's mother had often joked that in this life, she was meant to be a mother only. That in another life, she would find someone.

Perhaps it was the same for Faith. She was fine with that. Her work was fulfilling enough to stave off the lonely nights. Not that she allowed herself those kinds of nights. There was always too much work to do.

She blinked through the windshield as the wipers worked frantically to clear it of water. The white flap of one of the remaining tents could be seen through the downpour.

Had they already arrived? She couldn't believe she'd spent the entire drive lost in her thoughts. Apparently, that didn't bother Tamir as he seemed lost just as deeply in his own mind.

He parked the van close to the main tent. "It's much worse here than in the village."

"It sure seems that way." She leaned one way and then the other, hoping for a glimpse of Muscles. "Surely he saw our lights."

"Unless he's in the cave."

Of course. "Do you know his cell number?"

Tamir pulled out his phone and tried to call, but the line wouldn't connect. "I think it's the storm."

"I'm not leaving without him."

"You can't seriously be considering propelling down the cliff in this weather?"

She zipped up her jacket. "I wouldn't leave you out there."

"Yeah, but he'll survive it. Have you seen those muscles of his?"

She'd done more than that. She'd felt them. And how glorious they were. "It doesn't matter. I've lost one member of my team. I'll not lose another."

"And we can't lose our leader. I'll go."

She grabbed his arm to stop him from leaving the van. "You don't want to be here at all. I'm not letting you go down."

He looked out the window, his lips flattening. "All right. Let's compromise. I'll go down, but you stay at the top and watch. I'm a better climber than you anyway."

"Deal," she said. Tamir *was* a better climber, and she wasn't in any hurry to die. "Let's get moving so we can get back to the village and into warm clothes."

They got out of the vehicle and walked as fast as they could against the gale-force winds to the cliff. The gusts stung her face, making it impossible to see anything while she faced the storm. The only relief came when she put her back to it, but the power of the rain made it feel like blunt bullets slamming into her.

Finally, Tamir was harnessed and went over the side. She put her hand over her eyes to shield them as she turned and looked down.

Tamir shouted something.

"What?" she yelled.

He pointed to her. She straightened, confused. Then she began to turn around.

Just as a hand slammed between her shoulder blades and sent her over the cliff.

CHAPTER TWELVE

Dmitri's breath locked in his chest when he saw Faith tumble off the cliff. He didn't think, didn't worry about the outcome. He jumped, shifting into a dragon and unfurling his wings.

He caught a current and headed straight to her. Faith's screams were drowned out by the storm, but he could hear the terrified pitch.

There was no time for him to make a mistake. He dipped a wing, turning as close to the cliffs as he could. His back leg scraped against the jagged rocks. With a flap of wings, he was able to reach out a claw and snatch her out of the air.

As he flew past, he looked into Tamir's eyes before he altered his course and headed to the cave. There, he landed and set her inside.

When he drew back, Faith stood staring at him with wide, unblinking eyes. For all her talk of dragons, she obviously wasn't prepared to see one in the flesh.

"I . . . I was pushed," she stuttered.

Dmitri looked to the cliff. He fell backward, opening his wings and twisting as he righted himself. Even with the storm, he didn't want to take the chance of someone other than Faith's assailant being there.

So he stayed out at sea and flew straight up into the clouds as lightning streaked around him. Once he was high enough, he remained in the clouds and flew over the cliffs. When he looked down, he spotted the Dark Fae.

The bastard was looking to the sky, waiting for a Dragon King to strike. Though the Dark hadn't known for sure that a King was here, they suspected. Now by saving Faith, Dmitri had confirmed it.

It took every ounce of control for Dmitri to turn away. The Dark wanted him to strike, and that could only mean trouble. He would take care of the Fae when the pricks weren't expecting it. Until then, he would bide his time until he could exact his revenge.

The Dark Fae spread his arms and shouted to the heavens in an Irish accent, "Where are you, you fekkers?"

Dmitri snarled. It would be so easy to kill the scum now. Then he thought of Faith. He needed to get back to her.

He turned and made another pass over the Dark. As he did, he released his magic, directing it at the Fae. It took seconds to cancel the Dark's thoughts, but that was all Dmitri needed.

He waited long enough for the Dark to turn away while he tried to remember what he was doing. That's when Dmitri tucked his wings and dove to the cave. Right before he reached the entrance, he spread his wings to halt his plunge.

Landing lightly, he folded his wings and walked on all fours inside before shaking off the rain from his scales. He spotted Faith standing against the far wall as soon as he alighted. Since he didn't want to frighten her, he didn't look her way.

He wanted to lie down and let her take her time looking

him over, hopefully ease some of her curiosity. But nothing good could come from her and Tamir seeing him in his true form.

Dmitri returned to human form. He could feel her gaze moving over his naked body, and he responded instantly. His balls tightened, and the blood rushed to his cock.

It was only the sound of Tamir lowering himself to the cave from above that prevented Dmitri from showing Faith what he thought of her perusal.

Both archeologists had seen him. Both would have questions, questions he didn't want to answer—and couldn't. However, there was no way around it. His power could cancel thoughts for a short period, but it wasn't permanent. Not like Guy, who could erase memories.

Despite the situation, he felt good for being able to shift and fly. Even that short span of time had done wonders mentally, physically, and emotionally.

None of the Dragon Kings were meant to remain in human form forever.

His thoughts skidded to Ulrik. Countless centuries had passed in the time Ulrik was locked in his human body. It was a wonder he hadn't attacked the Kings thousands of years before.

"Faith!" Tamir called as he unhooked from the harness.

Dmitri backed into the shadows behind a grouping of waist-high rocks. He kept his head averted from her, but he still watched.

Faith slowly emerged. As soon as Tamir saw her, he rushed to her, wrapping his arms around her. To Dmitri's amazement, she looked his way.

"Are you all right?" Tamir leaned back, his hands on her upper arms as he looked her over. "Is anything broken? Hurt?"

"I'm fine," she replied.

Tamir then dropped his arms. "My God. Did you see that creature?"

She nodded woodenly. "Kinda hard not to."

"That was a . . . it was a—"

"Dragon," Faith said, supplying the word.

Tamir wiped the water from his face as the shock began to subside. "Where is Dmitri?"

"I don't know."

So she was going to lie for him. Dmitri was glad for it, but Tamir would eventually piece it all together. The time Faith had given him was appreciated. He would make the most of it.

"I saw someone behind you up top. Was it Dmitri who pushed you from the cliff?"

"No," Faith stated. "Though Muscles might be hurt up there."

Tamir blew out a breath. "You're right. Let me get up there and see if I can find him. It's better if you remain here."

"Of course."

It felt like eternity until Tamir began the climb up the cliff. After he'd left, Dmitri remained in the shadows, waiting to see what Faith would do. She had lied for him, but that didn't mean she would continue to help.

He watched as she made her way over to him with a bit of hesitation in her steps. She was scared but curious. Her inquisitiveness would overcome whatever fear she felt.

"Who are you?" she demanded.

"It's better if you doona know."

She gave a firm shake of her head. "No. I want the truth. I deserve the truth."

"You think my saving you gives you that right?"

"I . . ." She paused and inhaled deeply. "You're right. You owe me nothing. I deserve nothing."

He glanced down the tunnel to where the dragon skeleton rested. "What do you see when you look at those bones?"

A small frown creased her forehead. Her sherry eyes moved around him to the tunnel as if she were looking at the skeleton in her mind's eye. She shoved aside her wet, blond locks. "I see a creature that should be nothing but a myth. I see the theory that there were more. I see something unique and impossible." Her gaze returned to him. "I see truth."

He'd hoped that she would say something that would confirm his need to tell her lies. Unfortunately, the opposite had occurred. Now, he wanted to tell her everything.

Standing before him was one of those rare mortals who saw the dragons for what they were—nothing bad or wicked.

"You saved me from falling to my death," she said into the silence. "You had to know I would see you. Yet you shifted before my eyes. Why do all of that if you didn't want me to know?"

She had a point. He could've flown away and never shown her who he was. But he hadn't done that. Was it because he subconsciously wanted her to know?

"Who are you?" she asked again. "What are you?"

He held her gaze, looking deep into her eyes. Then he found himself saying, "You've seen what I am. A verra long time ago, I ruled these isles. Fair Isle was where I was born. It was my home."

"And the skeleton I found?"

"One of my people."

"Where are the others?"

A memory of all the dragons leaving popped into his head. He stopped the grief before it could assault him. "Gone."

"But not you. Why?"

Dmitri looked away. "You are treading dangerous ground, Dr. Reynolds. It's better if you stop asking questions."

"I can't. I want to know everything."

"Just discovering that skeleton back there has put your life in danger. Already, one of your workers is dead. More will die if you doona stop."

Her brows rose as her gaze hardened. "Why do these bones matter so much?"

"You've found evidence of something that was never supposed to be."

"Killing me won't stop the bones from being seen."

He shrugged. "I'll make sure that never happens."

"Is that why you're here? To make sure I stop digging?" she asked angrily, her arms folding over her chest.

He appreciated her pluck. She was going to need that courage. "I'm no' the one who tried to kill you. But I was sent to destroy the bones."

"You can't," she cried, her arms dropping.

"The thing that tried to kill you doesna want you to stop. He wants to scare you away so his people can retrieve the skeleton."

She briefly pressed her lips together. "Thing? You know what pushed me?"

"Aye."

"Is it the same . . . thing . . . that killed Roger Thomas?"

"Aye."

"You're a dragon. Which means that whatever is after that skeleton isn't a friend of yours."

He wanted to lie. He tried, but that wasn't what came out. "Aye."

"Who is it?"

"Once more, you're treading dangerous ground. You say you want to know, but you're better off as you are."

She lifted her chin, determination glinting in her eyes. "Thank you for saving me. I should've said that first."

"You're welcome."

"If you're worried I'll tell someone what I saw, I won't."

He didn't bother to mention that Tamir saw him, as well. "Why are you no' scared?"

"How could I be after you rescued me?" she asked in surprise.

"Most are terrified."

"I'm not most people."

That was a fact. And something he was liking more and more. He noticed how she kept her gaze on his face now. Unlike earlier when she'd ogled his nudity.

She really wasn't afraid of him. Intrigued, curious, and even mesmerized, but not fearful. She made demands and stood her ground, despite knowing that he could shift and end her life with a swipe of his tail.

Her bravery sent desire burning hotly through him. But all that vanished the moment he saw her shiver. How could he have forgotten that she was soaked through? Then there was the shock of falling and being grasped out of the air by a dragon.

"You need to get warm."

As if it just now dawned on her how cold she was, Faith wrapped her arms around herself and nodded. "It is rather chilly."

He looked around helplessly. He had no clothes to give her. His had been shredded the moment he'd shifted. He could light a fire simply by breathing, but there was no wood.

"The sleeping bags are still there. You need to get inside one," he said

She was shaking her head before he'd finished. "Not until I can get Tamir away."

"Sending him back to the village could lead to his death."

"And here?" she asked. "Is he safer here?"

Dmitri shook his head as he heard Tamir descending the cliff. "Nay."

"Tamir recognizes the evil. He's asked that I leave."

"Can you send him away from the isle?"

Her teeth began to chatter. "Maybe."

"Faith!" Tamir shouted, interrupting them.

He turned his head to the entrance to see Tamir's feet dangling at the top of the cave's opening.

"I'll take care of this," she said and walked to her assistant.

Dmitri watched her go, knowing it was his time to escape and never look back. But he remained. Whether it was for him or Faith, he didn't know yet.

CHAPTER THIRTEEN

"I didn't find Dmitri," Tamir said as he dropped a leather bag to the ground before he lowered himself.

Faith recognized Muscles' bag and dragged it inside the cave. It was really too bad there were clothes in there to cover that magnificent body of his. "He's here."

Tamir was unhooking his harness when his head jerked up. "Is he all right?"

"He . . . was attacked." Damn. How she hated lying, especially to Tamir.

"It was by that dragon, wasn't it?"

She didn't bother to deny it. He wouldn't listen to her. "I think it was the same man who pushed me. Dmitri is just a little banged up, and his clothes are wet. It's a good thing you brought his bag."

"I actually brought it for you." Tamir glanced at the leather satchel. "It was the only bag still at the site, and I knew you would need something dry to wear."

She smiled, truly grateful to have someone like Tamir in her life. "Thank you."

"Let's get both of you warmed up before we head up."

"No," she said and hurriedly stepped in front of him

when he tried to walk around her. "Tamir, you were right about this place. Roger's death, someone attacking Dmitri, and pushing me . . . It's time we leave."

His face clouded. "Do you mean it?"

"I do. The storm is only going to get worse. Get back to town and send everyone home before it does."

"And you?"

"After my fall, I'm not going back up until the storm is gone. I'll stay with Dmitri. Once the storm abates, we'll head into town."

Tamir's lips flattened. "And the dragon?"

She had hoped he would drop it, but she should've known better. "Look, I—"

"I'd better get back to the others, then," Tamir suddenly said. His eyes seemed almost unfocused, as if he had just woken from a deep sleep. "I'll return after the storm."

"Let him go," whispered a deep voice behind her.

Muscles. What had he done to Tamir? And why hadn't he done it to her?

She watched Tamir work the rope and begin the ascent back up the cliffs. Even though she was so cold she could no longer feel her toes and fingers, she remained at the entrance until she saw Tamir make it to the top.

"Enough," Muscles said and turned her away from the opening.

She didn't need to be told twice. He grabbed his bag and remained behind her as they walked to the sleeping bags.

"Get undressed and inside," he ordered as he dropped the duffle and strode back toward the front.

Faith was too cold to ask him where he was going. Her fingers were numb, and her hands were shaking, making it nearly impossible to get out of her wet garments.

When she was finally free of her soaked clothes, she crawled into a sleeping bag and burrowed beneath the heavy, wool blanket to curl into a ball for warmth.

It was only then that she realized that none of the lights were on in the cave. Had the cold affected her brain so she wouldn't notice something like that?

There was a flicker of light in the darkness that grew until it took shape as fire at the end of a branch, held by none other than Muscles.

He squatted down, dropping a stack of wood far away from the skeleton. Then he touched the tip of the burning branch to it. In moments, the wood roared to life, emitting heat that made her sigh.

She looked through the flames at Dmitri. His face was bathed in the red-orange glow. His gaze was locked on the fire. Then he stood.

Unable to look away, Faith drank in the sight of him. She'd looked her fill earlier, in the dim light. But now, she saw every glorious, splendid inch of him.

A man with a sculpted body like his should never cover it with clothes. His shoulders were wide and thick with sinew. She saw the tattoo of a dragon head over Dmitri's heart with the body of the dragon disappearing over his shoulder. Along the top of his right arm was more of the tattoo—the dragon's tail that ended atop his hand. Where was the rest of the tat?

She soon forgot as her gaze traveled to his chest and abdomen that were corded with muscles before tapering to his waist and hips—and his cock that hung thick and semi-hard. Her mouth watered at the sight of his member.

His legs were fashioned of more chiseled sinew. He turned to the side, and she bit back a groan at the sight of his butt. She never knew an ass could look that amazing.

Her gaze followed him, and she got to see the rest of the dragon tattoo. It lay along his shoulders with its wings tucked against its body, as if sleeping.

She watched the muscles in Dmitri's back move, wishing she could get a closer look at his tat. He pulled some items from his bag and placed them on rocks near the fire. Then he turned, their eyes clashing.

He said nothing as he walked to her and climbed beneath the covers. His hand found her hip and pulled her back against him.

The feel of his warmth was enthralling. While he rubbed his hand up and down her arm and leg to get her circulation moving, she lay there, soaking it all in.

From neck to feet they were skin-to-skin. She might crave him with all of her being, but he had given no such inclination toward her. It was upsetting, but the world wasn't a perfect place—as she well knew.

She wanted to wait for him to talk, but she didn't think he would. His secret was powerful, and not one that he would readily share.

It was after he was settled behind her that she asked, "What did you do to Tamir?"

"It's my ability. I can cancel someone's thoughts."

He said it as if it was nothing, when it was certainly something. "Have you done it with me?"

"Nay."

"So Tamir forgot what he saw?"

Muscles sighed. "Eventually, he will remember again. But by then, it will almost be like a dream, and he willna be sure if it was real."

"What else can you do?"

"Faith—"

She turned in his arms to look at him. Their position was extremely intimate. If she couldn't run her hands over that mouthwatering body, then she would get answers.

"You've already told me you ruled this land. I've seen you—" She had to stop as she recalled the majesty that had been the white dragon standing before her. "I can be trusted."

"But no' all humans can."

She licked her lips. "Please."

His gaze lowered to her mouth for a heartbeat before he said, "I'm a Dragon King, ruler of the Whites. I reigned upon these isles for thousands of years."

Just hearing him say the words gave her a thrill. A Dragon King. She'd thought him kingly, and now, he'd confirmed it. "What happened?"

"For millions of years, this world was ours. The dragons'."

"Were there lots of you?"

"Billions."

She smiled, excited. "Sizes?"

"All sizes."

"Were you the largest?"

"One of," he replied with a crooked grin. "Every color had a king."

She cocked a brow. "No queen?"

"The Kings were no' chosen based on popularity. It was the magic inside us that chose who would lead. The strongest with the most magic were given the right."

"And males are typically stronger than females."

He lifted one shoulder in a shrug. "Aye."

"So you ruled."

"We ruled." He rolled to his back and looked at the firelight dancing on the ceiling. "It wasna always peaceful, but that was why we have a King of Kings. One that is more powerful than any of us, with more magic."

"Is he still around?"

Muscles turned his head to her. "Oh, aye. His name is Constantine."

"How do we humans fit in?"

Dmitri's face tightened. "One day, your kind arrived. Con called all the Kings together, and upon seeing your race, we were able to shift into your form in order to communicate.

"No' all humans had magic, and we knew what was out in the universe. We made room for you in our world, and every King made a vow to protect your race."

She could only stare at him, she was so shocked at his words. "That was very kind. I doubt we would do the same if the situation were reversed."

"I know your kind wouldna."

That statement didn't bode well for the humans. "How did billions of dragons disappear, then?"

"Mortals reproduced quickly. Their numbers grew exponentially, and we had to keep taking land from dragons to give to the humans. Tensions increased. It was made worse when the occasional dragon would eat a mortal, and in turn, the humans would hunt dragons."

Faith could see where this story was going, and he'd been right. She didn't want to know.

"We managed through it all," he continued. "Some mortals found safety and comfort in the homes of the Kings. There were even females who became our lovers."

"Did you take one?" She didn't know why she'd asked that, but she suddenly had to know the answer.

Muscles shook his head. "Nay."

She found that hard to believe with him looking good enough to lick. "Just how old are you?"

"I'm immortal." His head turned to her once more. "I've been alive for an untold number of eons."

Holy shit. Her mind literally halted at the thought of that. Scientists claimed that if a human were immortal, they would go insane after about a century, and here a dragon lay beside her, millions of years old. And he looked as sane as they came.

"Does that bother you?" he asked, grinning.

She chuckled. "I'm just taking it all in."

"There are many differences between dragons and humans. For instance, dragons mate for life."

"We don't," she said, her thoughts immediately going to her father.

He tucked his outer arm beneath his head and once more looked at the ceiling. "Con was closest to a dragon named Ulrik. They were brothers in every way except blood. Ulrik was to be the first of us who mated with a mortal. He didna just want her as his lover. He wanted her as his mate. By doing so, he was condemning his line—the Silvers—to become obsolete."

"Why?" she asked.

"No matter how many try, a dragon and human can no' produce offspring. A few mortals get pregnant but quickly miscarry. Even rarer are the females who can carry the baby to term, only to have those children stillborn."

"That's horrible."

"Ulrik didna care. He loved her deeply. During all of this, Con discovered that Ulrik's woman wasna all she said. Con learned that she planned to kill Ulrik and begin a war."

Faith was flabbergasted. She knew some people were that horrible, but still, it never failed to surprise her.

Dmitri went on, unaware of her reaction. "Con sent Ulrik away and told all of us his findings. Everyone loved Ulrik. We were outraged on his behalf. So we tracked down the mortal. She refused to answer Con's questions and ran. To us, that was proof of her guilt."

"What did you do?"

"We killed her. We did it to save Ulrik the pain of doing it himself."

There was something in his tone that told her things didn't go as planned. "Ulrik didn't see it that way, did he?"

"Nay, he didna. He was consumed with grief and rage against the mortals and us. He wouldna turn on us, so he focused his fury on the humans. Ulrik began a war that day.

"Some Kings set their dragons up to protect the mortals,

only the humans didna want them there. They murdered those dragons, slaughtered them because the dragons were under orders no' to harm the mortals and wouldna fight back."

Faith covered her mouth with her hand, tears gathering in her eyes.

"The humans exterminated some species of dragons while those of us left either took Ulrik's side or Con's."

"Which did you take?" she asked.

Dmitri was silent for a moment before he said, "Con's."

CHAPTER FOURTEEN

Dmitri thought back to that day so very long ago when the Dragon Kings had been divided. It wasn't so cut and dried for many of them, him included.

"Do you regret your choice?"

Faith's seductive voice was like music to his ears. And his body reacted in a primal, visceral way that both alarmed and thrilled him.

It was why he had turned away from her. She no longer needed his body heat, but he couldn't make himself leave. To remain so close to her nude form was a special kind of Hell that he endured because it felt so good.

"Nay," he replied. Anything to take his mind off the need burning inside him.

It would be so easy to turn to her and take her in his arms. He'd felt her interest, seen her response to him. Yet he didn't wish to test Fate. Too many Kings had returned to Dreagan with mates. And with his reaction to her, it was best to leave things as they stood.

He swallowed hard as he recalled the feel of her soft body against him, her delightful curves and intoxicating scent. His balls tightened.

"Nay," he said again. "I followed my King."

She moved a lock of hair out of her face. "So you didn't agree with Ulrik at all?"

"I didna say that. Many of us did, but we took an oath. Whether we liked it or not, we would defend the mortals against the rogue dragons."

"Wow," she said, looking at him curiously. "Do men like you really exist?"

He glanced at her. "I'm no' a man. I'm a dragon."

"Then that definitely explains it," she murmured. "So the dragons were split. What happened then?"

He didn't want to talk about it, but in order to tell her the entire story, he had to also share this part. "Con worked hard to bring all of the Kings back to his side except for Ulrik. No one could get through to him, no matter how hard we tried.

"The humans wouldna stop attacking dragons. We attempted to broker a truce, but the mortals wouldna even talk to us. It became obvious that the two races couldna live in the same realm together."

"Why didn't you just send the humans away?" she asked. "It's what they deserved."

He looked at her, amazed at her thoughts. "Both sides were to blame."

"This was your home."

"We were also more powerful and gifted with magic. It would be like you getting rid of ants."

She wrinkled her nose. "Do you have any idea how many ant species there are?"

"Aye."

Her eyes widened at the analogy. "Oh. I see."

"If we wanted our families, friends . . . the verra dragons we were responsible for to live in peace, we had to send our kith and kin away. We built a dragon bridge with magic and sent them to another realm."

"Why didn't all of you go?"

"Our vow," he reminded her. "However, no' all the dragons listened to Con's command. Ulrik and four of his largest Silvers remained. They attacked villages. We then trapped the Silvers and used a spell to make them sleep."

Her face went slack. "They're still here, aren't they?"

"Aye. But no' anywhere they can be found."

"And Ulrik? What about him?"

Dmitri gave a shake of his head. "The worst happened to our friend. Ulrik wouldna listen to reason. He left us no choice but to take drastic measures. We cornered him and united our magic to bind his. That left him in human form. In a fit of anger, Con banished Ulrik from our home."

Several seconds passed before Faith said, "That's . . . horrible. And incredibly cruel to lock Ulrik in the very form of the beings he detested."

"Ulrik killed thousands of your ancestors. And we couldna allow him to be in his true form when all of us were going into hiding."

"Hiding?"

"We remaining Kings gathered together in one place and slept away centuries as we waited for mortals to forget about us."

She nodded slowly. "The story of your species turned to myth."

"Just as we wanted."

Her sherry eyes narrowed slightly. "You're Scottish. Your home is these isles, but you said all of you gathered. That was in Scotland, wasn't it?"

"It was. It is."

"Where?" she pressed.

After everything he'd already told her, what harm would there be to tell her more? "In the Highlands. We've a large piece of land that gives us room. Or rather, it did."

"Meaning?"

"We've enemies. No' to mention we are no' the only magical creatures in this realm."

Worry shone in her beautiful eyes. He wanted to run his hands down her face and erase the anxiety forever. His gaze lowered, and he saw her breasts—and the tip of one pink nipple.

He clenched his hand into a fist to prevent himself from reaching for her and giving in to the rising tide of desire. His mouth watered at the thought of wrapping his lips around that nipple. He tore his eyes away from such temptation and looked back at her face.

"There's more than just dragons?" she asked. "Who? What are they?"

Her questions were just what he needed to keep his thoughts from all the different ways he wanted to claim her body. "In your race, there are Druids."

"My life is based on science. I don't believe in magic. Or I didn't . . . until tonight. You shattered my beliefs into oblivion by showing me your true form. I find it easier to accept you than I do the idea of humans having magic."

"And yet, it's true."

She pressed her lips together briefly. "Hmm. The Romans did write about Druids."

He raised a brow, grinning as he saw the thoughts running through her mind as she considered what he'd imparted.

"The other species?" she asked.

His smile faded. "The Fae. They discovered this realm and chose to remain because humans are a food source for them."

"They *eat* us?" she asked, repulsed enough to scrunch up her face in distaste.

"No' as you're imagining. They draw you in because

you can no' resist them. The Fae are stunningly gorgeous, and emit pheromones that a mortal is powerless to ignore. Once in their arms, you experience the most amazing sex of your life.

"If you're lucky enough to be snared by a Light Fae, they will leave you after that one time. However, you'll never find fulfillment in the arms of another again."

She made a sound in the back of her throat. "You call that lucky?"

"I do. For if it's a Dark Fae, they continue to have sex with you until they drain you of your soul. You die happy, unaware that you were freely giving yourself to your murderer."

"Oh," she mumbled.

He turned on his side toward her. "If you feel that kind of attraction to another, do your best to fight it. The Fae have the ability to use glamour to hide their coloring. A Light has black hair and silver eyes, while a Dark will have silver in their black hair and red eyes."

"Evil."

"Aye. They're evil."

"Tamir said he felt evil."

Dmitri moved his hand as close to her arm as he could without actually touching her. He wanted to feel her smooth skin against his hand, to have her body against his once more. "It was a Dark who pushed you from the cliff."

She didn't become outraged at his words. Instead, she calmly nodded. "Is it here for the skeleton, or you?"

"I think he did it to see if a Dragon King was here."

"And you showed him you were by saving me."

He shrugged. "I made sure he forgot about me. For now."

"He'll be back, won't he?"

"Without a doubt."

Her frown deepened. "Was Roger killed by one of these . . . Dark?"

Dmitri nodded.

"Why do they want the dragon skeleton?"

"Through all these millennia, Ulrik has walked this Earth with revenge eating away at him. He wants retribution for what Con and the rest of us did to him."

"It was partly his fault," she interjected.

"Be that at as it may, he's set a course. Aligning with the Dark is part of his plan. Ulrik wants to show your kind that we're here. He's already taken one step. He had the Dark record us as we fought."

Realization dawned. "That video of the dragons. That was you?"

"Aye."

Her mouth went slack. "You're part of Dreagan."

"I am."

She leaned up on her elbow and put her head in her hand, not grasping that the blanket had slipped to further expose her mouth-watering breasts.

And he wasn't about to tell her either.

"Ulrik wants another battle between humans and dragons," she guessed.

He pulled his gaze away from her hardened nipples. "That's part of it. He wants to fight Con and take over as the King of Kings."

"Then kill all the mortals."

"Aye."

"Well, that sucks," she stated.

It was difficult not to smile at her response. "We are no' going to let that happen."

"Perhaps you should force Ulrik's hand. Make him fight Con now. Don't play his games."

She had a point. They *were* playing Ulrik's games,

allowing him to dictate what happened. If Dmitri could convince Con that this was the way to go, they would no longer be chasing Ulrik. Instead, they would be the ones in charge.

Dmitri liked that idea a lot.

"You spend an awful lot of energy making sure we don't know of your existence," she said.

He looked into her eyes and wished the rest of the humans could be as open as she. "We doona have a choice. There can no' be another war between our species."

"Not now that we have weapons to kill you."

He couldn't help but smile then. The humans always thought their weapons could kill anything. How very wrong they were. "You could try, but we're no' just immortal. We're verra hard to kill."

"You mean Ulrik's woman couldn't have killed him?"

"That's exactly what I mean, though she didna know it. You see, only a Dragon King can kill a Dragon King."

She blinked, a smile growing. "You're indestructible."

"Pretty much."

"Even against a nuclear bomb."

"Aye."

"Flying, magic, shifting, immortality," she said in awe. Then sorrow filled her sherry eyes. "All of that, and you hide. It's not right that you can't be who you are."

"Our lives would be so much simpler if every mortal thought as you do."

"Why would an immortal want to be with a mortal?" she asked breathlessly.

He found it difficult to swallow as his gaze locked on her lips. "When a King takes a mortal as his mate, she becomes immortal. Living as long as he does."

"Oh."

He rubbed his thumb on her lower lip. She had an amazing mouth. Her lips parted as her breathing quickened. Then she took his thumb into her mouth and sucked on it.

Whatever thoughts he might've had about keeping his hands from her vanished in a blink. He groaned at the feel of her tongue lapping at his skin.

She grinned and kissed the tip of his finger before she sidled closer to him. "Man or dragon, I want you, Muscles."

CHAPTER FIFTEEN

In the next heartbeat, Faith found herself beneath Dmitri. His weight atop her felt amazing—as did his obvious arousal.

"You doona know what you're doing," he whispered.

She looked up into his azure eyes, her heart thundering with delight and anticipation. "I do, actually."

"They'll be no turning from this."

"Shut up and kiss me."

His eyes lowered to her mouth. She found it difficult to breathe through the haze of desire. Her lips were parted, anxiously—and impatiently—waiting.

She lifted her head to take action herself, but he pulled back while tangling his fingers in her hair, holding her head immobile. His blue eyes burned with need, but he held himself in check.

Her fingers dug into his arms, her body tense. Yet still, he held back. She was used to taking what she wanted, and she never apologized for being a sexual creature.

Then again, she'd never been with a dragon before.

Her heart thumped against her ribs the longer he held

her gaze. His other hand pulled her arm out to her side, caressing the skin from her shoulder to her wrist.

Then he slid his fingers against hers, intertwining them. That simple act was so tender and sensual that it caused her breath to lock in her chest.

Being with Muscles wasn't going to be the normal quick "roll in the hay." Because he was so much more than that. It was in his touch, in the way he held her—in the way he looked at her.

Slowly, his head lowered, inch by agonizing inch. His hand in her hair held her firmly in place as his mouth hovered over hers.

Their breaths mixed, mingled.

Mated.

She saw the pale blue band circling his irises. In his depths, she found herself sinking into an ocean of blue that stretched endlessly before her, behind her, and around her.

Yet she wasn't afraid. She'd seen the dragon, touched him. Even now, as she looked into his eyes, she welcomed all that she'd learned.

He'd said she didn't know what she was doing. Perhaps she didn't. But that wasn't going to stop her.

She gripped his hand tighter, silently begging him to end her torment and kiss her. Still, he held fast, watching her with desire that flamed within his gaze.

Witnessing his yearning made a rush of excitement run along her nerve endings. Her nipples puckered tighter, aching as they pressed against his chest.

His hand holding her hair tugged downward, causing her face to lift and expose her neck. The moment his warm lips touched her, her lids fell shut.

She moaned as his tongue scraped sensuously along her skin. He placed kisses leisurely from one side of her throat to the other, driving her wild in the process.

He was merciless in his endeavor to tease her. And she loved every fucking moment of it.

But she *burned* for more.

His kisses continued down the column of her neck to her collarbone. Then he made his way upward to her jaw. She held still, afraid to even breathe lest he change his mind.

"Open your eyes," he commanded.

She complied to find him watching her. She was panting now, desire flooding her body. If he demanded it, she was sure she could climax right then. She was *that* turned on.

And he hadn't even touched her. Not really.

A sizzle of delight ran through her when she realized that if she felt this way now, then she would soon be soaring with pleasure once he did begin.

"I doona share."

Excitement tore through her as she realized what he was stating. Words were impossible now. She tried to nod, but his hold wouldn't allow it.

The only sound was the crackle of the fire as they looked at each other. Then his mouth was on hers, moving seductively. She returned his kiss, opening for him when his tongue swept against her lips.

He enticed, he tempted.

He tantalized, he seduced.

And it was glorious.

His kiss was intoxicating, enthralling. He masterfully pulled her along with him into a sea of desire so deep and yawning that she knew she could drown in it.

She went willingly, eagerly. The more she tasted him, the more she craved. She knew this moment in time would forever change her, and she was glad.

He deepened the kiss, a moan rumbling in his chest. She flattened her free hand and ran it over his shoulder, along his neck over the tattoo, and up into his hair. She held him as he did her, wordlessly demanding that he continue.

They could've kissed for years or centuries. She didn't know or care. His taste was addictive, and she couldn't get enough.

And when he ended it, she wanted to cry out. Then her eyes opened, and she stared into a face set in hard lines, a visage inflamed with desire and need.

"You're mine," he whispered hoarsely.

She grinned up at him. "And you're mine."

He issued another growl full of approval before he took her lips in another fierce kiss. She felt his longing, the yearning inside him.

She tore her mouth from his when he cupped her breast and pinched a nipple, crying out with pleasure so profound that she was sure time halted.

His lips soon replaced his fingers, and his tongue swirled around her peak before sucking. Her back arched as she clung to his head.

Finally, he released his hold on her hand. Then he had both of his on her breasts, massaging them as his mouth moved from one nipple to the other, licking, nipping, and sucking.

Dmitri didn't stop until Faith was crying out for more, her head moving from side to side. He loved her small breasts and sensitive nipples. He could feast on them all day.

He kept his gaze on her face as he ran his hand down her side to the indent of her waist and over the flare of one hip to her thigh.

A smile pulled at his lips when he felt a shiver run through her as his hand paused. He altered his path and slid his hand to the inside of her thigh. Her breathing hitched, her body stilling as she waited.

He didn't make her wait long. His fingers slid against trimmed curls to her sex. His cock jumped when he discovered how wet she was.

Unable to help himself, he dipped a finger inside her. Instantly, her hips lifted, a strangled moan falling from her swollen lips.

It exhilarated him to bring her such pleasure. Her body was an instrument made for playing. And he intended to spend hours mastering her.

Her back arched, causing her breasts to thrust into the air. His lips sought the puckered peaks once more, nipping lightly. Her cries grew louder. All the while, thunder rumbled so fiercely in the distance, it shook the earth. Flashes of lightning could be seen even in the depths of the cave.

A storm raged outside. Inside, another type of storm was brewing. One of desire and pleasure, of craving and hunger that wouldn't be denied.

He gazed down at her pale flesh accented by the red-orange glow of the flames. Her beauty was incomparable, her spirit unparalleled. Yet it was her thirst for knowledge and acceptance of him that touched something deep within.

With his eyes locked on her face to see her reaction, he pushed his finger deeper. Her hands fisted in the sleeping bag as her breaths came quicker.

"Please," she begged.

He ignored her plea and moved down her body so that his mouth was over her swollen sex. Then he licked her, lingering at her clit.

Her cries mixed with the thunder were music to his ears. His eyes closed at the taste of her desire on his tongue. He swirled his tongue over and around her clitoris until she was trembling.

Then he returned his fingers to her opening and pushed two inside her while continuing to tease her with his tongue. Within moments, she stiffened, and her body clamped around his fingers.

He looked up and watched the pleasure spread across her face as her mouth opened on a silent scream. As her body convulsed from the climax, a flush covered her skin.

She lifted her head, her gaze meeting his. Her hands pulled him until he once more leaned over her. He kissed her, letting her taste herself on his tongue.

When she ground her hips against him, he moaned. He couldn't remember ever being this hard for someone. He craved her, ached for her.

The top of his cock brushed her sex. Her responding groan sent him to the edge of his control, tumbling past any sort of reason or restraint.

She turned his face to the side and bit his earlobe before whispering, "Dmitri, I need you inside me. I'm burning."

In answer, he rose up on his hands and grinned. Her pupils were dilated, her lips swollen as she reached between them and wrapped her hands around him.

His lids closed when she squeezed and slowly pumped her fist. Her touch felt so good. He rocked in time with her as she increased her tempo.

Then she suddenly stopped. His gaze snapped open to see her focus was between them. He looked down to see her moving his rod to her sex.

She bit her lip as she rubbed him against her clit. His cock jumped at the erotic image before him. She had no idea how she turned him on.

As soon as he was at her entrance, he pushed inside. The moment he was fully seated, he paused, enjoying the feel of her tight walls gripping him.

Faith dropped her head back as soon as he filled her. Her body stretched to accommodate his width even as her hands wished they were still holding him.

Finally, he began to move. Her legs fell open as she ran her hands up his arms to his shoulders. As he thrust, one of his hands caressed her neck and face between his kisses.

It was the first time she'd ever felt so . . . wanted. And beautiful. The way he worshipped her with his touch and kisses left her floating so high she was sure she could touch the stars.

Her arms tightened around his neck. She never wanted this to end. It was perfection in every way, a dream come true, a fantasy that she hadn't known she wanted until that moment.

Thoughts ceased as the hunger once more took hold. She wrapped her legs around his waist and met him thrust for thrust as he plunged harder and deeper with every heartbeat.

Desire sharpened, tightening inside her and pushing her to the edge of another orgasm. She was on a precipice waiting for . . . she wasn't sure what she waited on.

Then she knew—Muscles.

She heard her name whispered. When she forced her eyes open, he was looking at her. Once more, she was drowning, but she wouldn't go alone. He was right there with her.

He pushed her over the edge, the climax taking her swiftly. She never looked away, even when the pleasure was so intense she screamed. He peaked with her.

As their pleasure swirled and melded before slowly fading away, they remained locked in each other's arms, their limbs tangled in the blanket.

Only when he lowered his head to rest beside hers did she close her eyes. With her breathing evening out and her heart slowing, she heard the fire pop.

Then she heard the thunder roll around them before the

crack of lightning. It seemed right that she'd had such fierce lovemaking in the midst of a storm.

The woman and her dragon.

"You're mine," he said.

She smiled. "And you're mine."

CHAPTER SIXTEEN

Perth, Scotland

There were many degrees of rage. Mikkel had thought he'd experienced the top of the arc the day his brother died and the role of King of the Silvers passed to his nephew instead of him.

But the violence he felt now far surpassed anything from before.

He wanted to destroy everything around him for a thousand miles. He wanted to find Ulrik and bash his skull in with a rock before cutting his head off with a jagged piece of iron.

Instead, he stood in the middle of The Silver Dragon at two in the morning and fumed in silence amid the dimmed lighting of the store. He should've known Ulrik wouldn't be there. The coward was running.

Or was he?

That thought drew Mikkel up short. He'd underestimated his nephew. To continue to do so might bring an end to his existence, and Mikkel wasn't ready to die. Not when he was about to have everything he'd ever dreamed of.

Ulrik wasn't running. If anything, his nephew was getting things ready. It's what *he* would do in Ulrik's place. But what could Ulrik be planning?

Mikkel walked through the shop, seeing through the priceless antiques and looking for something that would be important to a Dragon King.

His gaze landed on the desk. But a thorough search yielded nothing. Mikkel didn't bother with the computer. Ulrik wouldn't put anything on it that could be used against him by humans or dragons.

In order to discover just what his nephew was up to, Mikkel was going to have to find him—and leash him. It was what he should've done to begin with.

But he'd believed Ulrik was still attempting to get his magic back. It was the first—and last—time his nephew would get the upper hand.

Mikkel hadn't waited ages while his father and then brother ruled as King of the Silvers only to step aside for Ulrik.

He'd thought he could control Ulrik as he had before his nephew's banishment from Dreagan. The exile from Dreagan had changed Ulrik in ways Mikkel hadn't expected.

Then again, that could be used to his advantage.

For all of Ulrik's hate and rage, there was one thing he couldn't change—he was a part of Dreagan. No matter what Ulrik said, he wanted to return to the place he'd helped to create.

Ulrik might have more magic than he, but that didn't mean Mikkel didn't have ways to overcome such an obstacle. His plans were larger than merely becoming King of the Silvers. His goal was to remove Con and lead the defeated Dragon Kings back to their original glory as King of Kings.

The door to the shop was thrown open as a leggy brunette walked in. He turned and smiled when he saw her standing with one hand on her cocked hip.

She wore all black, from the leather pants to the sheer tank that showed her lace bra to the leather motorcycle jacket. She tapped the toe of her stiletto boot and raised a dark brow.

Eyes an exotic mixture of green and gold watched him. He put his hands behind his back so he wouldn't be tempted to touch her mocha skin.

The fireball before him was lethal in more ways than one. And Eilish was an ace Ulrik knew nothing about.

"What do you want?" she demanded.

Few people dared to talk to him in such a way. Most did it without realizing who he was. But she knew exactly who—and what—he was.

And she didn't care.

He allowed her to speak in such a fashion because he enjoyed her American accent and the way she faced the world as if everything rested in the palm of her hand to do with as she pleased.

"What do you think of the place?" he asked.

She didn't take her eyes from him. "I was working."

"I think that distasteful pub in the middle of nowhere can do without you for a while."

"*My* pub can run without me for decades. That's not the point." She dropped her arm and walked a couple of steps to him. Light glinted off her left hand where she wore silver claws that ran down her finger to her second knuckle in elaborate Celtic designs. "Don't dis my place."

He smiled at her, wishing she wasn't immune to his charms. But no matter how he tried to woo her, Eilish would have none of it. "You could have the best pub in the middle of Dublin. Why settle elsewhere?"

"It's what I want. Now," she said and crossed her arms over her chest as she glared at him. "I'll ask again. What do you want?"

Mikkel held out his arms. "This place is Ulrik's."

"Good for him. Shall I clap?" she asked sarcastically.

"You were right."

She continued staring with undisguised annoyance. "Which time?"

"He has all of his magic."

At this, her arms slowly dropped. Her attitude shifted as she suddenly became interested in everything around her. "I knew it."

"Can you stop him?"

Eilish walked past him, touching and looking over items as she passed. "You want me to stop a Dragon King?"

"You can do it," he said as he turned to watch her.

She shrugged. "Of course, I can." She came to a stop at the back of the shop and pivoted to face him. "Ulrik is more powerful than you now. You've lost your chance."

"Not with you by my side."

"True. But you still need Ulrik to kill Constantine. I might be able to help you with Ulrik, but I wouldn't be able to do it so soon after with Con. It's one or the other."

Mikkel wasn't going to accept that. "It's both. I know what you can do. I'll even let you choose how you kill Con. Make it quick or make him suffer. It's your choice, my dear."

She held his gaze before slowly smiling. "Consider it done."

He drew in her scent of lavender as she meandered her way to him. Eilish slowly walked around him before she went to Ulrik's desk and sat.

"I'm going to need some time here. Alone," she quickly added.

"I'll see it done."

Mikkel waited until he was outside before he smiled. Ulrik only thought he would win. The anticipation of looking into his nephew's eyes as Ulrik realized that he'd lost and was dying eased Mikkel's anger.

It was going to be a glorious beginning for the new age of dragons.

Dark Palace, Ireland

Balladyn walked the halls of the palace. He wanted to return to Rhi, to hold her in his arms again. Although it was ridiculous, he worried that she might still feel something for her Dragon King.

Rhi was nothing if not loyal. She'd loved her King for too many centuries. Even if she had closed herself off to that love, it was still inside her.

It would always be inside her.

Balladyn stopped by a window and braced his hands on either side of it as he stared into the night sky. Before him lay Ireland at its best with fields of green and forests thick with life.

Yet he saw none of it because his mind remained on Rhi. He wanted to bring her with him, to have her by his side. First, he had to get rid of Taraeth. Then he could rule the Dark Fae with Rhi.

Except she wouldn't come. He knew it, but he still held out hope. Rhi belonged with him, and he with her. He'd loved her for so long, then had sat back and watched as she fell in love with the Dragon King.

It was his turn now. She had come to him. They were lovers, and he would do anything for her. Destiny had given him this opportunity to rule. He wasn't about to let it pass him by. Eventually, she would understand that.

It was the sound of several pairs of boots approaching that caught his attention. He looked into the window's reflection and caught sight of Mikkel along with four Dark making their way to the throne room.

He turned and quickly hurried to the room by a back hallway, reaching it before Mikkel. He entered to find Taraeth finishing off a human female.

The king of the Dark patted the woman's now pallid face and said, "Thank you, dear. You were delicious."

Taraeth rose and zipped his pants one-handed as two guards collected the now dead human and left the room. Balladyn noticed that Taraeth continued to reach for his missing left arm.

"A new shipment has come in if you wish to sample them," Taraeth said.

Balladyn inclined his head. "Thank you, sire."

There was a knock at the double doors before they opened and Mikkel strode inside and greeted Taraeth with a bright smile.

"I didn't expect a visit," Taraeth said and motioned for his guest to take a seat.

"I didn't expect to make a trip, but something has come up." Mikkel's gaze stopped on Balladyn, his annoyance visible.

Balladyn remained by the throne as Taraeth poured two drinks and walked to Mikkel, handing him a glass.

"Do tell," the king urged.

Mikkel nodded at Balladyn. "Perhaps this is better done in private."

"I trust Balladyn above all others. He'll be the one carrying out my orders. He stays," Taraeth stated.

From the beginning, Balladyn hadn't liked Mikkel. It wasn't that he particularly had an affection for Ulrik either, being that he was a Dragon King, but Balladyn had already chosen to side with Ulrik when the time came for battle.

Because it was coming. Ulrik would fight Con for the right to rule the Kings. Taraeth had promised both Mikkel and Ulrik that he would help.

Taraeth didn't care who fought Con, as long as Con was killed. But Balladyn knew the only one who had a chance of taking down the King of Kings was Ulrik.

Yet Taraeth had already hinted at siding with Mikkel when the time came. Taraeth wouldn't make such a claim unless he knew Mikkel had an advantage. Either way, Balladyn wasn't going to allow that to happen.

Maybe it was because he believed Rhi hadn't betrayed him all those years ago.

Perhaps it was because Ulrik was the rightful King of Silvers.

Or it could be because Balladyn's love for Rhi was changing him.

Whatever the reason, he'd decided to back Ulrik. That meant he might have to take out Taraeth sooner than he'd anticipated. Not that it mattered. It was time the Dark had a new leader.

He'd kill Taraeth today if he could, but he was waiting to convince Rhi to come back to the palace with him. With her by his side, the brightest of the Light, they could unite their race once more.

It had come to him as she lay spent in his arms on her beach. He couldn't believe he hadn't thought of it sooner. It was the perfect plan.

Once united, no one could stand against the Fae. Not even the Dragon Kings.

Mikkel tossed back the whisky. "If Ulrik comes to you, trap him."

Taraeth raised a brow. "Why would I do that?"

"He's betrayed me."

"You mean the way you were going to betray him?" Balladyn asked.

Mikkel shot him a hard look, his gold eyes cold. "I saw him shift in Paris."

"Ah," Taraeth said, nodding slowly. "So the prodigal dragon has all of his magic once more."

"He's had it," Mikkel said through clenched teeth. "He lied to me."

Taraeth raised a black and silver brow. "Lying is part of who we are. You're not angry because Ulrik lied to you. You're pissed because you didn't see it."

Balladyn inwardly smiled as Mikkel seethed.

"I suppose you're right," Mikkel stated as a vein bulged in his temple. "Right now, he has more power than me."

"He is the King of Silvers," Balladyn said.

Taraeth glanced his way. "Balladyn's right."

"Not for long," Mikkel announced with a gleam in his gold eyes.

"Why is that?" Balladyn asked.

"I've someone that is going to give me the upper hand with Ulrik. And Con."

At this news, the first thing Balladyn wanted to do was go to Rhi and tell her. Then he paused. She might want to help the Kings, but he didn't.

Nor would he.

CHAPTER SEVENTEEN

Desire still burned fervently, feverishly. Dmitri reached for Faith upon opening his eyes—only to find the spot empty. He sat up, searching for her. The worry faded as he spotted her wrapped in the blanket, standing before the dragon skeleton.

He got to his feet and went to her. Her gaze was riveted to the bones. He tucked a thick strand of sandy blond hair behind her ear. "What is it?"

"You said all the dragons were called to leave."

"They were."

"Why did this one not go?"

He turned his head to the remains of one of his Whites. "I'm hoping to find out. As King of the Whites, I was— still am—responsible for every last one of them. I need to know if I failed."

"He could've already been dead," she said, looking at Dmitri.

He shook his head. "As a precaution, every King returned to their lands to find the dead."

"To destroy them," she said with a nod.

He didn't like the feelings plaguing him. The fact that

he might have forsaken one of his dragons weighed heavily upon him. "We couldna leave any evidence behind to be found by the mortals. I searched every cave on all the isles."

"The answers lie with the bones. The sooner I uncover the full skeleton, the sooner we can determine how he died."

When he looked at her, he found her smile wide, the certainty in her sherry eyes absolute. And it soothed him. "And if I failed one of my own?"

"We'll deal with that when the time comes," she stated. Then she turned and hurried back to the fire and their clothes where she dropped the blanket.

He took in her naked body, a smile forming as he re-called having her in his arms. He wanted her again.

As if sensing his gaze, she looked over her shoulder at him and winked before wiggling her ass. It made him chuckle. He walked to her, slapping one plump butt cheek as she bent to check on her jeans and see if they were dry.

He couldn't help wondering what it was that kept him going to the Fae for sex. Then he realized it was because he hadn't met Faith yet.

They had rested long enough that the fire was able to dry her sweater, but the jeans would take much longer. Dmitri squatted and rummaged through his bag. He tossed her a pair of lounge pants that she had to roll up several times just to keep on.

He quickly dressed before they returned to the skele-ton. Since she'd left her tools, they had something to work with. So while she sorted everything, he turned on the lights closest to them.

In moments, she was focused on the bones once more. He watched her for long minutes. He found it amazing how she dedicated herself to uncovering the past.

He'd feared that she was one of those wanting to expose

the dragons, when in fact, it was her love of history and the past that drove her.

She wouldn't have cared if it were a dragon skeleton or a centuries-old chest. She was more concerned with discovering the secrets of the past.

The way she gently and lovingly—and gradually—exposed the bones was a painstaking process that she seemed to get the utmost enjoyment from.

He used his magic to keep the fire going before he went to the cave's entrance to have a look around. The storm still raged as the sea churned angrily.

It was only a matter of time before the Dark came calling, and he was going to be prepared. If luck was on his side, he'd have the answers to the dragon's death, the bones and any evidence of dragons obliterated, and Faith, along with her entire team, safely away from Fair.

As much as he hoped for such an outcome, he was pragmatic. Once the tempest passed, Tamir would return. Which would bring the Dark.

He looked up at the thick clouds. The storm seemed to hover above them, giving them another few hours to work. Dawn was approaching, not that the sun could be seen through the dense cloud cover.

Apprehension perched contentedly upon his shoulders. No matter what they eventually uncovered about the death of the dragon, the simple fact was that Dmitri had let one of his own down.

Now he had Faith, her team, and the occupants of Fair Isle to protect. He couldn't fail them.

Briefly, he considered calling for Rhi. The Light Fae was usually eager to help the Kings, but he hesitated. Rhi remaining around the Kings only prolonged the ache within her heart.

It wasn't fair to do that to her. Perhaps if the Kings

didn't turn to her so often, she might be able to put the past behind her and forget the love she'd once had with her King.

Having another King there would greatly increase Dmitri's chances of winning against the Dark. But it would also increase the probability of someone seeing something.

There was no easy way to fix the problem. Either he brought in help and risked exposure, or he dealt with everyone and everything on his own.

He put his hand on the side of the cave opening and let his palm soak in the dampness of the rock smoothed by centuries of exposure to wind, water, and sun.

This was his homeland. The place he had been born. The place where he had learned to fly and hone his magic. The place where he had become King.

He'd defended these isles for thousands of years on his own. He could—and *would*—do so again.

It wasn't until he reached for his mobile phone that he realized it had been lost somewhere in the sea below when he'd shifted to save Faith.

He opened the mental link and said, *"Con."*

After a minute or so, Con answered. *"Is it done?"*

"No' exactly."

"Meaning?"

He heard the concern in Con's voice. The same worry he had. *"Things have . . . it's complicated."*

Con sighed heavily. *"Please tell me you didna sleep with the woman."*

That was none of Con's business, regardless if he was King of Kings or not. *"The Dark pushed Dr. Reynolds off the cliff in order to see if a Dragon King was here."*

"I gather you saved her."

"Of course."

"Is it too much to ask that you did it in human form?"

Dmitri looked at the cliffs. *"A wee bit, aye."*

"Damn. So she saw you?"

"That she did. I managed to make the Dark forget that he saw me, but he'll be back. One of the Dark has killed a member of Dr. Reynolds' team."

Con let loose a string of curses. *"Just destroy the skeleton. I'll send Guy to erase everyone's memories."*

"Nay."

There was a long pause before Con asked, *"Excuse me?"*

Dmitri knew he was pushing boundaries, but when it came to Fair Isle, he was in charge. *"I have to know how the dragon died. I searched every one of these caves, Con. They were all empty when I returned to Dreagan."*

"You can no' blame yourself for this dragon being left behind."

"But I do. I'm responsible. Before you ask, Faith knows about us. She's working to help me discover how the dragon died."

"Then will you destroy the bones?"

He was about to consent when he thought of another way. *"No one will find the bones."*

"Just what I wanted to hear. Now, about Dr. Reynolds . . ."

"I'll no' be discussing her yet."

"Dmitri—"

"I know what you'll say. I've heard you voice it to many of us. Let me have this time to figure things out."

Con released a long breath. *"Then I'll give you the time."*

"I know why you doona like any of us to find mates. Matter of fact, I agree with you."

"But?"

"There is no but. I'm merely pointing out a fact."

"Do you need help there?"

Dmitri looked out into the driving rain, watching the wind move it one way and then another. *"I can handle it."*

"Good luck, old friend."

The link was severed. Dmitri didn't want to interrupt Faith as she worked. Besides, she might try to stop him from finding the Dark. He removed his clothes and piled them together. Then he walked onto the ledge and jumped.

He shifted, his wings spread wide as he angled himself upward to soar through the clouds. To be able to return to his true form twice in such a short period of time felt amazing. Since his brethren couldn't do the same, he would keep it to himself.

The Dark needed to be taken care of. The quicker he could be rid of them, the better. With his dragon eyes searching for the scum, he flew from the cliffs to the village.

He found the first Fae standing over a prone woman. Dmitri didn't need to check her pulse to know that she was dead. He could see it in her blank eyes that stared upward.

Rage filled him at the loss of life, he flew low enough for the Fae to hear him. He circled back around, and just as he'd hoped, the Dark teleported away.

There was no need to find the second one. They would be coming to him.

Within moments, he was back at the cliffs. He saw the two Dark appear in the spot where Faith had been pushed. He could still hear her scream on the wind, still see the fear reflected in her eyes.

The thunder masked the sound of his wings while the wind and rain hid him from view. Fire licked at his throat, itching to be released and turn the Dark to ash, but that would leave evidence for the mortals.

Dmitri wasn't deterred, though. He tucked his wings and dove from the clouds, his eye on one of the Fae. The Dark turned just before Dmitri reached him.

He opened his jaws and clamped his teeth around the Fae. The Dark screamed in pain and tried to gather enough magic to use. Dmitri didn't give him the chance. He grasped the Dark and yanked, tearing the Fae in half.

With a roar, he dipped a wing and turned back for the second Fae. Only to be hit with a blast of magic.

It burned through him like acid, seizing his muscles—and returned him to human form. Then he was falling through the air, tumbling this way and that. He hit the water with a bone-jarring thud that knocked the breath from him.

The violent sea tossed him about while the currents grabbed hold and attempted to pull him under. Since the Dark had used a spell to ensure that it would be hours before Dmitri could shift back into a dragon, he would have to fight the fucker in his present state. Which only infuriated him.

Dmitri immediately thought of Faith. She was in the cave alone with no one to protect her. He renewed his efforts and kicked and fought his way to the surface.

A second later, he was slammed against the rocks. He caught hold and clung even as the shards sliced open his arm and his entire right side, only to have the injuries heal instantly.

With his teeth gritted, he pulled himself from the water and began the climb up the cliff. Dmitri chanced a look upward to find the Dark standing on the ledge outside the cave with a smile on his face.

It was all the warning he had before the Dark began throwing bubbles of magic his way. The iridescent orbs packed a wallop.

The evil within the magic penetrated Dmitri's skin and sank through muscle and into bone. There was no dodging the magic in his present condition. All he could do was hope the Dark had poor aim.

The storm helped to shield Dmitri from several of the magical orbs, but not all. And the more that landed on him, the more difficult it became to climb—or even hang on.

CHAPTER EIGHTEEN

If evil were a spirit, it just raked ghostly claws down Faith's spine. She stilled and looked up from the bones to listen. At first, all she could perceive was the thunder and rain. Then she heard it.

A sinister, menacing laugh that made her skin crawl with fright. Evil was in the cave. But where was Dmitri?

She set down the brush and grabbed the trowel with a shaking hand. It was the only weapon she had, but it was better than nothing. If evil had come, she was going to meet it head-on.

Slowly, she got to her feet and searched the area for some sign of Muscles. When she didn't find him, she hesitantly made her way toward the entrance.

Her heart knocked against her ribs, and her legs trembled, threatening to buckle with every step. The closer she got to the cave opening, the louder the laughter—and the more certain she was that she wanted to run the opposite way.

Yet she kept going. She wasn't sure why. Some unfamiliar and unknown force guided her. She didn't need to see the intruder to know it was a Dark Fae. The evil that permeated the very air told her that.

It was only a matter of time before the Dark would turn and see her. Then, according to Dmitri, she'd been unable to withstand the lure of the Fae and succumb to his advances, only to die in the end.

That's not how she wanted to go out.

She refused for that to be how she left this world.

Faith raised her chin even as her knees knocked together. She gripped the trowel tighter and rounded the corner. That's when she got her first look at the Dark.

He had his back to her as he stood on the ledge and looked down. His short, black hair was flattened to his head because of the rain, but there was no denying the streaks of silver running through it.

Something had his attention, causing him to howl with laughter as a sphere formed in his hands. She crept closer and saw what looked like bowling ball-sized bubbles that he threw down the cliff.

After one such toss, he flung back his head and cackled with joy. "Not long now, you fekking dragon!"

Dragon? Her heart literally stopped at the Irish accent. That was Muscles out there.

A calm suddenly overtook her. She stalked to the Dark and lifted her hand over her head before plunging the trowel into the back of the Fae's neck, severing his spine.

He jerkingly turned around, his eyes meeting hers a split second before he fell over the side of the cliff, trying to reach the trowel. She didn't know if a Fae could be killed. For all she knew, she'd only managed to wound the Dark, and he'd return for her.

The force of the wind struck her in the face. She ducked her head and got on all fours to peer over the ledge. When she spotted Dmitri hanging on by one hand, she screamed his name.

He looked up at her and gave her a heart-stopping smile. Her relief was short-lived when she saw the white lines of pain bracketing his mouth.

She lay flat and reached as far down as she could. "You can make it!"

He was at least twelve feet below her, and struggling against the storm. As she watched, she saw the large burn marks covering his body.

Was that what those bubbles did to him? Though he'd said a Dragon King couldn't be killed, he'd never said they couldn't be hurt.

"Please," she whispered. "Please make it up to me."

Her heart was in her throat as she watched helplessly while he attempted to grab hold of the rocks with his dangling hand several times.

After three tries, he held on. Then he let loose a loud bellow as he pulled himself up and began to climb. She wanted to clap and shout with joy. Instead, she remained with her hand outstretched, waiting for him.

A muscle ticked in his jaw as he pulled back his lips and showed his clenched teeth as he fought against the pain. Bands of smoke wafted from his wounds as the rain hit them.

If that's what happened to a dragon when struck by Fae magic, she hoped to never find out what it did to a human. A shudder went through her.

It felt like ages before Dmitri got close enough for her to reach. She grabbed his arm and pulled with all her might to give him what little strength she could.

He heaved himself up and onto the ledge, only to roll to his back. Her stomach knotted at the damage the Dark had inflicted.

She smoothed Dmitri's hair off his forehead and leaned

over him to block the rain from his face. His eyes opened, the corners crinkling as he smiled. She put her hand over his when he touched her cheek.

His smile vanished, replaced by a frown. "You shouldna be out in this weather."

Faith couldn't help but laugh. Once he'd gotten to his feet, she put his arm around her shoulders and walked him inside the cave to the waiting fire.

"What happened?" she asked as she stripped off her clothes and laid them around the fire to dry. Then she climbed atop the sleeping bag only to hesitate from touching him.

"The Dark needed to die." He closed his eyes and remained still.

Though she shook from the cold, it didn't seem to affect him, and she wasn't sure how the course, wool blanket would feel against his wounds.

"Of course, they did. But it doesn't explain what happened," she said.

He cracked open one eye and looked at her for a moment before closing it again. "I lured them here to fight them. I couldn't burn them with dragon fire because it would've left evidence. So I opted for another approach. I killed one, but the other used a spell that prevents us from remaining in dragon form."

She swallowed. He'd been in the middle of battle, and she hadn't even known it because she'd been absorbed by unearthing bones. While she'd been brushing away dirt, he'd been fighting evil.

"I fell into the sea," Muscles continued. "I started to climb up, but he was already at the entrance of the cave."

"It was magic he was throwing, wasn't it?"

"Aye. That shite burns."

"Will you heal?"

He nodded slowly. "What did you do to the Fae?"

"I shoved my trowel into his neck. Please tell me I killed him."

"I didna realize you were an archeologist and a warrior," he said with a grin turning up his lips, though he kept his eyes closed.

If he could joke, then he would be all right. Most of the tension left her. "I was scared."

"But you did it anyway." His hand covered hers and squeezed. "Come here and warm me."

She eyed his wounds. "But you're not cold. And what of your injuries?"

"I hurt worse no' being able to touch you."

She didn't point out that he was holding her hand because she wanted to feel him, as well. Faith let him guide her where he wanted her.

Her eyes closed when the side of her face rested against his chest. His heat was already seeping into her, warming her. He felt so damn wonderful.

"You did good," he whispered.

She smiled, moved by his praise. "Thank you."

"Hmm."

With his heartbeat in her ear, her thoughts drifted to seeing him hanging on to the rocks by one hand. Even though she knew he couldn't die, she'd been terrified that he would.

She barely knew Muscles, but what she couldn't deny—especially after what she'd just experienced—was that he mattered to her.

His masterful lovemaking and the fact that he was a Dragon King aside, she'd taken notice of him immediately. Especially when she hadn't wanted to.

Now that she'd felt his touch and had been brought to such heights of pleasure, she wasn't sure anyone could ever compare to him.

To make matters worse, she didn't like even thinking of being with any other man.

And that drew her up short.

Her feelings notwithstanding, there was more to this situation than just her. There were Dmitri and the others at Dreagan. She didn't know how many Kings lived there, and it didn't matter. They had sacrificed everything already.

It was time to give them a win. So as much as she wanted to be the one to discover such a find as the dragon, it would remain a secret. Right after she helped Muscles figure out how the dragon had died.

Dmitri didn't allow himself to sleep even with the two Dark dead. More could come.

Instead, he allowed his body the time it needed to heal. Oddly, the rain had helped to wash away some of the dark magic from his injuries.

But he couldn't heal quickly enough.

His arm tightened around Faith. She slept once more. He liked how easily she trusted him to keep her safe. What he really enjoyed was *her.*

If he could turn off whatever feelings she rallied, he would. She'd been doing fine before she stumbled upon the bones. She had a good career, but the dragon would've put her name on the map, so to speak.

He wished he could give that to her. If he didn't care about the humans learning about him and the other Kings, he'd give her the skeleton without a second thought.

She deserved that and so much more. He couldn't seem to stop extolling her, which was odd since he never did that with humans.

As the minutes passed, and as he healed, he imagined returning to Dreagan without her. Ryder had let Kinsey go for three years. The King had done it for Kinsey so she could have a life outside of theirs.

Dmitri could do the same for Faith. All it would take was a call to Guy, who would erase every memory she had of dragons, the Fae, and him. She could go on about her life as if none of this had ever happened. It was probably the right thing to do.

Why then did he want to howl at the very thought of it?

An hour later, the last of his injuries had healed. Faith's leg lifted, brushing his thigh and cock. He hissed in a breath, aching and hard.

He wanted to roll her over and take her again, to hear her cries of pleasure and see the ecstasy cross her face as she peaked.

But time was not on their side.

She drew in a breath and stretched. Her eyes opened and met his. "How do you feel?"

"Better."

She moved the blanket aside and looked for herself. Her head snapped back to him. "You're healed."

"That's usually what it means when someone says they're immortal."

"Yeah, but. . . . Wow."

He chuckled and gave her a kiss.

She leaned back and looked at him oddly. "You should be relaxed now that the two Dark Fae are dead, but you aren't."

"Because more will come."

"I knew you were going to say that." She sat up with a sigh, wrapping the blanket around her. "How long do we have?"

"That I can no' say."

"Then we need to get busy."

He rose and walked to the cave opening to get his

clothes and dress. When he returned, she had on her jeans and one of his black t-shirts. It looked really good on her.

"Do you think when this is over, we can do something normal?" she asked.

Intrigued, he asked, "What do you consider normal?"

"Oh, is this a typical day for you?"

He shrugged, nodding. "Unfortunately, it is."

"Well, I'm thinking something very mundane. Like going grocery shopping or even weeding my flowerbeds."

The image her words projected made him laugh. "That's definitely mundane."

"Exactly!" she said as she ran her fingers through her sandy blond locks. "Sounds exciting, doesn't it?"

Her enthusiasm was infectious. "I'm a pretty good cook. I'd choose grocery shopping."

"Truly?" She shot him a suspicious look. "I detest meal planning, cooking, and anything to do with buying food. I just want to sit down and eat it. If you take care of the meals, I'll take care of the weeds."

He walked to her and gave her a quick, hard kiss. "Consider it a deal, then."

"I think I came out the winner in this," she said as she gave him a sassy look and turned away.

Dmitri would have to disagree with her. He was the one who was coming out the winner at finding her. And to think, he was actually looking forward to cooking for her.

When Faith began working, he lay down beside her and helped. It was a slow process that was as time-consuming as it was monotonous. Dmitri thought he would hate it, but each time more of the bones were revealed, he smiled.

"You like it," she said, looking at him sideways.

He shrugged. "Perhaps.

"I'll make an archeologist out of you yet."

The idea of being with her on other digs gave him a little thrill.

But he kept that to himself.

CHAPTER NINETEEN

Rhi walked the halls of the Light Castle with her watcher by her side. She ignored the stares coming from everyone, but it was harder to pretend she didn't hear the whispers.

"She's back."

"Do you think that means she'll return to the Queen's Guard?"

"Perhaps she knows where the queen is."

"Do you think she has information on this Reaper issue?"

"I wish she'd look my way."

"Do you think she's upset about the queen and King of Kings?"

"I wish I could be like her."

"I hope she stays this time."

It was on the tip of her tongue to answer all of them, but she kept walking. Her watcher was veiled and silent—as always. If only she could see him.

She turned down a long corridor and blinked against the sun pouring through the bank of windows on her left side. Her gaze moved to the wall on her right, and the world tumbled to a halt as the room tilted and spun.

Stumbling, she grabbed the wall as images flashed rapidly through her mind, but they were too quick for her to see any of them clearly.

However, there was one thing she knew with certainty. She had been in this exact corridor, this exact place with her watcher before.

No matter how hard she tried, she couldn't pull up any memories of such an occurrence, though. Humans called it déjà vu. Among the Fae, it was proof that magic had been used.

She felt her watcher close. He didn't touch her, but he was there, waiting to see if he was needed. She kept her eyes closed and her head down as she wondered what he would do if she had fallen.

Once the room stopped spinning, she straightened and took a step away from the wall in order to look at it. There was nothing but marble. Why then was she sure that something had been written or drawn there?

"What did you do to me?" she demanded in a soft voice to her watcher.

Silence greeted her. Not that she actually expected him to answer, but she wanted him to know that she was going to find out.

"We were here. In this spot. Together. Why can't I remember?"

The thought of having her memories altered enraged her. What had she overheard?

Or seen?

Her watcher. She'd seen him. The circumstances and outcome were beyond her now, but that much was obvious. What could've happened that he'd shown himself to her?

Rhi pivoted and continued down the corridor, anger in every step. Her thoughts were firing rapid questions, all of which had no answers. Nor did she imagine that she would find those resolutions anytime soon.

She came upon three women standing together. One was wiping away tears. Since Rhi didn't want to be seen, she hurried past them. Only to stop when their conversation reached her ears.

"It's so sad," sniffled one.

Another nodded. "No one really knows what happened to the Everwood family."

The third wiped at her tears. "All of them dead. Some say it was the Reapers."

Rhi turned and looked in the spot where she knew her watcher was. Was it coincidence that her memories being changed coincided with the Everwoods dying?

"How did they die?" Rhi dropped the veil and asked the group.

All three turned to her, staring wide-eyed when they realized who she was. She sighed, waiting for one of them to answer.

Finally, it was the one who had been crying who said, "All four of them were killed."

Rhi's mind rebelled at the thought. "Are you sure?"

"The parents' bodies were found first."

"What about Neve and Atris?" Rhi asked.

The Fae nodded. "Neve's body is still missing, but they found Atris outside the castle. Everyone is worried about which family will die next."

Rhi whirled around. "No one else is going to die."

Daire clenched his jaw. How the hell was Rhi piecing together her memories? Nothing should've been able to work through Death's magic.

But the proof was before him in brilliant, epic display.

He thought back to that fateful day when the Reapers

had had the showdown with Bran. It had been Daire's job to keep Rhi away, and yet she'd managed to use her magic in a way that shouldn't have been possible to follow where Neve had been taken by the Reapers' nemesis, Bran.

Once there, Daire had made sure to envelop Rhi in his veil so that Bran wouldn't see her. Everything after that had happened so fast.

Neve was attacked, Talin and the other Reapers fought the Dark, and before he could blink, Rhi had touched Daire's face and pushed out of his arms.

It allowed him to fight alongside the other Reapers while seeing Rhi, in all her radiance, battle the Dark.

When Bran's magic began to shatter the world around them, it was Rhi who'd fought back with her magic, creating a vortex. Unfortunately, that maelstrom had been about to pull in their leader, Cael. Until Eoghan pushed him out of the way and was taken instead.

Rhi was the one who'd healed Cael from a wound inflicted by Bran. Something else she hadn't known she could do.

But the worst part came when Rhi had brought Neve and her brother, Atris, to her rooms at the Light Castle. Because Bran had turned Atris to the Dark side.

To seal it, all Atris had to do was take a life. He did that by killing Neve.

Rhi hadn't just seen all of that, she had also seen the Reapers, knew of them. Death's rules were clear. No Fae could ever learn the truth, lest they be killed.

Death had knocked Rhi unconscious and removed her memories of the entire disaster.

For that small fraction of time, Rhi had looked into Daire's eyes, and he into hers. No longer was he hidden. She had *seen* him. She had known him.

Then it was gone. Forgotten.

It was for the best since it had saved her life. The fact

that Death had gone to such extremes for her meant that Death saw something in the future in regards to Rhi.

If only he knew what it was. There was no doubt that Rhi wasn't just powerful but also respected among the Light. He saw it in the way they watched her and spoke about her.

His thoughts had been running wildly as he followed Rhi. He didn't realize where she had taken them until he stood inside her rooms. Then she whirled around to face him. Though she couldn't see him because of his veil, she always knew where he was.

For several tense minutes, she stared in his direction. Then she began to pace. "I don't take kindly to anyone messing with my memories," she bit out.

It caused him to smile. Some might be fearful once they discovered such things. But not Rhi. She was livid at the idea of anyone daring to do that to her.

"You know, I've known from day one that you followed me," she said, shooting him a look as she continued moving back and forth before him. "I ignored you at first, and then I began talking to you. I thought you were my friend."

He was, though he couldn't tell her that. His orders were simple: watch Rhi without interfering.

She halted before him. "I'm going to piece together those memories. No matter how long it takes."

He didn't doubt that she could.

"Whoever you are, stop following me."

That he couldn't do. Besides, he liked being around Rhi and seeing a part of her life. As long as it didn't involve Balladyn. That part, he could do without.

"Do you hear me?" she shouted.

Since he was standing two feet away, he definitely heard her. But he didn't drop his veil or talk to her.

Her nostrils flared in anger. "This is no longer amusing.

I don't care if you're Light or Dark Fae or another race al-together. You're no longer welcome around me."

She stormed out of her rooms, and he made to follow her. Only he couldn't get past the doorway. Somehow, she'd managed to prevent him from shadowing her.

Daire frowned. Though Usaeil as queen had decreed—with magic—that no one could teleport in or out of the castle, a Reaper's magic trumped even that of a queen of the Light.

He dropped the veil and thought of the Reapers and found himself standing inside the concrete building on Inchmickery, a tiny isle off the coast of Edinburgh.

Cael looked up from some papers and frowned. "What's happened?"

"Rhi's memories are returning," Daire explained.

Cael set down the papers and walked around the table. "We need to tell Death."

No sooner had the words left Cael's mouth than Death stood before them.

It wasn't the grim reaper with a scythe and black robes as the humans thought. Death was a woman, and stunningly beautiful at that.

Her blue-black hair hung to her waist in soft curls. The front part was pulled away from her face with intricate braids and held together by a spray of petite purple roses.

Death wore a regal, strapless gown. The top portion was a vivid, deep purple without a single adornment. From the waist down, it was a voluptuous skirt of satin and tulle in solid black with matching purple roses made of material sewn into the skirt in various places.

Lavender eyes framed by thick, black lashes watched him. Her flawless complexion was the color of soft cream. She had high cheekbones and full lips that he noticed Cael looking at.

"It must be important for you to call me here," she said in a soft, ethereal voice to Cael.

Daire nodded. Even though Death chose Reapers and was judge and jury to the Fae, it was rare for them to see her. Cael was her chosen leader of the Reapers, and the two of them interacted regularly.

"Tell me," Erith urged.

"Rhi went to the Light Castle," Daire began. "As soon as she came to the corridor where the Reaper symbol had been painted in blood, she stumbled to a halt. When she straightened, she somehow knew her memories had been altered."

"Interesting," Death said.

"She overheard some Fae talking about the Everwoods. I think Rhi figured out that she was involved. She told me she was going to piece all her memories together."

Erith's lips lifted in a small smile. "I believe she can do it."

"Against your magic?" Cael asked her in surprise.

Death merely gave him an enigmatic look. "Go on, Daire."

Daire swallowed, watching Erith and Cael with curiosity. "Rhi then said I was no longer welcome. She left the room, but when I tried to follow, I couldn't."

At this news, Death clasped her hands before her and lowered her gaze to the floor for a few seconds. Then she looked at Daire. "You'll still be able to track her. Though you won't be able to get close, you'll be able to see where she's going. Stay as close to her as you can. From now on, I want to receive daily reports."

"From me?" Cael asked.

Erith didn't take her eyes from Daire. "From Daire."

"I'll see it done." What else was Daire supposed to say? Death walked until her wide skirt touched his shoe, then she stopped. "Has Rhi confronted Con about the picture of him and Usaeil."

"Yes. It wasn't the violent clash I expected it to be."

Cael crossed his arms over his chest and said, "You think Rhi is going to confront the queen."

Death's smile was slow. "I'm counting on it."

CHAPTER TWENTY

"We'll never finish before the storm stops," Faith said as she continued brushing aside dirt around the bones from her position on her stomach. It was the first time she had ever wanted to hurry a dig.

Muscles turned his head to her, causing a lock of dark hair to fall over his forehead. "We'll deal with that when the time comes."

"The thing is, I'm a planner. I like to know what's coming, that way I can figure out a way to deal with it."

He shot her a wink. "I wasna planned, and you handled that situation well."

It was a fact, but then again, who could ever prepare for a man like Dmitri?

He was in the same position as she on his stomach, working diligently beside her. A dragon. A freaking real-life dragon. Her scientific mind couldn't believe it.

And yet, she accepted his explanations easily. Mainly because she'd seen it firsthand before the words ever came out of his mouth. It was hard to discount him saying he was a dragon when she'd been in his clutches—literally.

While she worked, she thought about the white talons

that had held her so gently. How he'd scooped her out of the air without cutting her was puzzling, but done it he had.

If only she hadn't been so terrified that she was falling to her death, she could've taken more notice of the dragon. But her eyes had been on the fast-approaching rocks and water.

It wasn't until she'd been set down inside the cave that she comprehended that she wasn't going to die. That's when she stumbled back and saw the freaking giant dragon.

The one thing she did remember was how the water had trickled over metallic, white scales. And unblinking umber eyes scrutinizing her.

There had been an instant of fear that had quickly morphed to wonder and awe. Now she wished she'd taken a longer look at Muscles in his true form.

She stood up to stretch her back, her eyes taking in the bones before her. While she worked on the neck, Dmitri had been carefully freeing the other side of the skull from the confines of the earth.

"I need to make sure everyone goes home," she said, thinking of all the people involved with the dig.

He paused in mid-brush and looked up at her. "Aye."

"Roger's death is a good reason." There was something in Dmitri's azure eyes that caught her attention. "What aren't you telling me?"

Blowing out a breath, he pushed onto all fours before sitting back on his haunches. "When I went to draw out the Dark, I saw that they had killed again. A woman."

"Oh, God," she murmured and put her hand to her forehead as her stomach rolled with the news. "I've got to get these people out immediately."

"We need to remove what the Dark wants—the bones."

She cocked her head at him. "I thought you wanted to destroy them."

"That's what I'm supposed to do." He drew in a deep

breath, causing his shoulders to lift as he looked at the dragon. "He's one of mine, and he's been waiting for me to find him. I'm going to take him back to Dreagan where he belongs."

She didn't consider herself a weeper, and yet, her eyes teared up listening to him talk. She blinked rapidly to dispel the threatening waterworks.

"This could take us weeks. You're telling me that as long as the bones are here, the Dark will be, as well?"

Muscles nodded slowly. "I'm afraid so."

"That's unacceptable. I can't have any more deaths on my conscience."

"This isna your fault."

"I disagree." She waved away his words when he tried to argue more with her. "First things first, we need to get my team away."

Dmitri raised a dark brow. "Will Tamir leave you?"

"He will if he thinks I'm going."

He rested his hands on his thighs and gave her a hard look. "What are you planning?"

"Nothing," she said with a shrug. "I'm going to remain here and free this dragon from the earth."

"I doona—"

"I know," she interrupted him. "But I'm staying. If care isn't taken, the bones could be damaged because of their age."

Muscles blew out a breath and climbed to his feet. He scrubbed a hand over his jaw, the scrape of whiskers loud in the cave. "I think you should leave with the others."

"What?" She couldn't believe what he'd just said. How could he want such a thing after their night together? After the passion? The raw hunger that had taken them?

Then it hit her. Maybe she felt more than he did. That made her cringe because she never gave a lover more of herself than what was given to her.

In fact, she was the one who normally walked away. The one who used the "It's not you, it's me" line. The one who crept away in the night so as not to have to explain why she didn't want to see them again.

Was it happening to her now? Others had warned her that it would eventually return to her tenfold.

And that thought chilled her.

Muscles dropped the brush and closed the distance between them. "You've only got a taste of what it's like to be mixed up with the Dragon Kings. We're in a war, and our enemies are coming at us from all sides. Any association with us, however slight, puts you under a microscope so our foes can see how they can use you against us."

It was on the tip of her tongue to say that she could take care of herself, but, in fact, she couldn't. Not against magic. She was the proverbial slug waiting to be stepped on.

"I'm giving you a choice," he continued. "I could go through each story of the women who now live at Dreagan as examples."

"There are women at Dreagan?" she asked in surprise. And hope.

A muscle in his jaw clenched. "I didna get to finish the story earlier."

"So finish it now. I'm curious." She was chomping at the bit to know every detail, but she was managing to hold it all in beautifully.

He gave a small shake of his head. "When we woke centuries after going to sleep in our effort to hide, the first thing we did was use magic to ensure that we would never feel deeply for humans in any way. Hatred, love, or even friendship."

It was like a kick in the stomach. So even if he wanted to care, he couldn't. Well, wasn't Karma a bitch?

And she could swear that Karma was somewhere giv-

ing her a wink and a very innocent—if not mocking—
smile.

Faith felt the despondency threaten, but she refused to
give in. She reminded herself why she liked being on her
own. Except it didn't work as well this time.

"That spell remained in place until a few years ago."

Hope soared so powerfully that she couldn't breathe.

Dmitri twisted his lips ruefully. "Despite our precau-
tions, Kings began to fall in love with mortals. Hal was
the first to take a woman as his mate."

"How . . . how many have taken mates?"

"Fourteen."

Her brows rose at the news. "That's a significant
number."

"One of them is a Fae. The other thirteen are mortals,
though one is a Druid. My point is that they are now in
the midst of this war."

"They chose to love."

"Aye. That they did. Though only one or two had the
choice I'm about to give you. Before I tell you what the
options are, let me explain that every woman has been tar-
geted by Ulrik. He's either attempted to kill them or
thought to bring them to his side."

The killing part worried her. She liked life and wanted
it to continue. "That's if Ulrik ever discovers me."

"It is something I verra much want to prevent. You've
gotten a small taste of our war with the Dark, but it's far
worse than you can imagine. Because of that, you have the
choice to either continue on as you are where I will do my
utmost to protect you . . ."

"Or?" she urged when he paused.

"Or your memories can be wiped of anything to do with
me, dragons, or anything else I've told you."

She would return to the world she'd known before

Dmitri, the one she'd loved for years. It was a safe place, but now, she knew it was all an illusion. Which, in fact, was more dangerous than her current circumstances.

"For better or worse, I'm going to keep this new knowledge."

He grasped her arms. "Please, reconsider."

"You told me I had a choice. I made it."

He dropped his arms and turned around, walking a few steps away. "You could die."

"I almost did. You saved me," she reminded him.

He turned back to her and gazed at her with blue eyes filled with concern before he raked a hand through his dark locks. "Is there anything I can do to change your mind?"

She strode to him, dropping the brush from her hand before grasping his face. "Enough," she said before she rose up on her toes and kissed him.

His arms snaked around her, crushing her against his chest. It was no soft kiss, but one filled with fire and hunger. The kind that consumed them as desire raged.

He spun them, pushing her against the stone wall. With one hand behind the back of her head to protect her, he deepened the kiss. She eagerly followed as he led her down the path of pleasure.

She gave a moan of annoyance when he ended the kiss. When she opened her eyes, he was staring down at her.

Her heart melted when he gently ran a finger along the shape of her face. "I doona want you hurt."

"Then don't stop kissing me."

"You should get far away from me."

She splayed her hands over his chest. "That's not happening."

With a sound that was half-growl, half-moan, he claimed her lips again. The kiss was savage, the desire between them wild.

Within moments, their clothes were discarded as they stood skin-to-skin, kissing. She reached around and sank her nails into his ass, feeling the muscles clench in response.

Then she kissed down his chest, her gaze on his face. He watched her as his chest heaved. She knelt before him and smiled when his eyes darkened with need.

She slowly wrapped her fingers around his cock and stroked. He groaned and fisted his hands in her hair. The feel of him was intoxicating. She knew what it was like to have him inside her, filling her. But she wanted to know his taste.

Watching him, she brought the head of his rod to her mouth. She then slowly parted her lips and slid them over the tip, guiding him deeper into her throat.

His head fell back, and his hips started to thrust as she began to suck. Her hand tightened as she pumped it in time with the movements of her head.

The first taste of him that touched her tongue made her moan and her sex clench with need. She closed her eyes and sucked harder.

In the next moment, he pulled away. She looked up, a question on her lips. Then she saw his face.

He grabbed her, carrying her to their pallet where he set her down and turned her around. Then he pushed her onto all fours.

She looked over her shoulder as he knelt behind her. Their gazes met as he touched her sex. A satisfied smile pulled at his lips when he found her wet.

Then he gripped her hips and thrust, filling her completely. Her head dropped down as her sex ached for more. She bit her lip and tried to move, but he held her still.

After what felt like an eternity, he began to move. Soon, he was plunging hard and fast. He bent over her, cupping one of her breasts and squeezing the nipple.

He bit her shoulder before licking it. His hand slid to her throat and turned her head toward him. Their lips met, tongues tangling in time with his thrusts.

She gasped when he reached between them and circled her clit.

"Come for me," he demanded in her ear.

CHAPTER TWENTY-ONE

The sound of Faith's breathing as it hitched right before she climaxed was music to Dmitri's ears. He felt her walls clamping around him, pushing him closer to reaching his own pleasure.

Her body quivered as cries of ecstasy fell unheeded from her lips. He continued to move, extending her orgasm.

"Dmitri," she cried hoarsely.

Her fingers clutched the blanket, and chill bumps covered her skin. But still, he pounded into her.

What was it about her that drove him to the brink of wildness? What was it that made him want to mark her physically and mentally as his?

What was it that tied them closer and closer together with each passing heartbeat?

And why didn't he care more that it was happening?

As his desire mounted, he forgot about his ridiculous questions and concentrated on the magnificent woman in his arms.

Her arms gave out, and she fell forward. He gripped her hips again and began to plunge hard and fast. No longer could he wait to join her in the sublime aftermath of their lovemaking, which was almost as good as the sex itself.

When he looked down, her face was turned to the side, flushed with pleasure. Her lips were parted and her eyes unfocused.

And just like that, his climax rushed him. He thrust deep and ground out her name as the bliss seized him, grasped him. For those amazing moments, he'd discovered true happiness—in the arms of a mortal.

Once he was able to regain thought, he pulled out of her and collapsed beside her. Her smile made his heart catch. He knew it was wrong to allow her to retain her memories, but he hadn't worked up the courage to leave her yet.

He told himself it was because of the skeleton, but that was a lie. He remained for her. The exact time his thinking changed couldn't be pinpointed, but then again, it didn't matter. He knew what he wanted—Faith.

Her eyes softened, and she blinked slowly. He touched her face, struck by just how stunning she was. Dmitri pulled her into his arms where she settled with a sigh of contentment.

They couldn't rest long. Already, the storm was abating. Soon, Tamir would arrive with news of the woman's death and to see about Faith. Hopefully, she would be able to convince him to leave and send everyone home.

That would alleviate his worries about protecting everyone on the team. Not that they would remain long. Fair Isle had seen its share of bloodshed. If he had his way, there would be no more.

The sooner he got the bones free, the sooner he could get back to Dreagan.

His thoughts skidded to a halt as he looked at Faith. The best thing would be for her to come with him. Con would balk, but Dmitri couldn't give a flying fuck what the King of Kings might say or do.

Unlike some of the other mates, Faith had a career. One that wouldn't fit in with anything to do with Dreagan. When Darius had brought Sophie home, she'd decided to open a medical clinic and be the village doctor.

With Kinsey and Ryder, Kinsey being a technical wizard allowed her to work alongside her mate.

There would be nothing of the sort for Faith. He saw how she sparkled as she worked. It was her passion, the thing that gave her purpose. There was no way he could take that away from her.

And if she weren't on Dreagan land—whether she had her memories or not—she would have a bright, shiny target on her.

He closed his eyes as the complications continued to rise. One of his dragons had been left behind and died. He refused to sentence Faith to the same fate. Yet bringing her with him and confining her to Dreagan might be just as bad.

With a sigh, he squeezed the bridge of his nose with his thumb and forefinger. There was no good outcome, no matter how he looked at it.

The best possible scenario would be to take the bones and leave Faith behind. He would ask Darcy, the Druid, and Shara, the Light Fae, to mix their magic with his and cast a protection spell over Faith so that Ulrik or no Dark could harm her.

As for her memories, he wanted her to keep them. It was for purely selfish reasons. He wanted her to think of him because he would be thinking of her.

"That's a serious look," she said and kissed his cheek.

He smiled and rolled her onto her back so he could kiss her soundly. Though he wanted to spend the day making love to her a thousand different ways, the weather had turned against them.

Reluctantly, he ended the kiss. "Listen."

She frowned and did as he asked. Her shoulders drooped. "The weather is changing."

"Which means Tamir is probably already on his way."

She smiled up at him with a mischievous glint in her eyes. "Can't you make sure he turns back? Or perhaps block the entrance somehow? I'm not ready to leave."

"Neither am I."

How odd, after so many years living as a human, that he wanted to remain in a cave with her. They had all they needed—except for food—right there. And the food issue could be easily remedied.

Her smile dropped as her face took on a solemn look. "I'm serious. I don't want to leave, and I don't want anyone to bother us."

"As soon as everyone is sent home, we'll be alone."

"For how long?"

He saw the skepticism in her eyes. "As long as we're given."

She pressed her lips together and nodded. "Then I'd better dress and get back to work."

He flopped onto his back and wished with everything he had that they weren't in the middle of a war. There had been a few times in his very long life that a female Fae had intrigued him enough to spend months or even years with her.

But Faith was different. He didn't know how or why, but he *knew* it with certainty. Though some Kings thought by doing the mating ceremony their women would be safe, he didn't feel the same.

For him, it made them more of a target. The mates couldn't die unless their Kings did, but that didn't mean the women couldn't experience pain or be tortured.

His thoughts had been one-sided up until now. With regards to Faith, he'd feel much better knowing that she was with him and protected by the magic on Dreagan.

Not that he wanted her as his mate.

Did he?

He sat upright, shock numbing even his brain.

"You plan on greeting Tamir in the buff?" Faith asked in a teasing tone.

"Um. Nay." He rose and dazedly went to his clothes where he began to dress.

When Faith passed him on the way to the dragon, she slapped his butt as he'd done to her earlier. He watched her, hungry for another taste of her already.

He was quickly forgotten as she returned to her work. With his clothes in place and the last boot tugged on, he made his way to the front of the cave.

The skeleton could easily be excavated with magic, but he didn't want to do that to her. Faith was already giving up any recognition she might have gained for discovering it. He didn't want to take away the joy she experienced from pulling it from the earth.

Though he didn't know where Ulrik was, the fact that Con hadn't alerted him to anything meant that Ulrik had yet to make his next move.

The Dark had gone into hiding after the attack across the UK on Halloween. But given how quiet things were, something big was in the works.

Dmitri thought of Asher, who was in Paris at the World Whisky Consortium. There was nothing there for Ulrik to wreak havoc with, so at least Asher was safe.

Most likely, Ulrik had his sights set on another team—Kinsey, Henry, and Esther—who were going to infiltrate a corporation to see how Kinsey and Esther had been exposed to Druid magic.

He wished he had his phone to call Henry. As the only

mortal allowed onto Dreagan who wasn't a mate, the fearless MI5 agent had earned his place among the Kings.

When his sister, Esther, had been pulled into their war and had had Druid magic used to get her to kill, Henry had proven his worth and boldness by standing up to Con and doing what had to be done to free his sister from the magic.

It was too bad Henry was in love with Rhi. He deserved love, and Rhi was in no position to give it since Dmitri suspected she was still very much in love with her King.

All of that made him realize that he had a while to himself before he'd be called back to Dreagan. It was time he was going to take.

For himself. And for Faith.

For so long, he'd done everything for Dreagan and his brethren. He couldn't remember the last time he'd done anything for himself.

Though he would never let his brothers down, he was going to allow himself to be selfish. Just this once.

He moved out of the cave onto the ledge and raised his face to the sky. With his eyes closed, the sprinkles of rain fell upon him.

No longer did thunder rumble the earth or lightning split the sky. The wind still blew, but not with gale force as before. The storm had raged—and so had his desires.

It was almost as if the tempest had sequestered him and Faith together. He smiled at the thought, because otherwise, he'd never have gotten that close to her.

He opened his eyes and looked at the sky. The clouds were a milky gray and moved rapidly, changing formations in a blink. With his arms out to his sides, he allowed himself to believe he was flying again.

Being in dragon form and feeling the wind rush over his scales as his wings navigated the currents had been amazing. It was a reminder of all that he and the other Dragon Kings had given up—and what they shouldn't have had to.

But they couldn't turn back time. What was done, was done.

He dropped his arms and lowered his head. Despondency filled him to the very brim. He was a dragon. A creature of magic and fire. A being that was lethal and dangerous.

The Kings had forgotten that. All but one.

Ulrik.

Dmitri thought of Faith, the mates at Dreagan, and Henry. Not all mortals were wicked or corrupt. Some were good, decent people. So while he didn't want to wipe the earth of them, he found that he was beginning to think more along the lines of Ulrik's agenda than Con's.

The sound of voices carrying upon the wind reached him. He recognized Tamir's, and within moments, the archeologist stood at the cliff's edge.

Dmitri had pushed aside his dark thoughts by the time Tamir climbed down the cliff. He helped Faith's assistant to the ledge and returned the man's smile.

"Let me guess," Tamir said. "She's working."

Dmitri nodded, noticing the bag in Tamir's hand. "Aye."

"I brought food for both of you. I can't believe that storm lasted as long as it did."

Dmitri nodded absently. "Thanks."

Tamir hesitated, looking him over. "How are you?"

It took a moment for Dmitri to remember that Faith had told Tamir he had been attacked earlier. "It was just a bump on the head. I'm fine."

"Glad to hear it."

Dmitri followed him into the cave and down the tunnel to Faith. She had her earbuds in, listening to music as she worked. He knew Tamir and the others wouldn't be there long, but he resented the intrusion into his world with Faith.

No matter how much he told himself to calm down, the longer Tamir was there, the angrier he became. Dmitri watched as Tamir sat beside Faith, and the way she smiled in welcome at seeing him.

He stood back and observed as she dug into the food and immediately opened a bag of chips, stuffing one in her mouth. Dmitri scrutinized every detail of her exchange with her assistant.

Then she asked Tamir, "How are the plans to get everyone home?"

It was all Dmitri could do not to grab Tamir by the collar of his shirt and toss him out of the cave so he could be alone with his woman again.

CHAPTER TWENTY-TWO

Faith was very aware of Dmitri's altered attitude. He was glaring at Tamir as if he wanted to do him harm, but she understood. Having food was good, yet Tamir's invasion seemed to change things.

"So you were really serious," Tamir said. "We're shutting down the dig?"

She licked her lips, enjoying the salt left by the chips. "Yes, of course. Things have gotten too dangerous."

"Yeah," Tamir said, his gaze lowering to the ground and going unfocused. "I was hoping you meant it, but I didn't do anything until I could talk to you again."

Faith laid a hand upon his arm. "It's fine. I'm going, as well."

His eyes jerked back to her. "What of the skeleton?"

"People's lives aren't worth it."

"Someone else will claim it if you leave now."

She couldn't exactly tell him that wouldn't happen and keep Dmitri's secret at the same time. "Hopefully, with Ronnie's help, we can prevent that."

"When will we return?"

"I haven't thought that far ahead."

Tamir glanced at Dmitri. "I'll feel better once we're clear of this place."

"I know," she said with a smile.

Tamir climbed to his feet. "I guess I'd better head back to town and let everyone know. A few have already left, and others were planning to leave."

It was all working out as it should. She stood and linked her arm through his, winking at Dmitri. "I have a proposition," she told Tamir.

"Really?" he asked eagerly.

"Do you remember the site in Montana that you wanted to check out? I think you should lead a team. You really wanted to go and explore the area more."

"Because I know there's something there to find." He stopped and looked at her. "You really want me to lead the dig?"

She met his dark gaze and smiled. "Without a doubt. You should've done it years ago."

"I'll still be your assistant, though. Right?" he asked excitedly.

"Whatever you want," she replied with a laugh.

He nodded and absently faced forward, his smile growing by the second. "My own dig."

Faith led him to the cave opening. By his astonished expression, she realized she should've pushed him to go out on his own years ago. But it was hard to let go of the ones you loved, and Tamir was family.

She hugged him, wondering if it would be the last time she saw Tamir. He'd recognized the evil straightaway. She should've listened to her friend. Mercifully, she hadn't lost him to a Dark attack.

"Thank you," he said and pulled back.

She waved away his words. "None needed."

Tamir glanced down the long corridor of the cave. "I

saw the way Dmitri looked at you. Is there something there?"

"I don't know what you mean."

He laughed wryly. "You most certainly do. You deserve this. Take him and don't look back."

She'd already done that. "Call me when you get to Montana."

"Aren't you coming back to town with me?" A frown wiped away his grin.

"I'm going to gather my things here. Then I plan to take a much-needed vacation."

He laughed, shaking his head. "Now I *know* something is wrong. You've not taken time off in three years."

She took his hands and squeezed. "This place has changed things. It has changed me. I saw how everyone reacted to the idea of what I might've discovered. People have died. I need some time to gather my thoughts before I decide on my next course."

It was a perfect excuse to step away from everything for a bit. She wasn't sure what would happen after her team left the isle, but she did know one thing: she wasn't ready to say good-bye to Dmitri.

"Muscles will look after me while I'm here," she added.

Tamir stared at her a long time before he finally nodded. "I'll do what I can with the authorities in town before I leave."

"I don't know what I'd do without you."

An impish smile curved his lips. "I know exactly who you've been doing."

She rolled her eyes at the entendre. "Perhaps you should go find someone yourself."

"Oh, I plan on it."

Faith remained, listening as Tamir talked about how excited he was while he affixed his harness to the rope.

With a wave and a wink, he was gone. She stayed, watching him until he was at the top of the cliff.

"You didna have to send him away," Dmitri said from behind her.

"It was time. I should've done it a long time ago. He's quite good, you know. He'll make a name for himself quickly."

Strong arms came around her from behind. Dmitri put his chin on her shoulder. "You made him verra happy."

"Yeah." But she felt like shit about it. Tamir was the closest thing to family she had. Was this how mothers felt when they watched their children go off to college? It sucked. "I don't know how my mother kept her smile in place when I left for school."

Dmitri's arms squeezed her.

She licked her lips. "After I left, Mom was all by herself. My father left us before I was born. My whole life, it was just her and me."

"Now I know why you're such an independent person. Your mother."

"She was an amazing woman."

There was a pause before Dmitri asked, "When did you lose her?"

"Six months ago. Giving Tamir that push to go out on his own reminded me of my mother doing much the same thing."

"She'd be proud of you."

That made her smile. "She loved dragons. It's too bad she couldn't have met you."

They shared a laugh before Dmitri asked, "So. Muscles, huh?"

She dropped her head back, grinning. Then she turned in his arms and met his gaze. "Yep."

"Is that what you think of me?"

"The first time I saw you, I wanted to rip off your clothes and see your body. 'Muscles' seemed to fit."

"I do believe I like it."

She rested her forearms on his shoulders and tried not to think about Tamir. "I'm glad."

"Tamir will be fine," Dmitri said as if reading her mind.

"I hope so." She didn't know how he knew what she was thinking, but it was nice that he did. "I should've listened to him when he first talked about the evil."

"You can no' blame yourself. You had a job to do, and that's where your priorities were."

"And those priorities got two people killed. My finding the bones is what brought the Dark. No one else did this. I did. So the fault lies totally with me."

He gave her a little shake. "I quite like that you're the one who found my dragon. Otherwise, how would I have met you?"

"Stop being so charming."

"I doona think I can."

She laughed, which was exactly what he wanted. Being around him made it tough to remember why she hadn't sought out relationships in the past.

He took her hand and led her back to the dragon. It felt comfortable and . . . right . . . to have their fingers interlocked, walking side by side. As if it were meant to be.

Which went against her "free will" concept of life. Because it was becoming hard to say that there wasn't such a thing as Fate or destiny.

"The authorities are going to want to talk to me about the deaths of my team members," she said.

"I can take care of that."

She raised a brow, curious. "And how do you propose to do that?"

"Did you forget that I'm from Dreagan?"

As a matter of fact, she had. "I suppose someone with that kind of clout and money can do a great many things."

"That is true," he said with a grin.

He grew silent as they approached the skeleton. She sat down before the bones and looked up at him. "Do you have a cell phone?"

"I doona need one. Dragons communicate via a mental link."

"Well, isn't that handy?" Something else she hadn't known. And she suspected there was more Muscles hadn't told her. Then again, it wasn't as if she'd told him stories of her life either.

He grinned and squatted beside her. "One of the Kings acts as a lawyer. Vaughn will be in contact with whoever is in charge."

"Impressive. Tell him thanks."

"You could do that yourself."

She paused as she lifted the brush. Was he asking what she thought he was? "What?"

"You could come with me to Dreagan."

There it was. The offer hung between them. She hadn't realized how very much she wanted it until he'd said the words. "I'd like that."

His bright smile made her heart trip over itself. "Good."

Inside, she was jumping for joy and shouting to the heavens. On the outside, she smiled and returned to work. "There's more to your world than you've told me, isn't there?"

"Oh, aye."

Damn, she loved his accent. It made her tingle all over. Or that could just be him. Not that it mattered. She loved the way he made her feel. "Tell me more."

"If you're sure."

"I'm sure." She glanced over to find him watching her.

He flipped the brush end over end, catching it. "Remember when I told you about the Fae?"

"Of course. Not something I can forget."

"The magical creatures doona end with us and them. There is another."

Intrigued, she found herself pulled between the bones and his story. "Tell me."

"They're called Warriors. They were mortals like you. Then one day, Rome came to conquer them."

She stopped working and gawked at him. "Were the Kings awake then?"

"We were."

"You allowed Rome to conquer England?"

He looked askance at her. "We didna *allow* Rome to do anything. We minded our own business. Though we vowed to protect mortals, that was from Fae and other magical creatures."

"You're right," she said, wrinkling her nose. "I'm sorry. Go on."

"The Celts turned to the Druids. Back then, Druids were healers and scholars. The leaders of the Celtic nations knew they would be able to help."

She faced the bones and started working again. "I gather they did."

"Within every species lives light and dark, good and evil. It is a balance that must be maintained. The Druids were divided into two such sects. There were the *mies* and *droughs*. Normally, the two didna mix, but Rome's impending invasion called for drastic action."

Faith shook her head. "They must've been terrified."

"Scared enough to do whatever it took to save their land. It was the first time in history the Druids combined their magic. They did so to call up long-forgotten gods locked in the pits of Hell."

She could no longer work. Setting aside her brush, she sat up. "This is . . . unbelievable. Tell me more."

"For a lass who is rooted in science, you're taking all of this well."

"I know." It was odd, but she didn't care.

He smiled and continued. "Each of the Celtic tribes asked for volunteers. No' unexpectedly, the best warriors stepped forward."

"Volunteers for what?"

"To give themselves up to the gods the Druids had freed."

She was flabbergasted. "They actually thought this would work?"

"It did. We watched from the skies as the gods each chose a warrior. It was because of the Druids that those men were able to ensure Rome never conquered Scotland."

"Holy shit," she murmured.

He chuckled, smiling. "Aye. It was a magnificent sight to see the Warriors in battle. The Druids' plans worked perfectly. Until Rome was gone and they tried to remove the gods. Now freed, the gods didna want to return to their prison. The Warriors began killing anyone and everyone because they couldna gain control of the gods. Their own families, their friends. It didna matter. The gods were demanding blood, and the Warriors were powerless to refuse."

"What happened?"

"The Druids came back together with their magic. As powerful as they were, the gods were more so. The gods couldna be removed. The only option the Druids had was to bind the gods, silencing them, and returning the Warriors to men once more."

She studied him a moment. "I can tell by your voice that things didn't go as planned."

"They did. Except the gods passed down through the

bloodline to the best warrior each generation. Then a verra powerful *drough* found the spell to unbind the gods. She thought to rule the world and control the Warriors."

"What happened?"

"The Warriors learned to master the gods within them. They rose up against the *drough* and defeated her. You've met one of them."

Her eyes widened. "Who?"

"Ronnie's husband, Arran."

"No way!" she gasped in surprise.

Dmitri's smile widened. "Then I suppose you didna know that Ronnie is a Druid."

She could only stare open-mouthed at him, internalizing the news that she had been surrounded by magic without even knowing it.

The next phone call with Ronnie was definitely going to be interesting.

"Tell me more," she insisted.

CHAPTER TWENTY-THREE

Dmitri loved to see the play of emotions wash over Faith's face—ranging from shock to disbelief and then changing to wonder.

"Ronnie is a Druid?" she asked in astonishment.

He gave a single nod. "All the women married to the Warriors are. Well, except for one. She's the only female Warrior."

"I . . . There's . . . I don't know what to say," Faith finally got out. "Ronnie is a Druid. Wow."

While she took it all in, Dmitri thought back to the day the Kings had approached the Warriors. It had been a long time coming, and the alliance had benefited both the Warriors and the Kings.

"Since Ronnie sent you, I gather they know who you are?" Faith asked.

"Aye," he replied. "We Kings agreed as a whole that it was time to let them know of our existence."

"There is so much on this earth that no one knows about."

"It's better that they doona. The Warriors and Druids

live at MacLeod Castle, which is shrouded by magic so it can no' be seen by mortals. Druids are everywhere, though the greatest concentration is on the Isle of Skye."

"And the Fae?"

"They choose Ireland when they're in this realm. Their civil wars have all but destroyed their realm. They tried it here, as well, but we put an end to the Fae Wars."

Faith ran a hand through her hair. "Is that all that's here?"

"For now. You never know what could come through from other realms, though."

"I think I need a drink. Oh, how you must have laughed at me saying I'm rooted in science. How naïve of me, when there seems to be magic everywhere."

He took her hand in his. "It isna naïve. It's what you believed. You didna know to look for the other or that it even existed."

"Right in front of my face," she admonished herself, turning her head away.

He put a finger beneath her chin and made her look at him. He saw the anger she directed inward, and he wanted to erase it. "Science is just as important as magic."

"I wish Ronnie would've told me."

"Druids rarely tell anyone other than other Druids of their magic. There are a few who announce it, but humans are quick to dismiss them."

She lifted their linked hands between them. "What do you see in me? I'm a mortal, descended from those who ruined your life."

"But you didna do it."

"You mean you can look at me and not feel even a kernel of anger?"

He cupped her face with one hand, looking deep into her sherry eyes. "When I look at you or even think about you, it's only desire and longing I feel."

"I need you to know that I wanted you before I knew what you were."

Without another word, he slipped his hand around to the back of her neck, blond locks sliding between his fingers, and brought her against him for a kiss. His body came alive instantly at the feel and taste of her.

"Why can't I get enough of you?" she asked between kisses.

"Do you want to?"

"Yes. And no."

Her admission was a reminder of their current predicament. He dropped his hand and looked at the bones. "I can move the skeleton to Dreagan now."

"Even though it's still in the earth?"

"The magic will fix that."

She looked away, her lips twisting. "It would keep the residents safe, at least."

"Aye."

"Do you still want me to come with you?"

"Without a doubt."

A smile formed on her lips. "Then perhaps we should do that."

Dmitri touched the bones. "He belongs here, but he'll find peace at Dreagan."

"Why didn't you mention this before?"

"Because I knew how much you enjoyed your job."

She laced her fingers with his. "You are a singular delight, Muscles."

Her words pleased him immensely.

"Though I am going to miss this place," she said, looking around the cave.

"There are plenty of caves to explore on Dreagan. But more importantly, there is good food, soft beds, and hot showers."

Her eyes closed as she moaned. "I don't know which I'd like first."

"Whichever you want."

"I want all of them. With you." Her eyes opened and her gaze moved to him.

He smiled, already hard thinking about it. "That can be arranged."

"So what now?"

"Now, I call us a ride."

As she watched, he opened his mind and called for Rhys. As soon as his friend answered, he asked, *"How does Lily feel about a flight to Fair Isle?"*

"Hang on." A few seconds later, Rhys said, *"She's up for it."*

"Give me a shout when she leaves. We're on the west coast of the isle."

The link severed, and Dmitri shrugged. "It's done. Lily will be here soon to fly us out."

"You have a plane?" she asked with a raised brow.

"Helicopter, actually."

She laughed and playfully punched his arm. "What else do you have?"

"The chopper is Lily's. She's Rhys's mate and wealthy in her own right. However, Dreagan has a helicopter of its own."

Faith's face clouded with concern. "Is everyone angry over my find? I know it jeopardized things."

"You did nothing maliciously. So, nay, no one is mad." Except maybe Con, but that was nothing unusual. Because of that, there was no need to tell her about the King of Kings' feelings regarding anything.

"I need to clean up the tents."

He jumped to his feet and held out his hand. "Let's get to it, then."

Once they were back at the entrance, she looked at him and asked, "Is there any way you can shift so I can see you again?"

More than anything, he wanted to do as she asked. "Within this cave I can."

"But you couldn't fly us out?"

He gave a shake of his head. "We're attempting to keep a low profile, remember. Too much attention is focused on Dreagan and anything to do with dragons. People keep an eye on the skies just to spot one of us."

"You hid in the rain the other day."

"Even that was a risk I hope I doona regret."

She licked her lips. "I want to look at you again."

He didn't have to be told twice. Her interest made his blood burn with desire. He kicked off his boots and began removing his clothes. As more of his skin was revealed, the longing in her eyes made his cock stir. Then her gaze locked on his tat.

He moved farther into the cave. With their eyes locked, he shifted. Her gasp wasn't one of fear but of wonderment— and it warmed his heart.

With his dragon eyes that could see in the dark as easily as the light, he watched the way her face held a look of reverence and amazement.

There wasn't enough room to unfurl his wings, but he sat and wrapped his tail around his body. He watched with joy as she walked to him and put a hand on his front leg.

Even if he had eternity to find the words for how she made him feel in that moment, he would never be able to aptly explain the exhilaration or happiness or serenity he felt.

With her palm on the warm, white scales, Faith looked at the glorious dragon before her. He was regal and imposing, majestic and daunting.

She dropped her head back and looked up at him. Dark, yellowish-brown eyes stared at her, but this time, she saw Dmitri in them.

At her foot was a paw or foot with four digits and gleaming white talons. She walked around him and saw the row of spines that ran from the base of his skull to his shoulders.

As she continued her inspection, she saw the four horns that sprouted from the back of his head.

She walked all the way around, looking at his long tail and leathery wings. When she stood in front of him again, she smiled up at him.

"Thank you. Seeing you makes me wish there were still dragons here. You're beautiful."

In a blink, he was human again. Before she could react, she was yanked against him as he took her mouth in a kiss that made her toes curl.

She barely felt the scrape of his whiskers, her need was so great. This kiss was savage and wild—just like him. And she loved every second of it.

He took her breath away in both of his forms, but she knew how incredibly lucky she was to experience what it felt like to be held by a Dragon King.

They were breathing hard by the time he ended the kiss. All she wanted to do was lead him back to their pallet and spend the rest of the day making love.

Then she thought of the people dying simply because of the skeleton she'd discovered. She rested her face against his bare chest, her eyes closed as he held her.

"I know we have to leave. It's the right thing to do," she began.

"I doona want to go either," he finished.

There were many reasons she wanted to remain. Mostly, she was afraid the world would intrude upon whatever it was they had found together.

While she wanted to see Dreagan, she was worried that the others there might attempt to dissuade him from her. Then she realized he was a King. He made his own decisions.

Which led to her true worry—that she was nothing more than a brief entertainment for him.

Because she really, really wanted it to be more. It was such a switch from how she normally felt that she knew right away that something was different.

With the new emotions swirling within her, she wanted to know how it would all play out. It was that planner part of who she was. Yet she knew that anything could happen.

She didn't want him to know how much turmoil she was in, so she put a smile on her face and stepped out of his arms. While he dressed, she got all her gear on to make the climb.

While she had to use rope and a harness to get to the top, Muscles did it in two jumps, proving once more that he was anything but ordinary.

At the summit, she felt as if she were on another world. Everything looked and felt different. Her eyes were open to the wonders of what surrounded her now. It was both remarkable and chilling.

Only the tents and a few scattered belongings had to be picked up. She wasn't surprised to find that Tamir had taken all the samples with him.

"Tamir will put the samples in storage," she told Dmitri. "No one will touch or see them."

"We'll need to get those."

She had assumed as much. "Of course."

Dmitri took her hand and walked with her to the edge of the cliff. "Look out. What do you see?"

"The sea. The unknown."

"An adventure perhaps?"

She glanced at him and grinned. "Yes, an adventure."

"What else?"

With blue stretching as far as the eye could see, she imagined what it would've been like to see white dragons living there.

To her, Fair Isle was a place to find remnants of the past. To Dmitri, it was home.

Ever since her mother's death, she hadn't called any place home. The closest anything had come was the cave. It made her see how gloomy her life was. Maybe that was why she remained out on digs, so she didn't have to return to her apartment alone.

She smiled and said, "I see the future."

CHAPTER TWENTY-FOUR

Somewhere in western Canada...

Rhi was veiled as she stood off to the side watching as the actors went through another take. It hadn't been easy to find Usaeil. The Light Queen had used magic to keep her location hidden.

But Rhi was never one to allow a little obstacle to stop her. After a brief discussion with some of the Queen's Guard, she'd discovered that Usaeil had told Inen that she had something private to do in the Fae realm.

Which was an outright lie. Rhi had kept many of Usaeil's confidences while she was a Guard. Now, those secrets burned inside her like dark magic.

Where she'd once revered Usaeil, she now reviled her.

Where she'd once honored the queen, she now spurned her.

Where she'd once sought out Usaeil, she now actively ignored her.

Because the queen wasn't acting like a queen. Usaeil didn't seem to care about her people or the imminent war between the Dark and the Dragon Kings.

Usaeil had forgotten what it meant to wear the crown and honor the duties involved. She pursued only her desires, and didn't care who or what might be destroyed in the process.

It was only by Fate's hand that the Dark hadn't yet realized how weak the Light were. The Dark's focus on the Kings gave the Light a narrow window in which to prepare.

Otherwise, the Dark would rise up and annihilate the Light.

That scared Rhi as nothing else could. She could see it all play out in her mind. It didn't matter who led the Dark—Taraeth or Balladyn or another—they would win.

But only the queen had the right to gather the army. If Rhi were still in the Queen's Guard, she might have been able to finagle a way to prepare them, but that was no longer an option.

No matter what she might say to Inen, he still believed Usaeil was the best thing for the Light. Rhi doubted there was another Fae out there who thought differently, besides her.

That was because she saw the big picture. Usaeil had given their people a false sense of security—one that everyone should realize was erroneous.

In all their civil wars, neither the Light nor the Dark had won. They'd each killed millions, gaining a slight upper hand that was soon whisked away.

The only time the Light every truly won against the Dark was when they'd joined the Kings in the Fae Wars. In all those scenarios, the Light had been ready for war.

The line drawn through Ireland to keep the Dark to the south and the Light to the north would soon be wiped away. No doubt the Light would be set upon in a surprise attack, and they would lose many.

The Light army would mobilize without orders from anyone at that point. But Rhi knew it would be too late by then.

Her anger and hatred grew as she watched Usaeil act out her part in the movie, kissing her male counterpart. The darkness within Rhi swelled considerably.

She knew it, felt it, but couldn't stop it. How could she when the very person who could save their people was off doing other things, human things?

At least she no longer had her watcher. Rhi's anger was divided between Usaeil and her unseen tracker at this point. She felt as if there was no place for her to turn, no one with whom she could talk.

Then she thought of Phelan. Yes, the Warrior who was like a brother would be there for her. Yet she hesitated to go to him.

He and Aisley had already been pulled into too much. After everything the Warriors and Druids endured and fought against, they should be allowed to live their lives in peace.

Normally, she would go to Rhys, but since he'd taken Lily as his mate, Rhi had kept her distance, allowing the pair to be alone.

Talking to Balladyn was pointless. He would steer her in the direction he wanted, and that wouldn't help.

So she was alone. Again.

Perhaps she should get accustomed to such a life. It seemed inevitable that this was her destiny. No matter how much light was inside her, no matter how hard she fought for her people, no matter how deeply she had loved her King—she was by herself.

Her eyes stung with unshed tears. She blinked them away, hardening herself against such emotion. Hadn't she cried enough throughout the last several millennia over her King and his abandonment?

Enough wailing in self-pity. She straightened her shoulders. So what if she'd always been there for others. So what if she gave 110% of herself to her King and friends and queen. So what if she never seemed to fit in anywhere.

She looked down at her hands where power sizzled through her fingertips. After everything she'd been through, she'd come to like the person she was—flaws and darkness and all.

"That's a wrap for the day!"

The voice broke into her thoughts. Rhi looked up, dropping her hands as she spied Usaeil smiling and laughing. Then a woman led the queen away.

Rhi followed them to a trailer parked amid a row of others. She ducked behind one of the mobile buildings and dropped her veil. Just as she was about to step out, someone grabbed her arm and jerked her back.

She spun around, shocked to her core to find Con. He was dressed in one of his usual handmade suits, looking too good with his blond hair and midnight eyes. "What are you doing here?" she demanded.

"Stopping you."

Admittedly, she was more than a little surprised by his words. She raised a brow. "You can't be serious? After what she did?"

"Exactly my point," he said in a low voice, looking around.

"Afraid she might see you?"

"Aye," he bit out. Then he sighed. "And I doona want anyone else to see us either."

Rhi crossed her arms over her chest. "No one else would dare confront her. So I will."

"No' here. No' now."

"Then where? When?" she demanded, her ire growing.

He clenched his jaw, his nostrils flaring. "I doona know yet. I agree with you, though. She needs to be confronted."

Her arms dropped loosely by her sides. She blinked, dumbfounded. "I'm sorry. Can you say that again so I can record it?"

"Verra funny," he said dryly and took her arm to move them away from an approaching group.

"I'm serious. I've never heard those words come out of your mouth about me before. I think it's useful material. Perhaps to go into the human's *Guinness Book of World Records*."

His face went hard. "Rhi."

She rolled her eyes. "What? I'm listening."

"Usaeil willna pay attention to me. I do believe she'll hear what you have to say."

Rhi glanced at the queen's trailer, and fury roiled within her, combining with the revulsion and disgust. "Oh, I have a lot I'd like to tell her."

"Can you do it now and no' lose control?"

She knew he was referring to her anger issue and how she'd begun to glow. She'd been known to blow up worlds before, so as much as she hated to admit it, he had a point.

"I see that you understand," Con said.

That didn't mean she was happy about it. "No one understands how vulnerable our people are."

"But you do."

She frowned, suddenly wary of the intense look in his eyes. "I've already thought about gathering the army. It won't work."

"Hmm."

Was that really all he was going to say? She narrowed her eyes at him, wondering just what was going through that head of his. She wouldn't admit it to him, but Con was a brilliant strategist. She just hoped he wasn't planning something she didn't agree with.

Then her thoughts halted. Of course he was planning

something she wouldn't agree with. How stupid of her to think otherwise.

She snorted, causing his brows to furrow as he gave her an odd look. Rhi ignored him completely.

"I can get her alone," he said.

I bet you can. Rhi was so glad the words never made it out of her mouth. "Then you want me to approach her? She's really going to be pissed at you."

"I can accept that."

"I don't think you fully understand. Right now, she wants you as hers. She'll do whatever you ask, whenever you ask it. In her reign, she's rarely taken lovers that anyone knew about. She's made it clear that she wants to be your mate, and you her king to rule beside her."

If it were possible, his eyes grew even blacker. "That isna going to happen."

"Be that as it may, once she realizes you don't want those same things, you're going to see the vindictive Usaeil. She'll be vengeful and cruel in how she reacts to anything having to do with the Kings."

"What are you getting at?"

Rhi sighed loudly in exasperation. "Ulrik. The Dark. Ring any bells?"

A muscle twitched in his jaw. "Aye," he bit out.

"You're going to need the Light. You'll never get them as long as Usaeil is pissed at you."

"I'll no' continue as her lover."

"Hey," she said and held up her hands, palms out. "You unmade that bed. You've got to lie in it."

"I'm no' amused."

She shrugged as she dropped her arms. "I am."

He ran a hand over his jaw, looking away. "There has to be another way."

"Why did you take her as your lover?"

His head jerked to her. "It doesna matter."

"It does. Your reasoning will have to come out. She's going to speculate all sorts of wild things. In order to counter that, you need to give her the tr—"

"I was in need."

She stopped mid-word at his interruption, so bewildered by his explanation that she literally couldn't form a thought for several seconds.

"You doona believe me," he said and tugged at the sleeves of his dress shirt, the gold dragon head cufflinks visible.

"Ah, nope. I sure don't."

"Why?"

She widened her eyes and held out her hands. "Have you looked in the mirror?"

"Aye? What of it?"

Rhi looked to the sky, shaking her head in exasperation. When she returned her gaze to him, he was watching her with what could only be described as confusion. "You're a Dragon King. King of Kings."

"This I know."

"Are you really that thick?" She blew out an annoyed breath. "Fine. I'll say it, but I'll deny it if you repeat it. You and every King are gorgeous. You could have any woman you want."

"You think I'm gorgeous?" he repeated.

She stared at him, trying to determine if he was teasing her or not. It was hard to tell since he kept emotion from his face and the tone of his words. Damn him!

"My point is that you didn't have to turn to Usaeil."

"I could be myself with her. No lies, no hiding."

That she could understand. "There's another reason isn't there?"

He gave a nod. "I knew I wouldna fall in love with her."

"So you wouldn't have to worry about bringing her to

Dreagan and explaining to the others that despite you hoping they wouldn't find happiness, you did."

"Aye."

"That's . . . sad."

"The truth normally is."

Rhi looked at the white trailer as his confession repeated in her head. "I'll hold off talking to her today, but we'd better come up with something soon."

"We will."

When she turned back, Con was gone.

CHAPTER TWENTY-FIVE

Dmitri heard the chopper long before it came into sight. He stood with Faith, staring at the horizon. Her words were inspiring.

He hadn't known what she might say when he'd asked her what she saw. In truth, he hadn't known what he wanted her to say. He knew what he saw—his home, his past, and now, his present.

The future . . . that was something he hadn't thought about in a very long time. As an immortal, it was best not to delve too far into the future or dwell too long on the past.

Together, he and Faith watched as the black and white helicopter landed some distance behind them. The whirling blades began to lose momentum as Lily shut off the power.

Dmitri kept hold of Faith's hand as they started toward the chopper. The door opened, and Lily climbed out in a pair of jeans and a ruby red sweater while her long, black hair was braided and fell over one shoulder.

Then another figure appeared from the other side of the helicopter—Rhys.

"You're no' surprised," Rhys said when they came together.

Dmitri shook his head. "I expected you to be with Lily."

Rhys's gaze lowered to Dmitri's hand, which was joined with Faith's. Dmitri waited for Rhys to make a comment, but nothing was said.

Dmitri then smiled at Lily. "Thank you for coming. This is Dr. Faith Reynolds. Faith, this is Lily and Rhys."

"It's such a pleasure," Lily said with a welcoming grin.

He felt Faith relax. She'd been more worried than she let on about meeting those from Dreagan. While he observed the girls greet each other, he couldn't stop thinking how incredible Faith was.

"*Dude. You've got it bad,*" Rhys said via their mental link.

His gaze jerked to Rhys to find the bastard smiling and nodding. It was on the tip of Dmitri's tongue to tell Rhys he was wrong, but he wasn't sure if he could.

Rhys then took Faith's hand. "Nice to meet you, Dr. Reynolds."

"Thank you, but please, call me Faith," she said, her smile wide as she looked from Lily to Rhys.

When Faith's gaze turned back to him, Dmitri basked in her glow. "I told you."

She laughed and briefly rested her forehead against his shoulder. "I know."

"You told her what?" Lily asked.

Faith gripped his hand tighter as she said, "I was worried how I'd be received."

"You did nothing wrong," Rhys told her.

It was Dmitri's turn to nudge her. "Did I no' tell you that?"

Faith's smile melted away. "The fact is, nothing can be found involving dragons. Few believed what I'd discovered, which is why I wanted it kept secret."

"But word got out," he finished. "No' your doing."

Rhys crossed his arms over his chest. "Dmitri is correct again. You're helping us, and for that, we're eternally grateful."

"Yes," Lily agreed in her English accent. "Very."

Rhys raised a dark brow, his aqua-ringed, dark blue eyes watching Dmitri carefully. "I suppose we'd best return to Dreagan."

"How are you thinking to bring the skeleton?" Faith asked.

Rhys smiled knowingly while Lily's eyes widened. She asked, "You haven't destroyed it?"

Dmitri looked around, thinking of the past before he slid his gaze to Lily. "This was my land. I checked each cave to make sure none of my Whites were left behind, but somehow, one was. He was killed by someone, and he's remained here all these thousands of years. I'll not burn his bones." He took a deep breath. "I'm bringing the dragon back with me to Dreagan to be buried in my mountain."

Rhys slapped him on the arm. "I'd do the same in your place."

"I'm sorry," Lily said, her big, dark eyes filled with anguish. "I didn't know."

"Doona think twice about it," Dmitri told her.

Rhys bent and kissed Lily. "You two beauties remain here while we go do the dirty work."

"So," he heard Faith ask Lily as he and Rhys walked away. "Are you the only one who's a pilot?"

"Denae is, as well," Lily said. "She got her chopper first. It wasn't long after, that Con bought one for general use," Lily explained.

Dmitri and Rhys hadn't gotten twenty feet from the girls before Rhys said, "I like her."

"Aye. What's no' to like?"

"Exactly. And she looks at you as if you hung the moon."

It took a moment for Dmitri to realize he was grinning like an idiot.

Rhys laughed and slapped him on the back as they reached the edge of the cliff. "Welcome to the love club, brother."

He jumped off before Dmitri could hit him. Love? No, that wasn't possible. He cared a great deal for Faith, but that's where it ended. Wasn't it?

"Come on!" Rhys shouted from the outcropping of the cave.

Dmitri looked back over his shoulder and locked eyes with Faith. They shared a smile before he stepped over the edge.

The wind whistled around him as he fell. He waited until he drew close to the cave before he outstretched his arms. A moment later, he landed with bent knees.

"Damn that felt good," Rhys said with a laugh. "Con wouldna be happy about it."

"There's no one looking." Dmitri walked into the cave to the bones.

As they passed the pallet, Rhys raised a brow. "Talk about privacy. I might have to do the same with Lily."

Talking ceased when they came upon the skeleton. Dmitri knew that taking the dragon from its home to Dreagan was the best thing, but it seemed wrong to do it somehow. Just as it had been wrong to send the dragons away.

"We had no choice," Rhys said as if reading Dmitri's mind.

"There is always a choice."

Rhys put his hand on the skull. "Every one of us— including Con—feels their loss, every second of every day."

"But you didna leave one behind."

"You said you searched the caves."

"I did. Twice."

Rhys's eyes narrowed. "Why? Did you no' trust yourself."

"I . . ." he paused, thinking back. Even though it had happened eons ago, he still recalled that day with clarity. "I had a feeling I was missing one. I was right."

"If you searched and didna find him, then he was hiding somewhere."

Dmitri squatted down and pointed to the neck bone. "There is one injury for sure. None of my Whites ever ignored my call. If he was hurt, I would've found him."

"It was a frantic time. We were in a hurry to save as many dragons as we could."

It still didn't excuse what he'd done. Now he would carry that guilt through eternity.

A sound behind them drew his attention. He looked back to find the girls. Lily walked slowly to the dragon and put her hand next to Rhys's.

"I wanted to get my things," Faith explained.

Dmitri wrapped an arm around her and held her tightly. The four of them stood in silence for a time. Then the girls stepped back so he could begin freeing the skeleton.

He felt the rush of magic run through him as he channeled it into pulling the bones from the dirt and stone. After countless centuries of time and the elements, the brittle bones had to be protected lest they shatter as they were pulled from the ground.

Rhys joined him, using his magic to help safeguard the skeleton while Dmitri did the rest. With every second that passed and more of the bones were exposed, Dmitri felt a curious case of urgency that he couldn't explain.

Finally, the entire skeleton was freed. He moved it over and gently set it down. Faith rushed to it, but he stopped her with an arm around her waist before dragging her back against him.

"Nay."

"What is it?" Rhys asked, immediately on alert.

Dmitri looked around. "I'm no' sure."

"Well, let's not find out," Lily stated.

Faith turned in his arms. "You killed the Dark."

"There were Dark?" Rhys demanded in a low tone.

Dmitri took a step back from the bones, keeping Faith with him. "The operative word there is 'were.' I killed one, and Faith killed the other."

"Well done," Rhys told her.

Faith smiled, obviously pleased by his words. "Thank you."

Unable to look away, Dmitri eyed the skeleton. "We should leave."

"Aye," Rhys said in agreement.

"What are you going to do with the bones?" Faith asked. Then her eyes brightened. "One of the tarps."

Rhys was already walking away as he said, "I'll get it."

"You took out the threat, Dmitri," Lily said. "There's nothing else here to harm Faith. It's going to be fine."

But was it? Because he sure didn't feel that way. The longer he stared at the skeleton, the more positive he was that something was definitely about to happen.

The feel of Faith's hands on his chest tugged his attention away from the dragon's remains. He looked into her sherry eyes. At that moment, he knew, without a doubt, that he would protect her with his very life if he had to.

He slipped his fingers into the cool locks of her sandy blond hair. She leaned against him and turned the corners of her lips up in a smile.

"Got it," Rhys said as he jogged to them, holding a folded tarp in his arms.

Dmitri reluctantly released Faith and waited until Rhys

had spread the tarp. With his magic, he lifted the skeleton in midair before moving it to the tarp.

Once the dragon had been set down, Rhys wrapped the tarp around it. He and Rhys then carried the bones to the entrance. After, with both of them using their strength and magic, they got the bundle to the top of the cliff and into the luxury chopper.

"I'll stand guard," Rhys said.

He nodded and pivoted to return to Faith. By the time he got back inside the cave, their pallet was dismantled and folded neatly.

Lily was gathering all the lights, while Faith made sure she had her tools. That needling insistence that they leave immediately doubled.

Dmitri gathered an armload and hurriedly made a trip back to the top. It took another two visits before the cave was as empty as when Faith had first found it.

Lily was already climbing up the cliff when Faith halted and started to turn back.

He grabbed her hand, stopping her. "What is it?"

"I need to have one last look. I can't leave anything behind."

"Hurry."

She shot him a grin. "Let go and I can."

With a sigh, he released her hand. He impatiently waited until she finally returned. Then he pulled her against him and said, "Hold on."

Once she had a firm grip, he jumped to the top. Rhys had loaded the chopper, and within moments, they were airborne.

A shiver of trepidation ran down his spine as they flew past the cave. He wondered why he hadn't felt anything remotely troubling until he'd used his magic to free the skeleton.

He glanced at the bones wrapped in the tarp on the floor

before them. Something wasn't right. He couldn't put his finger on what, but he needed to figure what it was and soon.

When Faith leaned her head on his shoulder, Dmitri wrapped an arm around her and settled back against the black leather seat. At least he had her with him.

That was enough to make him happier than he could ever remember being.

CHAPTER TWENTY-SIX

Con stared at the papers in his hand, but he couldn't concentrate. He tossed them down on his desk and leaned back in his chair with a sigh.

After his chat with Rhi—which went better than anticipated—he'd returned to Dreagan. He walked the halls of the manor, hearing the voices and laughter of the women.

Never had he thought his home would be filled with humans. He didn't begrudge the Kings their mates. . . . Actually, he did. His reasons were purely his own, and something that no one would ever know—not even Kellan, Keeper of History.

He leaned forward and reached for the report Henry had given him before leaving to follow Anson, Kinsey, and Esther to Kyvor in London. In the papers, Con saw that the Dark's movements had slowed considerably from even a few weeks before.

As he flipped through the pages of maps marked with red dots to indicate the Dark, he noticed that while there was still a high concentration of them in Ireland, they didn't seem to be gathering as if for war.

The Dark Fae would always be a problem until they were wiped from this realm, but in order to send them away, the Light would also have to leave. And Con knew there would be quite a few Kings—and Warriors—upset about Rhi no longer being around.

But that was the least of his worries.

The Dark's attacks on humans had ceased suddenly, which was a worry in and of itself. They were up to something.

Then there was Ulrik. Con squeezed the bridge of his nose with his thumb and forefinger as he thought of his old friend. Several of the Kings thought Con was responsible for Ulrik being what he was.

Perhaps he was. But the real person responsible was Ulrik. He could've let go of his rage and bitterness instead of letting it infect him to such a degree.

But passing the blame would do nothing to solve the current situation. Ulrik could shift. That still sent Con into a panic, because at any moment, Ulrik could wake the Silvers and call to them.

No amount of magic in the universe could stop the Silvers from getting to their King. Ulrik reunited with his dragons meant eradication of the mortals on a global scale.

If that wasn't enough, there was Usaeil. It was tough to admit, but Con had misjudged the situation with her. Epically. Now, he was trying to clean up his mess without dragging any of the Kings into it, while still keeping ahead of his enemies.

It was enough to make him want to bellow his rage and frustration. Yet he kept it all inside. Because to release it would only do more harm.

"Con!" Ryder's voice shouted in his head.

He immediately pushed away from his desk and stood, hurrying up the flight of stairs to the computer room. "What is it?" he asked.

Ryder's brows were drawn together as he furiously typed on the image of a keyboard that glowed atop the table. "Hang on."

Patience was still something Con worked to acquire. He walked around the rows of monitors to see what Ryder was doing. Each screen showed something different.

Some were for the hidden cameras monitoring the grounds—while keeping an eye on the MI5 agents still nosing around. Others were searching the realm using facial recognition for Ulrik.

"Look," Ryder said and pointed to a screen on the right.

Con's gaze moved to the monitor and froze when he saw an image in the background of a photo. "V."

"This was just posted, but it was taken a month ago. I'd love to have a full view of his face."

"It's him." Con leaned in closer to the screen. "Where was he?"

"Belgium."

Con straightened, dread filling him. As if he needed another problem to contend with. "Of all places. I didna expect him to go where the mortals are."

"They're everywhere now. Where could he go?"

"Have there been any deaths reported?"

"None."

For long seconds, Con started at the picture of V. His brown hair was longer than before, but there was no denying the wrath that dwelled in V's blue eyes. "Are you sure?"

"He's no' killed."

The 'yet' went unsaid. Con fisted his hands when Ryder showed another picture. This one had been taken in a pub, and there was a woman atop V's lap.

And then it hit Con. "I know what he's doing."

"Then please share, because I certainly don't."

He turned his head and met Ryder's hazel eyes. "He's searching for his sword."

"Fuck me."

Con took a deep breath and looked at the monitor once more. He recalled all too well what had occurred the last time V woke and went looking for his sword. There had been so much death. By the time Con realized what had happened, a mass extinction of human life had occurred.

"Maybe you shouldna have woken him," Ryder said.

"We're going to need everyone. Even V." He just thought he'd get to talk to V first.

Ryder reached into the box beside him and drew out a donut. "There's no use going to Belgium to find him. I'm sure he's already moved on. He willna stop looking for his sword. Though you could end his torment and tell him where to go."

Con counted to ten, then twenty, before he was calm enough to say, "I know the region. I doona know where the sword is. V will destroy that place if he knows where to go."

"He'll figure it out soon enough."

That much was true. If only he could talk to V, but the stubborn King wouldn't respond via the mental link. "Keep an eye out for V, but we've got bigger problems closer to home."

"The spy," Ryder said with a nod. "How are Kellan and Asher coming with that?"

That was a good question. "They're making progress."

"Listen, while you're here, I wanted to let you know that I got a hit regarding Ulrik."

Finally, some good news. He really needed some of that at the moment because he was drowning in shite. "What is it?"

On another monitor, an image filled the screen. Con's excitement faded. "That isna Ulrik."

"I know. At first, I thought it was. Whoever this is, looks so much like him that it even fooled my software."

"Who is he?"

Ryder shrugged. "As soon as I figure that out, I'll let you know."

There was something about the way the man in the picture tilted his head that made Con think of Ulrik.

"I guess it's true what the humans say, huh? We all have a twin."

"No' us," Con said.

Con left the computer room and made his way back to his office. With the door closed, he walked to his desk and sat. Then he opened the middle drawer and took out the file he'd begun.

One by one, he was removing each King's name from the list of suspects. He didn't for a moment believe it was one of his men who was passing Ulrik their secrets, but he wanted to be thorough.

Hopefully, the name he came up with matched what Kellan and Asher brought to him.

Con put his elbows on his desk and dropped his head into his hands. Ulrik had said he wanted to rip Con's world apart, and he was certainly doing it. There wasn't a single aspect that wasn't coming apart at the seams.

He couldn't remember the last time he'd slept or eaten. In order to deal with everything, he had to prioritize things. V, unfortunately, was last.

The King was a ticking time bomb. By believing V could wait, it could all blow up in Con's face worse than before.

The strange Light Fae who'd shown up a few days before and spoken to Roman was something else that Con shoved to the bottom of the list. The Fae had disappeared before they could talk to him or even find out who he was.

Though the Fae's arrival did prompt Con to have the magical shield surrounding Dreagan strengthened. It was meant to keep out the Dark, but with Usaeil bordering on neurotic, he was thinking of making sure *no* Fae could get in.

That would also include Rhi. But he wasn't sure that was a bad thing.

The Kings needed to remember that the Fae weren't part of their world. The Light were allies, but not friends.

Con winced as he realized he couldn't include the Light. Kiril would never forgive him if his mate, Shara, couldn't remain on Dreagan.

He squeezed his eyes closed. Why couldn't anything be easy? If he made even the slightest wrong decision, it could ruin everything they'd built.

The purpose of remaining in the realm was so that, one day, they could return the dragons. He'd already lost countless centuries with his family. However, that didn't compare to not knowing if the dragons had found a safe place to live. For all he knew, they'd been wiped out.

He clenched his hands into fists and slammed them down on his desk in aggravation.

There was a way to end it all. All he had to do was lift Ulrik's banishment and welcome him back to Dreagan. Then, together, they would lead the Kings on a worldwide hunt of every mortal until they were wiped out.

Ulrik would no longer be his enemy. No more would the Kings have to hide who they were from the mortals. The Fae would have no more reason to remain. But most of all, the dragons would be able to return.

It seemed like the easiest choice. Right up until he recalled the vow he'd made to protect the weak humans.

That promise ensured that he would remain on his path,

but the temptation to bring back his family and the Golds was so enticing that he could practically taste it.

If Ulrik knew his thoughts, his friend would laugh, but that's why Con kept his feelings and views to himself. None of the others could know how easily he could be swayed to join Ulrik.

It had been nearly impossible to refrain from helping Ulrik kill the first time. Now, after having lost so much and suffered for so long, he wouldn't be able to say no.

He was King of Kings, the one dragon who decided the course of action and made sure the others followed. Everyone trusted his decisions, even if they did balk every once in a while. They wouldn't be Dragon Kings if they didn't show their power.

He took a deep breath and relaxed his hands, stretching out his fingers. Then he lifted his head and looked at the names again.

Because of the size of Dreagan, they had many mortals working for them. As far as Con knew, none of the humans realized they worked for dragons.

Yet he'd learned that mortals could be crafty and devious when it served them. He needed to investigate each of them. It wouldn't matter how much Ulrik hated the humans if he could use one. More than likely, Ulrik had recruited one to spy, someone who was already a worker at Dreagan.

Since they hadn't hired any new employees in over a year, that left all one hundred and nineteen personnel to sort through.

Con turned in his chair and looked out his window. He saw the still house. The first name on the list was Travis MacBane. It was time Con learned all there was to know about Travis.

It would be so much easier if Ryder were gathering the information. Con might not have all of those computers at his disposal, but he knew his way around Ryder's software enough to use it.

Con retrieved the laptop from a drawer and logged into Ryder's system.

CHAPTER TWENTY-SEVEN

It was Dmitri's fingers on her cheek that woke her. Faith couldn't believe she'd fallen asleep. She looked at Muscles to find him watching her.

"I didn't snore, did I?" she asked.

"You only drooled a little," he replied with a straight face. Then he smiled.

She elbowed him, laughing. Despite everything that had happened, she was actually happy. Until she thought about the two deaths.

Turning her mind from that, she looked at the inside of the helicopter. The seats were mostly black with white accents, just like the outside of the chopper.

The luxury was staggering. It was so quiet, she could barely hear the blades. The leather was soft, the seats wide and comfortable.

She didn't get a chance to discover more about the aircraft because Dmitri pointed out the window. She looked to see rugged mountains capped with snow, waterfalls, and wide valleys. It was easy enough to trace a waterfall to a stream that fed into a wide, rock-lined river that snaked its way to a loch. Everywhere she turned was nature at its finest.

Faith wasn't sure when, but sometime while she took in the grandeur, she realized they were on Dreagan. She looked at Dmitri to find him gazing at the land with what could only be described as love.

It was there in his eyes, in the way he smiled. And if he spoke, she knew she would hear it in his voice and words, as well.

To have such feelings for two places. She'd seen his love of Fair Isle, though it held some bad memories, as well. It was Dreagan where he had gone to hide and remember he was a Dragon King.

It was Dreagan where he and the others had rooted themselves in the land and culture. They worked hard, giving the world the best—and most expensive—whisky available.

His head swung to her. She smiled and cupped his face. He loved two places, and she didn't love any. She wondered if he knew how lucky he was.

Her thoughts halted when Rhys turned around and told her to look out the other side. That's when she saw the white buildings with the red roofs.

Then she saw the mountain rising up behind them. Dreagan. People came from all over to tour the distillery, but she doubted many had the view she was getting.

Her mouth dropped open when she spied the gray stone manor. She could understand how she'd missed it since it seemed to be a part of the mountain.

Lily flew them around the manor so Faith could see the soaring towers. Though she didn't know much about architecture, she could see notes of Romanesque, Gothic, Baroque, as well as hints of Neoclassical in the manor.

And what a grand place it was.

She didn't need to go inside to see that history fairly dripped from every stone and window. That didn't even cover the manicured grounds surrounding the manor that then fed into a pasture where sheep and cattle grazed.

All too soon, they landed, and the engine was shut off. With the tour ended, she had no choice but to climb out of the helicopter.

She grabbed Dmitri's hand and took her first step on Dreagan land. Her gaze moved around her, trying to take in everything. It was Dmitri's laugh that made her stop.

"You can explore as much as you'd like," he told her as he squeezed her hand.

"I like the sound of that."

Rhys and Lily were already headed to the house when Dmitri made to follow. She tugged him to a stop. "What of the bones."

"They'll be fine for now."

She wasn't so sure of that, but he knew Dreagan better than she.

"No Dark can come onto Dreagan without us knowing," he said as they headed toward the manor.

"That's good to know."

They entered from a side door into what appeared to be a formal room of some kind since there were several sofas and chairs scattered about.

It was hard to miss that every painting on the walls had a dragon of some kind in it. As they passed out of that room into a corridor, Faith realized that there were dragons everywhere, not just in the paintings.

They were in the little touches of the architecture itself, carved into a door handle or in the molding around the doorways. How could anyone walk into the manor and not realize that it was the home of dragons?

"I love seeing people's faces," Lily said.

Faith blinked and noticed that Dmitri, Lily, and Rhys

were all watching her. She hadn't realized they'd stopped until then.

She held out her arms. "Look at this place. It's so beautiful I can hardly take it all in."

"We're glad you approve," Rhys said with a crooked grin.

Dmitri grunted. "Aye. We've only worked on it for a couple of millennia."

The four of them laughed in response. She couldn't believe how easy it was to fit in. Or maybe, she just wanted to so badly that she'd convinced herself she did.

Lily then said, "Why don't I show Faith to her room so she can shower and rest."

"I'm fine," she quickly replied. The thought of not being with Muscles frightened her.

Dmitri lifted her hand to his lips and kissed the back of it. "I need to check in with Con. Go with Lily. I'll be there shortly."

How could she say no when he asked in such a sexy voice? She leaned up and kissed him. "All right."

She and Lily walked around a corner to a massive staircase with a carved banister that also boasted dragons. When she was halfway up, she looked back to find Dmitri at the bottom watching her.

Faith was smiling when she looked forward, only to feel Lily's gaze on her. "What?"

"For any Dragon King to share his secret is a major event. That means there's something between the two of you."

Faith shrugged, unsure of how much to tell Lily. "I know it was a big deal for Dmitri to tell me anything."

"How did it happen?"

Their steps slowed as they reached the first landing and continued up to the second. "A Dark pushed me off a cliff. Dmitri made a decision to save me."

"He shifted," Lily said, her words laced with shock.

She nodded. "I saw him in his true form. Then I saw him change back."

"I'm not surprised he went against Con's orders not to shift. He did it to save you."

"I knew he wasn't supposed to shift, but I thought it was to keep people from seeing him."

Lily shrugged absently. "That's part of it. Ever since that video, people are actively searching for dragons. So, did you run from him?"

"No." She stopped and faced Lily. "I was scared, briefly. But then I realized that he wouldn't save me only to kill me. I also knew what I'd already found in that cave. A skeleton means there were—or are—dragons."

Lily's smile was wide. "I'm liking you more and more."

They continued walking. Faith then said, "I don't really know what to do here."

"You don't have to do anything."

"I'm not used to having nothing to occupy my time."

Lily turned and went up the next flight of stairs. "I'm sure Dmitri will take you to his mountain to bury the bones. You were the one who found them, after all."

"How did you come to Dreagan?"

Lily's smile held a bit of sadness. "I was hired to work in the shop, selling items to tourists. I was also hiding from an abusive ex-boyfriend."

"Oh."

"You can't run from the past, though. It always catches up with you. It did for me out there," she said, pointing through a window. "My brother and ex were working together with Ulrik. My brother killed me."

Faith tripped over her feet and stumbled to a halt. "Dead? As in, you died? Your heart stopped and all that?"

"Yes," Lily said with a small smile. "For a reason I've yet to figure out, Ulrik brought me back."

"That doesn't make sense. He wanted you dead."

"I know." Her gaze took a faraway look. "Con can heal anything, but the only one who can bring someone back from the dead is Ulrik."

That was a puzzle to be sure, one Faith thought might never be solved. "I'm glad you're not dead."

Lily blinked, focusing back on her. "I am, too. I found the love of my life with Rhys."

"Oh." She wasn't sure what else to say. 'Congratulations,' maybe? Or 'that's awesome?

With a perceptive look, Lily once more started walking. It wasn't long before she came to a door and opened it. "You'll find everything you need inside. Are you hungry?"

"I could eat."

"I'll bring some food up shortly."

Faith wasn't used to being waited on. "That's not necessary."

"Take some time to yourself. As soon as the others learn of your arrival, you'll be bombarded with questions."

That wasn't something she'd considered, but now that Lily mentioned it, she was going to soak up the alone time.

"Oh, and since it seems to be a common occurrence that when we first arrive at Dreagan we only have the clothes on our backs, some of us have set up a closet with various sizes and styles."

Clean clothes? Now that sounded heavenly. "I'll take you up on that offer."

"I can bring a few things. Any particular style you like?"

"Casual. I'm a jeans and t-shirt kind of girl."

Lily laughed and reached for the door. "That's easy enough. I'll be back in a bit."

When the door closed behind her, Faith let out a sigh. "I'm really at Dreagan. The center of the dragon world."

A place that seemed as if the world had been created

around it, but one she hadn't known existed until a few days ago. Everything seemed so . . . well, surreal.

She could picture her mother being so overcome with excitement at the idea of being surrounded by dragons that she squealed.

It made her laugh. And miss her mother all the more.

Faith then took notice of the room. It was spacious. On one side was a large fireplace with black marble and a thick mantel. Above the mantel was a sword. Two leather chairs with low backs sat angled before the fireplace with a small table between them.

On the other side of the room was a work of art that served as the bed. A grand four-poster antique with a canopy the same stunning dark wood as the rest of the furniture in the space.

It was the intricate and elaborate carving in the wood that took her breath away. She wasn't surprised to see dragons in what she now realized was Dmitri's home—Fair Isle—in the engravings.

Bedding in a solid, pale gray softened the heavy piece. On either side of the bed were matching tables. She ran her hand along one of the posts, amazed at the craftsmanship.

Out of the corner of her eye, a door caught her attention. She started toward it when she saw the painting of a white dragon soaring over the sea with cliffs in the background.

That's when she knew—she was in Dmitri's room.

"Oh, Muscles, we're going to have fun tonight."

She opened the door and sighed when she spotted the bathroom. Off-white rectangular floor tiles continued up the wall, mixing with the gray stone of the manor. The mix of old and new worked in ways she never would have expected.

Kicking off her shoes, she spotted the white sink before she caught sight of the pedestal tub and the shower behind it.

With a smile on her face, she turned on the water for the tub and stripped.

CHAPTER TWENTY-EIGHT

"You know he's no' going to be thrilled," Rhys said.

Dmitri made his way up the stairs to Con's office. "When is he ever delighted about anything? And since when do you care?"

"Who said I cared? This may come as a complete surprise, but I love agitating Con. It's become a favorite pastime," Rhys stated.

He saw the mischievous smile on Rhys's face and could only shake his head. "Oh, we all know just how much you love your pastime."

"I also enjoy it when others annoy him."

For all of Rhys's words, if anyone ever stepped over the line with Con, Rhys would be the first to knock them back into place.

Dmitri didn't have just one surprise for Con, but two. Neither was up for debate. Yet that wasn't why he was worried. It was that feeling he'd gotten back in the cave that continued to trouble him.

He stopped beside the closed door to Con's office but didn't reach for the knob.

"Everything worked out," Rhys said. "You got the bones

and the girl. Her team is leaving the isle, and you got rid of the Dark."

"After they'd murdered two people."

"They could've killed more."

He looked at Rhys. "Why did they no'?"

Rhys didn't have an answer, which only confirmed Dmitri's suspicions. He rapped his knuckles on the door and tried the handle, only to find it locked.

He and Rhys exchanged confused looks. Since when did Con lock his door?

"Enter," Con said from inside his office.

Rhys's gaze narrowed. "Interesting."

Dmitri wanted to ask him what he thought of Con and Usaeil, but that would have to wait until later. There were more pressing matters. He opened the now unlocked door and entered.

Con sat behind his desk. He closed a file and looked up at them. "I'm glad you're back. Tell me what happened."

Rhys sank into one of the chairs and linked his fingers across his abdomen. Dmitri decided to sit, as well. He looked across the massive desk to the King of Kings and wondered how Con did everything and still look unruffled and unaffected by it all.

"After our last conversation, things took a turn," Dmitri said. "The Dark killed a second member of the dig team, and I knew it would continue until they were dealt with."

Con nodded in silent agreement.

Dmitri stretched out his legs and crossed his ankles. "I lured them away from the village to the cliff. I killed one, but before I could take out the second, the Dark used magic."

Rhys's eyes went wide. "You fought in dragon form?"

That part he hadn't wanted to reveal, but there was no way around it now. "Aye. It was storming. No one saw me."

"Go on," Con said softly.

"I fell into the sea and started climbing up the cliff. The Dark was at the cave's opening, throwing magic."

Rhys made a sound at the back of his throat. "Evil fuckers."

"Dr. Reynolds was in the cave, and I knew if I didna get to her, the Dark would kill her and take the bones," he said.

Con merely watched him, not saying anything. That was more disconcerting than if he released his temper.

Dmitri continued. "I was losing my hold. One more hit of Dark magic, and I'd have fallen back into the sea. Then I saw the Fae tumble past me into the water. When I looked up, Faith was there."

"So she killed a Dark?" Con said.

"She stabbed him in the back of the neck."

Seemingly unimpressed, Con asked, "Who else saw this?"

"No one," Dmitri said. "The entire team was in the village. After the storm abated, she sent her team home."

"Where is Dr. Reynolds now?"

"Here."

There was a long, silent moment before Con leaned back in his chair. "I expected as much. But why? She's no' in danger."

Dmitri uncrossed his ankles and sat up. "I brought her because I wanted her here."

"And the bones?"

"Also here."

Con's face was devoid of any emotion, but anger rolled off him in waves. "Why?"

"The dragon was one of mine. He got left behind. I want to know why and how. Then I'm going to bring him to my mountain and bury him. No one will ever find the bones."

"Then see it done."

Dmitri blinked, unsure if he'd heard Con correctly. Apparently, Rhys had the same reaction because he was frowning.

"That's all?" Rhys asked. "You're no' going to say more? Maybe get angry that Dr. Reynolds is here and all that?"

Con's black eyes swung to Rhys. "That's all."

And that's when Dmitri realized that not every King knew of Con's affair with Usaeil. If Rhys knew, he wouldn't be sitting so casually beside him.

As if Con knew what Dmitri was thinking, his gaze returned to him. Dmitri opened the mental link and said to Con, *"The others need to know about Usaeil."*

"They will. Verra soon."

Dmitri didn't like keeping secrets. He never liked the way it seemed to eat at his soul. But he also wouldn't be the one to reveal it to any of the others. It was Con's story, and his right to tell it.

"Where is the skeleton now?" Con asked.

It was Rhys who answered. "Still in the chopper. We just returned."

"Once you find your answers, we'll have a proper burial," Con said.

Dmitri hadn't expected Con to agree without a fight, but he was pleased nonetheless. "I'll take the bones to the mountain where they can be examined."

"I doona want MI5 to see Dr. Reynolds."

"I'll make sure of it."

Rhys blew out a breath. "I thought we were getting rid of them."

"Vaughn has already begun the process. Hopefully, they'll be gone in a few days."

"Any word from Henry or the others?" Dmitri asked.

Con shook his head. "Nothing of significance."

"It was a bad idea," Rhys said. "It worked when Elena

went back to PureGems, but that was just Ulrik. This involves a Druid we have no' located yet."

Dmitri said, "I understand your concerns, but our enemies our growing. Ulrik's network of Dark and humans is larger than we anticipated. We have to find these people."

"And stop them," Con added.

Rhys leaned forward, his forearms on his knees. "And if Kinsey dies? She and Ryder have no' done the mating ceremony. Do you have any idea what that will do to him?"

"I know exactly what will happen."

Con's words, though expected, held a note of something that drew Dmitri's attention.

"Henry, Esther, and Kinsey, while all mortals, are part of Dreagan. Anson is there to protect them," Con said.

Rhys pushed to his feet. "This is our war. Any of the humans, willing or no', shouldna be doing our jobs."

A moment later, Rhys left the office. Dmitri waited until the door closed behind him before he looked at Con. "He has a point."

"Rhys usually does."

"But no one else could get into Kyvor besides Kinsey and Ester," Dmitri said.

Con lifted one shoulder in a shrug. "It was their idea. Henry may be mortal, but he's more than capable of looking after his sister and Kinsey."

"Henry would've made a good Dragon King."

"That he would've."

Dmitri asked, "Can I help with the Usaeil thing?"

"I believe it's under control."

"Let's hope it stays that way before Rhi finds out."

Con took something from his desk and tossed it to Dmitri. "She brought me that."

Dmitri looked down to find the magazine cover with the picture of a hotel room. It was obvious it was Usaeil. The man had his face turned away from the camera, but Dmitri knew it was Con.

But what really surprised him was the headline of "Who is our favorite actress's new lover?" He hadn't known Usaeil masqueraded as an actress.

"Those are all over the Light Castle," Con said.

"Is that where Rhi found it?"

Con shook his head. "She discovered that being sold on the streets."

"The fact that the manor still stands is good news, I suppose. Can I take that to mean Rhi isna angry?" he asked.

"Rhi and I have an understanding with regards to the queen."

"Why did you tell me about Usaeil?"

Con held out his hand for the magazine before shoving it back in the drawer. "I didna know how long you'd be gone. Anson needs to concentrate on this business with Kyvor, or I'd have told him, as well."

"The longer you put this off, the worse it'll be."

"I wanted everyone together to tell them about Usaeil and Ulrik."

Dmitri ran a hand down his face. "I doona think you can wait any longer."

"I agree. Tonight after dinner we'll gather in the cavern."

Dmitri got to his feet but he didn't leave. "There was something before we left Fair Isle."

"What?"

"I doona know exactly. A bad feeling. It happened when I used my magic to excavate the rest of the bones."

Con frowned at the news. "Maybe it was the idea of taking the skeleton off the isle."

"I thought the feeling would go away after we left Fair behind, but it hasna."

"You still feel it?" Con asked, worry tingeing his words.

"Aye."

"And there were only two Dark there?"

Dmitri nodded. "Only the two."

"You think it was too easy."

"I do. When was the last time we got to something before Ulrik or a Dark?"

Con sighed, his lips flattening. "We have no'."

"And when was the last time we got out without a huge fight?"

"We have no'."

"Exactly," Dmitri said. "No matter how I look at it, I can no' figure out what I'm missing."

"Perhaps you're overthinking it."

"You know I'm right."

Con ran a hand through his hair. "Aye, but I'm going to take the win in this. We need it."

That they did. After all they had suffered, the Kings were due a victory on a grand scale. But would they get it? It was going to be hard-won if they did, considering how many enemies they had.

"We'll start examining the bones immediately."

Con said, "Keep me posted. I'm also wondering how a dragon was left."

Dmitri walked from the office. He'd expected things with Con to go one way, but they had gone another. Lately, it was difficult to determine how Con would react to a situation.

But now that Dmitri knew why Con had been acting so weird of late, a lot of things made sense. What he still didn't know, however, was why Con had started the affair with Usaeil in the first place.

Dmitri could've told him that nothing good would come from getting too close to her. He'd only met Usaeil once, but there was something about the queen's diva mentality that rubbed him raw.

Queen or not, she didn't deserve the universe. Though she had helped Shara and Kiril. That won her some points, but not many.

He let all of that slip away as he reached the door to his bedroom. He opened it, eager to see Faith, but she was nowhere in sight. Then he heard a splash. He walked to the bathroom and opened the door to find her reclining in the tub with her eyes closed.

Her lids lifted, and a bright smile graced her face when she saw him. "I was beginning to wonder where you were, Muscles."

"Need some help?" he asked.

Her smile turned seductive. "I thought you'd never ask."

Just as he was taking off his shirt, a knock sounded. Then Lily's voice reached them. He bent and gave Faith a kiss. "It'll have to wait."

She wrinkled her nose. "Sorry. I'm starving, and Lily has food."

He was laughing as he walked to the door. It was odd how quickly things could change. He certainly never pictured sharing his room with anyone, let alone being so happy about it.

Then that feeling of dread returned tenfold.

CHAPTER TWENTY-NINE

A hot bath could do wonders to restore a person. The call of food is what drove her out of the tub. She dried off but left her hair wet, brushing her fingers through it.

The door started to open, only to be pulled quickly shut. Then Dmitri's voice came through the wood. "You're naked, are you no'?"

She looked down and smiled. "That would be a yes."

"If I walk in, we willna leave for hours. Nay, make that days."

"Ohh," she said with a sigh, thinking of being in his arms once more. "I love the sound of that."

His forehead plunked against the door before she heard his loud exhale. "I can no' go in there."

"What's wrong?" she asked as she turned to the door.

"We need to examine the bones so they can be buried."

There was more to it than that, she knew it. For some reason, he didn't want to tell her. She tried not to let it get to her, but it did.

"The clothes are by the door," he said.

She heard his steps fade away. Then she opened the bathroom door and saw him standing at the fireplace with his back to her. A fire was lit, reminding her of the cave and the bond they'd formed there.

Her gaze lowered to find the pile of clothes. She bent and picked them up, but didn't close the door behind her as she began to dress.

The jeans were a good fit, and the white V-neck t-shirt utter perfection. With her feet encased in new socks, she put on her boots, walked into the room, and saw the tray of food.

Dmitri turned to face her and smiled. "Come, eat."

She didn't need to be told twice. She sat in one of the chairs while the heat of the fire warmed her. "What aren't you telling me?"

"Remember that feeling I had in the cave?"

"Yes," she said around a mouthful of food.

"I still have it." He took the other chair and looked into the fire. "The bones need to be buried quickly."

"Then we'll get right on it."

He swung his head to her. "I can go without food or sleep for an extended period, but you can no'. Eat your fill. Then we'll go."

"Is it just the skeleton?"

"I warned you of our enemies. There is always something going on."

She didn't like thinking that he regretted bringing her. Faith wasn't one to let something fester. She'd rather know right up front where she stood. "Would it be better if I left?"

"No," he answered immediately. "Doona mistake my worry over our war to mean that I doona want you with me."

"Okay." She found it nearly impossible not to smile now.

His azure gaze locked on her. "I never asked if you had a man in your life."

"I don't."

"Good." After a second, he asked, "Why?"

She tore off a piece of bread and shrugged as she finished chewing. "I never wanted or needed anything like that. It's partly due to my absent father."

"Your mum never married?"

"She found that she couldn't trust men. I remember when I was ten and she went on a date but nothing came of it. Every so often, she would go out with a man, but rarely were there second dates, and never a third. She would tell me it was because she couldn't trust them. Perhaps if she could've put that aside, she might have found some happiness."

He frowned. "It sounds like she was happy. You made her happy."

"Yeah." Faith smiled as she thought of her mother. "She was a strong woman who overcame being left behind with a baby. In every way, she showed me how to be independent and not need a man. She encouraged me to find someone, but she wanted to make sure I was never dependent on anyone but myself."

"I'm sorry I willna get to meet her."

"Death is part of life." Then she remembered who she was talking to. "Well, it's part of a human's life."

"Dragons die. I know death well."

She lifted the wine glass to her lips and sipped the pinot noir. "My mom was my hero. I saw so many of my friends who defined themselves by the guys they were with. I dated my fair share of men, but no one ever seemed to measure up."

Until you. She wanted to say the words, but they locked in her throat. Talking about her feelings to a man in such a way wasn't something she'd ever done before. She was afraid of doing it wrong.

And she really didn't want to mess this up—whatever "this" was with Dmitri.

His soft smile was just what she needed. "I'm sure your mum was verra proud of you."

"I miss her terribly." Faith leaned back, no longer hungry.

His gaze lowered to the floor. "It's never easy to say good-bye to our family."

"Never."

As she looked at him, she understood how much he meant to her. The attraction was inconceivable, and the sex so amazing that she couldn't even think about it without becoming aroused.

Yet something far more profound joined those things. A word she'd never used with a man before darted through her mind. She was so alarmed, she refused to think about it further.

Whatever continued to draw them together and deepen their bond, she knew she liked it. Very much. But there was also a fear she'd never experienced before, one that had manifested after her mother's death.

Faith was afraid that Dmitri would leave her as her mother had. It was silly. Everyone died eventually. Well, except for Dragon Kings.

Death would never take Dmitri, but that didn't mean he wouldn't leave her. She inwardly shook herself because she didn't like the direction of her thoughts.

She looked up and saw that Dmitri was still lost in thought. "Shall we get to the bones?"

"If you're ready," he said as he looked up at her.

She got to her feet. "I'm used to working long hours, remember?"

They stood and walked out of the room. As they made their way toward the stairs, she saw that he carried her jacket.

"It's rather cool where we're going," he said.

She took the jacket and put it on as her excitement grew.

When they reached the bottom level, she looked around as they walked into a conservatory.

The array of plants and flowers made her feel as if she'd walked into a jungle—or a fantasy world. Then she saw the large fountain. There was no time to stop and look, but she intended to return later.

She let her fingers glide across the thick foliage until they came to what looked like a wall. Muscles glanced at her, smiling before he touched something and the wall turned into a secret entrance.

At his nod, she stepped through the doorway to find that she was inside the mountain. No wonder it looked as though the manor were part of the mountain—it was.

"This way," Dmitri said as he took her hand and led her down a lighted tunnel.

Though she saw no electrical wires. She rolled her eyes. Of course, there weren't any wires. This was Dreagan, the home of Dragon Kings. Magic was used here.

She saw several openings off the tunnel that looked to be smaller caverns. The explorer in her wanted to investigate each of them.

Dmitri stopped when they reached a wider part of the corridor. "Farther down the back entrance to the mountain, the opening is twice as large as the one to the cave on Fair."

Her eyes widened. "Really?"

"We use—*used*—it when we were out on patrol or simply spreading our wings. It's how we came in and out of the manor in dragon form."

"You will use it again," she declared.

He squeezed her hand. "I hope you're right."

"I am. Trust me," she said.

His lips softened, which was what she had wanted. He then pointed to the left. "That way is the special cavern we use for mating ceremonies. No one but Dragon Kings and those already mated to us can see it."

"Oh." She refused to be disappointed that she wasn't part of the group. What good would it do anyway? Hadn't she pushed every man out of her life?

"This way," Dmitri said, turning her to the right, "is something I do want to show you."

"Don't keep me in suspense," she said with a smile.

He tugged her after him as his strides ate up the distance. She hurriedly followed, then came to a jerky halt when she saw what it was he wanted to show her.

Her knees grew weak with delight and a bit of panic because she stood inside a cavern that held a large cage with four silver dragons inside.

"These are Ulrik's?" she asked in a quiet tone.

"You can talk as loud as you want. It's dragon magic keeping them asleep. And aye, these are Ulrik's."

There was a soft light overhead, spotlighting the cage. She took in the gleaming silver scales and the beasts' even breathing. They were beautiful and magnificent, but she was glad they slept.

Then it dawned on her. "Ulrik is the only one who has dragons on Earth."

"That's right."

"How often do you come see them?"

"Often. All of us do. They're a reminder of what we sacrificed, and what we'll do to one day return our dragons to their rightful home."

She leaned her head against him. "Can humans and dragons live together?"

"I doona know the answer to that."

"You have it. Look what happened. It'll happen again if you bring the dragons back."

He shrugged. "Con thinks it'll happen even if we doona."

She had to admit Con was probably correct. The odds of a woman betraying a King were high, especially with enemies like Ulrik and the Dark.

"There are seven billion people in the world," Faith said. "We're running out of room for ourselves. The humans would fight against sharing. I'd love to say it'd be different, but I don't see it."

"You're right. We all know this. It's why we've no' shown ourselves. We hide and watch as the world is slowly destroyed."

She turned her head to him. "Because you know we'll eventually annihilate ourselves?"

"All you have to do is look to the past to see the answer. There are some mortals who recycle and 'go green,' but no' enough to make a difference."

"That doesn't even count the animals that have gone extinct because we've either hunted them to extinction or destroyed their habitat."

He nodded slowly. "We only hope there is a world left for us when it is all finished."

She turned back to the Silvers. "We destroyed your lives and your world. Tell me again why you don't join Ulrik and be rid of us."

"Our vow."

"A promise made before you knew what we were capable of."

"It's still an oath."

She looked down at their joined hands. "How do you not hate us?"

"There are some Kings at Dreagan who do. They fought their instinct to kill mortals by answering to Con. It is a battle we fight every day."

"A human wouldn't."

"I know."

She turned away from the dragons to look up at him. "Honor and integrity aren't really our strong points. We're explorers and inventors. But you're right. We destroy without thought of the consequences or how it will affect generations after us.

"We worry about the here and now and let the difficulties our decisions make be the problems of others. Sea levels are already rising. How much longer do we have?"

"That's hard to say."

"We deserve whatever we get."

He touched her face before caressing her cheek to her ear. His fingers ran along the shell. "No' all of you warrant such a fate. You doona."

"How can you be sure?"

"Because I know you," he whispered right before he kissed her.

CHAPTER THIRTY

Dmitri was aware of everything Faith saw as they walked to a cavern where the skeleton waited. He smiled at her wide eyes and how she softly touched the dragons etched into the tunnel walls.

"This place is amazing," she whispered in reverence.

He'd always thought so, but it was nice that she saw it that way, as well. It was her outlook on life that gave him hope for humanity.

There were good people out there, but many were too wrapped up in their day-to-day lives to look at what was happening to their world.

"Oh. Look at that one," she pointed to one of the largest dragons carved into the stone.

"Ulrik did that."

She stopped walking, her head jerking to him. "Do you think he'll ever return here?"

"I'd like to think so."

"As King of Kings?"

"Ulrik is the only one who has a chance of beating Con." That didn't necessarily mean that it was what Dmitri wanted. "I wish things could be what they once were."

She turned her eyes back to the carving. "Whether Con wins or Ulrik does, everything will change."

"Aye."

He began to walk away when something caught his attention. Dmitri looked around the tunnel. He heard other Kings talking and moving about.

"What is it?"

He shrugged, unable to find the source because he was sure someone was watching them.

"Come on, Muscles," Faith teased and tugged on his arm. "I've got dragon bones I'm itching to see again."

He looked back to the entry of the cavern where the Silvers were, but he saw no one. Maybe he was just hyper-vigilant. After everything on Fair Isle, that could very well be the case.

Besides, Dreagan was safeguarded with dragon magic—millions of years of it. No matter how hard MI5 looked, they'd never find their way into the mountain. And no matter how many times the Dark tried, they would never get far onto Dreagan without being killed.

He let go of his worry and gave in to Faith. As soon as they reached the small grotto where the skeleton had been laid out exactly as it had been in the Fair Isle cave, she was immediately focused.

Another of the Kings had fallen.

Ulrik watched from the shadows as Dmitri and a cute blond walked away. By the way Dmitri acted, touched, talked, and kissed the woman, she was his mate.

Ulrik wondered if Con realized it yet. How many more would take a mortal as a mate? He pitied them because he—better than anyone—knew the treacherous ways of humans.

He might take one as his lover every once in a while, but it was rare. It was why he preferred the company of the Fae in his bed.

Never again would a human get close enough to hurt him the way he'd been hurt before. Because he hadn't realized how deceitful the mortals truly were, he'd allowed one into his heart and his home.

And in the process, he'd lost *everything*.

His family, his Silvers, his friends . . . his home. But most of all, he'd lost himself.

The more he returned to Dreagan, the more he hated the mortals. He came to see his Silvers. They had been loyal until the last. The only beings to ever be faithful.

When Dmitri and the woman moved out of sight, Ulrik turned back to his dragons. It was nearly time to unleash them upon the world. Yet they wouldn't help him in his quest for vengeance against Con.

No, that would only be between the two of them. It was a long time coming. A battle that needed to be fought for everyone involved.

It was time the Kings learned just who Con was and what lengths he would go to in order to get what he wanted. Ulrik knew all of Con's dirty little secrets.

But right now, that wasn't who Ulrik needed to concentrate on. Mikkel was the current problem.

There was a loud beep in his head, and then he saw Mikkel standing in his shop. The fact that it had taken several days for this to finally reach Ulrik told him that his uncle had attempted to use magic to prevent him from finding out.

Ulrik smiled as he inwardly laughed. Mikkel's magic paled in comparison to his.

Then his grin faded when there was another picture that displayed in his mind. It was of a woman. A woman he didn't recognize.

Ulrik touched the silver bracelet on his wrist and thought of Rhi's abandoned cabin in Italy. In a blink, he was there. He walked inside to the table where a laptop waited.

He yanked out the chair and sat, his fingers already moving over the keys as he brought up the video feed from the store. Ulrik used magic to alert him anytime someone entered his building be they human, dragon, or Fae.

But he anticipated that someone might try to prevent his cameras from recording, so he'd used magic to block that, as well.

He entered the data from the recorders and searched for the day Mikkel had seen his battle with Asher. It was in the early hours of the following morning that Ulrik found what he was looking for.

Turning up the volume, he listened to his uncle talk to the Druid—about him. Ulrik smiled. He might not know who she was, but he would soon enough.

She was American and owned a pub near enough that she could pay Mikkel a visit. How hard could finding her be? Ulrik captured a screenshot of her and quickly sent it out to his contacts so they could begin the search.

He leaned back with his fingers laced behind his head as he watched her remain behind after Mikkel departed and sit in his chair behind his desk. She didn't touch anything, simply looked around.

This Druid thought she was strong enough to take him and Con down. That would never happen. There was no magic stronger than dragon magic.

But, obviously, Mikkel believed she could do it. His uncle might think he was a step ahead, but Ulrik couldn't wait to prove him wrong.

Faith walked around the now clean dragon skeleton several times. She'd known he was going to be big after seeing Dmitri, but she hadn't truly understood because half of the body had been buried in the rock and earth.

"Why didn't the bones disintegrate?" she asked.

Dmitri frowned at her question. "They were protected in the cave."

"Not protected enough that the ground didn't take him."

"It's rock."

She gave him a flat look. "You saw for yourself how deeply the bones were buried. How long ago did you send the dragons away?"

"Long enough that the earth could've changed numerous time to claim the skeleton."

Which wasn't really an answer. Even through the surgical gloves, she could feel how hard the bones still were. She knelt beside the skull and carefully went over every part of it.

With Dmitri using magic to hold it in mid-air and turn it for her, she was able to look at it from all angles.

She then moved down the neck where she paused at the chip in the bone they'd found on Fair. Dmitri was sure it was from a blade, and now with the bones cleaned, she agreed with him.

When she shifted down to the front legs, she saw that one of the claws was broken off and two others chipped. It could be because of the age of the skeleton, but it was better to be sure.

Faith pointed to the talons. "Does this happen?"

"Imagine the talons on an eagle. They doona break. Neither do dragons'."

It was the way he stared at the talons, the rage barely leashed, that caught her attention. "You think this was done to him."

"I can no' imagine any other way for it to happen."

That wasn't a good sign. She went back to her examination with Dmitri doing his own on the other side of the skeleton. They were each looking for something different.

When she next looked up, she found Rhys and another man with shamrock green eyes and wheat-colored hair beside him. She gave them a wave and returned to her work.

Just when she thought she wouldn't find anything else, she saw a nick in a rib bone. Rubbing her finger over it, she felt the smoothness. Time could've worn the chip in the bone down, but she realized that wasn't the case when she felt the sharp edge of the bone cut through her glove and into her skin.

Faith yanked back her hand. Dmitri was by her side instantly. He took her hand in his and removed the glove. Then he put her finger in his mouth and set his tongue against the wound to stop the bleeding.

"I found another bone that could've had a blade scrape against it," she said as her eyes focused on his mouth.

She shivered when he sucked on her finger. His answering grin made her heart race with desire. But to her surprise, Muscles slowly pulled her finger from his mouth and kissed the tip.

"I see it," he said, nodding to the bone. "I also found something."

Her eyes widened. "What?"

"It's on the spine."

"Which I can't see," she told him.

In answer, he used his magic to lift, and then turn the bones toward her. "There," he said, pointing to the sixth vertebrae.

She touched the bone, her heart aching as she realized that this was how the dragon had been incapacitated. "They severed his spine."

"He couldna move, couldna fly," Dmitri said in a low, dangerous tone.

Rhys and the other man walked around to look at the bone. "A human did this," Rhys said.

"And kept the body where?" Dmitri asked in frustration. "I searched all of the isles."

Faith ached for the dragon and the pain he must have endured, but she also felt Dmitri's heartache. This had been done on purpose to one of his dragons, a dragon he was supposed to protect from the humans.

From her kind.

"Kiril, you're quiet," Rhys said.

Kiril moved next to Faith and peered closely at the bone. "One clean, downward plunge of a blade."

"Someone was on top of him," Dmitri said.

"Aye," Kiril said with a nod. "Did any of your Whites trust a human that much?"

Dmitri snorted. "Never."

She was trying to piece together the story that Dmitri told her with everything she was learning about the dragons. Something didn't quite fit.

"How long did it take to get the dragons out of this realm?" she asked.

The three men looked at each other before Dmitri said, "Days. Why?"

"What dragons were called first?"

"The Silvers, then Con's Golds."

"As I suspected." She gazed at the dragon, trying to put herself back in that time. "Tell me again about that day."

Rhys said, "Utter chaos."

"Hysteria," Kiril added.

There was movement beside her as Dmitri sidled closer. "Anger. There was lots of anger from dragons and humans. And Kings," he added. "We were all working hard to use our magic to create the bridge and try to protect the dragons."

"A fucking impossible task," Rhys mumbled.

Kiril made a sound. "I can still see all of our dead."

"There were so many dragons," Dmitri continued. "They couldna all go over at the same time. I've never felt anything drain my magic as I did holding open the dragon bridge."

Rhys said, "After each of our dragons went over, we would leave to go search our area for stragglers."

"Or those too wounded to fly on their own," Kiril added.

Rhys nodded slowly. "It was up to each King to get the remaining ones to the bridge."

Dmitri's fingers linked with Faith's. "With every day that passed, and as more dragons left this realm, the humans became bolder. When we couldn't reach the weak, old, or young in time, the mortals killed them. Black smoke filled the air as the humans burned anything we had built, whether it was for them or us. They wanted nothing to do with dragons.

"My ears rang from the shouts of humans and the roars of dragons. The mortals were frenzied, animalistic as they rushed upon dragons as a group."

Kiril looked down at the ground. "I saw such an incident. It was with one of my Burnt Oranges. I was hurrying to them. It was a young family. The baby was only a few months old. The mother was shielding her child, trying to coax it into the air when the humans saw them. The father stayed back to give his wife and child time to leave. By the time I reached them, the father was dead, but I got his wife and baby across the bridge."

Faith felt tears fall onto her cheeks. She'd asked for more information, and they were giving it to her in graphic detail.

"I was one of the last to check my area. The isles were isolated with verra few humans. I thought my Whites were safe from such harm," Dmitri said.

She turned her head to him, sniffing. Once the tears began, she couldn't stop them. She hurt for each of the Kings and all they and their dragons had endured.

"I was wrong," Dmitri stated. "Someone intentionally wounded this dragon so he couldna leave."

"But why? They didna tear him apart or burn him like the others," Rhys said.

Dmitri's face hardened. "That's a good question."

CHAPTER THIRTY-ONE

Dmitri was outraged at what they'd discovered. He couldn't wrap his head around the fact that someone would harm a dragon in such a way and leave it to slowly die.

That wasn't the murderous rage he'd witnessed during the war. This was something malicious and vindictive. This was someone who wanted to hurt a dragon—and him. It was the only explanation.

And it enraged him.

"Easy," Kiril said.

He lifted his gaze to Kiril. "Doona tell me to calm down. This wasna done to your dragons."

"He sees what I do," Rhys said in a calming tone.

Dmitri knew that tone. It was the one he used on those who couldn't control their anger. And it only pissed Dmitri off more.

"You have that same murderous look we saw in Ulrik's eyes right before he started the war," Rhys said.

Dmitri released Faith's hand and paced. He had to free some of the pent-up energy and anger because he felt like he might explode.

Kiril moved to block him. "You've never let your anger control you like this before."

"I know!" Dmitri bellowed, his muscles straining from the force of the violence within him. "I can no' contain it."

Nor did he want to.

It felt good to finally give in to the rage and resentment. He'd hidden it for so long, burying it along with his true nature of being a dragon.

And for what? To live out his days in a world that hated him?

"No' everyone hates us," Rhys said.

Dmitri looked up. Had he said those words aloud? He didn't even care anymore. The rage swallowed him until everything he saw was red.

Blood red.

The blood of the dragons that had covered this earth, slaughtered by the impudent, spiteful humans.

He growled. The mortals needed to die. They had done enough to the realm. And the dragons had given enough.

Suddenly, there was a shape before him. Soft hands touched his face. "I don't hate you, Muscles. In fact, I like you quite a lot."

"Faith," Kiril said in warning.

Dmitri growled again, this time directing it at Kiril. How dare his friend talk to Faith that way. Then it hit him. Faith. It was her hands on his face, her voice he heard.

He blinked, and the red faded away. As her face came into focus, he saw her spiked lashes and watery smile. What had just happened?

"Is it you?" she asked, her forehead furrowed.

He nodded, closing his eyes for a moment. "Aye."

"Good," Rhys stated, pleased. "Then tell us what the fuck just happened?"

Dmitri shrugged, his mind feeling as if it were shrouded in fog. Faith remained near him, even though she'd dropped her hands from his face. He sought her hand, and she eagerly accepted his.

"I doona know. Suddenly, I was filled with such rage that I wanted to kill," he said.

Kiril raised a brow. "Kill who?"

"Humans."

"This sounds like Ulrik," Rhys said.

Kiril crossed his arms over his chest. "For a moment there, he even looked like Ulrik."

"Do you think this was Ulrik's doing somehow?" Faith asked.

Dmitri shook his head. "There's no way. We bound his magic right after sending his Silvers across the dragon bridge."

"Who else could've done this?"

Rhys said, "A Druid."

"What happened to your dragon is appalling," Kiril said. "But it was thousands of years ago. Even if we manage to figure out who did it, we can do nothing. Those responsible are long gone."

Dmitri couldn't take his eyes off the bones. "I need to know. I have to know."

"That might prove impossible unless you know someone who can time travel," Kiril said.

Rhys snorted. "And if you do find someone, I know a couple of other things I'd like to change, as well."

"Aye," Kiril replied in a soft voice.

Dmitri released a breath and stepped back until he ran into the wall. Then he slowly slid down until he was sitting. All the while, Faith kept hold of his hand.

"If this dragon were on the isles, I should've found him." He kept imagining the pain and anguish the dragon had gone through waiting and hoping for Dmitri to find and help him.

It was too much to bear. The weight of what had occurred

kept pushing him under the waves of remorse, drowning him again and again for forsaking one of his clan.

Faith squatted beside him and looked into his eyes. "You did everything you could."

"No' enough."

"You said you searched every cave on those isles twice. He wasn't on land, in the water, or in the caves. You would've found him otherwise."

She had a point, but it left one glaring question. Dmitri looked at each of those in the cavern. "Then how did the bones get into that cave?"

No one had an answer, which only made matters worse the longer he thought about it. Something was wrong. Very, very wrong. A human had killed one of his dragons by severing his spine.

The other blade marks on the bones showed more wounds, but what about the ones that hadn't left evidence? The ones that went through scale and muscle.

His anger built rapidly, rising up and encasing him in a feral need for retribution. He heard a scream. The sound was music to his ears.

That's what the humans had sounded like when Ulrik attacked them. It was the sound that would soon fill the air again once he began the slaughter of all those responsible for ruining his life.

Something struck his jaw, whipping his head back against the rock. He felt his head split open and blood run down his neck.

"Dmitri!" someone bellowed.

But he was too caught up in how he was going to wake the Silvers and begin to cleanse the earth of the disgusting mortals.

He tried to get to his feet. There was another hit to his jaw, and then another. He laughed at the screaming that filled the cavern. The humans had once feared them.

And they would again.

It was time the mortals remembered whose land this was—and who ruled it. It was time they were shown the power and might of the Dragon Kings!

As if through a haze, he felt his wrist being broken. But he didn't care. It was already healing. The puny humans deserved the vicious end that was coming to them.

Dmitri felt himself lifted before he was tossed across the cavern into the opposite wall. His head slammed against the floor when he fell to the ground.

He blinked, shaking off the pain. The next second, someone had him by the throat and lifted him into the air. He grabbed the arm that was choking him.

And looked into cold, black eyes.

"Con?" he managed as he heard his larynx begin to break.

A final squeeze from Con crushed it. Dmitri choked even as his body began the healing process. He didn't understand why Con was attacking him, but he was going to find out.

No sooner had his trachea healed than Con crushed it a second time.

"Get. Yourself. Under. Control," Con bit out.

Control? Dmitri wanted to laugh. For the first time in eons, he felt as if he finally understood what he was supposed to do. He kicked out, trying to get out of Con's grip, but Con wasn't the King of Kings for nothing. He crushed Dmitri's windpipe a third time and let loose a growl loud and long enough to quiet the entire mountain.

But Dmitri was also a King.

He knocked Con's arm away, kicking him in the chest at the same time. Con fell backwards, rolling over his shoulder and coming up on his feet.

Dmitri landed on bent knees and glared at Con. "What the hell is wrong with you?"

"Me?" Con asked, his black eyes going frigid. "Perhaps you should ask yourself that."

Why weren't Rhys or Kiril saying anything? Rhys used every opportunity he could to irritate Con. Dmitri glanced to the side and saw Rhys and Kiril with their backs to him, kneeling beside something.

Then he recognized the boots attached to the unmoving legs.

"Faith."

"So you remember her," Con said sarcastically.

He jerked his head to Con. "Of course I do."

"You didna a moment ago."

Dmitri straightened, confused. "That's no' possible."

"I assure you, it is."

He heard a sniff. Was Faith crying? Just because he didn't remember who she was? Well, that was worrying for him, but it was nothing to get upset over.

"Con," Rhys called.

Without hesitation, Con pivoted and walked to the trio. Dmitri made to follow, and Kiril immediately rose and turned to stop him.

"I think it's better if you keep some distance."

He frowned at Kiril. "What? I brought Faith here to protect her. I kept her safe on Fair."

But Kiril didn't budge.

Dmitri looked around his shoulder and saw Con lay his hand on her. Con was healing her! The thought went through him as searing as lightning.

"What happened?" he demanded of Kiril. "How was she hurt?" When his friend didn't answer, Dmitri shouted, "Tell me!"

Kiril leaned close, his shamrock green eyes filled with censure. "It was you."

Dmitri reeled back. Him? He'd hurt Faith? That wasn't

possible. He shook his head, unable to comprehend what was going on.

Kiril advanced on him, his lips peeled back in anger. "You always told us how you preferred the Fae as lovers. Why choose a human now?"

"I didna choose her," Dmitri said, feeling his rage begin to bubble once more.

"Enough!" Con bellowed.

Rhys rose and walked to Dmitri, punching him in the face, followed by two punches in the gut. "Get your sword."

Dmitri flung out his arms, shoving the two aside and letting loose a roar. "I'll fight both of you."

"You willna do anything," Con declared. Then he got to his feet with Faith in his arms.

As soon as Dmitri saw the tear tracks down her face, he fell to his knees. Something had happened to her, and no one would tell him what. He knew without a doubt that he hadn't harmed her. There was no way he could.

"She's unconscious now," Con said. "I've healed her physically, but I'm no' sure anything will ever heal her emotionally or mentally."

All Dmitri could do was stare after Con as he walked out with Faith. He dropped back on his haunches, sick to know that something had happened and he hadn't been aware of it.

Kiril shook his head while Rhys squeezed his eyes closed several times. Dmitri put the heels of his palms to his temples as his head began to throb.

"What happened?" he asked again.

It was Kiril who said, "You became enraged, talking about how humans needed to die."

"And then you began squeezing Faith's hand," Rhys said.

Dmitri closed his eyes. No. Please, no. That couldn't have happened.

Kiril sighed loudly. "You broke every bone in her hand and wrist."

"We punched you to get you to release her, but nothing worked," Rhys said. "It was like you took pleasure in her screams and pain."

Dmitri opened his eyes and dropped his arms to his sides. "I doona remember anything until Con had his hand around my throat."

Kiril raised a brow. "That's no' good."

CHAPTER THIRTY-TWO

Con had never seen his men act like such . . . animals. The longer he thought about it, the angrier he became.

He stalked through the tunnel and into the manor without anyone asking him what had happened to Faith. It was to everyone's benefit because he wasn't fit to talk to anyone at the moment.

Faith was another example of why the Kings shouldn't bind themselves to humans. The mortals were weak. They didn't belong in a world that had been created with magic, for beings with magic.

When he reached the door to Dmitri's room, he found it open and Lily inside. He didn't look her way as he set Faith down on the bed and took a step back.

Had Faith not found the skeleton, he wouldn't have sent Dmitri there to destroy it. The Dark wouldn't have tried to kill her, and Dmitri wouldn't have saved her. Nor would she know of their world or be at Dreagan now.

"Where she doesna belong."

"I'm sorry?" Lily asked.

Con lifted his gaze to find Lily on the other side of the bed. "She doesna belong here."

"Dmitri wants her here."

He raised a brow. "Really? Then why did he just crush her hand as if it were a stick?"

Lily's eyes widened.

Con took a step toward the bed, anger churning viciously. "Did that shock you? Good. Because as long as you humans are on Dreagan, you put every King at risk."

"We're their mates."

"Mates? Humans were never meant to be immortals. Do you want to know why? Because your feeble little minds can no' handle the passage of time and the death of your friends!"

Lily jerked back at his words.

"How long do you think you'll have with your precious King before you go insane? He'll no' be able to end your misery, so it'll fall to me.

"It'll be either the passage of time or the yearning for a child that does you in. Either way, the outcome is the same. You'll lose your mind." He blew out a burst of air. "I'll do what I always do and watch over the Kings, which means I'll have to play the villain when I end your life. But if it saves my race, I'll gladly do it."

"You can't mean that," she said, lifting her chin.

He threw back his head and laughed. "Oh, I mean it. I mean every fucking word of it. Why do you think I work so verra hard to keep my men from taking any of you wretched humans as their mates?"

Lily met his stare. "I don't care what you say. I know you're a good man, Con."

"That's just it. I'm no' a man. I'm a dragon!"

By now, he could hardly breathe, the anger was so intense. The room and everything in it turned red. He fisted his hands, the need to kill strong. But he had only one quarry.

Mortals.

"You're King of Dragon Kings," Lily said. "The one with the icy demeanor and the cold eyes. You never show this much emotion."

She was right. He looked down at himself and smiled. He was holding nothing back, and it felt glorious! All the exasperating time suppressing his frustration and ire had been such a waste.

Now he could tell everyone exactly what he thought. And why not begin with the MI5 assholes who wouldn't leave? Then he would call the other Kings, and they could take to the skies as they were meant to.

No longer did he care if the humans knew of them or not. Hiding had done nothing but give the mortals more power over them. That stopped. Now.

"No more," he said.

Lily took another step back.

He cocked his head to the side, regarding her. "No longer will we hide. No longer will we protect the humans. We're going to take to the skies tonight. If the Fae want the mortals, then let them have them. The quicker the humans are gone, the sooner the Fae will leave."

"Con, please."

A smile pulled at his lips. "I doona know why I fought this idea for so long. It'll solve all of our problems. We'll be free of the Dark and the humans."

"And Ulrik?" she asked with a frown.

Ah, yes. His old friend. "I think I'll invite him to join us. Besides, what he did, he did for us. I should've seen that then."

"Not all the Kings will follow you."

He raised a brow, laughing. "If they doona follow me, then they die. And with them, their mates. Or perhaps I'll start by killing all of you first."

"You can't kill us."

"No' exactly true."

Her face paled. "We're linked to our mates. We live as long as they do."

"You've no idea the power I have as King of Kings or the responsibilities the title entails. Even mated, I could kill you."

"Rhys will never let you touch me," she said, her voice wobbling.

"He's no' here with us now, is he?" Con felt the rumble of fire in his chest. A growl formed as he said, "And let me remind you that I am King of Kings!"

Tired of her useless ramblings, Con walked from the room to the stairs. Lily had annoyed him for the last time. She would die tonight.

That would . . . show her just who . . . was in charge!

Con was halfway down the stairs when he felt the pain in his head. He looked around. How come he didn't remember getting there?

The last thing he recalled was being in the mountain and healing Faith. He didn't have a memory until now.

How much time had he lost?

He gripped his head with both hands, the pain making him dizzy. He tried to grab hold of the railing and missed. Then he pitched forward, tumbling down the stairs.

Thankfully, his body healed his broken back and tibia as well as the concussion immediately. He sat up, rubbing his temple. When he raised his gaze, he found Roman standing over him with a confused expression.

"What just happened?" Roman asked.

Con looked at the stairs, shaking his head. "I'm no' sure."

Shara stood at the foot of the bed, watching Faith as she listened to everything Lily told her about Con's visit. Something was off inside Dreagan Manor, and Shara had set about finding the source.

It led her straight to their newest visitor.

"Say something," Lily urged in her British accent. "You're freaking me out with that look."

Shara tucked her black hair with the thick strip of silver behind her ear. "I still haven't figured out what's wrong."

"You're Fae, can't you do magic to find out?"

She cut her eyes to Lily. "It's not that easy."

"You didn't hear Con."

No, but Shara had heard from Kiril about what had happened in the mountain with Dmitri. And she'd been on edge ever since.

"You know something," Lily pressed.

She shrugged, concern growing by the second. "I'm not sure, though."

"Just say it, please."

She saw the anxiousness in Lily's dark eyes. "The Kings should've felt it, too."

Lily threw out her hands before letting them slap against her legs. After a quick glance at Faith, she said, "That tells me nothing."

"I sense magic," Shara said.

Lily sank into the chair, her shoulders slumping. "I knew it. Is it Fae magic?"

"I . . . I'm not sure." Shara couldn't explain what she was feeling. The magic ebbed and flowed like waves crashing upon a shore.

At times, she was certain there was Fae magic being used, and then other times, she couldn't be sure of anything.

"Well, it doesn't seem to be affecting us."

She smiled at Lily. The English and their practicality. But Lily was right. Which made Shara ask, "Why are just the men affected?"

Lily crossed one leg over the other. "Maybe it's not the fact that they're men."

"They're dragons," Shara said, her heart lurching.

Breath passed Lily's lips in a harsh exhale. "It's Ulrik, then."

"I can't be sure."

"We'd better tell the others."

Shara gave a quick shake of her head. "Not until we know what's causing it. What was the common denominator? The dragon bones?"

"According to Rhys, Dmitri acted fine while at Fair, and even when they first arrived here."

"That's true. But while at Fair, the bones hadn't been removed until right before they left."

Lily bit her lip, her eyes moving to the bed. "Unless there's another culprit."

"You think Faith is working with Ulrik?" Shara knew the possibility was real, but she was hoping that wasn't the case.

Lily scrunched up her face. "Don't you think it's odd how she found the skeleton? Out of all those caves, she chose that one, only to find the bones."

Shara put her hands on the ornate wooden footboard. "That does bring a lot of things into question."

"We should talk to Ryder. He can do some digging."

"He's with the others in the cavern."

Lily fisted her hand and softly punched her other palm. "I forgot, Con called a meeting."

"Too many secrets are floating around," Shara said as she rubbed her neck where stress had tightened her muscles. "I hope Con clears the air. With the war and now this threat, the Kings need to be united."

"Have you had any luck talking to Usaeil about the Light helping?"

Just the mention of Usaeil made Shara want to hit something. "The queen won't answer me. So, I went to her."

Lily's eyes widened. "And?"

"She wasn't at the castle. But there is something going on there, as well. Every Fae is terrified and talking about the Reapers."

"Um. Excuse me? Did you just say Reapers?"

Shara sighed, forgetting that few at Dreagan knew about them. "We have a legend of Reapers. They are ruled by Death, who is judge and jury. The Reapers are the executioners."

"Sounds horrible. We also have such a myth. The Reaper is an entity who comes to a person when it's their time to die."

"The Light are told the stories of Reapers to scare them into not turning Dark. The Dark children learn of them so that they'll be too frightened to ever disobey their family."

"But you say they're real?"

Shara nodded slowly. "I believe so."

"Can't you find out who they are?"

"If you realize you're talking to a Reaper, then it's already too late. No one knows who they are, and I think it's that way for a reason."

Lily leaned back in the chair. "Well, I guess we can cross off the queen for help."

"No one can find her anyway."

"Great," Lily said sarcastically. "Our luck is horrible."

Shara looked to the bed once more. "It sure seems that way. I wish I could've spoken to Faith before the incident in the mountain."

"I'd like to talk to her now. I liked her. If she's working with Ulrik, she's good enough that I never guessed."

"Lily, you like everyone."

She shrugged, her face crestfallen. "I like to see the good in people."

It was because of that trait that she'd died, but Shara didn't mention that fact. "I know. The problem is that we don't have that luxury right now."

"If you look for the bad in people, you'll find it no matter what."

"We're surrounded by it, whether we like it or not."

Lily stood and straightened her shoulders. "You're right. I need to remember that our enemies outnumber us. We can't do anything until the meeting is over. Until then, I'm going to make Faith comfortable."

Shara smiled because Lily couldn't help but be that sweet. It's why everyone loved her.

While Lily began to remove Faith's jacket, Shara took off her boots and placed them side-by-side. When she straightened, she saw Lily checking the pockets of Faith's coat.

Lily looked up and grinned. "I may be nice, but I won't be taken advantage of again. Aha!" she cried.

The smile vanished from Shara when she spied the small wooden carving of a dragon that Lily held up. She reached out her hand for it. As soon as Shara touched it, images of other people, places, and times flashed in her head.

"Shara!"

She heard Lily's scream, but she couldn't answer because her mind was frozen.

CHAPTER THIRTY-THREE

Dmitri was still shaken from what had occurred with Faith when he'd joined the other Kings in the cavern. He had no answers, only the looks of consternation from Rhys and Kiril, which did nothing to ease his mind.

He wanted to go to Faith, to see for himself that she was all right. And tell her he was sorry for whatever it was he'd done. The longer he went without seeing her, the worse he felt.

Even though he knew why Con had gathered them, he was still uneasy about all of it. With half his mind on Con and the other on Faith, it seemed as if he were being split in two. All he wanted to do was see Faith, to try and explain himself.

But how could he when he couldn't clarify it for himself? No matter how hard he tried, there was time missing from his memories.

He looked at his friends. "I need to know every detail of what happened with Faith. Please."

Kiril and Rhys exchanged looks before they gave a nod. Dmitri listened as they told him everything that had happened, including the things he'd said about humans.

Dmitri cringed when he heard how Faith had screamed and tried to get away from him when he broke her hand. It had taken Con to breach whatever it was that had a hold of him.

As scary as all of that was, it was nothing compared to realizing that it could happen again unless he figured out how to stop it.

Which wouldn't be nearly as hard if he knew *what* it was.

The cavern quieted when Con climbed the boulder and looked over them. Dmitri eyed those around him to see if anyone else knew the secret Con was about to impart. By the look on Asher's and Kellan's faces, they did.

"There have been a lot of questions of late," Con said, his voice loud and clear. "I'm here to answer as many as I can, but first, there are a few things all of you need to know.

"There have been some recent developments. I wanted to wait until everyone was back under one roof, but this can no longer be put off."

Con paused and looked to Asher. "As most of you know, Asher took my place at the World Whisky Consortium in Paris. While there, he met Rachel, who was unknowingly recruited by Ulrik to write an article exposing us.

"She got close to Asher and learned our secrets. And Ulrik's. I'm sure you've seen Rachel around Dreagan since she arrived a few days ago. She didna just learn who we are, she discovered she was Asher's mate.

"That put her against Ulrik. He attempted to kill her, but Asher got to her in time. In the process, Asher learned Ulrik's biggest secret—he can shift."

The anger and concern that filled the cavern didn't surprise Dmitri. They were the same emotions he'd felt when Con told him. Because all of them knew that, at any moment, Ulrik could wake the Silvers.

It was the waiting that drove them all crazy.

"Ulrik has all of his magic," Con said. "We've known this was coming. *I've* known it was coming. The battle between Ulrik and I will most likely happen soon. Until then, we continue fighting him and the Dark."

Everyone nodded in agreement. They also knew that anything could happen in the battle to be King of Kings. Con could retain the title, or Ulrik could claim it for his own.

Con's shoulders lifted as he took a deep breath and released it. "There is another matter that needs to be addressed. I've heard the talk in regards to my private life and the speculation of who I've taken to my bed.

"I've never delved into your private lives, and I didna take kindly to you prying into mine. I still doona. I would be speaking to you about this now even if the questions hadna been raised because this matter is no longer concealed."

Dmitri stood with his arms crossed over his chest, watching Con. He couldn't imagine how hard this was for their King, because he was right. Their private lives should be private. Each of them had done wrong trying to probe into Con's.

"You've been asking who my lover is," Con continued. "I chose no' to share that information until now but she's left me no choice. It was Usaeil."

The silence in the cavern was deafening. Dmitri glanced at the ground, rocking back on his heels. "Why her?" he asked.

Con's gaze skated to him. For a long moment, the King of Kings stared at him. "I didna want the confines that having a mortal in my bed brings. I could be myself. Did no' have to lie. As beneficial as that was, it wasna why I sought Usaeil out.

"If we were going to continue hiding our presence from

the humans, we needed an ally. As I got closer to Usaeil, I came to discover that all Rhi had been saying about her is true."

Rhys snorted. "So Rhi was right all along?"

"Aye, she was," Con said. "The more I tried to untangle myself from Usaeil, the tighter the threads became. In the process, she claimed to have fallen in love with me. I used that to gain more information about Rhi and . . . other things."

Dmitri frowned at the mention of 'other things.' Just what did Con mean by that?

"The last time I saw Usaeil, she told me that she wanted to announce to the Fae and all of you that we were to be married," Con said.

None of the Kings would've cared about that since Kiril was already mated to a Fae. It was the way Usaeil had handled the situation that irritated them.

Con raised a magazine over his head. "Though part of our agreement was that our affair remain secret until we both agreed otherwise, she had our picture taken. You see, to the world, Usaeil is a well-known American actress. Photographers follow her everywhere. You can no' see my face, but it's me.

"This is her way of taking things out of my hands. I didna know of this until Rhi brought me the magazine. She saw it in Edinburgh, but someone posted it all over the Light Castle, as well. The Fae are speculating that the man is me."

Kiril gawked at Con. "Are you telling me Rhi didna blow up the manor in a rage?"

"I explained the state of things to her. We're working together on confronting Usaeil. And before you ask, I'm no' doing it now because there are other matters going on with the Fae that most of you are no' aware of yet. The Reapers."

There was something about the word that immediately set Dmitri on edge. As long as he'd known of the Fae and had dealings with them, he'd never heard of the Reapers.

Con lowered the magazine, letting it fall to the ground. He ran a hand down his face. The cavern remained quiet as Con told them the legend of the Reapers.

"You think the white-haired Fae I kept seeing in Edinburgh is a Reaper?" Darius asked.

Con shrugged. "It's a possibility. We had help dealing with the Dark that night."

Dmitri asked, "So they're our allies?"

"I didna say that." Con blew out a breath. "No one knows who the Reapers are. No' much is known about them at all."

"Not true," said a voice that everyone recognized.

They all turned to see Rhi making her way through the Kings. She reached Con and looked up at him. There was a brief moment of tension before he moved so she could stand beside him.

"The Reaper stories I heard as a child differ greatly from what they truly are," Rhi said. "They're meant to keep a balance between good and evil. The Reapers have more power and magic than Usaeil and Taraeth combined. There is a warning obscured in a book that counsels against messing with a Reaper. They are judge, jury, and executioner of the Fae."

Dmitri was growing more concerned by the moment. "How do you know so much about them?"

"I did some digging of my own. There have been whispers at court for months about the Reapers. Even the Dark are scared of them. It doesn't bode well for the Fae that they're here."

Con asked her, "You say they keep the balance of good and evil. Do you think it has something to do with our war?"

"They don't meddle in the affairs of other species. Just the Fae."

"What about half-Fae?" Dmitri asked.

Rhi's silver eyes turned to him. "I . . . don't know. All I know is that the Reapers aren't to be messed with. Usaeil's absence from court is only making things worse. I've tried asking her to gather the Fae army just in case, but she won't listen."

"I urged her to do the same thing," Con said. "She wouldna take me seriously."

Dmitri knew that most likely meant they couldn't count on the Light to help them. Unless . . . "Rhi, you were a Queen's Guard, a trusted friend to Usaeil. Can you no' lead the army?"

"No," she stated. "I might've had a chance if I were still in the Queen's Guard, but not now."

Rhys stepped forward. "Why no'?"

"I don't have the authority," she said.

Con raised a blond brow. "When has that ever stopped you before?"

She gaped at each of them. "If I try to take the army, Usaeil will see that as me attempting to take her throne. She'll cut me down where I stand."

Those words effectively ended that talk.

"Maybe we're looking at this wrong," Asher said.

Everyone looked to him, but it was Con who asked, "How so?"

"Rachel said something to me that I've no' been able to stop thinking about. She said that sooner or later, we'll have to make our presence known to the world again. We're going into battle with one hand tied behind our back as long as we try to keep hidden from the mortals."

Con put his hands in his pant's pockets. "She has a valid point, one I've considered often. The problem lies with the humans. We'll be battling them again, as well. They'll want to study us, run tests, and all manner of wretched things, and in order to do that, they'll want to capture one of us."

"Which means we'll have to keep away from them," Dmitri said as he realized what Con was getting at.

Con looked around the cavern. "I know well how much easier this would be if we didna have to keep what we are a secret, but the alternative isna any better."

"The Dark will bring the humans into your war," Rhi said.

Con turned his head to her. "We'll do what we've always done. Our vow to the mortals hasna changed."

Maybe it should.

Dmitri frowned as the words ran through his head. They weren't his. Well, they were, but he didn't mean them. Did he? He rubbed his temple as another headache began to pound.

The humans are nothing but trouble.

He clenched his teeth, hoping the words would stop. As the pain abated, he began to relax. It was only when he raised his head that he realized everyone was watching him.

Rhys and Kiril looked as dazed as he felt. But it was Con rubbing his temple that caught his attention.

Dmitri glanced around, but none of the other Kings was having the same reaction. It was just those who had been in the grotto with Faith and the bones.

"What's going on?" Kiril asked tightly.

Rhi jumped off the boulder and made her way to the three of them. "What is it?"

"An overwhelming urge to kill every human," Rhys said.

Dmitri closed his eyes and concentrated on his breathing because as soon as Rhys spoke the words, the anger surged again.

"Listen to me," Rhi said. "Listen to my voice."

Dmitri shook his head because it felt like a thick fog was enveloping him.

"Dmitri," Rhi said as she faced him. "You have to focus on one thing. Something that gives you strength."

Faith.

He saw her face in his mind. She was smiling at him, her sherry eyes filled with desire.

Human. Mortal!

"Nay!" he bellowed and clawed at his head.

Through his lids, he saw something bright flare, and then felt a zap of magic. When he next opened his eyes, Rhi was there.

She smiled and gave him a pat on the arm. "You worried me there for a sec, sweet cheeks."

Dmitri frowned. "What just happened?"

"Me," Rhi said with a wink.

"Rhys!"

"That's Lily," Rhys said, his head jerking toward the tunnel.

Dmitri followed Rhys and Kiril out of the cavern since it was Lily who was supposed to be watching Faith. Worry settled in his gut when he saw Lily throw herself into Rhys's arms, her black eyes wild with panic.

Rhys held her face in his hands. "Calm down, sweetheart. What happened?"

"She touched it and fell. She just fell, and now she won't wake up," Lily said.

Rhys nodded, keeping his voice soft. "Who?"

Lily turned her gaze to Kiril. "Shara."

Without a word, Kiril took off running.

CHAPTER THIRTY-FOUR

Life certainly had a way of knocking her flat on her ass. Faith opened her eyes and stared at the wooden canopy above her. She was in Dmitri's bed. The only difference was that she thought he'd be with her, and they would be making love.

Not that she would have a broken hand given to her by the very man who'd promised to protect her.

She paused, curious as to why she felt no pain. Cautiously, she tested her left hand, lifting one finger at a time. When everything felt fine, she made a fist. Then she rotated her wrist.

There was no bruising, no swelling. It was as if she'd dreamed the entire event. Except she hadn't. She could still recall what it had felt like to have her bones broken one at a time as Dmitri squeezed.

She'd screamed his name, begged him to release her. He'd been talking about how useless the humans were. And when he looked at her . . .

A shiver raced down her spine as she recalled the way his azure gaze had pierced her. The wealth of hatred reflected there had been staggering.

To think, she had given up the find of a lifetime. For what? A Dragon King? A man who'd turned on her the first chance he got?

It was time she left. She'd rather take her chances out in the world than stay at Dreagan for another moment. She sat up and saw her coat on the floor.

Next to it was a limp hand. She followed the hand up the arm to a face she didn't recognize. The woman was beautiful, but it was the thick lock of silver in her black hair that alarmed Faith.

Looking around, she searched for some assailant. When she determined she was alone, she slid off the bed and checked to see if the woman was alive.

As soon as she felt a strong pulse, Faith grabbed her jacket and put it on while searching for her shoes. She spotted them at the foot of the bed and hurriedly put them on.

She was headed to the door when she saw something on the floor. It was only a few inches tall. As she bent for a closer look, she realized that it was the item she'd found in the ground after the skeleton had been removed.

Faith glared at the woman who had dared to steal it. She picked it up and returned it to her jacket pocket. She'd been wrong about the Dragon Kings. Her ancestors had been justified to drive them away. Just look at what Dmitri had done to her.

It was proof that the dragons didn't know how to control themselves. They would never be able to stop hurting her race. But she could end it.

All she had to do was kill Dmitri.

Dmitri reached his room seconds after Kiril. While Kiril was on his knees, lifting his mate into his arms, Dmitri searched for Faith. He checked the bathroom, the closet, and even under the bed. But she was gone.

"Where is she?" he demanded of Lily, who stood with Rhys.

Lily pointed to the bed. "She was right there when I ran out."

"You were supposed to watch her!" Dmitri yelled as his apprehension swelled.

"All right, children," Rhi said as she walked between them before Lily could respond.

Con followed Rhi into the room and looked around. His gaze landed on Lily before he hastily looked away. Dmitri caught the exchange and wondered about it.

"What happened?" Kiril demanded of Lily as he sat on the floor with Shara in his arms.

Lily swallowed, shaking her head. "I was sitting over there, and Shara was standing at the foot of the bed watching Faith. She kept saying that something was off."

"Off?" Rhys repeated. "What did she mean?"

"She said it felt like magic, but when I asked her if it was Fae magic, she said she couldn't tell."

Dmitri, Kiril, Con, and Rhys all exchanged looks. Something definitely *was* off, and they were proof of it.

"I don't think this is the time for secrets," Rhi said as she looked at the four of them.

Con squatted beside Shara and touched her, but after a moment, he straightened. "My power is doing nothing to help her."

"Let me try," Rhi told him, shoving Con aside.

Rhys put a hand on Rhi. "You can't heal anyone."

"Y . . ." she began, only to trail off. "You're right. Why did I get this really strong feeling that I could?"

Dmitri watched as Rhi's gaze took on a faraway look. A moment later, her face shifted into a mask of anger as a subtle glow began around her.

"Rhi," Lily called.

It was Con who grabbed Rhi's arm. "You're glowing."

"I know," Rhi said through clenched teeth and jerked out of his grasp. "I just remembered something someone tried really hard to make me forget."

"What?" Rhys asked.

Rhi shook her head, refusing to speak of it.

Dmitri blew out a breath, wanting to get them back on track. "Is that all that happened, Lily?"

"No," she replied. "We talked for a bit, and then I took off Faith's jacket, and Shara removed her shoes. I found something in the pocket of the coat. Shara touched it and collapsed. I tried to wake her."

Rhys put an arm around Lily and held her tightly. "You didna do anything, sweetheart."

"Nay. That was Faith," Kiril said as he rocked Shara.

Dmitri took immediate offense. "How dare you blame Faith when she's no' here to defend herself?"

"That's right," Kiril said and glared up at him. "She was unconscious because you broke her hand and went crazy."

Con immediately moved between them. He looked at one and then the other before he said, "This isna helping."

"Perhaps we should begin with Dmitri breaking Faith's hand," Rhi said, her gaze directed at him.

Dmitri couldn't feel worse about it. "It was an accident."

"No' based on the things you were saying," Rhys said.

"Like what?" Rhi pushed.

Kiril smoothed the hair from Shara's face. "Like humans needed to be removed."

"He said they were a plague," Rhys added.

Dmitri grimaced, the words difficult to hear. "I wouldna have said such things."

"You did," Con said. "In order to get you to release Faith, I had to throw you across the room. You still wouldna stop going for her, so I broke your windpipe three times."

"How can I no' remember that?" he demanded, looking around.

Con's brows drew together. "When I left with Faith after healing her, I heard all three of you going at it, saying the same things."

At this, Kiril and Rhys both frowned in worry.

Con looked at Lily. "What happened when I brought Faith in here? I doona remember anything until I woke up from falling down the stairs."

"You were saying much the same things as the others," she replied.

Rhi raised her brows and whistled softly. "Sounds like there's definitely something in the air."

"That's what Shara and I were saying," Lily replied. "There were two common denominators. Faith, and the bones."

Dmitri rubbed the back of his neck. "Back in the cavern, I had a thought about the mortals."

Rhi turned her silver Fae eyes on him. "And what was that thought?"

"That humans were nothing but trouble."

Rhys cleared his throat. "I had that same thought."

"Me, too," Kiril added.

Con didn't move, didn't utter a word, but his entire attitude changed. Anger and rage were building, emanating from him to spread throughout the room.

"Someone brought this magic onto Dreagan," Con said in an icy voice laced with retribution.

Dmitri knew everyone was thinking about Faith. He had to turn them away from her. "What if it's the dragon?"

"Shara didna go near the skeleton," Kiril added.

Rhi held out her hand to Lily. "Let me see what it was that Shara touched."

"I dropped it," Lily answered.

Everyone searched the floor, and it didn't take long to draw the conclusion that Faith must have taken it with her.

Dmitri caught Con's gaze. "I was with Faith for days. I never felt anything off about her."

"You also didna dally with humans before her either," Con said. "What if she was waiting for you to bring her here."

"You think she's working with Ulrik?"

Rhi gave him a look of regret and put her hands in the back pockets of her jeans. "It's looking more and more like that's what happened, stud."

"Ronnie vouched for her," Dmitri argued. "Ryder did a background check on her."

"Druid magic." Rhys shrugged as he looked at each of them. "We've seen it recently with Kinsey and Esther. Perhaps Faith doesna know what she's doing."

"I have to find her." Dmitri turned to leave when Con said his name. He faced Con, knowing that no matter what the King of Kings said, he was going to find Faith.

Con met his gaze and said, "I'm coming with you."

Rhi stepped in front of Con, causing him to halt. "I'm not sure that's such a good idea."

"He's going to need help," Con argued.

"Without a doubt. It's why I'm going, and I think another King should, as well."

Rhys said, "I will."

"No," Rhi said. "You, like Con, have already been affected by whatever this is. It needs to be someone else."

Roman stepped into the doorway and leaned against it. "I'll go."

Rhi clapped her hands together, rubbing them. "Let's get going, sugar lips."

"Wait," Lily said and reached for Rhi's arm. "Whatever Faith has, don't touch it."

Rhi looked back at Shara. "I won't."

Dmitri turned on his heel and walked past Roman. He

didn't care if the others followed or not, he wasn't going to wait a moment longer.

He jumped from one landing to another until he reached the first floor, then he ran to the main entry. Once outside beneath the night sky, he looked left, then right.

Rhi came up on his right side. "Does she know the terrain?"

"She only arrived today, and we immediately went to the mountain."

Roman came up on his left side. "She'd go for cover since she doesna have a car to escape in."

"The Dragonwood," Dmitri said.

Rhi looked to the forest. "That's where I'd go."

Dmitri stopped her before she could teleport away. "Doona approach her. I want to talk to Faith first."

"And if she doesn't want to talk to you after what you did?"

That was a definite possibility. "She probably willna, but I must try."

"She's your mate," Roman said, surprise in his voice.

Rhi smiled sadly. "Have you thought about what you'll do if she is working with Ulrik and she won't change her thinking? You can't let her go with all that she knows."

"I'll no' kill her either." That wasn't an option no matter who said otherwise. Dmitri looked at the Dragonwood. "Guy can erase her memories."

Roman shook his head. "When magic has already been used on her, it might no' work."

Dmitri knew there were going to be obstacles, and he didn't have all the answers. Hell, he didn't have *any* answers. All he knew was that he had to find her. And quickly.

"Let's just locate her first. We'll worry about the rest after."

Rhi smiled and held out her arms. "After you, stud muffin."

CHAPTER THIRTY-FIVE

Being in the Dark Palace was a necessary evil. Ulrik didn't exactly like the Dark, but the enemy of his enemy was his friend.

No one hated the Dragon Kings like the Dark.

Before seeing Taraeth, Ulrik detoured to the south wing. Not a single Fae stopped him as he made his way through the compound.

When he came to the door he wanted, he rapped his knuckles on the wood. A moment later, it opened, and he smiled into red eyes he knew well.

"Hello, lover," Muriel purred in an Irish accent. Her black and silver hair hung long and loose down her back. "It's been a while."

Ulrik leaned a shoulder against the doorframe and grinned. "It certainly has."

She put a hand on his chest and covertly looked down the corridor to make sure no one else was near. Her voice lowered to a whisper as she said, "I've got news."

That's exactly what he'd been hoping for. He let her take his hand and pull him into the chamber. She wore a slinky red nightgown that hugged her lush curves and ended just below her amazing ass. He closed the door behind him and stood in the lavish apartment.

Muriel faced him and licked her lips. "I was getting worried."

"About me?" he asked.

She gave him an irritated glance. "We have a deal, remember?"

It was one of the best bargains he'd struck. She passed information to him from her sister, who spied on Mikkel. In exchange, he would help Muriel with her revenge when the time was right. And he was beginning to suspect the target of that reprisal was Taraeth.

After all, Taraeth kept the sisters as slaves.

"I doona go back on my word," Ulrik said.

She briefly closed her eyes. "I know. It's just with everything Sinny is discovering about Mikkel, I thought he'd killed you."

Ulrik took Muriel's hand and led her to the dark purple sofa. Once they'd sat, he looked into her red eyes. "I'm the King of Silvers. Only another Dragon King can kill me."

"So it's true," she said with a growing smile. "You do have all your magic."

"I have for a while now."

"You hid it on purpose, then. How did Mikkel find out?"

"He followed me." Something Ulrik had prepared for, but destroying the building in his battle with Asher had ruined his closely guarded secret.

Muriel leaned back and shifted to the side to face Ulrik, tucking her legs against her. "Mikkel doesn't seem worried at all."

"He has a Druid at his disposal. Stupid fool thinks a Druid can actually do anything against me."

Muriel's smile held a wealth of confidence. "A Druid's magic can't even harm us."

"I'm no longer worried about Mikkel."

"You should kill him now. The longer he's around, the more problems he can cause."

Ulrik rested one arm along the back of the sofa. "Oh, I plan to kill him. However, he's still part of my plans right now."

"Be careful. I don't trust him."

"No one does. How's Sinny?"

Muriel shrugged, though the worry was there in her gaze. "My sister is holding up. Your uncle takes his anger out on her, and Taraeth has given her orders that she can't protect herself against Mikkel."

"I'm surprised Mikkel hasn't moved on to another."

"He has, but he still likes to have Sinny around."

Ulrik met Muriel's gaze. "It willna be long now."

She glanced down at the wide silver bracelet on his wrist. "Has anyone noticed?"

"I make sure they doona. Your gift is our secret."

"If Taraeth finds out, he'll kill me."

"He'll never know of this."

She nodded, but he could see that she wasn't entirely convinced. His relationship with Muriel had been one of many in this chess game he played. She hadn't betrayed him or let him down.

And she was the only person he even came close to trusting.

Not that he would ever trust anyone fully again. That part of him had been ripped out and had shriveled to nothing long, long ago.

"You're here to see Taraeth, aren't you?" she asked.

He let her believe what she would. It was that trust issue again, but no one could know all that he was doing. "I'd better be going. I'll return soon."

"You sure you don't have time to stay?" she asked and shoved the thin straps of the gown she wore off her shoulders to reveal her breasts.

Ulrik leaned down and softly licked one pert nipple. "If only I had the time."

"Make sure you do next time."

"Of course."

He left Muriel's chamber with regret and made his way down the corridor, his thoughts on his uncle. Mikkel was a devious bastard. Though he hated to admit it, Mikkel was also smart.

Tugging his shirt and suit jacket sleeve down to cover the bracelet that allowed him to teleport wherever he wanted to go, Ulrik turned the corner. And came to a stop.

Balladyn was across the way, standing with his arms crossed over his chest, his gaze locked on him. Ulrik walked to Taraeth's lieutenant and stopped a few feet away.

"Have a nice visit?" Balladyn asked.

Ulrik looked over the black pants and silk button-down shirt the Dark Fae wore. Balladyn's long silver and black hair was pulled back in a queue at the base of his neck. "I did, actually."

"Mikkel has already been to see the king today."

"That's nice." It was also expected after his uncle had seen him shift. No doubt Mikkel was trying to convince Taraeth to go against him. Ulrik would have to keep a close eye on the Dark King.

Balladyn dropped his arms and took a step closer. "What are you waiting for? You have your magic. Take Dreagan."

"It's no' just about taking Dreagan."

"Right," Balladyn said with a roll of his red eyes. "You want to kill Con."

Ulrik smiled. "I'm no' the only one plotting a coup."

Balladyn's eyes narrowed. "Watch yourself. You don't know what you're saying."

"My mistake. I was obviously wrong."

Ulrik had known for some time that Balladyn would

end Taraeth's reign. No one had been so close to the king in a long time, and, oddly enough, Taraeth trusted Balladyn. The fool.

That trust was going to get Taraeth killed. Though perhaps it was time for the Dark to have a new ruler. Ulrik had thought the same about the Light for the last century.

They stared at each other for a long minute before Balladyn said, "Your uncle seems pretty confident that he can beat you and Con."

"Is that so?"

Balladyn's red eyes burned brightly. "Taraeth has agreed to lead the Dark army to Dreagan alongside Mikkel."

"When?" Ulrik demanded. This new development changed everything.

"I don't know. Tell me how Mikkel thinks he can best you and go after Con."

Oddly enough, he almost told Balladyn about the Druid. "He thinks he can position me so that he determines when I attack Con."

"If you win, you'll be King of Kings. Mikkel still wouldn't be able to kill you."

Ulrik's mind went through every scenario—and each time, it came back to the Druid. That was Mikkel's trump card. "He obviously believes he can."

"So why not go after Con himself and kill you now?"

He frowned at Balladyn's words as a new scenario played out in his mind. "With the Dark army behind him, Mikkel can keep the Kings occupied and isolate Con."

"Only a Dragon King can kill another Dragon King."

"As part of my clan, he can challenge me for the right to be King of the Silvers. Which is why he'll have to kill me first."

"That can't happen."

What a curious development. Ulrik looked at the Dark Fae with new eyes. "I didna know you cared."

Balladyn's face scrunched in revulsion. "Don't make me gag. I simply chose the better of the two options."

"Me?" Ulrik was astounded.

"You're the rightful King of Silvers. Mikkel had his chance, but you were chosen over him."

Ulrik was beginning to wonder if he could have another ally in the Dark court besides Muriel. "Some would say that if Mikkel were stronger, he'd win."

"That's not how it works with the Kings."

"That's right," he said. "You know a lot about us from Rhi."

A muscle ticked in Balladyn's jaw. "I also learned a lot here."

"And Con? How do you feel about him?"

"I want to see him burn," Balladyn said through clenched teeth.

Ulrik's smile was slow. "I see we want the same things."

"I believe we do."

"So where does that leave us?"

Balladyn's chest expanded as he drew in a deep breath. "It means we have to trust each other."

"That isna something I do."

"Me either."

Ulrik lifted one shoulder in a shrug. "Then I suppose we're at an impasse."

"Whether you want to admit it or not, you're going to need me."

"I have a massive network of individuals who I can call on for help."

"Not here," Balladyn said with a cocky smile.

Damn if the Dark didn't have a point. Ulrik might get information from Muriel and her sister, but that was limited only to Mikkel. Balladyn would know the inner workings of the Dark court as well as Taraeth's plans.

"It galls you, doesn't it?" Balladyn asked.

He met the Dark's gaze. "I do what has to be done."

"Good. I also think I have a solution for our trust issue."

Ulrik raised a brow. "What's that?"

"Rhi."

The Fae was a constant source of surprise. Ulrik was intrigued. Had the beautiful Rhi finally let go of her King and moved on?

By the look on Balladyn's face, and his certainty that Rhi would help them, Ulrik determined the two were lovers. No surprise since Balladyn had been in love with Rhi for eons.

But did Rhi love Balladyn?

"Is she up for this?" Ulrik asked.

Balladyn gave a single nod. "I think so."

"You think she'll willingly go against everyone at Dreagan, those who she's risked her life for again and again? I doona think you know her as well as you believe you do."

Balladyn closed the distance between them until they were nose to nose. "What I know is that Rhi will help take down Mikkel."

"You want her in such a battle?"

The Dark took two steps back, his brow deeply furrowed. "No."

"None of the Light Fae or the Kings know of Mikkel. I'd like to keep it that way." Ulrik paused as he considered Balladyn's proposal and then followed his gut. "Leave Rhi out of this. We'll muddle through this trust thing on our own."

Balladyn's quick agreement told him that the Fae hadn't thought about what Rhi's involvement could mean—or how it might affect her—until that moment.

"There is a cabin in the hills of Italy. It's isolated. It used to be Rhi's."

Balladyn's demeanor changed as he raised his red eyes to glare at Ulrik. "You took over Rhi's sanctuary?"

"She abandoned it. Besides, no one else will know of it."

"And Rhi will never go back," Balladyn said, nodding.

Ulrik held out his hand. "To our new partnership."

"To getting rid of the past," Balladyn said, clasping Ulrik's hand.

CHAPTER THIRTY-SIX

Snow flurries danced in the air like little fairies while Faith pressed her back against a tree as her breath billowed around her.

She closed her eyes and pressed her palms to the tree's bark. It bit into her skin, grounding her to the here and now. Something that was becoming an issue.

One moment, she knew exactly who she was and what she was doing, and the next, she wasn't certain of anything. Something had been done to her, of that she was certain.

She lifted her left hand and looked at it. Nothing was broken. So had she dreamed that Dmitri crushed it? Had she imagined the bones snapping in half?

"No," she whispered.

It had happened. Though she had no explanation for how she'd healed. Dmitri had been certain on Fair Isle that she possessed no magic, and she knew he was right.

Her heart skipped a beat at the thought of him. She squeezed her eyes closed, but the tears gathered and fell anyway. How could she have finally opened herself to someone only to have it be *him*?!

One of the Dragon Kings. The ones who would rain

death and destruction down upon all humanity. The ones who were supposed to have fled this world.

The ones who would enslave mankind.

She opened her eyes and angrily dashed away her tears. He wasn't worth crying over. No man—or dragon—was.

Faith pushed away from the tree and started running. The woods would give her cover, but she was only a mortal who had no defense other than her mind and determination.

"It'll get me home."

She wasn't sure what would happen after that, but she knew she had to get off Dreagan quickly and back to Houston. With her arms pumping, she jumped over a fallen tree and maneuvered the rocky, sloping ground.

Since she spent the majority of her time in a sedate lifestyle, this exertion was taking a toll on her. Every few minutes, she had to stop and catch her breath.

She hid behind another tree and braced her hands on her knees as she drew in deep gulps of air. A stitch had started in her side.

How long would it take for them to notice that she was gone? She didn't hear any alarms being raised. Then she recalled the MI5 agents. It was too bad she hadn't gone to one of them. She could've led them straight into the mountain and to the Silvers, giving them what the agents hoped to find.

It's what the Kings deserved.

In the back of her mind, she heard a faint, "No."

Where had that come from? There was no answer, which only made her more apprehensive. The only way to stop all of it was to get away from the magic.

She started running again, blinking rapidly as the flurries landed on her eyelashes. With the stitch getting worse, she held her side and ran faster.

The forest seemed to go on forever, and the darkness

was making it difficult to see. She tripped over a root and fell face-first onto the cold, hard ground with a grunt.

Taking stock of her body, she pushed up on her hands and knees in the snow before getting to her feet. She was going to have to stop soon since she couldn't see.

She raised her gaze to the sky, hoping for a full moon. Instead, she saw only a half moon and too many clouds to help her.

This had to be the Dragon Kings' fault. They were using magic somehow to keep her in the forest, unable to get away.

It didn't matter if she was blinded, she would go on. She took a deep breath and started running again.

Dmitri found Faith's tracks easily enough. She appeared to move quickly and rest often. It would take him no time to catch up with her, but he wasn't sure what he might find when he did.

"Doona approach Faith," he told Roman through their link.

He had no idea where Rhi was, but he knew the Light Fae would alert him if she came upon Faith first. At least, he hoped Rhi would.

They still didn't know what had affected them, or why it continued to do so. Or why Shara had been knocked unconscious. He was truly frightened of what was going on.

To be taken over by something and have no memory of it was terrifying. The amount of magic that would take was staggering. Faith running away made her look guilty.

But if it was her, why hadn't he been affected on Fair Isle? Why had the magic waited until Dreagan? The realization dawned like a knife to his heart—whoever or whatever it was wanted to make sure the magic reached as many Kings as possible.

Dmitri slowed to a jog and then to a walk. Had Faith

really done that to him? To his brothers? Was it permanent? Not that it mattered, they would fight with every bit of power and dragon magic they had to counter it.

Ulrik was a devious son of a bitch, but this was a new low. He was giving them no choice. Instead, Ulrik had decided to use magic to turn them all to his way of thinking.

The humans didn't stand a chance. Ulrik was getting everything he wanted without having to lift a finger. Dmitri had to give him credit. It was a brilliant move. A shitty one, but brilliant all the same.

Dmitri was glad it was night. It would disorient Faith and give him one more advantage on top of his enhanced senses, speed, and magic.

He stood atop the hill and looked down into the valley below, his gaze locking on a form. Faith was moving close to the trees and holding her side. Roman walked up on Dmitri's left seconds before Rhi stood to his right.

"We need to surround her," Dmitri said.

Roman jerked his chin toward his side of the forest. "There's a good spot to corner her."

Dmitri nodded as he remembered it. "We need to move her in that direction."

"Easy enough," Rhi said. But she wasn't wearing a smile.

He looked at her, worried. "What is it?"

"Something I'll deal with once this thing with Faith is over."

It had to be serious to affect Rhi in such a way. She'd had that look in her eye since she'd remembered something in his room.

"Let's get going," Roman said and started running.

Rhi teleported away, leaving Dmitri alone. He walked down the hill, keeping his eyes on Faith. He knew the moment she realized she was being followed because she ran faster.

He left it up to Rhi and Roman to direct Faith toward the semi-circle mountain wall. It was a sheer barrier, connecting two of the mountains. She ran, stumbling right in the direction they wanted.

Dmitri was the one who entered the area after her. It was going to be up to him to talk her down. If he couldn't, he would have no choice but to use his power.

Faith couldn't believe she was trapped. They had maneuvered her right to this point, and she'd let them. This was her own damn fault.

She looked up at the vertical wall of mountain. There was no climbing it. A look on either side of her showed how it made a semi-circle shape. It was a perfect spot to corner someone.

There was no need to look behind her. She knew Dmitri would be there. No doubt, he would tell her everything was in her mind. But she knew the truth.

"Faith."

The sound of her name on his lips made her sigh. Then she reminded herself that he wasn't the man she thought he was. It was the image of him killing humans that she needed to keep in her mind.

She frowned, wondering when she had seen such a thing.

"Faith."

"What?" she asked over her shoulder.

"Look at me."

That was going to be a mistake. She knew it even before she did it. Yet she turned to him. All she saw was his shape in the darkness. She couldn't see his face or his eyes.

Then a soft blue light flared off to her left. It rose, growing larger as it moved to hang above them. When she looked back at Dmitri, his face was visible.

"I'm sorry," he said. "About your hand. You may no' believe me, but I doona remember any of it."

She fisted her cold hands and put them in the pockets of her coat. Her fingers brushed against the wooden dragon. She wrapped her fingers around it, holding it tightly. "So that did happen."

He nodded solemnly, his face contorted with anguish. "I'm ashamed to say that it did. Con healed you."

"At least there's that."

Dmitri swallowed and glanced down at the ground. "Something happened to me, Rhys, Kiril, and Con. We think it might have to do with the skeleton."

"You're lying," she said with a laugh. She wasn't sure how she knew, she just did.

"I'm no'. I hope it's the bones because the other alternative is that you're working with Ulrik."

At this, she started laughing. "Everything always comes back to him, doesn't it? You told me you had several enemies, and yet anytime something happens to you Kings, you immediately point to Ulrik."

"Because it's usually him."

She shrugged. "It matters not. I don't know Ulrik."

"He goes by many aliases. Let me show you a picture."

"No," she hastily said. "I don't want to see a picture or have anything else to do with any of you. I know what you are. I know what you're planning."

A woman stepped out of the shadows. She was gorgeous with thick black hair and shining silver eyes. "And just what are the Kings planning?"

"They will exterminate all humans," Faith said with a lift of her chin. It was a defiant move.

Dmitri was shaking his head. "You've got that wrong. We could've done it at the start, but we didna. Remember the story I told you? Remember how we sent our dragons away and hid?"

She thought back to the cave on Fair where Muscles had shared his story, enthralling her with each word. The image suddenly distorted into something she couldn't piece together.

"It's magic," Rhi said to Dmitri.

He blew out a breath. "Aye."

"Stop!" Faith yelled.

"I can no'," Dmitri said. "We need answers, and I think you might have them."

She held up her hand to stop him, only vaguely realizing that she had the wooden dragon clasped in her fingers. "Don't come any closer."

"No' your choice," said a male voice from her right. A moment later, another Dragon King stepped into the light.

No. She wouldn't go back with them. She wouldn't be their first kill, starting the war all over again. Her head swung to Dmitri.

It had to end. All of it had to end. Tonight.

She rushed him, her arm over her head, a scream of outrage on her lips. He stood his ground, not backing away. When she reached him, his hands gripped her arms.

When she plunged the knife into his heart, his eyes widened in surprise, shock, and grief.

Faith started laughing when she saw the blood running down his chest. She'd won. She'd done what no one else had the courage to do.

Because of it, she would end the reign of the Kings once and for all.

Her mind suddenly went blank. She couldn't form a single thought as she was dragged unconscious.

CHAPTER THIRTY-SEVEN

Faith's words tolled through the Dragonwood like a bell. Dmitri was too shocked to do anything but look at her. Then her face went slack and her eyes closed. He caught her against him. He looked into her face that no longer held malice and contempt, but the peace of sleep.

She had believed every word she'd uttered.

"That was . . . eerie," Rhi said.

Roman was silent as he walked to stand beside Dmitri. Then he said, "I have this peculiar feeling that this entire episode wasna coincidental."

"It reminds me of what could've happened with Ulrik and his woman," Dmitri said.

Rhi looked around. "Magic was at work here."

"No' dragon magic," Roman said.

"I'd like to know what made her pass out," Rhi replied, looking at the ground.

Roman snorted. "I'm just glad she did."

Dmitri lifted Faith in his arms and spotted what had caught Rhi's attention. In the snow was a small wooden carving of a dragon that looked exactly like Con.

"I thought Lily said it was just a carving," Roman said.

Rhi squatted beside the object but didn't touch it. "She did. It is. Yet only a few minutes ago, it was a knife."

The memory pierced his heart like no knife could. Dmitri would never forget that moment. The physical pain had been nothing compared to the feeling of his soul bellowing at the thought of Faith turning against him.

"We need to take it back to the manor," Roman said.

Rhi made a sound and lifted her gaze to him. "I saw what it does to the Fae. I'm not touching it."

"And that could be what set Dmitri and the others off," Roman said. "I'm no' touching it either."

Dmitri winced as his head began to throb again. "Someone has to."

"What is it?" Rhi asked as she looked up at him, frowning.

"My head. The last time this happened, I had some . . . no' so good thoughts about mortals."

Rhi pointed toward Dreagan. "Take her out of here."

"What if it's Faith?" Roman argued.

Dmitri turned around. "It's a chance I'll take."

"We'll be right behind you," Rhi called.

Dmitri didn't bother to reply. Both of them were more than competent to deal with the wooden dragon in some way. His concern was Faith and what had changed her. Because the woman who'd shoved the knife into his heart wasn't the same one he'd made love to on Fair—or even the one who had been in the mountain examining the skeleton.

Whatever had been done to her, he was going to find a way to reverse it. No matter what, no matter how long it took. He wouldn't give up.

With every step, his headache began to dissipate. By the time the manor came into view, his worry had turned into a slow burning rage—against Ulrik. Dmitri wanted to find him and tear him to pieces for what he'd done to Faith.

He had no doubt it was Ulrik because no one hated the Kings like Ulrik did. After the many times Ulrik had gone after a woman a King had been seen with, he was the obvious answer.

Dmitri saw Hal holding open the door at the side entrance and made his way there. The snow was falling quicker, as if the sky itself were crying over what had happened to Faith.

"You found her," Hal said with a nod, his moonlit blue eyes locked on Faith.

Dmitri shouldered past his friend. "Aye."

Without a word to anyone else, Dmitri walked up the stairs to his room. He entered to find Con standing inside. Con's stance was casual, but the fact that he didn't have his suit jacket on said he was prepared for anything. They shared a look before Dmitri laid Faith upon the bed.

"Shara has woken," Con said.

That was a relief, at least. "Good."

"I take it by the blood on your shirt that things didna go well?"

Before he could answer, Roman and Rhi walked into the room. Roman said, "You could say that."

Dmitri looked at them to find a small sphere hovering before Rhi that confined the wooden dragon. "Is it contained?"

"Oh, yes," she said with a nod. "It's filled with magic, but I've made sure it won't leak out from the field around it."

Roman looked askance at it. "I'd feel better if we destroyed it."

"No' until we learn how it was made and why," Con said.

Shara and Kiril walked into the room then. Shara's gaze went to the orb as a shudder went through her. "We need to get that far away from all of us."

"What happened when you touched it?" Dmitri asked.

Her silver gaze moved to him. "I heard screams. Horrible chilling screams. In a blink, I was consumed by anger so terrible that I literally shook from it. Then it felt as if someone passed through me."

"Well, I won't be touching it," Rhi said, looking at the object with distaste.

Kiril put an arm around Shara. "We still doona know what it's for."

"Actually, I think we do," Roman said as she pointed to Dmitri.

Dmitri looked down at the blood on his shirt. "Have any of you ever thought what might've happened had we no' prevented Ulrik's woman from attempting to kill him?"

"Nay," Kiril said.

Con put his hands in his pant's pockets. "Aye."

Dmitri looked at Con and released a breath. Most of them had put what had happened with Ulrik out of their minds after he was banished because it was too painful. But it stood to reason that Con would continue to go over everything again and again while also looking at other scenarios for the way things could've gone.

"Faith drew that wooden dragon from her pocket," Dmitri told everyone. "Then she said that she wouldna go back with us. That she wouldna be our first kill, starting the war all over again."

He paused, still reeling from the hatred in her sherry eyes. "She said it had to end. All of it had to end. Tonight. Then she charged me. That dragon suddenly had a blade attached, and she plunged it into my chest."

The room was silent as death. Dmitri swung his head to the bed to look at Faith, who hadn't so much as stirred since she fell unconscious.

"That sounds like it was another person," Kiril said. "No' the Faith I met earlier."

Roman crossed his arms over his chest. "Unless this is the real Faith, and the earlier one was the fake."

"No," Dmitri said. "I spent days with her. What happened tonight wasna her."

Con removed his dragon head cufflinks and put them in his pocket before he rolled up the sleeves of his dress shirt. "This reeks of Ulrik."

"He didna use his magic because I didna sense dragon magic," Dmitri stated.

Con shrugged indifferently. "He has a legion of people that he can use. We saw what he does with Druids. Darcy unknowingly helped him release his magic, draining hers in the process. It wouldna surprise me to learn that he has other Druids willing to help him."

"I felt Fae magic," Rhi said.

Everyone looked at her. Dmitri said, "You didna mention that before."

"I knew I didn't feel dragon magic, but the rest . . . it was difficult to determine," she replied.

Con asked, "Why?"

"Because there are several different kinds of magic being used."

Shara began nodding earnestly. "Yes. That makes sense now after what I experienced."

"Great," Dmitri said. "How do we fix what it's done to us?"

Rhi turned the orb so she could look at the carving. "That would be easier to determine if we knew exactly what this was for."

"You mean who it was truly meant for," Con said.

She met his gaze and inclined her head. "Yes."

"The skeleton Faith found was one of my dragons," Dmitri said. "It was on Fair Isle, which was part of my domain. Con sent me there, and I interacted with Faith. It was meant for me."

Kiril scratched his cheek. "That's a possibility. It wouldna be a big stretch to determine that Con would send you to Fair Isle since the dragon was yours."

"Or that Dmitri would bring the remains back to Dreagan," Shara pointed out.

Dmitri didn't like anything he was hearing. "We willna know until we ask Ulrik."

"As if he'd tell us," Roman said with a snort.

That was true, but Dmitri could be persuasive. "We need answers."

"That willna come from Ulrik," Con stated. "We deal with this on our own. Now, we've been in this room with both Faith and the carving, and none of us have . . ."

"Gone crazy," Roman offered.

Con cut him a look. "Aye. For lack of a better word."

"Then it could be the skeleton," Kiril said.

Dmitri shook his head. "I was around the bones for days and felt nothing out of the ordinary."

"But did you no' tell Rhys you felt something odd when you pulled up the bones?" Kiril asked.

"I did," Dmitri admitted.

Con's brow puckered. "What did it feel like?"

"Like something wasna quite right."

"That could be anything," Rhi said.

Kiril nodded to the orb. "But it wasna. Look what came to Dreagan."

"Oh, you found it," Faith said as she sat up.

Dmitri watched as she put her hand to her head and swung her legs over the side of the bed. "Found what?" he asked.

She gave him an odd look as if she didn't understand why he wasn't getting what she said. She pointed to the wooden dragon. "The carving. I found it in the ground where the skeleton was."

"Why did you no' say anything?" he demanded in a soft tone.

She raised a brow as she rubbed her temples. "Because we were in a hurry to leave. I put it in my pocket and forgot about it."

"What do you remember?" Con asked her.

Faith looked at him, then at the others around the room. Her hands dropped to her lap, and then her gaze lowered to the hand Dmitri had crushed. "I remember coming here. I remember Dmitri taking me to the Silvers."

"And . . ." Dmitri pressed.

She met his gaze. "I remember examining the skeleton and finding the chipped vertebrae that showed us that the dragon had its spine severed. Then you crushed my hand."

He'd hoped that was something she had forgotten. No such luck. "I wasna myself then. I'm sorry for that."

"It's healed," she said as if only just now realizing that.

Dmitri pointed to his right. "Con healed you."

"Thank you," she told Con. Her gaze moved around the room to the others. "Why do I feel like everyone is in here because of me?"

Dmitri was struggling to find a way to tell her.

Then she asked, "And why do you have blood on your shirt?"

It was Rhi who came to his aid. She motioned to the orb and the wooden dragon inside. "We believe this little fellow had something to do with that."

"It's just a carving," Faith said with a chuckle. But her smile died and she looked to Dmitri. "Tell me. I need to know."

He swallowed and took a deep breath. Kiril then handed him a mobile phone with Ulrik's picture on it. Dmitri showed it to Faith. "Have you ever seen this man?"

"Never," she replied immediately.

He handed the mobile back to Kiril. "I doona remember hurting you. I doona recall what I said. Kiril, Rhys, and Con all had an episode, as well."

"You're telling me I had one," Faith said.

He hesitated because he wasn't sure how she would take the news. He felt like shite for hurting her when he was supposed to be protecting her.

"Just give it to me," she said. "Like a bandage being ripped off. It's better to just say it."

Dmitri looked into clear, sherry-colored eyes. This was the woman he'd known at Fair Isle, the woman who had captured his attention and made him ache.

This was the woman who had smiled and laughed with him, who had cried out in pleasure and gazed at him in wonder. This was the true Faith.

"You tried to kill me."

CHAPTER THIRTY-EIGHT

"I'm sorry. What?" Faith asked, flabbergasted.

Had Dmitri just said that she had tried to kill him? That couldn't be right. She'd never even thought about committing murder before, much less attempted it.

And with Dmitri? That would be ludicrous.

"You're a Dragon King. I couldn't kill you even if I wanted to," she said.

Dmitri's lips twisted. "I felt the blade. Wielded by your hand."

"Why don't I remember that?"

"The same reason none of us recall our episodes," Con said.

Faith looked at the two women. Both had silver eyes and black hair, but one had a thick silver stripe near her face. If she had to guess, they were Fae. The one with the sphere looked familiar, as if Faith had seen her before.

"You think you know me?" the Fae asked.

Faith nodded and replied, "It's like I recognize you, but I can't place why or from where."

"A little while ago, I was with Dmitri and Roman as we cornered you in the Dragonwood."

"Oh." She was mortified. Faith didn't even want to know everything she'd said, but what could be worse than attempted murder?

"Rhi," Dmitri admonished.

Faith waved away his words. "No, she's right to tell me. I have to know."

He blew out a breath. Then he pointed to the Fae near Rhi, "That's Shara, and on the other side of her and Kiril is Roman."

After a nod to each of them, Faith moved her gaze back to the wooden dragon encased in the orb hanging midair. "Are you telling me that someone put that carving with the skeleton, knowing that it would take many thousands of years to be uncovered?"

"Aye," Dmitri answered. "It looks that way."

"That makes no sense." She gazed at it with worry. "That means whoever planned this was patient enough to wait. If it wasn't activated until it was unearthed, then they took a chance that someone other than a Dragon King would come in contact with it. Not to mention, there was no guarantee it would end up on Dreagan."

A grin lifted the corner of Dmitri's lips. "Scientific?"

"Logic," she replied, unable to hide her own grin.

Dmitri's smile faded as he ran a hand over his jaw. "We hadna bound Ulrik's magic yet, but he was busy attacking the mortals with the four Silvers that remained with him."

Rhi rolled her eyes. "Haven't I already told you that I didn't feel any dragon magic?"

"Ulrik would've had to move quickly," Con said. "Having just had his magic bound and being banished from Dreagan, he would've had to make his way to Fair Isle and take down a dragon."

Kiril said, "The dragons would've recognized him."

"He could've done it," Dmitri said. "All of it except one crucial part. I searched those isles twice. I would've found Ulrik and the dragon had they been hiding there."

Roman crossed his arms over his chest. "So someone used magic to prevent that."

Rhi wrinkled her nose. "Which means it wasn't Ulrik."

"Then who?" Con asked.

Dmitri ran a hand down his face. "Someone who did all of that, then put enough magic into a carving—which looks a lot like Con with the body of the dragon—and waited for it to be found."

All eyes turned to Faith. She'd been listening with interest as they pieced it together. She was the outsider there, the one who was only just now learning the stories of the Dragon Kings.

"What?" she asked.

Con asked, "How did you know to look in that cave?"

Her normal answer wasn't going to suffice. She clasped her hands together. "I don't really have an explanation. As I've told Dmitri, I'm a student of science. I didn't believe in magic or someone's 'gut feeling' until after I met him and saw who he was. What he was."

She stopped and swallowed, her gaze lowering to the floor. "But every time I think of finding the dragon, I have no answer. I chose Fair because there were so many archeological digs on the island. There wasn't anything in particular I was looking for when I chose it, which was odd. I had a map of the isle, and looked at all the different cliffs and places where the caves were.

"I went for a walk on the beach and looked up. Right at the cave. I told my assistant we needed to look in that one. It was my 'gut feeling,' and in truth, it scared me. Right up until we went inside and I found the skeleton."

Faith raised her gaze to find everyone looking at her.

It was disconcerting, but they wanted answers. She could only hope she could tell them enough that it would help.

She knew she wasn't one of Ulrik's pawns, but she had no proof to show. Dmitri's blood-soaked shirt was confirmation that she hadn't been in control of herself.

Surely Tamir would've told her if something like that had happened before. So if the first occurrence was at Dreagan, then what did that mean?

If only her head would stop hurting, she might be able to think clearly. She rubbed her temples, wishing for some aspirin.

"What is it?" Dmitri asked.

She gave a shake of her head. "It's this headache. It won't stop."

"My head begins to pound right before the anger sets in," he said to the others.

Kiril's lips compressed. "As does mine."

"Make that three of us," Con said.

Faith jerked when Con moved to sit beside her. "Sorry," she mumbled. Con had never hurt her, but the reaction had been involuntary.

"It's fine." His smile, though kind, didn't reach his black eyes.

She had the absurd notion to ask him if he'd ever truly been happy. Then she realized the answer to that was probably yes, before the dragons had to be sent away. So she kept her mouth shut.

"I can help," Con told her and held out his hand.

She looked at it for a second before placing her hand in his. Almost instantly, the pounding in her head subsided. The relief was so great that she closed her eyes and sighed.

"Thank you."

Con patted her hand and returned it to her lap before he rose. "My pleasure."

Now that she no longer felt pain, Faith was able to look at the situation with a clear head. She opened her eyes, focusing on the wooden dragon.

"You've ruled out Ulrik in accomplishing this feat, correct?" she asked.

Dmitri made a sound at the back of his throat. "It looks that way."

"You said it wasna Ulrik in the woods," Roman said.

Rhi's eyes widened. "That's right. She did."

Faith really hated that she didn't recall any of what they claimed. "Then if it isn't Ulrik, who else could it be?"

"The Dark?" Kiril asked.

Shara shook her head. "That means they would have to work with a Druid."

"They would if that Druid were a *drough*," Rhi pointed out. "Evil always helps evil. The problem with that scenario is that I sensed both Light and Dark magic, as well as Druid magic from both a *mie* and a *drough*."

Dmitri let out a soft whistle. "Four sects of magic. The good and bad of two races. This wasna done lightly."

"It was intentional. And directed at Con," Rhi said.

Faith's eyes moved to Con, and she took a closer look. The King of Kings wasn't anything like she'd expected. He was gorgeous, yes, just like Rhys, Kiril, and Roman, but there was something else about him.

Con dressed immaculately in custom-made suits. He was tall and well formed with his golden blond hair. He kept cool and calm under strain. And while his black eyes were as emotionless as his face, it was the power within that drew others to him.

"The group wasna verra smart if they were coming after me," Con said. "Half of them are dead."

Dmitri's frown was deep as he said, "A new enemy? Now?"

"Is there a perfect time to learn we have another adversary?" Roman asked.

Kiril looked at Roman, nodding. "Good point."

"I get that," Shara said. "But Fae and Druids combining magic? I've never heard of it before."

Rhi turned her head to Shara. "Are you sure? Think back. Your family is one of the most powerful of the Dark. Can you remember hearing anything?"

"Need I remind you that I was locked away for a huge portion of time," Shara stated.

Faith almost asked what had happened, but by the way Kiril kissed his wife's forehead to soothe her, she decided it wasn't a good time. So Shara had been Dark but turned Light. How fascinating.

"We can talk to Darcy," Roman said.

Dmitri perked up at that. "She's part of the Skye Druids. They'll know."

"Why?" Faith asked.

Con said, "There have been Druids on the Isle of Skye from the verra first time a mortal found magic. As Dreagan houses magic, so does Skye. The Druids there may have answers for us."

"They're going to want to see this," Rhi said and motioned to the orb.

Faith looked at the dragon. "I could take samples of the wood to carbon date it."

"No one is touching it," Con said in a voice as chilly as the north.

"I think we need to be sure that object is what is causing all this hoopla," Faith pointed out.

Roman snorted. "I saw the blade come out of it when you raised it over your head."

"All right," she admitted with a nod. "What if that isn't the only thing that was imbued with magic?"

Dmitri raised a brow. "You mean the skeleton?"

Faith looked into his azure eyes. "Yes."

"As strong as a Druid or Fae—or even a combination—is, they are no' more powerful than dragon magic," Dmitri said.

She considered his words and then asked, "Even a dragon that was dying?"

"She's got a point," Con said.

"I'll check out the bones." Roman turned and walked out.

Kiril said, "I'll help him."

"We doona need another enemy," Dmitri stated.

Con withdrew something from his pocket. Faith saw a flash of gold in his hand as he turned it over and over with his fingers. She finally glimpsed the cufflinks—dragon heads.

"We doona have a choice," Con said.

Rhi tapped her toe on the wooden floor, her silver eyes narrowed on the globe. "None of this is coincidence."

"You think whoever did this is still alive?" Faith asked in surprise.

Rhi raised a black brow and looked at her. "I've seen stranger things."

"But humans aren't immortal," she contended.

Dmitri and Con exchanged a look before Muscles said, "They are if they're mated to a Dragon King."

"Right." That wasn't something Faith was likely to forget. "But you told me they die if their King is killed. So that rules out any mates."

Rhi winced. "Um. Actually, there was another way. The Druids of MacLeod Castle. Isla put a shield around the castle hiding it from view and protecting everyone inside. As long as they stayed within the wards, they were immortal."

"Until I gave them rings filled with dragon magic that allowed them to be immortal regardless if they were inside the shield or no'," Con said.

Faith looked at each of them. "You mean Ronnie? She would never do anything like this."

"None of those at MacLeod Castle would," Rhi said. "But there are other Druids."

Faith wrapped her arms around herself. It seemed that the Dragon Kings couldn't win no matter what they did. And where exactly did that leave her?

CHAPTER THIRTY-NINE

Dmitri felt a new kind of anger within him. He glanced at Faith, his gut twisting in fear and rage. "Are you saying that someone intentionally put Faith in danger?"

"We're speculating," Con said.

Rhi snorted. "Speak for yourself."

"There's no proof," Con argued.

But Dmitri knew that the confirmation was in the magic. "If you hadna put that wooden dragon within a force field, there's no telling what we would've done to each other or someone else."

"Dragon, human, or Fae," Faith said, her gaze on the floor as her face was filled with remorse.

"Nothing said or done was what any of you truly believe, correct?" Shara asked.

Dmitri nodded. "Correct."

"Someone wanted to force another war," Con said tightly.

Faith raised her gaze. "Who would benefit from another dragon and human war?"

"Fae," Rhi and Con said in unison.

Rhi then shrugged. "But only if the mortals won."

"That wouldna happen," Dmitri replied.

Con crossed his arms over his chest. "Nay, it wouldna. Which means this once again turns back to Ulrik."

"But you ruled him out as being a part of this," Faith said.

Dmitri ran a hand down his face. "We're going in circles with no answer. We know Ulrik wasna part of setting this up. The timeline doesna work."

"And we know that Fae and Druid magic are interwoven," Shara said.

Con turned his gaze to Rhi and frowned. "What is it? What do you see?"

Dmitri looked to the Light Fae to find her staring at the orb that hovered before her. Her silver eyes were startlingly bright as she put her hands on either side of the sphere just short of actually touching it.

The globe began to crackle before tiny bolts zigzagged from within it to her hands. She didn't seem fazed by it. Then she began to glow.

"Rhi," Dmitri called.

If she heard him, she didn't respond. The glowing increased, as did the bolts running back and forth between her hands and the sphere until it was difficult to tell where one ended and the other began.

Shara reached over and tried to grab Rhi, only to be zapped in the process. Shara gasped, jerking her hand back and moving away.

It was Con who lowered his voice and said, "Rhi."

She blinked and looked at Con. The glowing faded, as did the electrical currents.

"What the hell were you doing?" he demanded.

Rhi tilted her head, studying him. Her gaze then slid to Faith. "This was a beacon. One designed specifically for you."

Dmitri clenched his jaw. No. This couldn't be happening. Not to Faith. "You must be wrong."

"I'm not." Rhi turned her eyes to him. "I felt it. I saw it. It wasn't just digging up the skeleton that activated the carving. It was her touch."

Faith's eyes grew round. "How? I don't understand."

"The how is the easy part," Con said. "Your ancestors."

Dmitri shook his head. "Stop."

"No," Faith said. "I want to know. I want to get to the bottom of this."

"I doona. I'm a fighter. I've battled many things in my life, and I know I'll clash with many more."

"You can't fight my battles," she said.

"Why no'?" he demanded. He shot a hateful glare at the wooden dragon. "That . . . *thing* . . . didna just affect you. It touched others here."

"But I started it," she maintained.

Con returned his hand to his pocket. "You didna have a choice. It called you to it. You didna know it at the time, which puts everything you did after out of your control."

"She's a descendant," Rhi said. "That means something."

"Every fucking mortal on this planet is a descendant of the first humans!" Dmitri bellowed. Then he clutched his hands into fists to control his anger.

Faith swallowed hard, breaking the silence. She watched Rhi and Con exchange a look before she looked at Dmitri. He shook his head and glared at the hated orb.

"It's been a long day," Con said.

Rhi gave the sphere a cutting look. "With a lot of wacky stuff going on."

"Exactly," Con said with a nod. "Let's take a few hours to mull all of this over and attack it with clearer heads later."

Dmitri turned away to look into the fire as the others filed out of the room. He was disgusted with everything, including his inability to protect Faith. The one thing he'd always been good at was protecting others, and he was useless now.

As soon as he felt her arms come around him from behind, the tension in his muscles began to lessen. Then she rested her head against his back.

"Stop blaming yourself," she said.

He braced his arms against the mantel and hung his head. "We've another enemy. As if we doona have enough to contend with. But that I can deal with. It's you unwittingly being brought into this that has me tied in knots."

"I know I'm only human with no magical ability, but I'm not weak, Muscles. I can handle this."

He smiled despite everything. Then he dropped his arms and turned to face her. His hands cupped her face, and he looked into her sherry eyes. "Aye. I know you can."

"So stop worrying about me," she told him. "Rhi has that thing contained. Let's get to the bottom of why I was involved."

"And who put it all together," he finished.

Her smile was bright. "Exactly. Turn that vengeful fire inside you to those who deserve it. Not on yourself."

The truth of everything became clear in that moment. Perhaps he'd known before, but he hadn't been ready to accept it . . . to feel it. Until then.

"What?" she asked, a frown puckering her brow.

"I made a point of only taking Fae as lovers. I believed that becoming entangled with a mortal would only complicate things."

Her eyes dimmed. "Oh."

"I tell you that so you'll understand how profoundly you've touched my life. I can no' imagine it without you. You didna just open my eyes, but my soul, as well. I think

I stayed away from humans because I was waiting for you."
He smiled as he caressed her cheek. "Because I love you."

As the seconds ticked by without a response, he wanted
to bellow his fury. Instead, he remained beside her, touching her.

It was the first time he'd ever told a woman such words,
and though he hadn't planned it out, he had hoped for a
reply in some fashion.

Maybe that was the problem. He hadn't planned it. If
he had, he could've given her the flowery words women
needed. He could've come up with a better way to tell her
of his love and let her know how deeply she was embed-
ded in his heart.

But her message was loud and clear. He lowered his
arms, intending to leave her alone. As he turned away, she
grabbed his hand. His head jerked to her, hope springing
anew.

"So you drop something like that on me and then
leave?" she asked.

He swallowed, wondering what the correct response
was. "I . . . I." he paused and swallowed again. "I had to
tell you of my feelings."

"Then let me tell you of mine."

By the way she wouldn't meet his gaze, he wasn't so
sure he wanted to hear them. But he was a Dragon King.
He would stand before her and listen to all she said, no
matter how it might tear at his heart.

Because he loved her.

She released his hand and clasped hers together. Her
shoulders rose as she took a deep breath before slowly
releasing it. "I never wanted relationships. I saw that some
worked, but most didn't. I was too young to see the heartache my mother went through when my father left. But
him walking out left a scar upon her heart that never
healed.

"She didn't turn her back on love, despite what he'd done. She looked for it, hoped for it. Yet time and again, I witnessed how love let her down. My mother deserved to find happiness more than anyone I knew. She searched for it, and I actively ran from it."

Dmitri dropped his gaze to the floor. He didn't need to hear more. He knew exactly where this was going.

She said, "I was happy. Everything in my life was just where I wanted it. Then I went to Fair Isle and found the dragon. There was a feeling swirling in my gut that told me things were about to change.

"I'm a woman of science, so I disregarded it. I ignored Tamir's feelings, and didn't heed Ronnie's words of warning. Then you arrived."

He looked up to find her eyes on him. He couldn't tell what she was thinking or feeling, and he hated it.

"You protected me. You watched over me. Then you saved my life. I saw you. The real you. And I wanted you."

He searched her face, trying to determine if that was good or bad.

"In your arms, I found pleasure and ecstasy. I found myself. With that, I was able to look at this new world you showed me with fresh eyes. And I wanted you."

He fought to keep from reaching for her, dragging her against him and claiming her mouth.

"I killed a Dark. I watched you shift into a dragon. And I wanted you."

Their eyes locked, heat and desire coiled between them.

"You brought me to Dreagan. You showed me the Silvers. And I wanted you."

He moved closer, unable to stay away.

"I was affected by magic, and you saved me again. And I ached for you."

He could barely breathe as he watched her.

"I learned that I was somehow involved with this new

enemy. I saw you try to protect me once more. Then I heard your words. And I ached for you.

"I tell you all of this, so you'll understand when I say I love you, it comes from the depths of my soul."

Dmitri yanked her against him and plundered her lips savagely, the hunger consuming them both. Her nails clawed at his back through his shirt while he ground his arousal against her.

The pleasure and joy were so dazzling and deep that they engulfed him. She loved him.

She loved him!

"Say it again," she said between kisses.

He moaned. "I love you."

"And I love you."

Lifting her, he carried her to the bed. With a knee upon the mattress, he slowly lowered her. Her answering moan made his balls tighten.

He lifted his head to look down at her. "I want you as my mate. I know it might be too much right now—"

"It's not," she interrupted.

His smile was slow. "You'll be mine?"

"I've been yours since you arrived on Fair. And you've been mine since that first kiss."

"Nay, love. I was yours from the moment I returned to Fair."

Her fingers threaded through his dark hair. "I never thought I could be this happy. I didn't know this kind of delirious bliss was even possible."

"Anything is possible."

"I realize that now. I'll still look at things scientifically, though."

"I wouldna have it any other way," he said and placed a kiss on her lips.

She smiled, her arms wrapping around his neck. "This will work. We will work."

"I know."

She scraped her fingers across the stubble of his cheek. "We'll find this new enemy. I'll not be used as a pawn. I've made my choice in this war."

This was no mere mortal in his arms. Faith was a warrior. He'd never been more proud to have a human in his heart and his bed than in that moment. "You're mine."

"And you're mine," she said before bringing his head down for another kiss.

CHAPTER FORTY

Con closed the door to Dmitri's room behind him. He didn't need to be told that Faith was Dmitri's mate. It was clear, even to him.

"What now?" Shara asked as they stood in the hallway.

Rhi nodded toward the stairs. "Ask them."

Roman and Kiril stopped before them. Roman shrugged. "There's nothing. The bones are fine."

"So it *is* that," Con said, looking at the wooden dragon.

For the first time, he honestly hated a dragon. Which, he guessed, was the point. This new enemy wanted him to hate them because they detested dragons. Made even more evident by fashioning the piece to look like him.

"Ryder," Roman said. "He can start tracing Faith's ancestors."

Shara added, "I'll do more digging and see what I can find about Fae mixing magic with a Druid."

"I'll let the others know of this new enemy," Kiril said.

Con waited until the three departed before he looked to Rhi. "What are you going to do with that?"

She shrugged and turned, heading toward his office. He followed because he'd intended to go there anyway. The longer the orb was around him, the more irritated he became.

"You want it gone," Rhi said.

He gave a nod as he walked around his desk and sat. "I do."

"So do I." Rhi closed the door and leaned back against it. "I could destroy it, but it's going to take a lot."

"Can you take it to another realm?"

She twisted her lips, looking at the sphere. "Probably, but I don't think we should yet. The information we seek about those responsible is held within that piece of wood. If you want to find them, we can't destroy this."

That wasn't what he wanted to hear. For once, couldn't it be good news?

He rose and went to the sideboard where he poured himself a glass of whisky, tossing it back in one swallow. Another enemy. No matter what they did, they angered someone.

"You've not asked for my opinion, nor will you," Rhi said. "But I'm going to give it anyway."

He poured another drink and turned to face her. "You're going to say this is my fault."

"I'm not placing blame on anyone. I will tell you that you need to find this enemy soon. Ulrik hid in the shadows for too long, doing untold damage. If you don't put a stop to one of these enemies, they might join forces."

"We're protectors of this realm."

She pushed away from the wall and stalked to him, leaving the orb behind. She jabbed a finger in his shoulder. "Stop. Be a protector of Dreagan and your Kings. And yourself. You can't protect anyone until you have your own affairs in order."

He drank the whisky and set the empty glass aside to look into her silver eyes. "Mortals will be killed."

"So will Fae. So will Kings. This new foe is powerful."

"I can no' divide my time between Ulrik, the Dark, and this new enemy. Ulrik can attack at any time. I need to be ready."

She lifted her chin. "I'll look into it."

Immediately, he was suspicious. "What are you no' telling me?"

"Oh, puh-leeze," she said dramatically, rolling her eyes. "I try to do you a favor, and you think I have an ulterior motive.

Con stared, waiting.

She sighed, becoming serious. "Fine. I'll tell you that my motives have nothing to do with the Kings. This is about me. I need to do something, to feel a part of something."

"What of your people?"

"They don't need me."

He raised a brow. "Are you sure of that. What of the Reapers?"

"I can't do anything if I can't find them."

"You know something."

Rhi hesitated, glancing to her right. "Call it a hunch."

There was more she wasn't telling him, but he decided not to press. The Reapers weren't a threat—so far. He'd keep his ear to the ground about them, but until they were an enemy, he would back off.

"All right," Con agreed. "Look into which Fae might be involved."

"And the Druids."

He slowly nodded. "And the Druids."

"We need to look into Faith, as well. The fact that she heard the beacon means there is something in her past."

"Meaning what? A Druid?"

"Or a Fae."

Con walked to his desk. "Ryder can only go so far with the records he has access to."

"I can pick up where he runs out of information, especially if it's Fae," she said.

He couldn't believe he was willingly working with Rhi for the second time. Especially when the issue with-Usaeil hadn't been resolved.

"You can find out information on the Light, but no' the Dark."

She hastily glanced away. "That's not entirely true."

"Meaning?"

"I have an . . . ally."

He didn't like where this was going. "A Dark ally, you mean."

She lifted one shoulder. "Call it what you will. I can get answers."

"Who is your source?"

"Does it matter?"

"I want to know who to go to if something happens to you."

She gave him a seductive smile and fanned herself. "Oh, Con. I didn't know you cared that much," she said in a Southern accent.

He sank into his chair, annoyed. But that is what Rhi did when she didn't want to discuss something. She deflected. The idea of her having a Dark ally caused a significant amount of concern. "Who is it?"

"You need to learn to loosen up."

"You're stalling because you doona want to tell me."

"All right," she said. "Maybe I don't want to tell you."

It was something he'd heard Rhys say that gave him the idea to ask, "Is it Balladyn?"

She went still, which was all the answer he needed.

"Rhi. He kidnapped you, tortured you."

"I know," she replied.

He sat back in his chair, truly worried. The bond between the two Fae hadn't been severed despite everything—and that could spell trouble down the road. "You broke the Chains of Mordare that held you, but you never broke away from him, did you?"

"I tried to outrun him, and then I stopped caring if he caught me."

"And?" He shouldn't ask. He knew better. It was always wiser to stay out of someone's private life, but if she was going to be helping him, he had to know where she stood—in all things.

In other words, was she turning Dark?

"You really want the truth?" she asked.

"I wouldna have asked otherwise."

She moved to the two chairs and sat. "I fight the darkness inside me every day. Balladyn released it, allowed it to grow stronger while he held me captive. I hated him for what he did, and then I just got tired of running from him and who I might be turning into."

Con didn't utter a word, because if he did, he knew Rhi wouldn't tell him anything else.

"When Balladyn caught up with me, I went with him. But he didn't take me back to his compound or even to the Dark Palace. We went to the desert. We talked, and it continued that way for a while. I found myself turning to him for help. And he gave it. Then he told me that he'd been in love with me since he and my brother were friends."

Con had always known Balladyn carried a torch for Rhi, but he hadn't realized it was actually love. That changed . . . everything.

Rhi met his gaze. "I trust him with my life."

"He wants you to become Dark."

"He does, but I've already told him I won't do it."

Con lowered his eyes to his desk. What he didn't need to ask was if they were lovers. The confirmation was in the way she spoke about Balladyn. She protected him.

"Balladyn will help me," she stated.

Con looked at her and asked, "Even if it ultimately helps us?"

"Yes."

"I hope you're right, because regardless of the Fae you knew and were friends with—or the Fae you're sharing your bed with now—there is one fact that can no' be denied. He's Dark. Never forget their nature."

"You think I need a reminder?" she asked, her silver eyes flashing in anger.

He regarded her for a moment. "There was a time you would've never considered looking twice at a Dark."

"Things change. *I* changed."

"Aye, you have. We all have, but the core of who we are doesna alter so drastically."

She leaned forward, putting her hands on his desk. "You have no idea what I endured in that dungeon. You have no idea what it felt like."

"You're right, I doona. But I saw you. I came to free you."

The look on her face said she didn't quite believe him—not that he expected her to. There was too much history between them, too many centuries of strife and divide.

He'd often wondered if she'd broken the chains because she'd already been working on them, her magic growing with her anger. Or if it was him saying her name that did it.

Could it be the hatred between them that had caused it? Had the sound of his voice sent her over the edge that day? And did it really matter? She was free. Changed, but free.

As he looked into her eyes, her long, black hair falling over one shoulder, he wondered what her reaction would have been if Balladyn hadn't taken her prisoner.

The one thing Con was sure of—Rhi wouldn't be Balladyn's lover now.

"Has my new . . . association . . . made you doubt me?" she asked, steel in her eyes.

"Nay."

"Good. Then it doesn't matter who I take to my bed."

He slowly exhaled. "He's Dark."

"And she's the fekking queen."

"You might trust Balladyn, but what if Taraeth discovers you two? He'll no' stand for it. You'll once more be captured, but by Taraeth this time."

There was a flare of doubt in her gaze. "Balladyn wouldn't let that happen."

"Because he'll be the next King of the Dark?"

She shrugged. "The Dark change kings often."

That was a fact, but Taraeth had ruled longer than any other. He wouldn't go down easily. Con didn't need to tell her that. Rhi was well aware.

"Your concern for me is sweet, but I've always taken care of myself just fine," she replied.

He decided to shift their conversation since they were getting nowhere fast. "How long do you think it'll take you to find the Light and Dark who were involved with targeting us?"

"It shouldn't be long." She sat back in the chair. "When are we going to deal with Usaeil?"

"Soon."

"The sooner, the better, Con. If you don't do something, she's going to."

He raised a brow. "You mean worse than she already has? She's all but told the Light."

"You think you know her, but you don't. She cares about nothing but her own desires now."

"Sounds like the Dark," he said.

"I know."

CHAPTER FORTY-ONE

The tides of change had left their mark, cutting a deep trail that would forever alter Faith's path. She stood with Dmitri and watched the sun rise above the mountains. They had slept little, preferring to spend the hours making love.

But the ripples of their actions from the day before were still causing devastation.

"It's going to be fine," he said.

She rested her head back against him as his arms tightened around her from behind. "I hope so, but I have my doubts. I was a pawn. All these years, I didn't believe in destiny and Fate. I believed that each person made their own decisions. And the entire time, someone made sure I walked a certain path to put me exactly where I am."

"I doona regret where you are."

She turned to face him and smiled. "I don't regret it either. What infuriates me is that I was part of something much bigger. Something that could affect you."

"Then be a part of something even bigger than this Druid/Fae magic. Be a part of us striking it down."

"Now *that* I like," she said and rose up to place a quick kiss on his lips. "Let's go see what we can find."

"Are you sure you really want to do this?"

She nodded and took his hand as she walked to the door. "I am."

As they strolled to the computer room, Dmitri said, "I doona want to wait too long for us to be mated."

"Let's do it today."

He halted and looked at her. Slowly, a smile formed. "I'd like that verra much, but there is more that goes into it than that."

"Is it a big ceremony?"

"Aye. Every Dragon King is in attendance."

"All but Ulrik, you mean."

Dmitri looked away briefly, a glower forming. "That's right."

"We can do the ceremony whenever you want. I'm not going anywhere, Muscles."

He wrapped an arm around her and nuzzled her neck. Then he raised his head. "What of your work?"

That was one thing she hadn't been thinking of. Now that he'd brought it up, she didn't have an answer. "I don't know. Can I still be an archeologist?"

"I'd never forbid such a thing."

"Maybe Ronnie and I could work together now that I know her secret."

"I doona see that being a problem."

With a bright smile in place, she nodded. "Let's see what kind of dirt Ryder dug up on my family."

"I'm no' sure I'd be so happy about the prospect," Dmitri said hesitantly as they continued toward the computer room.

What he didn't understand was that she was deliriously happy. The kind of bliss that she never thought would be possible. It didn't matter what Ryder told her. Nothing was going to dim her happiness.

As soon as Dmitri opened the door, she was immersed

in a room full of all the latest technological gadgets someone like Ryder would like.

To her, it made her dizzy just looking at it. She could
work a computer well enough to do emails, check her
Facebook page, and even keep up with her expenses, but
as she walked around the rows of monitors to see the
screens, she felt as if she'd been thrown a million years into
the future.

And Ryder was looking at all the screens, keeping up
with everything on his own. His keyboard was integrated
into the table with glowing keys. Much of what he did was
by voice recognition, though, telling each screen to do
what he needed.

Then with a swipe of his hand, he took something from
one monitor and moved it to cover an entire wall that
was really one big screen. Faith studied it, realizing it was
a family tree. Her family tree.

"There are some missing parts."

She turned at the sound of the voice to find Ryder standing beside her. He had kind, hazel eyes and short blond
hair. Those eyes of his missed nothing.

Dmitri had told her about the cameras smaller than a
button that Ryder had designed and built that were placed
all over Dreagan, especially the distillery.

Listening to how Muscles talked of Ryder's expertise
and how he'd built everything in the computer room himself, she knew she was standing before a genius.

"It's sad that the world doesn't know what you can do,"
she said.

Ryder smiled and held out his hand. "It is a pleasure,
Dr. Reynolds."

"Faith, please," she told him. "Thank you for allowing
me to come and see what you've found."

He opened a box and took out a jelly donut as he walked

to the wall with her family tree. "As I said, there are some missing parts. I can no' find everyone due to destroyed or missing records. I'm working my own angle on some of these. The odd thing, I never found your father's name."

"I never wanted to know it," she said. "He walked out on us. I didn't want someone like that in my life."

Dmitri squeezed her hand. "Understandable."

But she caught the way the two men shared a look. "I don't like secrets, so there's no need to keep anything from me. I can take whatever it is."

"I've searched your mother's life, and though she did have a boyfriend or two, she wasn't with anyone before she conceived you," Ryder said before taking a bite of the donut.

"You think my mom lied about her and my father being in a relationship?" Faith thought about that a moment. "Mom was always honest with me about everything. She said they dated for a few months before she became pregnant. He wasn't thrilled with it and bailed on her."

With a swipe of his hand, Ryder pulled up a daily timeline of her mother's activities before she'd gotten pregnant, and who she saw for a six-month period during that time.

Faith walked to the wall, reading it. "How did you put all this together?"

"Ryder is that good at what he does," Dmitri replied.

"It's accurate," Ryder said.

She turned to look at Ryder. "This is over thirty years old. People didn't keep these kinds of records back then."

"Actually, the governments always have," Ryder stated.

Her mind was officially blown. She turned back to the wall and realized that the dates were the months before and after she was conceived.

Yet no matter how hard she looked, she couldn't find a

man's name connected with her mother. Ryder hadn't been lying. Her mother hadn't been seeing anyone.

"I don't understand," she said.

Dmitri said, "We doona either."

"I wasn't magically conceived. There had to be a man somewhere." She sorted through her memories of the times her mother had spoken of her father—it hadn't been often. "Maybe she had a one-night stand and didn't want to tell me."

Dmitri shook his head. "You always said she spoke the truth about everything. There was no need to lie to you about this, right?"

"And what if you'd wanted to know your father's name?" Ryder asked. "I bet she was prepared to tell you."

"She was. It was written down. After she died, I burned the letter without opening it." Now she wished she had read it, just so she could give the name now.

Ryder returned to the family tree. "We'll get back to your father in a moment. How far can you trace your family line?"

Faith glanced at him, laughing. "My great-grandmother. I was never into learning my family history, why?"

"Ryder traced you all the way back to the tenth century," Dmitri explained.

Now her mind was truly blown. She ran her gaze up the tree, the names all a blur. "How?"

"It was simply a matter of designing a program and plugging in your name," Ryder said.

He made it sound as if he'd just baked a cake, not detailed her family history back eleven hundred years. She didn't recognize any names, then again, she might be able to if she could see clearly.

But the shock had a discernable effect on her.

Dmitri pushed her down into a chair, which was a good thing because her knees had been about to give out.

"How does an archeologist who loves history not care about her own?" Ryder asked.

Faith blinked. He was right. She loved history, craved it. Why then had she never cared about discovering where she came from? "I don't know. It never mattered."

"I think it did," Dmitri said. With a motion to Ryder, the family tree shrank, and a map was pulled up beside it. "Look at the places you went to dig."

She leaned forward as he pointed out places her family was from on the tree to the exact places she'd gone to dig. Had she been looking for her past the entire time?

And once more, her theory on there being no destiny was kicked right out the door.

"What does this mean?" she asked.

Ryder finished off his donut and crossed his arms over his chest as he stood next to her. "It means that you were subconsciously looking for answers. It took you to Fair Isle."

"I thought a beacon took me there."

Dmitri smiled. "Ryder found your notes. Six years ago, you wrote down places you would visit to excavate. Fair Isle was one of them. And last on the list."

Long before she'd felt drawn to go there. "I think my head is going to explode."

"Now you understand why we find it so curious that there's no mention of your father," Ryder said. "I'll find it. I always do. It's just taking me longer than usual."

Faith rubbed her hands along her thighs as her gaze went to Fair Isle on the map. If she went there, then that meant she had family there. Which meant . . . Her gaze slid to Dmitri.

"Aye," he said. "I believe that your ancestors were some of the same mortals who inhabited the isles I ruled."

"But you said no humans were on Fair then."

"They took over as we were leaving."

She swallowed past the lump in her throat. "Please tell

me that one of my ancestors isn't the person responsible for all of this."

"I can no' say that for certain," Ryder said.

She could read between the lines. "But it looks that way. Right?"

Dmitri nodded. "It does."

"This just gets better and better," she said, wanting to sink into a hole.

Dmitri squatted beside her and took her hand. "It doesna change how I feel about you. It never will."

"Don't be too hasty with that promise. Ryder isn't finished digging into my past."

"Your family's past," Ryder corrected.

She shrugged. "Same difference."

"It's no'," Dmitri said. "This has nothing to do with you. You're connected to these people by blood, but you were no' there to make decisions with them. So doona carry the weight of their actions."

It made her feel a little better, though the embarrassment of having such a family might never go away. "What now?" she asked. "How do we link my family to the Druids or the Fae?"

Ryder tapped his chin. "It willna be easy, but I'll see how the dots connect."

"How much time do we have?"

"As long as that damn wooden dragon is contained, we should be fine," Dmitri said.

She rose to her feet and faced them. "This could happen again. On top of Ulrik's and the Dark's attacks. Let me help. My skills at digging don't stop with the earth. I'm skilled at following the past and ascertaining details."

Ryder turned to retrieve something. He faced her and held out a laptop. "Everything you need is on there."

"You knew I'd ask?"

Dmitri smiled when Ryder looked his way. "I might've suggested that you would most likely want to be involved."

One of many reasons she'd fallen so hard and so quick for her dragon. "I love you. Now, let's get to work."

CHAPTER FORTY-TWO

While Faith was lost in her searches on the laptop, Dmitri made his way to Con's office. The door was open, and he walked in to find Con staring at a file.

Suddenly, the King of Kings looked up at Dmitri. "Come in," Con bade.

Dmitri entered and lowered himself into one of the chairs. "I suppose Ryder has already filled you in on what he discovered about Faith?"

"Aye. I also know she's helping. That's no' what really brought you in here, though, is it?"

Dmitri shook his head. "I'm taking her as my mate."

"I assumed as much."

Dmitri expected a fight, or an argument, at least. This was something entirely different. It made him a little uneasy, especially knowing everything that had occurred since Faith was brought to Dreagan.

"I've surprised you," Con said.

"You could say that."

"Maybe I'm tired of fighting what seems to be inevitable."

Dmitri frowned, something in Con's voice setting off warning bells. "What's that supposed to mean?"

"History is repeating itself. It always does."

"It doesna have to."

"And yet, it will."

"You still believe a human will betray us?"

Con blew out a long breath. "I do. We bring them to Dreagan for protection. A few we've sussed out were working with Ulrik. We managed to change their way of thinking, but when will it happen that we doona realize their connection to him? When will it happen that we can no' make them see our side of the story?"

"When will the betrayal come?" Dmitri asked. Damn. Con was right. It was coming. It was simply a matter of time.

Constantine nodded. "Now do you understand why I worry each time one of you falls in love with a mortal? Now do you comprehend why I try so hard to stop any of you from bringing them here?"

"And yet you doona prevent us."

"Our pledge to protect the humans willna end. As long as one of them is brought into our war and turns to us for help, it is our duty to shield them as best we can."

Dmitri rested his ankle atop his knee. "And you wait."

"I wait, and I observe. Ryder digs into every mortal's life that is brought to Dreagan. I'll find out if there is another betrayal."

"You discovered it the first time, as well. How?"

Con didn't flinch, didn't so much as bat an eye. But Dmitri still noticed a subtle difference in him. It was so faint that anyone could've missed it.

Then again, Dmitri had been looking for just such a sign.

"One of Ulrik's Silvers noticed some strange things. He

came to me with his suspicions because he was concerned. The misgivings were such that I took action."

"How? You didna have Ryder."

"You think because Ryder didna have his computers and electronics that he couldna poke into a life? Even then, Ryder found a way to learn all there was. But you're right. I didna turn to Ryder. If my fears were true, I didna want anyone else involved until I knew the facts."

Dmitri sat straighter in the chair, dropping his foot to the floor. "You dug into the mortal's life?"

"Doona sound so surprised. This was my best friend's, my brother's happiness on the line. I wanted absolute definitive proof. I needed it."

"I suppose you found it."

"It was no odd thing for me to visit Ulrik. We were often at each other's settlements, so my appearance didna draw attention. On the surface, everything appeared as it was supposed to. It went on like that for several months. I saw how much Ulrik loved his mortal, and how much she doted on him."

Dmitri linked his fingers over his midsection. "What changed?"

"It was so slight that if I hadna been looking for it, I would've missed it. We were at dinner. Do you remember the huge feasts Ulrik gave?"

"Aye," Dmitri said with a nod. "He left his doors open for anyone who wanted to join."

"That night, his hall was bursting with mortals. The day of his mating ceremony was approaching rapidly, and he was in great spirits. We'd spent the afternoon with his Silvers, flying, training, and feasting. That night was his time with the humans.

"Ulrik was able to be in both our world and theirs with ease. I think it was his jovial nature and how easily he trusted. Because he trusted everyone, I felt it was my job to mistrust all to keep the balance."

It was still easy for Dmitri to remember the old Ulrik, the dragon who everyone loved. Ulrik hadn't had a single enemy—that they knew of.

"That night, Ulrik leaned over to kiss his woman," Con continued. "She returned the kiss, but it was when she turned away that I saw her look of utter disgust. And that's when I knew everything I'd suspected was true."

"Is that when you sent Ulrik away and called for us?" Dmitri asked.

"I watched her for a few days first. She would wait until Ulrik left to be with his Silvers, and then she rushed from the house into the village to another residence."

Dmitri's lips compressed for a moment. "It was a mortal's dwelling, and you'd have no reason to go in after her."

"Exactly. She remained there most of the day, returning to Ulrik's house shortly before he returned home. He kept to a schedule that allowed her such movements. So, I then turned my attention to the place she visited. I watched it for days, but never saw anyone leave but her."

"I still doona know how you pieced together that she was going to try and kill him."

Con shrugged and lowered his black eyes to his desk. "I wasna able to go into the home, but I got close enough to hear what she was planning."

Con grew quiet, and Dmitri knew he was reliving that day. "Was she alone?"

"Nay," Con said and looked up at him. "There was someone with her, but I couldna tell if it was a man or a woman. They disguised their voice as if they knew I was listening."

"Or thought someone might be."

"True," Con said with a twist of his lips. "The mortal

was planning to kill Ulrik. I knew she couldna harm him, but I also knew what her actions would do to him. I had to prevent that."

"You thought to save your friend."

"And I lost him instead." Con sighed and leaned forward to rest his forearms on the desk. "I put the spell in place that we would never feel anything for the humans again because I knew that debacle would happen again. I lost one brother. I didna want to lose another."

Dmitri ran a hand through his hair. "Why did you never tell us that story?"

"None of you really wanted to know. Because none of you have ever asked."

"I never wanted a mate."

Con nodded slowly. "You preferred the Fae. Yet you're here, telling me you're going to mate a mortal."

"I love Faith."

"I know."

Dmitri held Con's gaze. "Are you worried that she'll be controlled or called again by whoever used the Fae/Druid magic?"

"Without a doubt. I was affected by it, as well. Though I doona remember what I said, Lily gives me a wide berth. I've asked her repeatedly to tell me everything that happened, but she refuses. She says it willna do anyone any good."

"Which means it was quite dreadful."

Con smiled ruefully. "I heard the things you said when I came upon you in the cavern with Faith. If my tirade was anything like yours, I can only imagine how awful it was."

"Rhi has the magic contained, though," Dmitri said.

"She does. Rhi's magic is strong and should hold that piece of wood so that nothing else happens, but I want to be prepared in case something else does."

Dmitri looked around. "Where is the orb with the dragon?"

"Rhi took it to get it away from Dreagan."

That brought Dmitri to Ulrik. "What about Ulrik? He didna approach Faith or me as he has with the others."

Con raised a brow as he shook his head. "I doona know, but be thankful."

"Ulrik could be getting ready to attack."

"Most likely, but I'll be his focus. Let me worry about my upcoming battle."

Dmitri leaned an elbow on the arm of his chair. "Did you ever tell Ulrik about his woman? About how you followed her?"

"I tried. He didna want to hear it."

"I doona guess he would."

Dmitri couldn't imagine how he'd feel if he learned Faith wanted to kill him. No wonder Ulrik had been lost to his grief and anger. None of them had understood it then, but they were slowly beginning to as each of them fell in love.

And it also made sense why Ulrik made a point of going after the women the Kings were interested in. Ulrik wanted his fellow dragons to hurt as he'd hurt.

"When do you and Faith want the ceremony?" Con asked.

Dmitri blinked. "Soon."

"Darius and Sophie, Ryder and Kinsey, as well as Asher and Rachel have also requested to be mated."

It was the first Dmitri had heard of the others, but he wasn't surprised. "One big ceremony, then?"

"After we bury your White."

"I'll let Faith know." He got to his feet and looked to the King of Kings. "Thank you."

Con didn't seem to hear him as his attention returned to the open folder. Dmitri briefly thought of trying to see what was in that file, but he decided to return to Faith instead.

As he entered his bedchamber, he smiled at the sight of his woman. She sat cross-legged on the bed with the laptop resting on her legs. The light from the screen illuminated her face, showing a small frown as her eyes moved back and forth while she read.

"It's rude to stare," she said without looking up.

He closed the door behind him. "I can no' help myself from gazing at such beauty."

Her eyes snapped to his, a smile forming. She closed the computer and set it on the bedside table before getting to her knees and throwing off her shirt.

"What are you waiting for?" she asked with a wink.

Dmitri quickly undressed as he made his way to the bed. He wrapped an arm around her as he put a knee on the bed and turned, falling back onto the mattress.

"Where did you disappear to?" she asked before kissing him.

A long kiss later, Dmitri answered. "Con."

She straddled his chest. "Ah. And what did he have to say?"

"We willna be the only ones doing the mating ceremony."

Her eyes widened. "So he's okay with me? Even after everything?"

"It was no' your doing."

"But it could happen again."

"Which is why Rhi is helping us."

Faith wrinkled her nose. "I think we should talk to Ronnie, as well."

"No doubt the Druids will be brought into this eventually. For now, let's enjoy the quiet and peace."

"And the bed," she said with a wicked gleam in her eye.

With a flick of his fingers, he unhooked her bra. "Most definitely the bed."

She tossed aside the garment and looked down at him with her sandy blond hair framing her face and her sherry eyes filled with love. "I hate what brought us together, but I can't deny that I'm happy to be with you."

"I can certainly agree with that." He slid his hands into her hair and brought her face down to his. "I love you."

"I love you. For you are mine."

"And you are mine."

EPILOGUE

Two days later ...

Faith stood alongside Dmitri at the front of the gathered
Dragon Kings and mates. The mood was somber as they
entered Dmitri's mountain.

The day before, Lily had flown her over the entire sixty
thousand acres of Dreagan and shown her Dmitri's mountain. It should've been a day of celebration because Vaughn's
legal expertise had come through and all the MI5 agents
were ordered off Dreagan.

Yet, there was a dark cloud still hanging over them
because of the wooden dragon she'd found on Fair Isle.
Thanks to Ryder's amazing software program, she'd found
more relatives that confirmed her link to Fair.

What she—or Ryder—still hadn't found was her father.

Dmitri's fingers squeezed hers as they finally came to
the cavern he'd chosen for the burial. Then Con, Roman,
Cain, and Nikolai carried in the dragon bones on a pallet
draped in white.

As what was left of the dragon who had been tortured
and died alone was gently set down, tears filled Faith's
eyes. She didn't stop them as they flowed down her face.

After everything she'd learned of the dragons, to

know that one had suffered so left her bereft. It was cruel and brutal, something someone truly and wickedly evil would do.

And it terrified her that she might be connected to such a person.

She bowed her head and closed her eyes as Dmitri began a chant in a language she didn't know. Soon, all the Dragon Kings joined in.

Though she might not know the words, she knew they were ones of love and devotion, of strength and tenderness. Of sorrow and regret.

Her tears ran faster. She hadn't known the dragon, but she had discovered him. Whether it was by Fate or magic, she'd had a part in bringing him home to finally find some peace.

When the chant finished, one by one, the Kings and mates walked to the bones and touched what remained of the dragon before walking out.

Faith stayed by Dmitri's side until it was only the two of them and Con left in the cavern. Wiping her eyes, she sent up a silent prayer that justice be brought to those responsible for such a horrendous act on a creature that had done no harm.

"You did a good thing," Con said to Dmitri. "You brought a dragon home."

Dmitri nodded. "I hope the others we bring home are no' dead, as well."

Con knelt before the dragon, his hand on the skull as he bowed his head and whispered words Faith couldn't hear. When he rose, he walked out of the cavern without looking their way.

She looked at Dmitri to find that his eyes were red with unshed tears. And her heart broke all over again. "We'll find who did this."

"I know."

With a deep breath, she released his hand and walked to the skeleton. There she ran her hand over the skull. "I hope you find serenity now. You are back with your King."

She swiped away the new tears and walked out to join Con, who stood at the cavern entrance. There she watched Dmitri go to his dragon and kneel before him with his head bowed.

"He's saying farewell," Con told her.

She nodded, unable to speak because of the tears.

"Thank you for helping Dmitri bring him home."

Surprised, she turned her head to Con. "Look what else I did, though."

"It wasna your doing." He jerked his chin to Dmitri. "Take him and celebrate the life of that dragon as well as the future before both of you."

"Will you ever take a mate?"

He looked away quickly. "I made a choice to lead. It's what I'm meant to do."

"It's a lonely choice."

"No' when I have all of you."

She didn't get to say more as Dmitri walked to her. She took his hand, and stood between two Dragon Kings as they sealed the cavern with magic.

When they walked from the mountain, Dmitri released a breath and smiled, raising his face to the sun. "I'm glad you were beside me for that."

She grinned as he looked down at her. "There's no other place I'd rather be than by your side."

"That's good, since I doona ever plan to let you go."

"I love the sound of that."

"Let's go home."

She felt her heart warm at the thought. Home. She had a home now, a place she loved almost as much as the dragon she was going to marry.

No matter what came next, no matter what she unearthed about her family, it wouldn't touch the happiness and love that she'd found with her Dragon King.

Rhys walked the Dragonwood with Lily. "You're going to have to tell me."

"Wait," she said.

He frowned but kept silent as they walked. It wasn't long before they came to a shallow valley. There he saw Guy and Elena, Banan and Jane, Tristan and Sammi, Warrick and Darcy, Thorn and Lexi, Darius and Sophie, and Kiril and Shara.

"What's going on?" he asked Lily.

She looked at everyone who stood in a circle. "Each of you have asked me why I'm keeping my distance from Con. I'm here to tell you why."

Rhys frowned as he looked at Kiril. He had a bad feeling about this. "You told me it was because of the things he said."

"Yes." She paused and took a deep breath. "I know the things he said were because of the wooden dragon Faith found on Fair Isle. At first, I discounted everything he told me because of that. But the longer I thought about it, the more I wondered about it."

Kiril shrugged. "He wasna the only one affected. Both Rhys and I were, as well."

"I know. It's not about who was touched by the magic, but rather something Con said," Lily replied.

Lexi moved closer to Thorn. "Just tell us."

Rhys took Lily's hand, sensing her distress. He became more concerned when he felt her shaking, and he knew it had nothing to do with the cold temperature.

"Lily," Elena urged.

When Rhys turned Lily's face to him and he looked into her black eyes to see them swimming in tears, he felt a band constrict around his heart. "What is it, sweetheart?"

"Con said that humans were never meant to be immortal. He said that we'd go insane," Lily said.

Guy shook his head. "If that were true, Con would've told us."

"I don't think so," Lily said as she looked at him. "He said that's why he's tried to dissuade all of you from taking mortals as mates, because when we go insane, we'll need to be killed. And he'll have to do it since none of you will be able to kill your own mate."

Rhys wanted to deny all of it, but in the back recesses of his mind, an old memory stirred.

"I don't like the sound of this at all," Sammi said.

Jane shrugged. "It's done now. There's nothing we can do."

"I'll certainly look for something," Darcy said.

Warrick wrapped an arm around Darcy. "We all will."

"At least Shara and Kiril don't have to worry about this," Darius said.

Sophie nodded at his words. "He's right, but it's not the end for us now either. We've got plenty of time to deal with this. We're aware of it now. That's what matters."

"Sophie has a point," Shara said. "And I know that I'll use my Fae magic if needed to help all of you. Right now, we've got to stop our enemies."

Talk began between the couples, but Rhys didn't hear any of it. He took Lily's hand and turned her to face him. "Why did you no' tell me?"

"I was trying to come to terms with it. Con said that it would either be the passage of time or us unable to have children that makes us go insane."

Rhys ran a hand through his hair. "I doona understand this. Look how long the Druids at MacLeod Castle have been immortal. Hundreds of years. None of them are insane."

"Con seemed adamant about it."

Because there was truth to his words. Rhys wouldn't mention that now. "It'll be fine. We'll find a way to stop anything like that from happening."

Rhys prayed that he could follow through with that promise.

Rhi stood, staring at the display of OPI polish in the middle of the store. She walked to the counter with five bottles to add to her collection.

Humidi-Tea, a nude shimmer. Crawfishin' For a Compliment, a creamy orange. Take a Right on Bourbon, a metallic pewter. I'm Sooo Swamped, a verdant, creamy green. And to her surprise, a pale pink called Passion.

Her next stop was Jesse. She handed the bag of polish to her favorite nail tech to let Jesse choose the shade. Rhi didn't look at her nails as they were being done.

Instead, her mind was on her watcher—or, rather, his absence. He'd become such a familiar part of her life that it felt weird not having him there.

Yet, to know that her memories had been taken from her sent her over the edge of reason. Except those memories had returned.

Every. Single. One.

Fear mixed with her anger. Reapers. She had met and fought alongside Reapers. What she wished she knew more about was Bran. And the woman who had appeared in her chambers at the castle.

Rhi paid Jesse and walked out of the nail shop to teleport to her island. She stood on the shores, listening to the waves roll in as she went over everything that had happened with Neve and Talin.

For a long while, she'd had a suspicion that her watcher was a Reaper. Now she knew. It didn't bode well that a Reaper was watching her. But what did he want?

It was the tingle along her back that alerted her that she

wasn't alone. Her reprieve from her Reaper was over, though he wasn't able to get as close to her as before.

Rhi held out her hands and looked at her nails. They were painted the pale pink—Passion—and the metallic pewter—Take a Right on Bourbon—in a beautiful mix of swirls.

Strong arms came around her from behind. "I like them," Balladyn said.

She leaned back against him. "I've missed you."

"As I've missed you." He kissed the side of her neck. "You're troubled. What is it?"

She turned in his arms and looped hers around his neck while she looked into his red eyes. "Nothing. Everything."

"Rhi," he said, concern in his deep red eyes.

She put a finger to his lips. There was so much she couldn't tell him—that she didn't want him to know. About the Reapers, Dragon Kings, and Usaeil.

He nipped at her finger, smiling seductively. "Let me help."

"Hold me. Make me forget everything," she begged.

"Gladly," he murmured before taking her lips.

Read on for an excerpt from the next book by
Donna Grant

BLAZE

Coming soon from St. Martin's Paperbacks

There was no denying it. She had well and truly lost her mind.

But it felt *heavenly*.

Devon could barely fill her lungs with air as she perched on the few inches of the sofa not taken up by Anson's powerfully built body.

It might be practical to say something, but for the life of her, she couldn't think of anything. Ever since he'd pressed that hard physique against her, she hadn't been able to think about anything other him.

Running her hands over those muscles.

Sliding her hands into his black hair.

Feeling the weight of him atop her.

Having him inside her.

When he'd tried to kiss her in the hallway, she'd been so shocked that she looked away. *Looked away*! What idiot does that?

Her apparently.

She'd tried to read. She'd even tried to sleep. But he filled her mind completely. So she decided to do something she'd never done before—make a move.

Now here she was sitting beside him as he lay on the couch. His eyes watched her curiously—and with a touch of anticipation. The fact he *wanted* her to kiss him gave her the boost of confidence to finish what she'd begun.

Her heart hammered against her ribs. But not in fear or even anxiety. In *eagerness*.

She leaned down and pressed her lips against his. There was a second where he didn't move. Then he let loose a groan that rumbled his chest.

A sigh escaped her when his fingers entwined with her hair once again. Her head tipped to the side as the kiss deepened. She could tell he was holding back, and after she had turned away upstairs, she didn't blame him.

But if she was going to do this, she wanted all of him.

Devon ended the kiss and straightened. Confusion filled his gaze. She smiled and got her to feet before she unbelted her robe. There was a millisecond where it felt as if she had an out of body experience and was looking down upon the room.

Despite this being so out of the ordinary for her, it felt good. Right, even. There was a grin upon her lips as she pulled open the robe and let it fall to her feet to reveal she had nothing on underneath.

His gaze heated her skin as he gradually looked her up and down. He slowly sat up and reached for her. Large hands were placed upon her hips as he pulled her toward him. Then he stood, lifting her as he did.

Her legs wrapped around his waist and her arms around his neck. Their gazes clashed. Her stomach quivered with excitement when she saw the desire he didn't try to hide.

He held her easily as he made his way to the stairs. Before she knew it, they were inside her bedroom. He stopped in the middle of the room and set her down as it if physically pained him to do so.

She didn't want to let go of him. It felt good to be in his

arms, and she wanted to return there. Reluctantly, she let go of him. As soon as she did, he began to undress.

His white shirt was the first to go. Her lips parted as she took in his finely sculpted chest to his stomach where she counted each and every one of his abs.

With arms that rippled with chiseled sinew, her hands itched to touch him. Before she got the chance, he removed his boots and pants.

When he straightened she bit her lip at the absolute perfection that stood before her. It was the sight of his arousal that caused her sex to clench in need. Her desire blazed out of control—and she loved it.

In the next heartbeat he had her against him, his mouth plundering hers. He kissed her hungrily, greedily. Ravenously.

She moaned, her hands clutching him as she fought to get closer. It wasn't until she felt something against her back that she realized he'd moved them against the wall.

His kiss stole her breath.

It gave her life.

As if she had been sleepwalking up until that moment. Everything became crystal clear. The more their tongues mated, the more she felt herself changing. Like a caterpillar becoming a butterfly.

He pulled on her hair, causing her to expose her neck. She gasped in pleasure as he kissed down the column of her throat to lick her pulse point.

Everything he did was erotic, sensual. Utterly carnal.

Her fingers slid into the cool locks of his hair as he continued to her breasts. She groaned when his lips grazed a nipple. Then those lips wrapped around the peak and sucked before his tongue teased it.

She was gasping for breath at the pleasure that filled her. All the while his hands roamed over her leisurely, learning every inch of and leaving a trail of heat in his wake.

"Anson," she whispered when he moved to her other breast and began to flick his tongue over the peak.

It wasn't long until she was rocking her hips in need. She relished the thought of being so thoroughly in his control. Helpless.

Ensnared by his skill.

He was better than any fantasy she'd ever had—or ever would have. With her head moving side to side, she waited—breathlessly—for more.

As his lips trailed down her stomach and lower, she moaned at what was to come. He then lifted one of her legs and placed it on her shoulder, exposing her sex. She kept expecting to feel his fingers or tongue on her. But there was nothing.

She opened her eyes and looked down to find him gazing up at her. The look of hunger, of need she saw there made her heart skip a beat.

But it was the promise that he wouldn't stop until she was fully satisfied that had her panting.